Millie Conway grew up in the UK and has lived in many countries and cities, including Amsterdam, Shanghai, Hong Kong, London and New York. She also writes for newspapers, magazines and is a regular contributor to various radio shows. Her time is split between Glasgow and Los Angeles, although most of her latest book, *From Essex to Chelsea with Love*, was written on a balcony in Portugal. When not writing, Millie shops too much, chats too much and watches far too much reality television.

From

ESSEX

to

CHELSEA

with Love

MILLIE CONWAY

headline
review

First published in Great Britain in 2012 by
HEADLINE REVIEW
An imprint of HEADLINE PUBLISHING GROUP

1

Cataloguing in Publication Data is available from the British Library

ISBN 978 1 4722 0036 5

Typeset in New Baskerville by Palimpsest Book Production Limited,
Falkirk, Stirlingshire

Printed and bound in Great Britain by
Clays Ltd, St Ives plc

Headline's policy is to use papers that are natural, renewable and
recyclable products and made from wood grown in sustainable forests.
The logging and manufacturing processes are expected to conform
to the environmental regulations of the country of origin.

HEADLINE PUBLISHING GROUP
An Hachette UK Company
338 Euston Road
London NW1 3BH

www.headline.co.uk
www.hachette.co.uk

This book is dedicated to the wonderful Sheila Crowley – an agent and friend who is unsurpassed in Essex, Chelsea or anywhere else. xxx

Prologue

Contracts. She'd never been particularly good at dealing with them. Not that she'd had much experience in these things. The man in front of her cleared his throat, impatient about the delay. If it was meant to intimidate her, it was succeeding.

She should sign. Definitely. But . . .

Her eyes flicked to the large black clock on the yellow wall. Noon.

The pen was making a ridge in the inside of her index finger, yet she couldn't release the pressure. This would change so much. Everything. It was too soon. She needed more time, but the expectant faces around her made it clear this was a one-shot deal.

Little beads of sweat popped out on the palms of her hands, natty accessories to the flushed face and the heart that was hammering louder than that ticking clock.

1

That bloody clock.

12.01.

OK, so it had to be now. She had to sign it right now and consequences bedamned.

The pen touched the paper, then moved with a flourish to complete the first letter of her name.

Suddenly she stopped. Looked up. The guy with the obnoxious cough stared at her with puzzlement.

'I'm sorry, but I don't think this pen is working.'

He looked at her, then down at the page, then met her eyes again before repeatedly patting down all his pockets.

Everyone in the room was now mimicking his movements, searching their pockets, their anxious faces giving them the appearance of a stressed-out formation dance team.

Perversely, the situation was having the opposite effect on her as, for the first time since she woke up this morning, a sense of calm started at her perfectly manicured toes and worked its way north.

The paper in front of her was still blank.

It had to be a sign.

Chapter One

Talli

17 October 3013

The ringing of her mobile phone cut through Talli's panic. She rifled through the piles of papers nearest her on the desk, dislodging three hardback catalogues and sending them crashing to the floor.

Still the phone rang.

Bending to pick up the books, her elbow knocked over the Venti Coffee Frappuccino with whipped cream twist she'd picked up at Starbucks ten minutes ago.

The coffee splashed all over her bare feet, making her yell with pain and instinctively jerk her knees up. This jolted the desk, causing another pile of documents, samples and a large crystal 18 sign to fall.

It smashed. But still the phone rang.

With wet feet and a sinking heart, Talli realised that her right breast was vibrating. With a defeated sigh, she fished her phone out of the pocket of her coffee-splattered white Calvin Klein shirt.

'Good morning, Grand Affairs of Chelsea, Event Management, can I help you?'

'Tallulah Caston-Jones, please,' came the clipped reply.

Talli instinctively shuddered at the sound of her full name. Her mother had insisted she have it printed on her business cards, despite Talli's insistence since the age of twelve that she should be known simply as Talli Jones.

'This is Tallulah,' she replied, keen for the call to be over so she could get back to having a full-scale anxiety attack over an imminent eighteenth birthday party at the Dorchester. Note to self – order new crystal 18 sign with immediate urgency. The party was less than a week away and the birthday girl, Cosima Carlton, had just decided that the Snow Queen theme she'd been absolutely set on was 'so last year's Narnia' and decided to go for 'Vamps and Vixens' instead. Talli now had to dispense with the services of a snow machine, twelve igloos, thirty-six ice sculptures and a dozen little people lined up to play marauding wolves. She had five days to come up with coffins, crucifixes and several gallons of fake blood.

'This is Tabitha Deloite, Cosima Carlton's BFF. Can you do me a huge fave, yah? A few of us want to buy Cosima a fabulous piece of jewellery for her big night. A surprise of course. Could you possibly send me over a picture of the gown she'll be wearing? We want to make sure the piece we pick is perfect for her look.'

'Erm, sure. Of course.'

'Oh, you're a star. A star!'

Click.

Talli immediately started searching for the catwalk image of the scarlet Dior gown, depressingly certain that if she didn't do it straight away, she'd forget. Where was it? Where? She frantically leafed through piles of brochures, invoices and pages ripped from magazines. Organisation had never been her strong point.

'Yes!' she muttered to no one as she found the image she was looking for: an Amazonian goddess stomping down the catwalk in a creation so elaborate it bordered on art. It was a stunning dress, but not one she herself could ever imagine wearing. She might have the model's height, and could just about pour herself into a size 10 dress, but there was way too much effort required to pull off this look. Her beauty regime ran to soap, moisturiser and a bit of lip balm after her daily workout. As for her style, she was strictly jeans and T-shirts.

She took a quick snap of the dress on her iPhone and sent it to the mobile number that had just called.

One job done. Later, she'd recognise the irony of that moment. She'd thought she was being unusually efficient. But as she pulled her thick honey-blonde hair up into a twist and stuck a pencil in to hold it there, she was blissfully unaware that her actions would actually fall in line with the theme of the party by opening the gates to hell.

Chapter Two

Zac

17 October 3013

Sleb! magazine, 15 October 2012:

> *Big news for the cast of* Lovin' Essex *this week as their show topped the million-viewer mark for the first time since it hit the air two years ago. Set up to rival the huge success of the mighty* TOWIE, Lovin' Essex, *set in Chelmsford, has proved that great things come in small packages. The production team is smaller, the cast is tighter, the budgets don't kerching like* TOWIE, *yet they still pack in just as much drama as their friends over in Brentwood.* Lovin' Essex *leading lady Kiki Spooner had this to say. 'We love* TOWIE *and we're thrilled to be sharing the spotlight. Essex is definitely big enough for both of us!'*

Four of the five female stars of *Lovin' Essex* were deep in conversation, their inch-long eyelashes wide with surprise. 'Shut up! Like, proper shut up! OMG, what a troll! I'm sick of Porsche, she just thinks that she's like, total queen bee around here and she's so not. I knew her when she was still giving BJs to that DJ down the Beach Box.' Shiraz spoke like an AK-47 spraying lip-gloss-coated bullets around the room.

The others nodded in agreement. It was, Zac thought, like looking at a shelf of picture-perfect Barbie dolls in the supermarket. There were twin dolls on the TV show: his stunning sisters Lena and Minx. Almost identical, they differed mainly in the shade and cut of their pink hair and their style. Lena's baby pink extensions fell to her waist and she was dressed as always in girlie pastels, while Minx was the tomboy with the bright pink elfin cut. Or at least her version of tomboy: full make-up, tiny denim shorts and trainers with four-inch wedge heels. Zac's girlfriend Kiki was Sexy Barbie, the smoky-eyed brunette who played the part of a wild free spirit. Then there was Glamour Barbie, Porsche, who was missing from this shoot so that the rest could have a good old rant about her. Porsche prided herself on sharing her assets with the world and every weekly celebrity mag. And finally raven-haired Shiraz was Bondage Barbie: glossy curls, short leather skirt, the owner of the salon bought by her father, a property mogul with more build-ings and land than the local council. Spa Shiraz was the mother ship for the girls' grooming upkeep, chat and hardcore bitching sessions, not to mention the best place in Essex for hair extensions, false eyelashes, gel nails and fake tan. For a reality show that now had over a million viewers per episode, there sure wasn't much on *Lovin' Essex* that was real, but that kind of discipline and effort had always impressed Zac. These were girls who knew how to make the most of themselves, looked sensational and most of them were really sweet too. He'd known Shiraz and Porsche for years, because they'd hung out with his sisters since they were kids. Back then, Lena was always the sensible, diplomatic one. Nothing much had changed.

'Look, it's not worth gettin' frazzed about.' Lena was speaking now, playing out her part as the peacemaker of the group. The lines weren't scripted as such, but the girls all had defined roles, exaggerated versions of themselves.

Shiraz, the hard nut, was on the warpath again. 'Yeah, but it's, like, time she got told to get a grip. C'mon, let's get over to the club.' She was on her feet now, her Versace mini riding up to give a peek of her gold sequinned thong. 'And if I see that slapper, she'll be proper sorry.'

'And CUT!' Edwina, the director of the show, barked out the order and everyone on set immediately obeyed. She stood up from her chair. 'Great, well done, girls. Shiraz, I was really feeling your frustration there. Kiki, can we see you for a quick moment, luvly? Zac, my darling torso of hotness, could you come too?'

Zac raised his eyebrows in surprise at the invitation.

He hoped Edwina wasn't going to try to get him on the show again. She was always saying that with his looks, he would be a massive ratings booster, but there was no chance. The thought of all that attention made his teeth grind. He was strictly background in this whole affair. He'd only popped on to set today because he was picking up Lena and Minx and taking them shopping to buy their Auntie Dot a birthday present.

They followed Edwina into one of the side rooms, a massage suite that played weird music even though there was no one there. Zac had a sinking sense of being marched to the headmistress's office, unaware as to what crime against school rules or property had been committed. Edwina had that presence about her, made all the more jarring by her towering height, slightly chunky frame and cropped dark hair with wisps of grey. Criminal that she didn't get that fixed. Added years to her and she must only be about thirty. No make-up either. And God knows, that nose could do with a bit of strategic shading.

Bloody hell, he was hanging out with those girls too much. He was becoming scarily bilingual – speaking in fluent English and Max Factor.

Edwina, however, was pure posh London and now, hand on hips, she was commanding their attention. 'I'll get to the point. There's been another one of those fucking letters. We've passed a copy of it on to the police because it had a photograph of you taken at your book signing last week.'

Kiki started to physically shake. 'Let me see it.'

'I don't think . . .' Edwina began to argue.

'I want to see it. Please.'

Edwina picked up a black clipboard from the counter beside her, flicked over a couple of pages, then removed an A4 sheet of paper. The image in the middle clearly showed Kiki sitting at a table in Waterstones at Lakeside Shopping Centre with a pile of *Lovin' Essex* Christmas annuals piled in front of her. It had been taken last Wednesday, Zac knew, because he'd been there. It was easy to make him out, standing behind Kiki, looking for all intents and purposes like one of the security guys that had been hired by her management company.

But it wasn't the picture that concerned him most; it was the words above it, made out of letters cut from magazines.

Die bitch. Die!

Chapter Three

Talli's mother gave her the stare of death, a look of such disappointment that it made Talli's Burberry biker boots curl up at the toes.

At least she thought it was the stare of death. Ever since the surgery two weeks before, Arabella Caston-Jones's furious yet frozen, tightly tucked, swollen face bore a striking resemblance to her happy face, her anxious face, her sad face and, more disturbingly, the face of a puffer fish.

One face it bore absolutely no resemblance to was that of her idol, Carole Middleton, mother of the most recent addition to the British royal family. Judging by the results, the Harley Street surgeon had taken one look at the picture Arabella had brandished at their first consultation (an image from the *Daily Mail* featuring both the Windsor and Middleton families at

11

Wills and Kate's wedding), and mistakenly thought the new client wished to hand over several thousand pounds of her cash in return for the aesthetic visage of Prince Andrew.

'Tallulah, how could this happen? The Carltons are refusing to pay their bill. They claim they've had to pay thousands to the Dorchester in compensation and little Cosima is so overwrought she's had to flee to their house on Grand Bahama. Poor darling. You know how fragile that child is.'

Talli bit her bottom lip to stop the rant that was brewing in her head. Little Cosima? She was a spoiled, malicious bitch who had thrown the mother of all tantrums when Tabitha Deloite, her Former (with a capital F for oh fuck) best friend had shown up at her birthday party wearing the same dress, a stunning scarlet Dior gown that cost more than the team of waiters got paid in six months. For anyone else it would be a mildly upsetting glitch on an otherwise fabulous night. But no, not for little Cosima. The shrieks could be heard in several London postcodes, as could the sirens belonging to the emergency services that were called after little Cosima threw an almighty tantrum and launched a Jimmy Choo at the wall, which – thanks to the gods of attention-seeking prima donnas – somehow set off a fire alarm. The hotel was forced to evacuate the premises of all guests, including three American rappers, several Cabinet members and Gwyneth Paltrow.

Everyone, in fact, except little Cosima, who took to a

nearby bathroom with several grams of coke and a bottle of tequila and was only found when her father demanded a full search or he'd call in a specialist team from one of the intelligence services. Apparently you could do that when you were someone important in the Ministry of Defence.

Talli had visions of being arrested, or shipped to Guantanamo, or wherever the British government sent people who seriously pissed them off.

Apparently she'd broken one of the solemn commandments of party planning – one must guard the secrets of the client's outfit with one's life. It didn't help that the whole debacle was further exacerbated when Tabitha took to Facebook, Twitter and email – hell, she did everything but hire a plane and write it on the sky – boasting that she'd utterly humiliated Cosima because she looked so much better in the dress. Oh, and thanks to the nice girl at the event planning company for showing her a snap of the gown that the birthday girl planned to wear.

Talli wasn't sure what stung most – the fact that the party had been such a huge disaster or the ignominy of having the cashmere pulled over her eyes by an eighteen-year-old with an evil streak. The girl had sounded so plausible on the phone. And surely Cosima had to shoulder an element of the blame? If she hadn't got caught giving a blow job to Tabitha's boyfriend in the marble washroom of the Carlton private jet, none of this would have happened.

God, when did kids get so evil? thought Talli with a resigned sigh.

Her mother had on her impatient face now. Perhaps.

Talli decided there was no point in getting into an argument that could result in a family rift and several burst stitches behind her mother's ear lobes.

'Sorry, Mother, but you know I'm just not very good at this.'

Arabella eyed her daughter with blatant disappointment. Or perhaps it was sympathy.

'Do not dare give me that speech again,' she hissed. 'Grand Affairs needs you right now, darling.' Definitely disappointment.

Her mother's fourth child, the party planning company Grand Affairs of Chelsea (yes, their internet website did receive enquiries from twenty-two-year-old ladies looking for a benefactor in the SW1 or SW3 postcode areas) was another element of the Caston-Jones life that came courtesy of the almost-royals. Arabella had been perfectly happy with a little hobby organising small, exclusive parties for friends until Carole Middleton came along.

Arabella's ruthless competitive streak kicked in and she set about pushing for larger, more ostentatious commissions, enlisting Talli's help along the way whenever necessary.

'Let me remind you that we are a family. We swoop in to help each other out in times of challenge . . .'

And really bad cosmetic surgery. Talli didn't say that out loud. Nor did she question why she was the only one of her siblings who was 'helping out'. True, she was currently unemployed in the strict do-work-receive-payment sense. Since leaving university clutching a respectable degree in sports science two years ago, Talli had floundered, unable to choose between a postgrad in teaching and voluntary coaching work that would make her CV more attractive to the seventy-eight football, rugby and tennis clubs she'd sent applications to. She'd managed to secure one interview – a junior football team in Bolton, with a manager who called her 'Posh Totty' and looked surprised that she knew a goal kick from a groin strain. She didn't get the job.

Her brother Persimmon at least had a fully employed excuse not to pitch in, given that he worked long hours as vice president of Gambond Paper, the largest toilet-roll supplier in the country, owned for five generations by the family of his fiancée, TV director Edwina Gambond.

Meanwhile, on a bejewelled, designer-adorned branch of the family tree, Talli's twenty-one-year-old sister Dessi (Desdemona by birth) was still 'finding herself'. So far, she'd found out that she loved coffee and lunchtime champagne at bijou bistros on the King's Road, and weekends in Cap Ferrat.

There had never been any doubt in Talli's mind that she would agree to her mother's demands that she take the job. It had always been that way. Her siblings were loud, headstrong, so sure of themselves, utterly firm in their convictions, whereas Talli's resolve was more of the consistency of toothpaste. Whatever it took to keep the peace. She was a people pleaser.

Only it seemed that right now she wasn't pleasing anyone.

'Bambi Abercrombie was at the party and she witnessed the whole thing,' Arabella continued. 'Now the Abercrombies have cancelled their Christmas party. I don't have to tell you that it was the biggest event of our year!'

Talli was caught between a twinge of concern that those stitches could pop at any moment and a desire to punch the air in glee. Thankfully there were only a couple of small events booked between now and Christmas, run-of-the-mill birthdays that even she would struggle to screw up.

There was an uncomfortable pause, the silence broken only by her mother rearranging the fur throw that was draped casually across her Louis XVI chaise longue. If Marie Antoinette had lived today in an elegant town house in Chelsea Square, dressed in Halston and developed an obsession with plastic surgery, she'd be called Arabella Caston-Jones.

Talli realised that her Marie Antoinette was still talking.

'Naturally, I'm devastated that they've chosen to take their business elsewhere. However, it may actually be a blessing in disguise. Persimmon called this morning. He's frightfully thrilled. You know that he and Edwina have had their hearts set on marrying at Highdrow Castle, but there was a three-year waiting list?'

Talli nodded, unsure as to where this was going and wondering how long it would be until she could excuse herself from the crosshairs of the firing squad.

'Well, they've now been offered a cancellation. I think it's because Lord Highdrow remembers me. We had a minor flirtation before I met your father.'

Talli's spirits soared. This was great news. Not only would it soften the blow of the Carlton debacle, but her mother would now completely immerse herself in wedding research, allowing Talli to slide a little further under her demanding radar.

'Good morning! How are we all today, my favourite ladies?' The bellowing voice of Persimmon made her mother beam with joy. Maybe. Still difficult to tell.

'Persimmon, darling, so wonderful to see you. Oh, that suit is divine.'

Persimmon kissed Talli on the cheek and gave her shoulders a squeeze as he passed her. She melted just a little. Her brother was undoubtedly the favourite child, a huge burden that Talli was glad she didn't need to share. Mild indifference and partial obscurity were far easier to handle in this family. Poor Simmy carried the pressure of expectation well. Not traditionally handsome, he made up for it with a cheeky sense of humour and a sharp business mind. On top of that, he'd scored a million Brownie points by embarking on a relationship with Edwina, heiress to a toilet-roll fortune. The two families shared neighbouring summer houses in Brighton and a beach house kiss at the age of thirteen had ignited a relationship that was still going strong almost sixteen years later.

Persimmon greeted his mother with a kiss that Talli noticed landed in mid air a few inches above her head. Probably wasn't safe to go any closer without a nurse and a packet of antiseptic wipes.

He then plonked himself down on a gilt Louis XVI armchair and put his expensively-shod feet on a coffee table that had been in the family since Napoleon was a toddler.

'Have you told Talli the great news yet?'

'Oh, yes. Erm, congratulations. A wedding at Highdrow will be gorgeous.'

'I knew you'd take it well. Thank you so much, Talli – you're a rock.'

A strange prickling feeling told her she was missing something. A few days ago she'd been called a star, and that hadn't ended well. Now she was a rock?

'Actually, I was just getting to that part, darling,' Arabella said, turning – slowly – back to face Talli. 'Yes, well, there's one tiny hitch. The wedding is on Christmas Eve.'

'But that's lovely. It's a wonderful time of year for a wedding – and we now have great contacts for ice sculptures,' offered Talli, contemplating the leftover Narnia props and deciding the igloos and the marauding wolves might not be in keeping with the occasion.

'But it's so soon!' Simmy said apologetically.

Talli's brow furrowed with confusion. Fourteen months

was plenty of time to plan a wedding. Her mother would be back in charge in just a few weeks and then she could spend the whole of next year being the party-planning version of a cross between the mother of the groom and a Third World dictator.

Talli looked quizzically at her mother. 'I don't understand.'

'Tallulah, don't frown like that. I do wish you'd reconsider Botox. Anyway, it's *this* Christmas Eve. So while it's not ideal, there's nothing to be done but get on with it. You're in charge. I'd help, but I leave for Switzerland in the morning. If I'm going to be ready to face the world in eight weeks' time, I'm going to need to spend time at the spa.'

Eight weeks.

Talli repeated it several times in the hope she would stop hyperventilating long enough to absorb the reality of it.

Eight weeks from now. Christmas Eve. And apparently she was on her own because her mother was returning to the spa – which was a cover name for an extortionate Swiss clinic that had in the past starved her, cleansed her and injected her face with fat cells from sheep. Not all at the same time.

'Darling, don't worry, you'll be fine. If Pippa Middleton could make it all the way down that aisle without falling flat at the feet of the Archbishop of Canterbury, you can organise a simple wedding.'

A simple wedding. The thought gave Talli a glimmer

of hope. Perhaps if it was an intimate affair, just close family and her mother's Swiss doctor, it might be manageable.

'We'll only be inviting two hundred,' Persimmon casually informed her. 'Oh, and darling, you might want to book the doves now. Edwina wants one for every guest. Terrible idea. The vile things crap on everything.'

Closing her eyes, Talli reflected that the doves might not yet be here, but somehow she already felt like she was getting crapped on from a great height.

Chapter Four

34 October 3013

'He's out there again, babes. I just know it,' Kiki Spooner wailed as she squinted through the venetian blinds. Zac jumped off the brown Dralon couch and shot to the window, where he scanned the street outside.

Nothing. Or at least, nothing out of the ordinary. There was a geezer standing at the bus stop a few yards down the road, chatting to a woman in a pink raincoat. On the other side of the road a paparazzo was lounging against a motorbike, but Jezzer was a familiar face who had been tracking the cast of *Lovin' Essex* since the very first episode. The drug dealer from two doors up was giving him shifty looks as he passed with his two pit bull terriers, obviously trying to ascertain whether Jezzer was an undercover cop and his house was on the verge of getting raided for the third time in a month.

But other than that, nothing suspicious.

Two years he'd been with Kiki and he'd never seen her in such a state. Not that he blamed her for being jumpy. For the last few weeks she'd been terrified after the bigwigs at the show had first sat her down and warned her that she'd been getting vile, malicious mail, including grainy photographs of her out and about in Chelmsford. The snaps clearly showed that someone was tracking her, and given the content of the letters, it wasn't an adoring fan. Sick bastard. Zac wasn't one for violence, but if he caught the creep that was doing this he'd . . . he'd . . .

They both jumped when his Auntie Dot barged into the room brandishing a tray with five mugs of tea, a brown cake and a plate of Penguins.

'What's going on, love?' Auntie Dot asked as she placed the tray on the tallest of the teak nest of tables that sat in the corner of the room. They'd been there since Zac was a boy, but Dot Parker had resisted all attempts and offers to refurnish the house. She was from the mend-and-make-do generation that came genetically attached to their patterned carpets, pink lampshades and furniture that must have caused a global teak shortage some-time around 1975.

'It's OK, Auntie Dot – Kiki thought she might have spotted that weirdo, but there's no one there.'

'If I get my hands on him he'll be sorry,' Dot muttered, shaking her head and causing her Ivana Trump beehive to wobble as she put five doilies on plates and then loaded each one up with a Penguin and a slice of Swiss roll. Zac recognised it as home-made, and the thought compelled him to open the window. Dot was marvellous at many things, but baking wasn't one of them. The roses directly outside the window had suffered years of bombardment from discarded cupcakes and rock-solid slices of Victoria sponge. 'I mean, imagine treating a young girl like that. Wouldn't have got that in my day. We said what we thought to people's faces – none of this interweb and Facepage stuff.'

Neither Zac nor Kiki even considered correcting her. Interrupting Dot when she was on a rant was akin to attempting to hold back a tsunami with an umbrella and an extra-large cagoule.

The door opened again and Lena came tottering in on pink bejewelled platforms with eight-inch heels, followed by Minx in skin-tight shorts and white suede boots. Minx plonked herself down on the floor while Lena carefully eased herself down on the couch, leaving three feet between her and Kiki, the distance required to accommodate two hairstyles that were the approximate diameter of five-year-old leylandiis. Their elaborately groomed appearance today wasn't just for the *Lovin' Essex* shoot they'd be working on later. Minx, Lena and Kiki had looked like this long before they got parts in the show. While Minx was comparatively low-maintenance, with her cute crop, the other two had hair extensions that reached down to their waists, Lena's pale pink, Kiki's a deep shade of conker. They all had eyelash extensions that caused a draught when they blinked, and their Roberto Cavalli outfits (hot pants for Minx, mini-dresses for Lena and Kiki) revealed tans that matched Auntie Dot's nest of tables. All three had made the top ten in *Heat*'s Reality TV Babe of The Year awards. Zac was totally made up for Lena and Minx, who came joint fourth. And Kiki would get over coming second to some bird from *Made in Chelsea* eventually. Like when hell froze over.

Lena took one look at the Swiss roll and took evasive action that involved much pointing at her gold Dolce & Gabbana cuff watch. 'Aw, Auntie Dot, thanks ever so much, but we need to get going to work. Don't we, babes?' Lena loved their Auntie Dot dearly and would never hurt her feelings, so her expression implored Minx, Zac and Kiki to agree. They didn't need persuading.

'Er, yes, we do, Mrs Parker. But thanks ever so much for the cake.' Kiki flashed her polar-white perfectly shaped gnashers.

Dot was having none of it. 'You haven't eaten any yet. How about I put a couple of slices in a Tupperware for you to take with you? Minx, you'll have a bit, won't you?'

Zac watched Minx grimace as she nodded and reached for a large slab of cake. That was Minx all over. While Lena was the peacemaker and the calm, reasoned one, Minx was the more adventurous. At nineteen, she'd moved out of Dot's to live with her boyfriend, Dale. They were the show's 'cool' couple, devoted to each other, glued together by their mutual love of parties and extreme sports. The episode featuring their tandem bungee jump off Tower Bridge had been a ratings winner, and now they were waiting for permission to abseil down the Shard. Since she'd moved to the other side of town, he didn't see Minx as often as he saw Lena, but he loved her to bits.

Thus, action was required to save her from allowing her adventurous streak to land her in trouble. Or A&E.

Zac threw his arm around Dot's shoulder, something he'd been doing since he was tall enough to reach. At sixty-four, Dot Parker was their mum's older sister by almost two decades, and had brought them up since their mum walked out on them twenty years before. She had willingly accepted five-year-old Zac and the three-year-old twins and had never complained about taking them on.

They didn't know their dad. Auntie Dot said she thought it was the guy who used to do the catalogue deliveries but told them their mother had refused to confirm the gory details, so they could never be sure.

Divorced from a market trader and with no kids of her own, Dot spent most of her life with a mug of tea in one hand and a cigarette in the other. It was a life that had left her with lined skin and a throaty laugh that could be heard in neighbouring streets when she got going. Throughout their childhood she'd worked two cleaning jobs to make sure they never went without, but she still wore her red lippy and her smartest shoes and could craft a beehive in world-record time. She was a tough, optimistic diamond who'd instilled in them the importance of family, the principals of a hard day's graft and her motto for life, 'As long as there's bingo, there's hope.'

'Tell you what, Auntie Dot, I'll be back round tomorrow and we'll tuck into it then.' Zac gave her a kiss on the cheek, then laughed as she swatted him away with a smile. He was a grown man who lived in his own flat, made a good living as a personal trainer, looked like he'd just walked off the pages of *Men's Health* magazine, had travelled the world (Benidorm, Fuengirola, Marbella), yet the thought of upsetting Dot Parker still chilled him to the bone. He didn't care if it made him look soft.

'Far too handsome for your own good,' she said with a proud grin, repeating the line she'd been cooing to him since he was a boy. Minx threw him a grateful wink for the distraction and sidestepped the food tray on her way to the door.

Zac kissed Dot on the cheek again, then took Lena's hand.

'Right then, let's go. Lena, Minx – Jezzer is out there, so you walk beside me. Kiki, you go first.'

The subterfuge was necessary because over the two series of *Lovin' Essex*, Kiki had been billed as the wild child of the show, resistant to commitment and permanently bikini-waxed, ready for action. Of course, it was all a sham – but her 165,000 followers on Twitter didn't realise that.

To keep the facade going, the producers had warned her that she wasn't allowed to mention Zac or anything about their relationship on the telly. It suited them both fine. They'd met just before the first episode was aired, when he'd run a five-day residential boot camp designed to get the female stars of the show in perfect shape before the cameras rolled. He'd broken one of his ten commandments (number 3 – Thou Shalt Not Shag Thy Clients) and hooked up with her on the last night. They'd been together ever since. One day he'd definitely do something about making it more permanent . . . if Auntie Dot didn't kill Kiki with a toxic banoffee pie first.

As they emerged from the front door, Jezzer threw his bacon roll to the ground, flicked on his Nikon and shot snap after snap as the foursome climbed into Zac's black convertible BMW. It was an old model, but with meticulous care and a personal plate, it was every bit as flash as some of the newer ones on the roads. Kiki was always on at him to upgrade it, but he had other things on his mind. Other plans for his cash. The thought made his muscles clench with anxiety. He shook his head to clear it of the scenario that was stressing him out and never far from his mind. He needed to fix it and quick, but there was no point worrying about it right this minute. He'd come up with something. He always did.

Jezzer was at the passenger side of the car now, getting great shots of Kiki as she did her best 'ignoring-the-camera-but-don't-I-look-gorg' pout. Meanwhile, Lena and Minx smiled with amusement, knowing that the paps would use the picture of Kiki mincing up the path before they'd use the one of them with their hulk of a brother taking up most of the frame. Zac knew it didn't bother them. Lena thought Kiki's fixation with press and publicity was exhausting and she'd no desire to stress herself out with all that. And Minx was sure that spending every daylight moment with your back arched, hand on hip and boobs projected outwards could result in spinal problems later in life.

Less than fifteen minutes later, they pulled into the car park of Density Fitness, a gym in Chelmsford that was owned by Zac's mate Den. The gym was the epicentre of the daytime action on the show, with the guys working out while delivering updates on the previous night's activities. It was the perfect location because it shared the building with Shiraz's ground-floor beauty salon.

Today's shoot was to be in the salon, recording the girls gossiping as they got ready for a big night out at the Beach Box, the top night spot in the county. Shiraz and Porsche were already there. 'Bitches always have to steal the best spots,' Kiki murmured to Lena, before screeching, 'Hi, babes!' and air-kissing the other two. Zac shook his head, then offered a 'Hey, guys' to the crew. Three cameramen in the standard T-shirts, jeans and rigger boots, the sound bloke and one of the junior directors all returned his greeting then went back to setting up. Zac didn't see the appeal in any of this. Despite Edwina's approaches, he wasn't interested in joining them on screen. Give us a break. Who would ever want their whole lives to be played out in public? Some things just weren't worth free waxing for life and a VIP pass to the Beach Box. Besides, if he dared talk about some of the stuff that lot discussed on the show, he would soon experience Dot's hand across the back of his head. It was a peculiar double standard. As far as Dot was concerned, it was fine for Lena and her cast girlfriends to discuss the blokes they were seeing, but when the guys on the show spilled the details of their sex lives, Dot came over all militant, muttering declarations like 'Robert DeNiro would never have been so indiscreet' and threatening to picket the set.

Suddenly a deafening screech struck the whole room into stillness, as Edwina marched on to the set. 'Right, my little fucking wonders, let's get going.'

Zac felt his back molars crunch together. How the hell did Edwina's boyfriend put up with that all day? She had a voice like an Exocet missile being shot through the Dartford Tunnel.

Edwina consulted the notes on the clipboard she was carrying. 'Right, Lena, you're in chair number five. We want to know whether or not you shagged Max last night, and if so, whether he's going to tell his wife before she gets back from Vilamoura. No, don't say anything right now – I want it authentic and fresh on camera.'

Zac winced. He was going to have to send Dot to bingo the night this one aired. Dot didn't mind Lena's chat, but she drew the line at relationships with married blokes, so whenever this was going to be mentioned, they took evasive action involving a dabber pen and a taxi for her and her chums to the Full House Funhouse. If Dot ever got Sky+, Lena was screwed. There was no way their aunt would believe that it was all a set-up, and Max and his glamour model wife Coco had actually been separated for months. Zac wasn't sure about this storyline at all, and neither was Lena – it was painting her out to be something she definitely wasn't.

'Porsche, we want to hear about the results from the STD clinic, and give us the latest on the rash.'

'It was an allergic reaction to the nail glue she used when she stuck Ramone's initial on my vajayjay,' she raged, throwing daggers at Shiraz. 'I had to cancel my *Loaded* shoot and everything.'

Edwina's expression brightened at the prospect of a potential catfight. The episode where Kiki had taken a pair of kitchen scissors to Porsche's hair extensions had come a close second in the ratings to the one in which Lena had made a move on the (allegedly) married Max.

'All right, love, save it for when it's rolling. Kiki, you were considering Toby's offer to go to Dubai for a dirty weekend.'

That one didn't bother Zac. He'd known Toby since they were in school together and he'd always been the best-looking guy in Essex – but he was more likely to want a rampant affair with Zac than Kiki. Toby's decision to come out was being saved as a season finale.

Toby was fairly new to the show and had been happy to be open about his sexuality from the start, but after long conversations with the producers, they felt that watching him come out would be a storyline their teenage gay fans could relate to. Not to mention a ratings winner. Massive press coverage was planned, with a road-show and a phone hotline campaign – although no one was sure who had started the rumour that Elton John would pitch up for the coming-out special.

Edwina was still barking out information.

'Minx, you're announcing that you've been thinking about talking to Dale about getting engaged.'

Minx giggled. 'We're going to have to get him proper drunk when I tell him how much the ring I want costs.'

'And Shiraz, the police are considering legal action after the whole naked-riding-a-motorbike-into-Lakeside. Our lawyers are looking into it, love, so don't worry about a thing. But if we don't get a *TV Times* Award for that episode, I'm Janet Street-Fucking-Porter.'

Shiraz couldn't hide a slight squirm of uncharacteristic discomfort.

No one was in any doubt how far Edwina would go to ramp up the drama, and having Shiraz carted off in handcuffs would be the perfect secondary storyline to Toby's outing for the final show of this series. Doing time inside for indecent exposure would play havoc with her tan and her chances of getting an American visa when the time was right to leave Essex and go crack Hollywood.

Edwina moved to wrap it up, then paused. 'Oh, and Porsche, what's this I hear about you wanting away early today?'

'Is it for that meeting about promoting the thongs?' Shiraz piped up with mischievous innocence and barely restrained glee. The temperature in the room dropped several degrees. The cast's endorsement deals and personal appearances were a major source of irritation to Edwina, who viewed them as proof that her little band of TV stars were believing their own hype. Zac knew that Kiki had been trying to pluck up the courage to tell her about her new range of gel bra inserts for a fortnight.

Keen to escape the imminent blowout, Zac decided to nip upstairs to see if Den was in the office. Den might be close to double his age, but they'd been best mates since the owner of the gym had shown him how to work the front lat pull-down machine when Zac first walked into Density Fitness as a puny fifteen-year-old. The two of them had just clicked. He thought about confiding in Den about the problem that was keeping him awake at night, but right now his pride was stopping him. He should be able to sort it himself. What kind of bloke was he if he couldn't? He'd already made progress. Twenty grand they said they wanted, and he'd already raised ten. He'd quietly sold just about everything of value that he owned, and his car would go for another five Gs. The bank had knocked him back for a loan, but that wasn't really surprising given that he was self-employed and business had slumped a bit, what with the credit crunch. It didn't help that Kiki wanted him with her all the time since the whole stalker thing started. Not that he begrudged that – he'd never let anyone lay a finger on her. He knew he could ask her for the money – she was minted these days – but he never, ever would.

He checked his Tag, only still on his wrist instead of eBay because it had been a present from Lena and Minx and was inscribed with 'To our big bro, with all our love' on the back.

Maybe he'd get a quick workout in now. He reckoned there would be at least a couple of hours before they moved filming to the Beach Box, and he hadn't done his pecs, delts and lats yet this week. It was all part of the job. He'd been a personal trainer now for five years and he knew his best advert was his own body. Every muscle was perfectly toned, every curve defined, and if he lay down, his abdominal area could be used as a toast rack. Not that he ate carbs when he was in training.

'Freeze!' Edwina screeched just as he got to the door. She descended on him like a deadly python preying on a mouse. He braced himself for yet another barrage of reasons why he should join the show. The profile. The fame. The babes. The fact that if he didn't, she might just dislocate her jaw and swallow him whole.

'Den tells me that your skills as a personal trainer verge on the fucking miraculous,' she said. He tried not to wince at the sheer volume of her voice. Hanging out near this woman came with a definite risk of tinnitus.

He nodded, unwilling to argue the point. If he wasn't going to have faith in his own abilities then no one else would. He waited for the inevitable. They obviously wanted a personal trainer on the show and were going to offer the part to him. No way. He couldn't. He'd rather do the whole naked-motorbike-through-Lakeside thing than share his life with the British viewing public.

'Here's the deal, Schwarzenegger. I've just found out I'm getting married in eight weeks in front of the whole fucking world. I am not parading down the aisle with every pair of eyes trained on this arse.' She pointed to her back end.

Bloody hell, she was offering him a job. That was all he needed right now – a new, demanding client, just when he had other more important problems to solve. No doubt she'd want one or two hours a week, expect a miracle and then bad-mouth him right across the south-east if he failed. It wasn't worth it. He needed to focus on raising some serious cash to get everything sorted.

'I'm sorry, but I'm not taking on new clients just now. I can recommend someone else though.'

He could swear he heard the click of her jaws separating.

'I don't think you understand me,' she said slowly, with added menace. 'This arse has to be at least three sizes smaller than it is now. I need you to train me. Eight weeks, thirty pounds off and I want Kelly Brook's buttocks by the end of it. Her tits too. I want your services for at least four hours every day and I'm willing to pay for it. What's your price, Muscles?'

This changed everything. He did a quick calculation. Two months. He needed at least five grand to cover his flat, bills and spenders, but he got that from his regulars. He could do this too. He'd need to shuffle things around a bit, but it was manageable. His heart started to beat just a little bit faster at the prospect of what this could mean. Not that he would show the python. He shrugged and did his best impression of nonchalance.

'Five grand. And an extra grand bonus at the end if we achieve the target. And we will,' he told her in a tone of confidence he definitely didn't feel.

Edwina's eyes narrowed as she summed up the offer.

'Six grand. OK, Muscles, let me tell you how it's going to work. Two grand now, call it an advance against future services. Then four grand bonus if you succeed. And you will, isn't that right?'

There was an edge of challenge in her voice that would have made the hairs on his back stand on end, if he'd had any. He didn't consider it a sign of weakness or vanity that the waxing pot was his friend. Kiki wasn't the only one in the relationship who took pride in their appearance.

Six grand. This could solve everything, could make the difference. He held out his hand.

'Deal.'

Edwina barely had time to reciprocate when she was called to set. 'Right, Muscles, tomorrow morning, eight a.m., upstairs, and don't be late.'

'Done,' he agreed. Yes! This was incredible. Problem solved. He just had to . . .

His thoughts were interrupted by his phone ringing in his pocket. Across the room, the sound guy threw him a filthy look.

Zac stepped outside to check the screen. Blocked number. He considered flipping it to answering machine, then thought better of it. It might just be another client he could squeeze into a free slot – which given his most recent commitment would have to be between midnight and four a.m.

'Hello?'

'Zac, love, it's me. Look, it's nothing to worry about, but I need you to come down to Chelmsford cop shop and get me out. There's been a bit of bother.'

'What? Are you OK? Shit, Auntie Dot, what happened?'

'I got arrested, love. Saw someone in the rose bushes outside the window so I went for him. Turns out he was a junkie looking for the house up the street. You know how frail I am. Don't know what came over me – fear, I 'spect.'

Zac had two conflicting emotions – a massive wave of concern, tempered by the urge to laugh at Dot Parker describing herself as frail and scared. She was obviously playing up to an audience.

'But the nice copper here says they won't be pressing

charges on account of me being elderly. And, you know, not hitting him with a proper weapon.'

'What did you use, Auntie Dot?'

'Don't be disappointed, love, but I grabbed the first thing that came to hand. I thumped him with my Swiss roll.'

Chapter Five

Talli drained her coffee and put her mug on the granite draining board. Theresa, the housekeeper, got borderline murderous if anyone dared to interfere with the way she stacked the dishwasher. Theresa had been with the family for ever, and ran the house with a rod of iron that intimidated everyone except Arabella and Dessi. When Talli was a child, Theresa used to tell her that she'd been trained by the Honduran rebel militia, and given her temperamental outbursts over the years, Talli was one hundred per cent certain that the militia had lost their best member.

The white Georgian town house on Chelsea Square was spotless from the attic room Talli inhabited, down four floors to Theresa's basement apartment. Directly below Talli were Dessi's suite, two guest rooms, and Simmy's old room, last inhabited before he'd moved into Edwina's river-view flat in Richmond. The Richmond flat was closer to his paper plant in Twickenham and far enough away from Theresa's disapproving glare, but he still regularly stayed in his old room when he had early meetings in the city and didn't want to tackle the morning rush hour.

Her parents' suites, dressing rooms and bathrooms and her mother's fully kitted-out professional beauty salon were on the first floor. The three reception rooms, her father's study and the Smallbone of Devizes kitchen were on the ground level, with the gym, garage and Theresa's apartment below. In the grounds at the back there was a garden room that housed a fifteen-metre swimming pool that was only ever used by Talli. Her mother had decided sometime around the mid nineties that the chlorine was ageing her skin.

'Why do you have a face like you've been chewing a wasp?' Dessi's arrival came with a customary good-natured jibe, as she wandered in wearing black cashmere lounge pants and a tiny matching vest top, her make-up-free face glowing with health and her mane of caramel hair pulled up into a high ponytail. Everyone said how much the sisters looked alike, but Talli knew they were just being kind. The one thing they had in common was their height, but while Dessi used it in the manner of a supermodel, Talli was all clumsy arms and gangly legs.

They were completely different in personality, too. At twenty-one, her sister had the looks of a model and the debating skills of a politician, but chose to conserve both by resisting work, stress and boredom. Instead she went from brunch at noon with her chums, to the shops or salons of Chelsea, Kensington and Knightsbridge, then on to dinner and a club. She called it her networking stage – apparently it came between the education stage and the 'oh fuck, I'd better do something for charity and then think about getting a job' stage.

Talli couldn't think of anything more mind-numbingly boring – not to mention stressful. If there was a choice between an afternoon trying on clothes in Bottega Veneta and Theresa pulling out her toenails using a garlic press, she'd probably opt for the latter.

Dessi plopped a bowl of melon and strawberries, freshly prepared by Theresa, on the counter, then leaned in to give Talli a kiss on the cheek.

'Cheer up, sweetie. What's the worst that can happen?' she asked with a grin.

Talli shrugged. 'I'm thinking nuclear apocalypse might be worse. Nah, maybe not.'

Dessi roared with laughter. Despite being such different personalities – or perhaps because of that – the two women were friends as well as sisters, even sharing the same social group. Talli just didn't join them on a daily basis.

'Mother has put me in charge of Simmy's wedding and I need to organise the whole thing in eight weeks. Hang on, I'm feeling the urge to put my head down for a moment.'

Talli dropped her forehead on to the solid oak table, making Dessi cackle with laughter again.

'Say no!' she giggled. 'What could she do? She can't force you to do it.'

They both knew that wasn't true. Talli lifted her head. 'You know, you could always help me. Make it a family effort.'

Dessi scooped some natural Greek yogurt out of a tub and landed a dollop on her fruit. 'I'd love to . . .'

'You would?' Talli asked, her voice full of hope and astonishment.

'I would,' Dessi replied firmly. 'But I can't, because my speciality areas are fashion and shoes. And besides, if I actually participated in this, the 'rents might realise there's a work ethic in here somewhere and coerce me into gainful employment.'

The last line was delivered with an accompanying shudder. 'So . . . heard from Fliss this week?'

Talli and Fliss Bramwell, another lifelong member of their group, had been inseparable since their nannies used to take them to Kensington Gardens on sunny afternoons. Later, they'd spent countless sunny days in Fliss's gardens (plural – there were several, one of which provided specimens for the Chelsea Flower Show), playing at schools. Fliss was always the headmistress and Talli was the PE teacher who ran at the Olympics in her spare time.

Those childhood games had clearly mapped out a career path for at least one of them. Talli might now be the most reluctant wedding planner in London, but Fliss had just qualified as a teacher and had left the month before to take up her first post.

Talli shook her head. 'No. She's at the school in Malawi now. I won't hear any more until she gets back to civilisation. Apparently they make a trip for supplies once a month, so she'll try to get to somewhere with a phone signal then.'

Dessi was aghast. 'No phone, no internet – you know what that means?'

'None of the needless, time-wasting trappings of modern life?' Talli replied, while mentally betting her entire worldly goods that wasn't the point Dessi was hinting at.

'No phone sex, no Skype sex and no way to hook up for sex! The poor girl. I'll give it a month and then I'm arranging a helicopter and flying in supplies of men and make-up. Poor Fliss will be desperate by then.'

'You're right, that will be just what she needs while she's fighting disease, infection, lack of sanitary conditions, language barriers and the challenge of educating a hundred children using nothing but chalk. Thank God you've got her back, Dessi,' Talli replied with a smile, then jumped up from the table and grabbed her black Mulberry Daria satchel from the floor beside her. It was one of Dessi's cast-offs, but Talli didn't mind. Spending £700 on a handbag seemed pointless to her.

'Where are you off to?'

'Meeting Domenic for a quick lunch, then out to see Edwina. She's working somewhere in Essex so it'll take me a while to get there.'

'Call the car service,' her sister suggested, like it was the most natural thing in the world.

Talli ignored the suggestion, stole a large strawberry from Dessi's bowl and headed for the door. As she passed the huge antique Venetian mirror in the hallway, she wondered if she should have made a bit more of an effort, rather than sticking to her standard uniform of grey skinny jeans, white T-shirt, biker boots and a black waterfall cardi. It was Nicole Farhi, but she'd had it so long, it was definitely on the well-worn side of this season.

A clicking noise distracted her from her thoughts, even more so when she realised that it was coming from Daddy's study. She was sure he'd left for work hours ago, as usual.

Pushing the door open, she saw him sitting at his desk, his face a picture of surprise at the interruption. Was it her imagination or did he suddenly flush a subtle shade of pink?

A couple of rapid clicks on his computer mouse didn't help alleviate her fears. Oh God, she'd caught him watching porn. It was the only explanation for his flustered reaction. Her mother had only left for the Alps two hours before, and already her dad had turned to the Playboy website for amusement.

'Talli, darling, didn't see you there,' he lied unconvincingly. Giles Caston-Jones had been a handsome man in his time, but few hints of that remained. Years of lunches at the club and long hours at the bank had stretched his midriff to breaking point, and the lack of any grooming regime other than soap and water had left him looking every one of his sixty-five years. Talli was sure her mother tried to inject him with Restylane as he slept.

'Just out then, are you?'

His forced joviality made Talli's heart ache. For all her mother's self-obsessed criticisms and carping, her daddy made up for it with a lifetime of quiet love and understated pride. Her parents' marriage had always puzzled her, but somewhere along the line she'd decided that her mother had traded excitement and passion for the perks that came with being married to her father. The Caston-Jones heritage could be traced back centuries. They were an old London family with an illustrious record in finance and philanthropy in the male line – only Simmy had bucked tradition by going to work for Edwina's father over at Gambond Paper. Daddy didn't mind, though. He wasn't the type to make demands of his children. He was just happy with his clubs and an easy life – courtesy of a glamorous wife who ran things with military precision. But now that he seemed to have taken the pedal off the gas a little at work, he'd obviously turned to new outlets of amusement.

'Yes, Daddy, just going to meet Dom. Can I get you anything?'

Another wave of pink crossed his cheeks.

'Erm, no. Thanks, darling. I'm fine. Thanks. You have a lovely day.'

She took a step forward to kiss him, decided against it in case he had a pile of *Hustler* magazines stashed under the desk and blew him a kiss instead.

A quick cab ride to Kensington High Street later, she reached Bon Auberge just ten minutes late. Domenic was already waiting for her at the corner table he frequented every day for lunch. Her boyfriend was a creature of habit. He grinned and rose a couple of inches off his seat as she approached, then leaned over to kiss her once on each cheek.

'Hello, munchkin, you're looking lovely.' He always said that. It was his cursory opening line every time they met.

'I look like I've been dragged through a spin cycle,' she retorted with a giggle, motioning to her explosion of hair. It was never great in the rain. When she was a kid, there had been a doll whose hair expanded when you wetted it. Talli had realised then that it was the closest she was ever going to get to being immortalised in plastic. Pulling her mane back from her face, she grabbed a black band off her wrist and twisted her locks into a ponytail.

Sitting across from Domenic Stritch-Leeson (yes, she was aware that her children could potentially be called Caston-Jones-Stritch-Leeson, which would be a bugger to fit on all those school name tags) always made her feel a bit better about the world.

They'd been dating for five years, but their parents moved in the same circles so they'd known each other all their lives. They'd first kissed at Talli's eighteenth birthday party, when he scooped her up after she fell off her platforms. Unlike every other smartly dressed young man in the room, she'd immediately loved Domenic because he was wearing a vintage Stone Roses T-shirt and boots that looked like Adam Levine had battered them to death with a club. Today his outfit wasn't a radical departure from that look. His black skinny jeans sat on top of black leather Diesel boots. His oversize T-shirt was monochrome except for the red lips on the image of Marilyn Monroe that covered the entire front. The contrast between his formal upbringing and the casual guy before her was viewed as a (disturbingly enduring) passing phase by his parents, who were convinced it had happened because they'd smoked a lot of dope with famous rock bands in the eighties.

Every now and then Domenic and Talli talked about moving in together, but they had never quite got around to it. Maybe they should. It would be life progress of some kind. She had no career, no plan and these days she spent a disproportionate amount of time talking about bunting and Portaloos – maybe it was time to move things along in the 'personal relationships' area.

'Horrible business with the Carltons. What a hellish situation for you. Although the general consensus was that Cossie had it coming.'

Talli exhaled and reached across the red checked table cover for his hand, smiling a thank you to the waiter who appeared as if by magic to lay down two menus and fill her water glass.

'Domenic, do you love me?'

'Of course I do.' He looked almost offended by the question.

'Then never mention the names Carlton or Deloite to me again.'

He laughed and gave her hand a squeeze. 'It wasn't your fault – you thought you were doing the right thing!'

'It was my fault, but thanks for defending me,' she mumbled, on account of the fact that she'd torn off a large piece of the sun-dried tomato and rosemary loaf in front of her and was healing her pain with stodge.

Domenic took another sip of his mineral water. Sparkling. Always. 'I bumped into James Abercrombie this morning and he tells me they're no longer using Grand Affairs for their Christmas party.'

'I *know*. Can we add Abercrombie to the veto list?' This was excruciating. Stodge alone obviously wasn't going to cut it. 'Can I have a large white wine, please? Any one will do – you choose,' Talli whispered to the waiter, who was still hovering beside them.

Domenic carried on regardless. 'So I was thinking, darling, let's get away for a few weeks. You've been so busy lately, and some of the gang . . .'

Was it wrong that Talli had the sudden thought that a twenty-five-year-old man shouldn't still be referring to their friends as a 'gang'? God, what was wrong with her? Had her mother's venomous side been lying dormant in her for twenty-three years only to erupt like that Icelandic volcano when she least expected it? No, it was the stress, she decided. The prospect of the meeting with Edwina this afternoon had switched her terror dial up to maximum and she was having a minor meltdown in anticipation.

'Talli, sweetheart, are you listening?'

'Sorry, I'm . . . just . . . yes, I am. I just missed that last bit.'

Domenic rolled his eyes and handed her another chunk of bread.

'Some of the gang are going over to Courchevel mid-December to get a bit of skiing in. You know how everything practically shuts down at the office in December and January . . .'

The reason why Domenic perennially looked like he was down to his last trust fund was that he had rebelled against working in the family wine business and instead joined the A&R department of Embankment Records, the second largest music company in the country. His credibility had gone through the ceiling and catapulted him up several floors when he'd discovered the latest rap sensation, Big Up D, busking outside the Brixton Academy. Now Domenic was the 'go to' guy at the label for anything to do with Big. Or was it Up D?

'. . . and we could have a couple of weeks on the piste and then come back for Christmas.'

Domenic sat back with an excited grin and she so wanted to leave him with that feeling. She suddenly realised that he looked even better now than he did when they first hooked up. Back then he'd been a university lacrosse champion, with a floppy fringe and a tanned, muscular frame. Now his face was softer, a little rounder, and the hair was a bit of a shaggy mess, but it suited him. Made him look like the kind of guy you could hang out with on a Sunday morning, eating bagels in the park. Which, actually, they never did due to his wheat intolerance. And his dislike of grass. For a laid-back rock/rap guy, there were a disproportionate number of things he liked to avoid.

'I can't.'

'What?'

'I can't go. Persimmon and Edwina got a last-minute cancellation at Highdrow Castle and they're getting married on Christmas Eve.'

'But we can ensure we're back by then,' he argued.

'My mother has put me in charge of arranging the wedding.'

Even Domenic, who supported her, valued her skills and encouraged her when she was full of self-doubt, looked at her now like she'd just suggested climbing Everest in a wetsuit.

'Your mother does know what happened at the Carlton party, doesn't she?'

Talli nodded.

'And she knows that the marquee collapsed at the Goldberg bar mitzvah and that you set the Dunlops' kitchen on fire with a crème brûlée torch?'

Talli nodded.

'And yet she's put you in charge of the wedding. My God, she must be desperate.'

Talli tried hard to conjure up some indignant outrage, but actually he was just vocalising her own thoughts.

'You have to get out of it and come with us instead. We're all going. Dessi has already booked her ticket . . .' Of course her sister was going. Of course. 'And Verity and India are in,' he added, confident that having two of her girlfriends there would change her mind. 'Tell her you're not doing it. Insist she gets in a real . . .'

Discomfort stopped him, as they both realised he was about to say 'a real party planner'. Again, he was only stating the obvious, but she appreciated the tact.

'What can I get for you today?' The smiling waiter was back, looking at them expectantly.

'I'll have a burger, with pepper fries, and a large Coke, please.'

As always, Domenic raised one eyebrow at her order. He never tired of telling her that she had the eating habits of a twelve-year-old from Acton.

'A grilled chicken breast, well done, salad on the side, no cheese, croutons or rocket. And another water. Sparkling. Perrier.'

There was a pause as the waiter drifted away. Finally Talli ended it.

'I can't.'

'Of course you can. Talli, you're a twenty-three-year-old woman – you are allowed to stick up for yourself. Do you want to do this?'

'Of course I don't.'

'Well, put your foot down. Tell her you're not doing it, that you're coming to Courchevel with me and that's final.'

Coming to Courchevel. He said 'coming'. So he'd already made up his mind.

It suddenly occurred to Talli that he was telling her to back out of what her mother wanted so that she could do what he wanted.

Did anyone give a damn what *she* wanted?

The thought made her wince. Bugger, this stress was making her act crazy. Of course she wanted to go with Domenic and the posse. Or gang. Or whatever he was calling it. They'd have a lovely time. But she knew that if she went against her mother on this, Arabella would pull contacts at Interpol and have her hunted down and returned to Chelsea in a Louis Vuitton chest to fulfil her duties.

Fifteen minutes later their lunch arrived, by which time Domenic had realised that argument was futile and settled for quiet seething. The frustration was that she knew he was right and he was just disappointed that his lovely plans for them would be spoiled. After a couple of half-hearted attempts to engage him in conversation, she gave up and consumed the rest of her pre-teen meal in silence.

'Coffees or desserts?' the cute, smiley waiter asked as he cleared away their plates.

'No thank you,' Talli answered, even though she felt like she desperately needed an erotic encounter with a tiramisu. It would just irritate Dominic even more – he didn't do dairy.

Shoving up the arm of her cardi, she checked the Omega her parents had bought her for her last birthday, then reached out and put her hand over his in a conciliatory gesture. 'Look, I have to go. I'm meeting Edwina in Essex in two hours and I have to work out the best way to get there.'

He didn't even offer suggestions. Shit, he must really be pissed off if he wasn't trying to utilise his encyclopaedic knowledge of London geography and transport, gathered over years of going to gigs in out-of-the-way places in a bid to sign the next Puff Diddy. Or Daddy. Or Puffy. Talli was never quite sure. She was much more of a Snow Patrol and The Script kind of girl.

They parted with a frosty peck on the cheek before Domenic marched off in the direction of the office, leaving everything but her stomach feeling deflated. This was obviously National Upset the People You Love week.

'Sis! What are you doing here? Ooh, is that the gorgeous Domenic's arse I see departing?'

'What's the maximum sentence for assault with a Mulberry?' Talli asked a drooling Dessi. The creature in front of her bore no resemblance to the one from their earlier meeting in the kitchen. Now Dessi was a glam goddess, in a pair of butt-clenchingly tight white jeans, over-the-knee leather Louboutin boots, a white wisp of a chiffon vest top and a studded black Dolce and Gabbana jacket that fitted like an obscenely expensive glove. A Chanel 2.55 with silver hardwear was casually slung over her shoulder, a perfect match for the sunglasses that sat on top of her head, holding back her wavy tresses. Yes, sunglasses in October. This was a page from Italian *Cosmo* come to life, plonked in the middle of Kensington High Street and given the power of speech to mock her dearest family member.

'Oh, for Mulberry you'd probably get community service,' Dessi replied with a grin. 'But if it was a Chanel I'd call for maximum sentencing and refuse to let Theresa smuggle in a nail file in one of her carrot cakes.'

Despite herself, Talli laughed. It was so difficult to be irritated with her sister.

'Who are you meeting?' she asked.

'Verity and India. I think Simmy is joining us too. He's in the city for a . . . actually I've no idea why he's in the city – I tune out when he mentions work.'

A prickle of annoyance forced Talli to reverse her last conclusion regarding the inability to be annoyed at her sister. And brother, for that matter. Her life had been hijacked by his wedding plans, yet he was having a lovely sociable lunch while she was cutting hers short to get to work on his behalf. 'Simmy? But . . . but . . .'

'Here he is now! Fabulous! What great timing.'

A large black Mercedes drew into the kerb beside them, and her brother stepped out, looking none too pleased with life. Despite her one-track mind being firmly on the road to blind fury, Talli was struck by the regular observation that while she and Dessi had dived into their mother's side of the gene pool, Persimmon had clearly stayed for a paddle in their father's side. He was so much shorter than his sisters, dashing in an old-fashioned, somehow-crumpled-in-a-Savile-Row-suit sort of way.

'Sorry, I'm late, Dessi – traffic was bloody murder. This is why I don't come into the city unless it's life or bloody death. I've been here twice this week and I'm in need of a lie-down in a dark room. Talli, darling, I didn't realise you were joining us.'

'I'm not,' Talli said with an embarrassed shrug. 'I'm just heading out to Essex to meet your fiancée to talk about weddings.'

'Ah, you're a rock.' She didn't point out that he had already informed her of this at their previous meeting. 'Thanks again for stepping in, lovely – Edwina is terribly stressed out with all that crowd she works with. Unbelievable what they get up to. Unbelievable. How are you getting over there?'

'I'm not sure yet. Taxi to Liverpool Street and then train, I think.'

'That's absurd, it's bloody miles away. Look, take my car. I'm not using it again today anyway. I'm staying with the 'rents tonight because I've got another meeting here tomorrow and there's no point heading back out to Richmond when Edwina is shacked up in a hotel in some godforsaken suburb.'

'No, it's fine, I'll—'

'Talli, stop!' Dessi interjected. 'Simmy is helping you out here. It will make your life so much easier and it's a little act of appreciation for what you're doing. Take it. Gift horse. Mouth. Fucking great big Mercedes.'

Talli laughed and got in the car. Dessi was right. Sometimes her natural urge to resist a bit of gratuitous luxury got in the way. Her sister had clearly floated right past that trait in the genetic pool.

Two hours later, Simmy's driver pulled into a parking lot in front of a huge sign announcing the 'Density Fitness Gym'. It would probably have taken Talli less time if she'd used public transport, but at least she'd had a chance to snooze without the worry of waking up with her head on some random stranger's shoulder.

The car drew to a stop in front of a large window on the ground floor, with 'Spa Shiraz' written in pink on the glass.

Talli checked her notes. This was definitely the place.

The receptionist directed her upstairs, and she'd barely stepped foot on the black rubber floor of the massive gym when she was ambushed by a greeting that broke the sound barrier.

'Talli! Thank fuck you're here!' Edwina screeched. Shocked and mildly traumatised by the decibel level of her voice, a nearby elderly gent missed his footing on the Versaclimber and was now dangling two feet in the air.

Talli bustled across the room, did the air-kissing thing and barely had time to snatch her notepad out of her bag before Edwina got started with a bang.

'OK, darling, as you know, my mother's dead, I've got

no sisters and my friends are all far too fucking busy. My father's a sweetheart, but unless it results in the production of toilet rolls, he's no help. So as far as this wedding goes, you're it. Now, here's what I want.'

Talli wondered if treatment for compulsive use of the word 'fuck' would be on the list. They were such an odd couple, her brother and Edwina. He was so straight, so Establishment, while Edwina, six inches taller, was wildly extrovert and tough as nails, with a mouth like a Navy Seal.

Talli started scribbling, her stomach twisting a little more with every mention of words like 'sensational', 'magnificent' and – oh, dear God – 'wedding of the decade'.

'Are you OK? You look a bit pale, love.' It took a few moments for Talli to realise that the enquiry was directed at her and came from a guy on the other side of the treadmill. Well, not really a guy. More of a god – a barely dressed one, with visible muscles on his tanned arms and torso, dark blond hair and long black eyelashes women would kill for. This guy made Ryan Gosling look ordinary. And she'd watched *The Notebook* at least ten times.

Edwina banged the stop button on the treadmill. 'Soz, forgot to introduce you, darling. Talli, this is Zac Parker, my personal trainer. Zac, this is Talli, my future sister-in-law. Now. What's fucking next?'

Chapter Six

Zac chided himself for taking his eye off the calorie counter on Edwina's treadmill and staring at the new arrival. Focus. It was all about work. No distractions. No stupid moves. He'd seen too many guys before him get distracted by living it large or booze or chicks – chicks like the one standing at the other side of the treadmill. Man, she was gorgeous. No make-up, but cracking skin and the kind of long, thick hair that didn't spend the first years of its life on someone else's head.

Posh, though. You could tell just by looking at her. Some wavy strands of long, honey-coloured hair had escaped from her ponytail, and as she pushed them away from her face, she swayed a little.

'Are you OK? You look a bit pale, love.' She seemed confused by the question, muttered something into her notebook. That was when Edwina banged the stop button on the treadmill, ten minutes early. That time would have to be made up later. She'd given him strict instructions – at least four hours a day for the next eight weeks. It was hard-core bridezilla training. There was no way he'd fail to get her into that size ten dress by Christmas. More than just the dosh depended on it.

Looking at her now, though, face a shade of purple, he knew it was going to take some work. And while he was confident he could change her body, there was bugger all he could do about the personality. She was like a cross between a sergeant major and a bulldog.

'OK, so here's what I'm thinking . . .' He listened as Edwina barked out orders to her sister-in-law. Was it Tabby? Sally? It didn't matter. She was looking like a rabbit in headlights as Edwina continued to rant. 'Highdrow Castle is only twenty minutes east of here. I'm going to be staying at the hotel down the road until we get this series in the can, so I think you should check in too. Let's use suppliers in this area and make this as seamless as possible. I've had my assistant book a room for you.' Sally/Tabby swayed again, her skin tone somewhere close to grey now. A twinge of sympathy crossed with irritation at the distraction forced Zac to intervene.

'Look, let's take a break. Edwina, what time do you finish filming tonight?'

'Eight o'clock. It's all salon shoots today.'

'OK, meet me back up here at half past.' He knew from collecting Kiki that they always ran over time.

Turning on his heel, he headed off before she had a chance to argue. He was beginning to realise that that was the best way to deal with Edwina – bossy, assured, no opportunity for discussion or debate, and preferably wearing ear muffs.

The gym was busy with the usual assortment of clients. A group of young women chatted as they rode side by side on spin bikes. A few middle-aged blokes grunted as they pounded the treadmills. And dotted all over were serious trainers, faces etched with concentration as they focused on the muscle/mind connection. In the free weights section, two huge bodybuilders were sitting on parallel benches doing perfect slow-motion concentration curls with twenty-five-pound dumbbells. Zac picked up a skipping rope and did a sixty-second warm up. There was time for a quick workout before his next client arrived in an hour. If he was going to juggle this new job with all his existing clients, he knew he had to keep his fitness up to deal with the stress of it. Hard work didn't faze him in the least. He'd been grafting for years and he intended to keep going after this little bump in the road had been smoothed out by six grand of Edwina's cash. One day he was going to have his own gym – he didn't doubt it for a second. His business plan was done and he'd started saving a bit for the deposit. Yeah, he'd definitely been on the way, before it had all gone tits up.

Over at the door, three of the male members of the *Lovin' Essex* cast, Toby, Max and Ramone, appeared. Immediately every chick in the room sucked in her stomach and smiled in their direction.

Zac greeted them with a collective 'All right?' They were OK, these blokes. Max was older than him, around thirty, and had that whole laid-back, cool vibe going. He'd met his soon-to-be-ex-wife Coco on the glamour circuit and was a snapper on a couple of those modelling competition shows before he joined *Lovin' Essex*. Zac admitted to a reservation or two when he'd hooked up with Lena, but in fairness, they seemed pretty well matched. Both of them were smart and low key, probably craving the limelight least out of all the cast members.

Ramone, on the other hand, was the perfect partner for Porsche. He was currently on half the billboards in town wearing nothing but his new range of boxer shorts. And Toby was just class. Pure class. The bloke was a dark-haired version of Beckham, when Becks was in one of his slick phases, all square jaw, piercing eyes and ripped body.

These guys were treated like movie stars around here, with every wannabe who'd ever set her heart on stardom and fortune desperate for the exposure that would come from dating them. It didn't make Zac jealous in the least. Good luck to them. The guys were making a great life out of it and he didn't begrudge them the spotlight – it just wasn't for him. The thought of having his cock bulge highlighted in a circle on a page of *Heat* magazine made his teeth grind. Nah, he'd take obscurity any day of the week.

Like that bloke from the Bible who parted the Red Sea, a gap formed in the crowd as Kiki arrived and strutted towards him, loving the fact that all eyes – both male and female – were now on her. That girl was made for stardom from the minute she was conceived, during the last episode of *Dallas* in 1991. Her mother had wanted to call her Sue Ellen, but thankfully her dad had a thing for that singer Kiki Dee and won the name debate.

'Hey, babes, we've got a break in filming so I'm heading in to pick up something to wear for the club shoot tomorrow night. Come with me?'

Of the dozen or so blokes within a ten-metre radius, Zac was the only one who hadn't stopped what he was doing and turned to stare, open-mouthed, at Kiki.

Just as well jealousy wasn't his thing. In fact, he didn't blame them. If she wasn't his bird, he'd stare at those legs too. And that outfit . . . Actually wasn't much of an outfit as such. A tiny white T-shirt tied in a knot under her boobs, abs that he'd trained to look like they'd been carved into her stomach, legs that were far too long to belong to someone who barely touched five foot four. Granted, that might have had something to do with the ten-inch heels she was wearing. Den would go fucking mental if they left indentations on his gym floor.

'I can't, babes. Want to get a quick workout in before the next client.'

Kiki's pout went all the way down to her chin. He waited for her to stomp off like she usually did when she didn't get what she wanted, but she stood rooted to the floor. Maybe those heels were stuck in the rubber mat after all.

Nope, she'd just started slowly walking closer to him, still clearly aware that her adoring public were watching. She was a cracking girl, Kiki, but she did love to lap up the attention. She curled her hand around his neck and pulled his ear down to the level of her mouth.

'Come with me and I'll shag you senseless in the back of the car.'

Thank Christ she'd whispered it so quietly that no one else could hear.

A bloke at the barbell weight stack groaned, turned and headed for the changing rooms. Maybe one or two people *had* heard, then.

Despite a definite wish to stay focused, Zac felt his resistance wilting. Actually, not so much wilting as being squeezed into submission by the erection that had formed in his shorts. Sod the focus. Sex was a cardiovascular exercise that burned over five hundred calories an hour. And if they did it in the back of the car, it had the flexibility advantages of yoga.

As soon as they left the gym, the flash of the cameras alerted them to the fact that Jezzer and a couple of other paps were waiting for them. So much for the in-car quickie.

'C'mon, let's go back to my place,' he whispered in Kiki's ear, while keeping his expression perfectly sullen. The cast had spread it around the press that Lena's brother acted as a bodyguard for them, to throw the tabloids off any hint of a romance.

As soon as they jumped into the BMW, Kiki pouted,

'But babes, I really need that new dress for tonight. Just take me shopping. Please, baby. Come on, I'll do you on the way there.' Thankfully the paps weren't following them, or they just might have drawn up alongside them and got a front page, pixelated snap of Kiki releasing Zac's cock from the zipper of his shorts. Man, he wanted her to carry on, he really did. But they were in the middle of traffic and he didn't fancy explaining this one in court.

Instead, he gently removed her hand, tucked himself back in and carried on driving.

'You know, you're just not as much fun as you used to be,' Kiki moaned, flicking her chestnut hair back and pulling her Gucci sunglasses down on to her face.

Zac sighed. There was no point arguing. She was right. Sometimes he wished they could go back to the early days just before the series aired, before Kiki got really famous and was told to keep their relationship on the down low. Before the weird stalker that was freaking her out. When she was just a normal girl who could go out without spending two hours in hair and make-up. Before he realised there was a whole big shit storm out there that he was going to have to fix.

Sitting on a gold chesterfield sofa outside the changing rooms at Perfect, the boutique that all the girls in the show frequented, he checked his watch a dozen times, following each gesture with a 'Ready, babes?' or 'Kiki, I really need to get back.' She preened. She pouted. She gazed at her reflection for an irritatingly long amount of time. It was supposed to annoy him, and it was succeeding.

Eventually he stood up. 'Sorry, Kiki, I need to go, love. I told you I only had an hour,' he said to the back of a fitting-room curtain.

The silver velour swished open and Kiki stood there wearing nothing but a thong. 'But I'm not ready.' She stared at him, eyes challenging, hands on hips.

Well, hello again, serious erection. Mandy, the owner of the shop, disappeared into the back store. After ten years in the business, there was nothing she hadn't seen – although this reality TV lot were the wildest ones yet. Sometimes she longed for the return of the low-level malice of competitive WAG-dom.

Zac spoke slowly. 'I need to get back to the gym. I had a client booked five minutes ago.'

Fuck, she was gorgeous. What the hell had happened to him? Was he seriously going to knock her back twice in one day?

But client equalled cash, and right now that was more important.

'I'm going. You've got five minutes if you're coming with me.'

He was sure Mandy thought Kiki's strangled scream was caused by something other than a furious sulk. He ducked to avoid the Louboutin that came flying in his direction.

The second hand on his watch was ticking down to the five minutes when she strutted past him and straight out towards the car.

Hanging a few feet behind her, he was torn between

irritation and amusement. No one ever said going out with a chick like this would be easy.

Later, he wasn't sure what made his senses tingle. The guy standing beside the car looked like any one of the dozens of fans that popped up every time the cast members went anywhere. Twitter and Facebook helped to broadcast their locations to thousands in a split second, and occasionally it was the guys in the cast that started the hype. A mob scene was always great in pap shots. Kiki had probably posted a dozen tweets while she was in the fitting room.

The dude was about twenty-one, skinny jeans, long black hair, T-shirt, and standing a foot or two away from the car. 'Kiki, can I have your autograph? I, like, really love you.'

Kiki immediately stopped and flashed on the mega-watt smile. Zac was about to move round to the driver's door when he stopped, reversed, opened the passenger-side door instead. 'Kiki?'

His girlfriend ignored him, deliberately playing up to the fan. Shit, she was petty sometimes, just trying even harder now to yank his chain. If he hadn't had three protein shakes already today, this carry-on would be making him seriously weary.

The geezer was grinning now, telling her how gorgeous she was, how he adored her, how . . .

Zac saw the bloke's hand slip into a gap in the back-pack that was slung over his shoulder. Saw it come back out holding something. The guy's expression darkened.

A glint of silver. Raised toward Kiki's face. Her expression changing as she noticed. A flicker of fear. A—

'Knife!' Zac roared as he flew towards it, pushing Kiki out of the way before crashing to the ground on top of the guy.

There was a struggle, grabbing, chaos, screaming – and in the midst of the madness, it was no surprise that he didn't register the click of the camera shutters.

Chapter Seven

Talli struggled into the gym, buckling under the weight of a huge Prada holdall stacked with countless brochures for crockery, cutlery and table linens. Trevor, the very nice wedding director at Highdrow Castle, had offered to allow the couple to use the in-house range, but Edwina had refused on the grounds that she didn't want to eat her first meal off a plate that had been used by brides who were 'probably already fucking divorced by now'. Yep, that was the kind of logic Talli was dealing with.

The 'small, intimate wedding' was gaining momentum by the day. Six weeks to go and already they were up to 250 guests, while Edwina's demands were getting more and more outlandish. She now wanted the ceremony officiated by both a vicar and a rabbi. She wanted a fanfare of trumpets as she walked back down the aisle.

Oh, and Kylie. She wanted Kylie Minogue to sing at the reception.

'All right, duchess?' shouted Den, maintaining a smile despite the fact that he was holding a boxing bag that was being pummelled by a bloke who was a dead ringer for Lennox Lewis.

'Morning, Den,' Talli replied, grinning. His cheeky banter was the only bright spot in an otherwise miserable existence. The last fortnight had dragged by in a drudge of hotel food, Edwina's demands and endless hours trying to find suppliers that specialised in flavoured almonds and gold-leaf confetti. The only thing that kept her going was that Den had given her a temporary membership for the gym, so she headed back here every night for a late workout after the rest of them had gone off to the Beach Box or whatever other club they planned to terrorise. Chronic boredom had set in a few nights before and she'd watched an episode of *Lovin' Essex* on her laptop. It was the TV equivalent of crack. At four a.m. she was still awake, on her sixth episode, and didn't want to turn off. These girls were amazing – so strong and confident. A couple of them were scary. Really, really scary. If she was ever stuck in a siege situation, she would request that they bypass the SAS and let Shiraz and Porsche from *Lovin' Essex* storm the building. The hostages would be released after the removal of all body hair and the application of a tan in a sexy shade of St Moriz. Den was great in the show, though. The cheeky older guy who treated the girls with respect and threatened to thump any bloke who stepped out of line. But it was his back story that endeared him even more to the TV-watching world. As a teenager, he'd gone off the rails, living in junkie squats and anywhere else he could find a bed, eventually overdosing and ending up in hospital close to death. It was enough to make him turn his life around. Jobs as a labourer followed, hard graft replaced the drugs, and he built a new life, capitalising on the fitness boom in the nineties and staying on top of it ever since.

'Big Bird's over at the bikes,' Den shouted with a raucous laugh. He had a different name for Edwina every day. Talli tried her best not to encourage him, but it was difficult not to giggle.

Assertive, she told herself as she headed in the direction of the cardiovascular equipment. I will be assertive. Today she needed to pin Edwina down, by force if necessary, and get her out of Chelmsford and into Vera Wang in Brook Street, in the city centre. They'd already cancelled three appointments, and she was pretty sure that Vera's emissaries in London wouldn't be best pleased.

Her heart sank when she saw that Edwina was on the stationary bike, with that Zac guy cycling beside her. He was so monosyllabic he bordered on rude. And he was a thug. He'd been on the front page of the *Daily Mirror*, sitting on top of some poor fan of the show. Who behaved like that? She hadn't even bothered to read the full piece. Obviously he was one of those louts who used fear and intimidation to get what he wanted – a bully who crushed everyone in his path. She wasn't sure if she'd just described Zac or her mother.

'Erm . . . hi,' she greeted Edwina, who was dressed in bright yellow Lycra, her grey-streaked hair having bypassed all stops on the way from 'well groomed' to 'frizz'. Den probably had a point.

'Morning, darling,' Edwina chirped.

Best get this over with. Talli took a deep breath and jumped straight in. 'Listen, did you remember that we have to head into the city today? And it's a two-day thing – we've got another appointment there tomorrow too.'

'No.' The objection wasn't coming from the bride-to-be. Flustered, Talli dropped her notebook as she caught the bruiser's steely glare.

'We're behind, 'cause shooting ran late last night. I need her here all day today. Tomorrow too,' he informed her, his voice absolutely firm and resolute. This obviously wasn't a man who was used to hearing an argument.

Something inside Talli snapped. No. No way. She had been pushed around by her mother, by Edwina, by the whole bloody world. She was stuck in a hotel miles from home. She was working her ass off. And she bloody hated almonds anyway. She was desperate to get home, even for a night. She was not – NOT – going to take any crap from this bloke, even if he looked like he could kill her with his thumbs.

'Well, I need her to come with me,' she hissed.

'No,' he replied calmly.

Edwina sat back in her seat, an amused grin revealing her feelings. 'God, I wish this was on camera. Why didn't we do a show about this wedding? It would have been TV fucking gold.'

Talli ignored her. 'She's coming with me,' she argued, surprising herself with a voice that was low and edged with steel. Who the hell did this guy think he was? What gave him the right to come over all arrogant and macho? That stuff didn't work with her. When she'd been doing her degree, she'd done work experience placements at plenty of schools with teenagers who thought they could get a bit of credibility by mouthing off at the student teacher and had realised that if you let them do it once, it would keep happening. It was just unfortunate that she'd learned the lesson after her childhood acquiescences had awarded her the position of family doormat.

Edwina was looking at her now, enjoying the debate.

'Look, princess . . .' he said.

'I'm not a bloody princess,' she bit back.

Edwina's head was swinging, pendulum style, like she was watching a Wimbledon final.

'OK, then, love. I'm sorry if this is bursting your thong, but I need her to stay here for at least another two hours.'

Talli checked her watch. 'First, my thong remains decidedly unburst,' she deadpanned. 'And as for the two-hour delay, no can do. We need to be in central London by two o'clock.' Turning to Edwina, she continued to explain. 'It's almost eleven now. And because we've missed so many appointments, they're squeezing you in. You have to pick your gown today and they've gone out of their way to schedule your first fitting for tomorrow.'

'You still can't go,' he interrupted again.

'Do you want to phone and explain that to Vera bloody Wang?' Talli retorted, refusing to back down.

'OK, children, play nice. Here's what we'll do,' Big Bird adjudicated. 'Zac, do you have any other clients today?'

He shook his head.

'OK. So I've got to check in on the set-up downstairs for tomorrow afternoon's shoot. Then we can head into the city. I'll do Vera Wang and then train with Zac. We can have another session in the morning before the fitting, then head back out here.'

'Train where?' Talli asked, with trepidation. She had a horrible feeling she already knew the answer.

'At your house. Your mother did say that everything was at my disposal. Simmy is crashing there tonight because he's working in the city, so I'll get to see my honey and we can fit in two workouts in your mother's gym. It's perfect.'

Looking at the guy in front of her, Talli decided it wasn't perfect. In fact, it was far from bloody perfect.

The only consolation was that he appeared to be as horrified at the prospect as she was.

Chapter Eight

Sleb! magazine: 12 November 2012

So who do you think is the coolest couple in reality TV?

We've mooched around Made in Chelsea. *We've gone gaga over* Geordie Shore. *We've scoped out the* Scousewives *and tested* TOWIE.

Now we're getting in between the heavy breathing at Lovin' Essex, *with four truly adorable twosomes that are never slow to get their pash on.*

a) Minx and Dale – the daredevil duo and yes, we're dying to know if the engagement rumours are true.

b) Porsche and Ramone – beautifully formed and not afraid to show it off.

c) Kiki and Toby – has the hunk finally tamed the wild and free spirit?

d) Lena and Max – and we're guessing these two won't get Coco's vote.

Enter our draw to win a box set of Series One by texting your answer to 948484.

Oh and PS – Why is the gorgeous Shiraz still single? Is no bloke brave enough to take her on? Guys, if you think you're hard enough, drop us a line. Time for Sleb! *Cupid to step in!*

Kiki was in one of the treatment rooms getting her fake tan topped up, rustling up support for the *Sleb!* competition by tweeting her adoring followers as Fran, the tanning technician, sprayed.

'Is that you multitasking there, babes?' Zac teased her as he stepped into the room.

He found it ironic that her popularity had soared even higher since the incident with the weirdo. She couldn't have come up with a better PR stunt if she'd planned it herself. Rumour had it that Shiraz and Porsche were now trying to work out how they could find themselves in a life-threatening situation of their choosing, all of which would of course be captured by the cameras.

The incident wasn't exactly having a bonus effect for Zac, though. Turned out the young guy from Crazy Central hadn't had a knife, but a pair of scissors. He hadn't planned to harm Kiki, just wanted to snip off a lock of her hair.

Still freaking weird, though.

Thankfully, it was enough of a provocation to stop the Old Bill pressing charges, and they even did a few checks to ensure the guy wasn't Kiki's stalker. When they searched his bedsit, though, the most deadly things they found were the entire *Twilight* series on DVD and a cupboard full of instant noodles.

They'd eventually cleared him, but the guy had already sold stories to a couple of magazines and was threatening to sue Zac for injury and hurt feelings or some other bollocks. Like that was all he needed right now. Auntie Dot was threatening to countersue for what she announced was 'defecation of character'. They corrected her terminology and talked her out of it, but not before she'd phoned Lenny's Lawyers, the no-win-no-fee crowd up the High Street, and demanded a free consultation.

Fran looked happy to see him. She gave him a big grin and scoped him out from the top of his grey Armani T-shirt down to the black Adidas shorts. 'Hey, Zac, you're looking great,' she whistled.

He gave her a wink. Fran was Shiraz's younger sister and one of the gang that had hung out with his sisters at school. Just before he met Kiki, he'd bumped into Fran in a club and they'd had a bit of a fling. She was a good girl and his entirely hair-free body was testimony to her skill with the wax pot.

'Hi, babes,' Kiki purred. Man, that was a sight to behold. Totally naked except one of those paper hat thingies to keep her hair dry. Her boobs were the most spectacular ones he'd ever seen in his life, and they weren't even fake. Sometimes she didn't half give him earache, but he was well aware that a million guys would kill to be in his Nikes. Now she was arching her back just a little, putting on the bee-stung pout, and he knew it was down to the presence of Fran. Kiki had a bit of a jealous streak. Wasn't a bad thing – but she wasn't gonna love the news he was about to deliver.

'Babe, I'm just going to nip back to the flat and grab a kit bag. Edwina wants me to go into the city with her and stay there tonight so I can train her later and in the morning.'

Kiki's expression went from annoyance, to fury, to thoughtful, to understanding. Which basically meant that she was really pissed off, but then considered the fact that Edwina was her boss and in charge of cast selection, so it was therefore in her best interests to make sure she pulled strings with her any way she could – and if one of those strings meant hiring out her boyfriend for the night, she could live with it.

'OK, babes, but I'll miss you. Aw, and you'll miss the party at the Beach Box tonight. Shiraz and Porsche are launching their new range of condoms. It's gonna be, like, such a train wreck.'

The glee in her voice suggested that wasn't necessarily a bad thing. Much to the rest of the cast's disgust, Kiki had got in there first with hair products and a false eyelashes range that was outselling at least three of the Girls Aloud collection. Not to mention her latest endorsement, the glitter chicken fillets guaranteed to inflate a bra two cup sizes. Now the rest of the cast were putting their names to everything from cleansing wipes to dog beds.

'I've asked Den to come with you tonight. Keep an

eye. Just in case of any bother.' There had been no threatening letters for two weeks now, but Zac wasn't taking any chances, especially as the *Lovin' Essex* crew wouldn't be there for extra protection. Edwina refused to film anything that was connected with the cast's personal endorsements.

'Aw, you're a honey,' Kiki replied as she turned around so that her perfect backside was facing him. Tight buttocks, gorgeous legs and two intertwined gold stars at the base of her spine. She'd had them done one weekend in Marbs when they first got together. He had resisted her encouragement to get the same one. Tattoos weren't for him – too much of a distraction from what was underneath. In his opinion, the only bloke who got away with them was Becks, and that was because he was a living god.

'Have a chat with Edwina, you know, if you're alone together, babes. I'm totally not getting as much airtime as Lena or Minx.' They both knew that wasn't true. Kiki got the most airtime of all – she was just greedy for more.

'Course I will, babe.' Fran gave him a look that confirmed they were the only two in the room who knew for sure that he wouldn't.

Half an hour later he was back at the gym, carrying a suit bag and a holdall containing his training gear.

'Fucking hell, are you coming for a week?' Edwina asked, as he threw the bag into the back of her company Merc.

The posh bird, Talli – yeah, he'd found out that was

definitely her name – didn't say a word. Sulky cow. She just got into the back of the car, buried her head in some catalogue and kept shtum the whole way into town.

Even in the showroom at the bridal place, she didn't crack a smile – obviously totally used to people running around after her. They probably weren't grovelling enough.

The Vera Wang shop was a bit smart, though. A huge showroom on a corner, with deep charcoal carpets and loads of natural light from floor-to-ceiling street-level windows. The chairs in the middle of the room were black and boxy, the kind he'd have one day in the reception of his gym. Yeah, it was going to be a classy place. Exclusive. Small, though – just big enough to do one-on-one sessions with personal clients who wanted to train but didn't want to mingle with the masses.

'Nope, it's not right,' Edwina bellowed from a plinth in the middle of the floor. An hour in, and he wished he'd stayed in the car. Edwina had tried on ten dresses, only to dismiss every one of them. Only thing keeping him going was the champagne they'd been offered when they walked in the door. He hadn't intended to break his 'no alcohol on week nights' rule, but Edwina's drama had him knocking back the bubbles.

The crew of people around them bustled her off back into the changing rooms. He was glad he'd put on his True Religion jeans and grey Versace shirt. It was the right look for a place like this. Kiki would love it here.

He suddenly conjured up an image of her wearing one of these wedding dresses and was immediately overcome by a weird sense of sadness. She'd look beautiful in any of them. Before the show got huge, they used to talk about getting married all the time. Now he couldn't remember the last time they'd discussed it. It wasn't that he didn't want to, but somehow all the personal stuff had got shoved out of the way by the show.

He glanced over at Talli, who was sitting with her head back against a wall, eyes closed. Obviously thought she was too good to talk to him. 'Stuck up' didn't even begin to describe this chick. Den reckoned she was OK, but he must just be tripping or trying to get into her knickers. Two weeks and he hadn't seen her smile or offer a bit of chat.

No manners at all. None.

'You don't fancy any of this lark, then?' he asked her. The outburst came from nowhere and surprised him as much as it obviously surprised her. In all honesty, he realised, he wasn't particularly interested in her reply. He was just bored, and irritating her by gassing would pass the time of day.

Her eyes flew open and she seemed lost for words. 'What? Erm . . . no. No. Not my kind of thing. Wedding dresses.'

Lesbian, then. Definitely. He'd never encountered a single female in his entire life who wouldn't love all this palaver.

She closed her eyes again.

'So. Not married, then?' he persisted, trying not to let her see that he was playing with her.

'Erm, no. Not married.'

'Boyfriend?'

'Yes.'

Not a lesbian then.

'How long?'

'What?'

'How long? The boyfriend.'

'Oh. Erm, not sure. About four years? Five. Long time.'

That took him totally by surprise. He didn't have her pegged as the loving partner type. Too self-obsessed. Although that clearly didn't apply when it came to her fashion choices. Did she ever wear anything but jeans and biker boots? Granted, she was well fit, but no make-up, scraggy hair – no effort at all. He should lock her in a cupboard with Shiraz and Kiki for a couple of hours and she'd come out a totally different bird.

'Engaged?'

'No.'

They both looked equally relieved when Edwina came back out of the changing room wearing an ivory silk strapless gown that wouldn't have looked out of place on the cover of *Vogue*. Yeah, so he read *Vogue*. Nothing wrong with admitting it. Always good to see what that David Gandy bloke was wearing.

'That's . . . gorgeous,' Talli said hesitantly, even smiling a bit for the first time all day.

'I love it. LOVE!' Edwina screeched, clapping her hands. 'This is it. Zac, what do you think?'

Surprised to be asked, he immediately scrutinised it from a professional point of view, noticing that the Talli bird was giving him the evil eye again. What was her problem?

'Top looks great, really shows off the delts. Bottom half needs work, though. It's straining across the hips where it should flow, and it's pinching at the waist . . .'

'Well of course, structured undergarments will help,' one of the assistants suggested.

Zac shook his head. 'No amount of magic knick-knacks are gonna sort that, love. But we've got six weeks. We can fix it.'

Edwina moved forward as if she was going to kiss him, then realised she was stuck on a pedestal and due to the restrictions of the frock only had a ten-inch span between her ankles at maximum stretch. She stayed put and smiled gratefully instead.

'Phone. Phone please. Take a pic,' she ordered, pointing to her Hermès Birkin discarded on a nearby chair.

Talli found Edwina's iPhone, took a snap of her in the frock and then handed it over. Edwina immediately pressed a button and then put it to her ear.

'Darling, I found it! Yes, the perfect one. I'm going to send you a picture. No, I don't stand for all that nonsense; I've bonked you so it's a bit late for traditions and superstitions. I want to know if you like it. What?

Right. Yes, she's here. With Zac, my trainer, too. Great. OK, darling, kiss kiss.'

Edwina hung up and tossed the handset back to Posh Bird with a 'There you go, darling. Now, your brother is so thrilled, he's insisting on taking us all out for dinner tonight!'

'No!' Their simultaneous outburst took them by surprise, and Zac realised it was the first time he and Talli had ever agreed on anything.

'I mean . . . it's not necessary. Really. And I was, erm . . . planning on catching up with Domenic tonight.'

She was stuttering a bit now, and Zac couldn't say he blamed her. He didn't fancy hanging out with Edwina and her mob tonight either. He'd seen her every single day for over two weeks now, and he was starting to have nightmares about her. He actually fancied an early night. It would be the first time in months he'd be on his own in bed, on sheets that weren't streaked with Kiki's fake tan, with her watching endless reruns of the show so that she could 'examine her performance'. Every bleeding night.

Edwina was still arguing with Posh Bird.

'Simmy is inviting Domenic too – he's calling him right now.'

'Oh,' Talli replied weakly. The tense smile gave a hint that her get-out-of-jail card had just been shredded. Zac suddenly realised he should be using this valuable stalling time to come up with his own excuse not to go. Damn.

'Great! Settled! Now get me out of this dress before I fucking faint from lack of oxygen.'

The minute Edwina was gone, Zac watched Talli close her eyes and lean her head back against the wall again.

'Well, that sounds like it will be fun,' he said in a teasing voice. When she opened her eyes, they looked a bit misty. Contact lenses must be bothering her.

'And I'll get to meet your lucky guy. Bonus.'

He downed the champagne and put the glass by his side, not entirely sure why taking the piss wasn't quite so much fun now.

Chapter Nine

Talli was considering crying. In public. The sort of real, proper, dramatic wailing that would embarrass everyone in the vicinity and possibly result in her father declaring loudly that she'd had too much wine and she must be taken home and put to bed immediately.

'You all right, munchkin? You're so quiet tonight,' Domenic asked her softly, his face full of concern. God, she'd missed him. Missed this. Sitting around a table with the people she loved, chatting about absolutely nothing in particular. A self-reprimand was quickly forthcoming – how pathetic could she be? She was turning into one of those contestants on *Big Brother* or *I'm a Celebrity . . . Get Me Out of Here* who burst into tears and wailed for their granny after only forty-eight hours away from home. It was time to get a grip, it really was. She was only staying in bloody Chelmsford, not the darkest depths of an Australian rainforest.

Watching all those episodes of *Lovin' Essex* was rocking her emotional equilibrium. Some of those girls, especially Kiki and Porsche, cried all the time. And they must be wearing some kind of revolutionary mascara, because it didn't run at all. They cried like movie stars, single tears running down their cheeks. Talli made it a point not to cry unless absolutely necessary, but she was fairly sure that in times of sobbing her face resembled a large tomato being squashed in a vice. She realised that Domenic was still looking at her questioningly.

'I'm fine, I promise! Just . . . listening to what everyone has to say. I've missed you all.'

Under the table, Domenic's hand gave her thigh a reassuring squeeze. He was such a sweetheart, really. When this was all done, they should definitely get away somewhere. Explore a mountain or go diving or . . . anything that put several thousand miles between her and anything to do with weddings.

She had almost lost it in Vera Wang today. It had taken every ounce of self-discipline she had, together with some meditation techniques her mother had forced her to learn in the hope it would stop her developing more frown-induced wrinkles, to stop herself from having a full-scale meltdown. All this nuptials stuff so wasn't her. Even when all her friends were planning their weddings as children, wearing their mothers' veils and strutting up and down the playroom, she'd been in a corner daydreaming about running in the Olympics. When she was a teenager, she'd realised she would never be fast enough to be a professional athlete, but she still loved the discipline and the freedom of running and the energy that working out gave her. Plus, given her fondness for burgers and cake, if she didn't train she'd need to reinforce her bed and book two seats on a plane to accommodate her girth.

Sometimes she wondered if she'd done the right thing, though. A sports degree had been a natural choice, but where had it got her? Sitting in Delaney Grill, a Michelin-starred restaurant in the middle of Chelsea, while worrying that the bridal honeymoon suite at the castle wouldn't have the 800-thread-count sheets Edwina had just insisted on. Spectacular career trajectory.

Edwina was busy regaling the table with stories from the *Lovin' Essex* set. Simmy, Domenic and her father were listening intently, until Dessi, India and Verity arrived, making a loud entrance in a flurry of air kisses and 'dahlings'.

Confidence had never been an issue with – what was it Domenic called them? Their *gang*. Verity and India were sisters and two of the founding members of their crowd. Talli loved them dearly, but there was no doubt that they shared Dessi's inherent values: live for today and spend like there's no tomorrow.

India's mane of red corkscrew curls swamped her as she ambushed Talli from behind and gave her a crushingly affectionate bear hug. India was the kind of girl who demanded attention when she entered a room. The wild hair, the wide green eyes, the enthusiastic greetings. And for someone with the frame of Lily Cole, she had the strength of a Russian shot-put champion, something she put down to a childhood climbing trees with Verity on their family's estate in Barbados.

'Where have you been, gorgeous? We've missed you.'

'Essex.'

'Oh Christ. Not to worry. As long as you got your inoculations before you went, you'll be fine.'

Embarrassed, Talli flicked her eyes to see if Zac had heard, but if he had, he wasn't reacting. Cutting sarcasm was just India's way. It was the reason she'd built up a massive following for her blog Rich Cows and Cartier, and was relied on by the *Guardian,* the *Independent* and the *Daily Mail* to give outrageously cutting commentary on anything involving royalty or London society. There were rumours that Camilla Parker Bowles had a contract out on her.

Talli sometimes wondered if there had been an accidental swapping of children around the time they were born. India and Dessi were so matched in personality; they were the posh, non-criminal version of serial killers who worked in pairs, feeding off each other's wants and fantasies. It was a dynamic that invariably ended up in a first-class lounge or the fitting rooms at YSL.

India's younger sister Verity was in full possession of the siblings' compassion and grace genes. As understated and elegant as her sister was effusive, Verity's lifelong love of ballet was obvious in her posture and every perfectly placed step. She'd never made professional ranks. At fifteen she'd shot up to five foot nine, discovered boys and realised there was more to life than pirouettes and blisters. As trust-fund offspring, the sisters would never have to work a day in their lives, but Verity used her organisational skills, exclusive contact list and shameless hustling to fund-raise for Save the Children, arranging monthly events and an annual ball that had raked in millions.

'Budge up, darling.' India was bumped out of the way, to be replaced by the sheets of glossy brunette belonging to Verity, who homed in for a kiss on each cheek. 'Hello, Talli, darling! Thought you'd been kidnapped.'

'I have,' Talli replied ruefully.

'Well, glad they let you out on day release. I'll call you tomorrow for a proper chat. Been weeks since we caught up, and I want to hear how Fliss is doing too.'

The mention of their absent friend sent another lump directly to Talli's throat. If this carried on, Ant and Dec would charge in any minute with a TV crew and a video tape of Fliss canoeing across Lake Malawi.

'Who in the name of holy shag is he?' Dessi whispered as she slid into the empty seat next to Talli – who still, to her own surprise, hadn't cried. Dessi's outfit immediately took her mind off her woes. It was designed to stun, and it succeeded. A black, indisputably Hervé Léger dress that barely reached mid thigh, bare, tanned legs and six-inch Louboutins with silver studs scattered around the toe. Her caramel hair fell in loose curves down her back, her smoky eyes making her a dead ringer for old pics of Brigitte Bardot.

'Who?'

'Brad fucking Pitt over there.'

Looking over at Zac, listening intently to Edwina's anecdotes from her last few shoots, she could see what had caught Dessi's attention. OK, so he was pretty hunky, in a male model, super-slick way. You just knew he spent a fortune on grooming products and hours in front of the mirror every morning. And, sure, his body was great. The thought made her blush, but come on, even in that black shirt and trousers it was obvious that he trained. His shoulders were as wide as an athlete's, but then his torso gradually narrowed in a perfect V shape to a tiny waist, hips and butt. Her eye was caught by the buckle on his belt. Was that Gucci? The sound of a clearing throat made her lift her eyes to meet his amused glare. Oh bugger, he'd just caught her studying his belt, but of course he was so conceited he probably thought she was staring at his groin. Shit! Bugger. Bugger. Shit.

'Talli?' Dessi pressed her.

'Oh, that's, erm, Zac. Edwina's personal trainer,' she replied, desperately hoping she sounded perfectly normal. Mr Self-Obsessed had turned back to listen to Edwina again.

Dessi let out a slow, soft whistle. 'Dear God, I could play with him for a week and still have ideas for more. Does he talk or just look good?'

'He talks. But only about things involving sweat.'

Dessi lifted Talli's wine glass and took a large gulp. 'That would suit me just fine.'

For the first time in two weeks, Talli's smile was genuine. Sometimes she wished she could be more like Dessi and India – wild, bold and perhaps even a tad more sexually active. It had been weeks since she'd had a bit of passion with Dom. Another bottle of wine and she might just correct that. The thought filled her with new resolve. Time to shake off the maudlin woes – she was here now, so there was no point in moping.

'Is he single? Not that it matters,' Dessi whispered.

'Are we still on this?' Talli laughed.

Dessi let out a long, appreciative breath. 'Not yet, but hopefully soon.'

And there it was – the reason why her sister had been expelled from two boarding schools and a Swiss finishing academy. None of those teachers would ever get another job. She'd worked her way through a geography professor, a maths teacher and a French master who still sent a Christmas card to '*ma chère Lolita*'.

Talli reclaimed her glass. 'He's seeing Kiki from the show, but they keep it out of the press.'

'Is she the one with the huge tits?'

Talli nodded and watched as Dessi subtly rearranged her bra, moving her cleavage up a couple of inches. 'No worries, I could take her,' her sister vowed as she leaned over the table, giving Zac a bird's-eye view as she held out her hand. 'I'm Desdemona, Talli and Simmy's sister. And this is Verity,' she motioned to her smiling chum, who had slipped into the seat next to Domenic, 'and India.' With a dramatic flourish, India broke off from chatting to Talli's dad, turned to Zac, who was seated on the other side of her, and bestowed a double air kiss on him as a welcome.

'So, Talli, how are the wedding plans going, darling?' her father asked. Was it her imagination, or was he slurring his words a little? Her dad was never knowingly caught after six p.m. without a glass of port in his hand, but he rarely showed the effects of it. Oh well, the old boy deserved to go a bit wild while her mother was away. But booze and porn? He'd be snorting coke and buying a mail-order mistress next.

The thought was enough to defuse the stress of the question.

'It's going fine, Daddy. We're . . . erm, making progress.'

'Good show, darling. Good show.' He rewarded her with a 'cheers' gesture and then drained his glass.

Dessi jumped in and commanded the conversation for the next hour, regaling them all with admittedly hilarious exploits from a birthday weekend they'd just spent at Stoke Poges Country Club, that she swore had ended with her playing pool and hustling over a grand off an ageing rock star.

Talli noticed that Zac was listening intently to Dessi, smiling, laughing at the punchlines. It was nothing new. Dessi had a knack for holding an audience.

Meanwhile, Domenic's hand was slowly working its

way up her thigh and she was enjoying the sensation. Yep, he was getting lucky tonight, and the sooner the better.

'Darling, I just wanted to say sorry,' he whispered, confident that everyone else was out of earshot and busy listening to Dessi's exploits.

'For what?' she asked, genuinely puzzled.

'The whole Courchevel thing. I just thought it would be fantastic for us to get away. You know. It feels like an age since we did anything fun.'

'I was just thinking the same thing. Let's do something after Christmas when this wedding is over and done with. Let's go somewhere amazing.'

'Munchkin, I'd love to, but Big Up D starts his European tour the first week in January, and you know how that is. I mean, you could come perhaps for a weekend, but you know how tied up I am when the show's on the road.'

She did. The year before, she'd popped over to see him in Barcelona when the tour stopped there for three days, and he hadn't even had time to pick her up at the airport. She'd spent the whole three days sitting in a coffee shop in Las Ramblas, working her way through the last three books by Jackie Collins. Not that it was his fault, and she couldn't complain, not when she was putting him on the back burner for the wedding of the century.

'Staying at my place tonight?' he whispered.

'Promise you won't mention Vera Wang?'

'Who?'

'She's a rap star out of Brixton,' Talli joked, now relishing the chat and the flirtation. If the food wasn't so delicious here, she'd insist they bail out now, go back home, watch a movie in bed and eat toast. Off their naked arses.

She furtively checked her watch. Another hour and it wouldn't be too rude to excuse themselves.

Her Cajun catfish arrived, and as soon as everyone else had been served, she tucked in.

After general chit-chat over dinner, Simmy took over the conversation as the main courses were being removed. 'So, Zac, how have you found training my wife-to-be?'

'Oh, yeah, she's . . . committed.'

As she took another sip of her wine, Talli realised that his voice seemed . . . different. Uncomfortable. Perhaps he found them all a bit too much. Her family were quite overwhelming when encountered for the first time. Thank God her mother wasn't there or he'd have tunnelled for freedom after the starter.

To her shame, she realised that she didn't actually mind the fact that he didn't seem to be enjoying himself. He was without a doubt the vainest, most arrogant, rudest guy she'd ever met. A total plank. Day in, day out, he'd argued with her, ignored her or wound her up – yep, she knew what that little performance was all about this afternoon. He was deliberately baiting her, making fun of her.

The sooner this whole wedding debacle was over and

he could go back to his large-bosomed plastic girlfriend the better.

She almost spat out her drink. Had she really just thought of Kiki as a large-bosomed plastic girlfriend? God, she had to get out more, she was beginning to sound like her mother. Perhaps Domenic had a rap star she could go hang out with for a while to get a bit more 'street'.

Edwina cackled her way into the conversation. 'Early training tomorrow, Zac, then Talli, we need to have a summit – I've changed my mind about the colour scheme. I'm thinking purple now.'

With a struggle, Talli swallowed the wine in her mouth, her shoulders falling into a slump. She fought the urge to resort to her usual stress reaction and put her head on the table. Which, coincidentally, was exactly what her father did. At speed and with a thud.

'Daddy!' Dessi screamed, jumping to her feet, but Talli was quicker. She was at his side in a split second, and immediately realised that everyone else was frozen, staring at her, doing nothing. Except Zac.

Zac was right next to her. 'OK, we're going to ease him off the chair and on to the floor, put him in the recovery position.'

'Start CPR. Start CPR!' Edwina screeched.

Zac and Talli both ignored her, too busy supporting Giles as they moved him to the floor beside the table. Talli was grateful they were in a private dining area, so at least they didn't have to deal with panicked onlookers.

Heart thudding, she turned her dad on his side and checked for a pulse, puzzled when she immediately found it, strong and regular.

'Start fucking CPR!' Edwina repeated.

Zac had his ear at Giles's mouth, then on his chest. 'Is he taking any medication? Got any health problems?'

Talli shook her head. 'Nothing.'

He put his hand on Giles's chest again. 'He's breathing fine,' he told Talli.

'And he's got a regular pulse,' she replied. 'But I think we'd better phone an ambulance. Could be a stroke? Some kind of cardiac blip?'

'Ambulance! I need an ambulance immediately!' Edwina was bellowing into her iPhone. 'It's my father-in-law. He's . . . he's . . .'

At that very moment, Giles inadvertently answered Talli's question with a slurred verdict on the matter. 'Good job, Talli. Jolly . . .' The sentence ended with a crooked grin and a sleepy snore.

'He's pissed, Edwina,' Zac told her calmly. 'Probably best cancel the ambulance.'

Talli stroked her dad's hair, relief flooding through her. The tension had evaporated as quickly as it had escalated.

'I'll call my car to take him home,' Simmy announced. As they got Giles up into a sitting position, Talli realised he was making a strange sound. She recognised it as the opening bars of 'You Raise Me Up'. Porn. Booze. Westlife. Who was this man?

'I'll come with you,' Simmy volunteered, as he texted his driver and told him they were ready to go.

'No, it's fine, honestly,' Talli said. She glanced at Domenic. The thought of going back to his place held no appeal now. She just wanted to get her father home and make sure he was OK.

'Darling, do you mind if I just head back to my own house tonight? Just want to keep an eye on Daddy.'

Dom shook his head. 'Of course not. You go on home. There's a gig in Camden tonight that I wanted to check out anyway, so I'll just head on over there.'

This was why she loved him. He had the odd petulant moment, but didn't everyone? At heart, though, he was a decent, lovely guy. One with intolerances to 564 different foods and chemical substances. At the last count.

Simmy checked the screen on his phone. 'The car's here. If you guys insist you're OK, you could go first, then send the car back for us.'

'No, honestly, stay and enjoy the rest of the night,' Talli insisted. 'We'll be fine.' She suddenly realised that the generic 'we' included Mr Muscles. He replied to her questioning gaze by nodding. 'Absolutely. No problem. I'll give you a hand.'

His voice was still odd. Was that relief she detected?

'I'll hitch a ride too, if you don't mind,' Dessi announced, flashing her veneers. 'Girlies, see you in the morning for breakfast.' India and Verity nodded. They all knew that meant early afternoon and brunch.

With the same degree of manoeuvring that it took to make an oil tanker do a three-point turn, they somehow got Giles into the car, out again, into the house and up into his bedroom. As soon as he was on the bed, Zac retreated. Determined not to heap on any more embarrassment, Talli removed her dad's socks and tie, but left the rest on. He was now quietly humming Barry Manilow's 'Mandy'. Her mother would burst her stitches if she could see him now. Pissed as a fart, lying on the top of the pure cashmere throw she'd bought in Harrods for more than the price of a small car. Daddy was normally cast out to the small bed in the annexe off his study when he'd been drinking. If he threw up on this throw, or damaged it in any other way, they were all going to have to flee the country and claim political asylum somewhere Mummy would never find them.

She sat with him for a while until he fell back into a deep sleep, watching his chest gently rise and fall. Concerned, she resolved to have a chat to him in the morning. This was all so out of character that she had to know if it was just a belated mid-life crisis or whether something was wrong.

Happy that he was settled for the night, she padded out of the room and headed back downstairs. Much as it pained her to admit it, she owed Zac an enormous thank-you. He'd been amazing, so quick to help, and the way he'd dealt with the whole drama had just been so impressive. As far as the blokes went, Simmy had been worse than useless and Domenic would only have served a purpose if he'd been called on to rate her father's vocal potential as a member of a Westlife tribute act.

OK, she could do this. She could go find Zac, be gracious and thank him sincerely for his swift assistance. It didn't mean they had to be friends, or that she had to like him or overlook the fact that he dinged the bell at the top of the arrogance scale. She could just say a simple thank-you and move on.

Where would he be? Already gone to bed? Should she nip upstairs and knock on the door of the guest suite he was sleeping in? No, that would be too excruciatingly embarrassing.

She'd do a quick sweep of downstairs, see if he was there, and if he wasn't, the thank-you could wait until morning. As she reached the ground floor, she immediately noticed that the kitchen door was ajar, a mumbling of voices coming from behind it. Of course! When they'd arrived home, Dessi had offered to put the kettle on. Her spirits soared. She'd get the thank-you over and done with, and right now a strong cup of tea sounded better than champagne. Actually, a strong cup of tea always sounded better than champagne.

Talli's hand was on the door, and she was just about to push when she caught what Dessi was saying.

'. . . from the moment I saw you tonight.'

'Oh really?' Zac answered. He had his back to the door so his voice was barely audible.

'I prefer to be direct about things,' Dessi was telling

him, her voice thick with raw sexual energy. 'So let's be straight. Upstairs. Now. Naked.'

There was a scraping of chairs and Talli jumped back from the door, turned on her heel and went flying up the stairs, stomach churning.

She'd got the big bloody heroic act so wrong. *That* was why he'd been so impressive tonight, she realised, as she peeled off her clothes and snuggled into the welcoming comfort of her own bed. He'd been trying to charm his way into her sister's La Perla knickers.

Chapter Ten

Zac woke up and automatically reached out for Kiki's sleeping body, patting the bed when he realised that his fingers were coming into contact with nothing but fresh air.

He opened one eye and was unable to stop the groan that came with the realisation of where he was.

Not just a bad dream then.

He headed for the en suite bathroom, not even stopping for his customary morning check that his abs were still in prime shape. He turned the shower on to cold and stepped in, using the icy shock as a distraction from his thoughts.

It didn't last long.

What a bloody night.

It had started off OK, nice restaurant, bit of civil chat. Edwina's boyfriend was a decent enough guy once you got past the fact that he snorted when he laughed. He wasn't so sure about that Domenic bloke though. What was with the tatty jeans and the AC/DC T-shirt? Looked more like he was going to a teenager's sleepover than a classy joint in Chelsea. Too skinny, too. Guy had never seen a gym in his life. Didn't even seem like he made Talli happy either, 'cause she sat there looking like she'd just been told her budgie had copped it.

When God gave out sunny personalities, that girl was obviously too busy waiting in the queue for stroppy expressions with intervals of misery.

Not conditions that affected the three who'd arrived late. Yep, that was when it had all started heading south. He'd been momentarily taken with the fact that they were all fit. Things could be worse, he'd decided, not realising that it was all about to go downhill pretty sharpish.

Zac lathered up the soap – Bvlgari – and rubbed it across his pecs and under his arms.

At first he'd thought it was a mistake. Although how India's hand could inadvertently find its way on to his leg, he wasn't sure. Talli's sister had spoken to him while it was happening and he'd been so mortified his throat started to close up. No bloody shame on that India one, though – she'd kept chatting the whole time, telling him about some trip to the Seychelles, while her fingers worked their way across his thigh. He was just about to remove them when they skimmed the end of his cock and . . . crash.

To be honest, it had been a relief when the old bloke had keeled over.

He had to give it to Talli, she'd been the only one who had reacted, diving right in there, but keeping calm and doing all the right things. Maybe he'd misjudged her. She clearly loved her old man, so she wasn't the frozen fish he'd taken her for.

He'd planned to tell her that when they got home, but then *Predator 2* had kicked off. Bloody hell, twice in one night. That sister came at him out of nowhere. 'So let's be straight. Upstairs. Now. Naked.' Before he knew it, he was backed up against a wall and stuttering like a crazy guy about having a girlfriend. Blustering like a fool, he was. His mates would have pissed themselves laughing if they'd seen him.

Not that he wasn't tempted. She was bloody gorgeous. But he'd never been one for messing around or one-night stands, and especially not with someone related to Edwina. He needed that cash and he wasn't going to blow it by getting fired now.

Besides, he wouldn't do that to Kiki. Two years was a long time to throw away, even if he could plead extreme provocation.

The cold water coursed over his face. He was all for equality, for a fifty/fifty balance of power, but these girls were like mercenaries. In for the kill, out, no casualties or prisoners.

Now he just wanted to finish the job and get out of here. After pulling on a white Lacoste T-shirt, grey shorts and black Puma trainers, he headed downstairs to the gym.

He was just about to open the door when the old bloke appeared.

'Terribly sorry about last night. I believe you stepped in to help. Don't know what came over me.'

Zac restrained from answering, 'Two bottles of red wine and half a bottle of Scotch.'

'That's OK. I'm just glad it was nothing serious. How are you feeling today?'

Giles sighed, and Zac realised this was where Talli got the whole 'miserable demeanour' thing from. 'Just like every other day, young man,' he answered wearily, before giving Zac a pat on the side of his shoulder. With a 'Thanks again,' he wandered off, shoulders slumped.

Zac shook his head. These people were a different breed. Auntie Dot's whole flat could fit into their kitchen, yet she would wake up in the morning chirping like the birds. This lot had everything, yet they were all either bloody miserable or sex-crazed.

In the gym, he put Edwina to work on the treadmill straight away, running next to her in an attempt to boost his endorphins. God knows, he needed a lift. They'd been running for thirty minutes, Edwina screaming into the headset connected to her BlackBerry the whole time, when Talli popped her head round the door. The first thing he noticed was that even for her she looked tired, with dark circles under her eyes and her hair resembling a burst couch.

'Hey, I was just—' he began.

'I'm here to see Edwina,' she cut him off, and he

reeled back. Cheeky cow. He'd been about to tell her that she'd been pretty sharp last night and she'd just dissed him big time.

'Edwina, can you come chat to me in the kitchen when you're done?' she asked. 'The table linen swatches are here.'

As soon as Edwina nodded, Talli was gone. Not another word. Zac's jaw clenched with irritation. What. A. Bloody. Cheek. It wasn't like he expected thanks from her, but now she was treating him like he didn't exist.

Sod her.

Even Edwina picked up on his fury. 'Ten more minutes and don't argue,' he told her, resetting both treadmills. For the first time since they started training weeks before, she didn't utter a peep.

Training done, he didn't even wait around for a lift back out to Essex with Edwina. He wasn't going to run the risk that Stroppy Tits would be joining them in the car, and he didn't trust himself not to say anything. Shagging one sister could end this job, but so could giving the other sister a piece of his mind, even if she totally deserved it.

He jumped in a cab to Liverpool Street, hopped on the train, and was opening his front door by noon. The noise of the TV in the bedroom told him that Kiki was still here. Pushing open the door, he saw her lying on her side on the bed, gloriously naked against the white cotton sheets, her hair still wet from the shower as she tapped away on her iPad.

'Babes!' she purred, giving him a beaming smile, before going straight back to her laptop. Zac pulled off his T-shirt, kicked off his shoes and joined her on the bed, spooning behind her, nuzzling into her neck. Man, it felt great to be back here.

'Babes, I'm updating my Twitter,' she said, playfully nudging him away with her shoulder. 'I've got four hundred and fifty-two new followers this morning after the *Sun* posted the pictures from last night. Me and Tobes were, like, totally in matching outfits and it was super-cute. I movie-star-snogged him outside the Beach Box – no tongues – but the paps went wild.'

Zac wasn't even listening. His hand came around and cupped her left breast, his index finger making slow circling motions around her nipple.

'Babes! I've, like, got to get this done . . .'

He answered by placing a trail of kisses along the side of her neck and over her shoulder. Her groan told him the Twitter page was no longer the sole focus of her attention. Still behind her, his hand slowly traced a line down until it found the soft seam between her legs. One of the recurring topics of conversation on the show was the girls' disdain for any form of body hair. Kiki had been going for the full Hollywood since he'd known her.

Cupping his hand, he slipped his fingers between her lips, immediately finding her clitoris. She gasped with pleasure and reached behind her for the thick, hard cock that was pressing into her back. Her iPad slipped to the white shag pile carpet on the floor, all thoughts of social networking now gone.

Still spooning, he slipped his other hand under her body to find her right breast. With both arms around her, simultaneously massaging her tit and her clit, he nuzzled close into her ear.

'I missed you, babe,' he whispered. 'All I've thought about all morning is coming home to fuck you. Here. Like this.'

Another groan.

'I'm going to do this for a little longer . . .' His fingers slipped inside her now, his thumb still rubbing her clit. His other hand was pinching her right nipple, just hard enough to send waves of pleasure to every nerve in her body. 'And then I'm going to lick every inch of you.'

'Just fuck me, Zac. Now. Just fuck me.'

'Sssshhh. Not yet.'

With the agility he had spent years developing, he used his right arm to take his full weight while he changed position, rolling Kiki on to her back as he moved on top of her. His wide shoulders dwarfing her tiny frame, he moved downwards, taking each nipple in his mouth, sucking hard, making her whimper for him never to stop. Down. Further down. He licked a path across her stomach until his mouth was between her legs, his tongue tracing slow, lazy circles on a clit that was already swollen with pleasure.

'I'm going to come, baby,' Kiki panted, her voice high.

Still he didn't stop, alternating now between flicking

her with his tongue and slipping it inside her to taste her wetness, a fusion of her juices and her favourite Miss Dior shower gel.

Suddenly her back arched and she cried out as she came. Only when the orgasm passed and her moans subsided did he slide his tongue between her lips one last time before moving upwards, every muscle on his back glistening with moisture. He retraced the path he'd taken earlier, pausing at Kiki's neck to kiss every contour. 'You are the most beautiful thing I've ever seen,' he told her, and she rewarded him by pulling his face towards her and kissing him, her tongue moving deep into his mouth. He flinched with surprise. She generally didn't allow him to kiss her after he'd been down on her.

Her legs were wide open now, and he felt her muscles contract around his cock as it slid inside her. Reaching down, he supported her buttocks with his hand, rotating them in perfect synchronisation with the undulations of his dick as it pushed inside her, pulled back, inside her, back . . .

'Oh babe. Oh God, babe . . .' Kiki's eyes were closed, her ecstasy building again.

Zac didn't reply, just pushed harder, faster, harder, faster, until she came again, screaming out his name. Only then did he allow himself to release, his arse muscles tight as drums as he flowed into her. Afterwards, he paused for a few seconds before lowering his torso down on to one elbow, his other hand stroking her damp face. 'You're gorgeous,' he told her. 'I love you.'

'Love you too, babes. S'pose I'm going to have to go shower again now,' she added, feigning petulance. At least he thought she was feigning it. 'I'm supposed to be out of here in half an hour. I'm doing a shoot with *OK!* – "Reality TV Royalty". If they put me next to that fat tart from Chelsea that beat me in the poll, I'm going to go, like, proper diva on them.'

With that, her perfectly shaped arse disappeared into the bathroom.

Ignoring her chatter, he realised that he'd needed that. Needed to be with her. Needed to have sex. Needed something to take his mind off the stress and the worry and the pressure to raise the money, and that whole load of twats he'd spent last night with.

So it was perfectly natural that as he drifted off to sleep, the image he would have in his mind would be of Kiki's perfect face.

Perfectly natural.

Except it wasn't strictly true.

Because to his complete and total irritation, the beautiful face he was seeing belonged to someone else.

Chapter Eleven

Talli reached over and squeezed the hand of one of her favourite people. 'Thanks for coming with me, V. Can't believe you ventured all the way out here just for lunch.'

'I know,' Verity replied. 'Alarms went off when I left the vicinity of the King's Road. My mother has probably sent out a search party, claiming I've been abducted by a cult. She's convinced Scientologists have got a list of rich targets and India and I are on it. If she ever meets Tom Cruise, it's bound to turn nasty.'

Talli laughed, and thanked the patron saint of wedding planners for throwing her a bone of relative sanity.

Five weeks to go.

Five weeks.

Edwina was adding more guests and changing her mind about key elements of the ceremony on an almost daily basis. The only things that had remained constant so far were the groom and the two bridesmaids. After her experience with Cosima Carlton, Talli had threatened India with certain death if she published pics of the dresses on Rich Cows and Cartier.

Not for the first time, Talli wondered at the eccentricity that surrounded her life. Maybe they were all normal and she was the one who was out of the ordinary by way of lack of neurosis, madness or remarkable qualities of any other kind.

'So. Tell me about the wedding plans,' Verity demanded, as she cut into her Nando's Peri-Peri Chicken.

'Well, she's gone off the Scottish theme – probably wise as I don't know that having a dead Scottish grandad constitutes grounds for a ceilidh and finding a piper was proving to be a complete bugger. Now she's going for monochrome. Which will be stunning. Although I just need to track down a complete new range of black and white table linen, crockery, cutlery and centrepieces. The florist we're using is saying there's no way she can source enough black flowers for the sprays and centrepieces Edwina wanted. The only consolation is that her mission to have Kylie has been ditched, thank God. She's demanding a Blues Brothers type band instead. Apparently she wants to unleash Simmy's inner funk. With an "n".'

A few moments passed before Verity dislodged the chicken that had stuck in her throat because she'd tried to laugh and swallow at the same time. Talli was on the verge of attempting the Heimlich when her friend finally cleared her throat and regained the power of speech. 'Doesn't Domenic's company manage that lot that won *Britain's Next Star*? You know, the ones that did all the Motown songs?'

Pausing mid-chomp of a corn cob, Talli nodded. 'Oh my God, you're right! I hadn't even thought of them. They'd be perfect. What are they called?'

'Billy and the Brass. I know because I tried to book them for the next fund-raiser but got nowhere. Apparently their PR people are insisting they keep a low profile until the album is ready in January.'

Talli picked up her phone and tapped out a message to Domenic. 'Darling, any chance of booking Billy and the Brass for the wedding? Would save my life.'

A reply was almost instant. 'Will see what I can do. Will be at least £20K, tho.'

The full-fat Coke in the glass Talli was holding splashed as she thumped it down. 'Bloody hell, twenty K,' she passed on to Verity, before biting her bottom lip as she thought about it. She was sure it was the right band for the wedding. Edwina and Simmy had been emphatic that they didn't want anyone stuffy, and they loved the whole soul/Motown thing. Billy was a gorgeous six-foot-tall black man with a voice like Otis Redding, and the Brass the title referred to comprised of a trumpet, horn and saxophone section that had driven the audiences wild at the live shows.

Twenty thousand pounds was a lot of money, but it was one of the few things her parents were footing the bill for and she was sure they wouldn't mind. Her mother spent more than that on cosmetic treatments every year.

Lifting her phone, she typed out another text, this time to Edwina. 'Billy and the Brass for band?'

'Fucking fabulous,' was the instant reply.

Talli felt her spirits soar. Brilliant. As long as Domenic could sort it out, and she was sure he would, it was another problem off the list.

'Verity, I love you.'

'I know, darling. It's understandable. But seriously, any help you need with this whole shebang, just let me know.'

A group of about twenty-four, complete with at least a dozen children, started filing into the table next to them, forcing Talli to lean closer to Verity. 'Thank you. But I feel like, you know, I have to do this myself. I love Simmy and want to make this a perfect day for them. Which probably means I should turn the whole thing over to someone who actually knows what they're doing. Besides, after the whole Cosima Carlton debacle, it would be good to redeem myself in the eyes of my mother and her merry band of so-called friends. The Abercrombies, the Deloites and the Carltons are all coming to the ceremony. I've upped the security in case of all-out warfare.'

Verity giggled. 'Anyway, change of subject. How are things with the hot guy from the restaurant?'

It took Talli a moment to catch on.

'Who?'

'Muscles.'

A wave of something between indigestion and heartburn seeped across Talli's chest.

'Urgh, he's vile.'

'That man is many things. Vile is not one of them. Is he gay?'

'No! Why would you think that?'

'Because I've never seen anyone so perfectly groomed who was straight.'

A kid at the next table sporting a huge badge announcing that he was four threw a baseball glove at his mother and demanded a Fanta.

Talli gestured to the kid. 'That little boy throwing the tantrum? More mature than Zac bloody Parker. Honestly, Verity, you know I never take a dislike to anyone, but he is the rudest guy I've ever met.'

'What is it they say, though? Fine line between love and hate?' Verity teased, moving her vintage white canvas Miu Miu satchel to her other side, out of the direct firing line of small, demanding children armed with orange drinks.

Talli shook her head so fiercely her ponytail slipped down a full inch. 'I promise there's no love there. Not on either side.'

'Well, he must be really hot on his girlfriend then, because India was groping him up under the table and he didn't respond. How often has that happened? She spent the next day in a state of shock, googling his girlfriend and watching reruns of that show. I think she viewed the rejection as a challenge. Talli, honey, don't leave your mouth open like that. I can see your fillings.'

'Sorry, but I'm just . . . just . . .' Talli stopped. Obviously he'd rejected India because he fancied Dessi. Or . . . Dessi had definitely been the one making the moves, so maybe he'd been hit on by both of them. Didn't matter who had kicked it off, she still couldn't look at him knowing he'd been unfaithful to Kiki with her sister. It wasn't that she was being judgemental . . . actually, yes, she *was* being judgemental. But what did it matter? As soon as this wedding was over, she'd never again have to look at Zac Parker's totally handsome square jawline, or his piercing green eyes, the ones that were framed by sweeping black lashes. Or his shoulders, so wide and strong that they could lift her up like Patrick Swayze at the end of her very favourite old movie, *Dirty Dancing*. She would never see that butt again, the one that looked like it had been carved out of steel. Or the thighs that flexed when he walked. And his smell. Like grapefruit, but with a woody, musky undertone. Or his wink. He winked a lot. Usually at the other girls, who all, for some strange reason, seemed to love him, but sometimes when he was messing around with Den too. He'd never winked at her, though. Not ever. He rarely smiled at her either. Sometimes she caught him looking really serious, distracted, and then someone would say hello to him and he'd break into this wide grin like he'd never known a moment's unhappiness in his life. Yep, when this was over, she'd never have to see that smile again.

'Talli, your mouth is still open. God, you're miles away. This wedding is really stressing you out, isn't it?'

She nodded, snapping out of whatever freaked-out place her mind had wandered to. Wow, she felt really weird. PMT. Definitely PMT. There was nothing she'd miss about Zac Parker. Absolutely bloody nothing – especially not the thought of him shagging her sister.

On the table, her phone buzzed and she automatically picked it up. 'Munchkin, spoke to band mgr. Gig booked. Send me full details and will pass them on.'

Talli immediately responded with the info. '24 December. Highdrow Castle. Sound check before 1 p.m. Play from 8 p.m.–midnight. U rock. See you Sat xx'

That left plenty of time for the sound check to be over by the four o'clock ceremony, which would be followed by dinner and speeches before the bride and groom hit the dance floor at eight.

The sound of another incoming text rattled on the tabletop. 'Mine this time,' Verity said, picking up a phone with a Prada insignia on the back and smiling when she saw the screen. 'India and Dessi are in Harvey Nicks buying shoes for the wedding. They want to know what we think.'

Verity turned the phone around to show Talli an image of two perfectly formed ankles, wearing red-soled shoes that differed only in colour. One pair was black, the other a gun-metal grey; both were completely covered in metal spikes that protruded about half an inch from the surface of the shoe.

'I think they'd come in handy for fighting off potential muggers,' Talli laughed.

'I'll call India. Tell her we adore,' Verity said, pressing a speed-dial key. Talli took advantage of the interlude to make a call of her own. May as well strike while the iron was hot. And expensive.

'Daddy, it's me.'

'Darling! How are you? I was just on the phone to your mother telling her what a splendid job you're doing with this wedding.'

'Thanks, Daddy. How is she?'

'Wonderful. Says the Alpine air is putting the colour back in her cheeks. Not sure if the cheeks can move yet, but I suppose that's some kind of progress. Bloody unnecessary if you ask me. She was perfectly lovely before all that nonsense.'

One of Talli's heartstrings tugged for him. He didn't have an iota of annoyance in his voice, just a genuine sadness and sincerity. Growing up, she'd never been in any doubt how much he loved her mother, and she thought, not for the first time, how they should be off enjoying this stage of their lives together, not spending it apart while their mother attempted to single-handedly defeat the ageing process.

'You're right, Daddy. Maybe you should have a holiday when she gets back, after the wedding. You could go down to the house in Brighton for a while, get some peace and quiet.'

116

'Yes, well, we'll, erm, we'll see, darling. I'm not sure I can spare the time.'

His response made her pause for a second. That was so unlike him. Usually he'd snatch every opportunity to steal away for a week or two to Beeches, their house on the Brighton coast. A worry niggled at her stomach, making her regret the second helping of buttered corn on the cob. Her dad was definitely going through some kind of late-life crisis. Perhaps he needed a hobby. Bowling. All the oldies seemed to like bowling out this way, and they all seemed happy enough. She'd definitely suggest he took it up as soon as this wedding was over.

Verity had finished her call now and gestured that she was nipping to the loo.

'Anyway, Daddy, what I'm calling for is to check with you on the band for Simmy's wedding. We've found the perfect one, but their fee is pretty high so I wanted to run it past you before I confirm.' Not strictly true, but she didn't like to say it was already booked. It was important to give him his place, even though she knew that he'd be fine with it. After all, Edwina's father was footing the majority of the bill and he'd set a £100K budget, but made it clear that was only a working guide – whatever Edwina wanted, she would get.

'How much is it, darling?'

Again, his response surprised her a little. She'd half expected him just to say it was fine without even asking. Her father had always been that way with money. Talli had made a point of earning her own way, working in restaurants and sports centres while studying at uni. Somehow supplementing a small allowance with a minimum wage made her feel that she was accomplishing more than just a final stage in her education. Dessi, however, had no such scruples. She'd been working her way through a two-grand-a-month clothes budget since she hit her teens.

'It's twenty thousand pounds. It's the band that won *Britain's Next Star*,' she added, quite unnecessarily, as her father never watched anything but *Question Time* or programmes presented by David Attenborough.

The pause stretched out so long she thought she'd lost her signal.

'Daddy, are you still there?'

Cough. 'Erm, yes, darling. That's fine. Of course. Absolutely fine.'

'OK, I'll go ahead and set it up then. I'll see you at the weekend – I'll be back Friday afternoon.'

'Splendid, darling.' His voice sounded odd, and she was sure she could hear the tapping of a keyboard. Oh God, was he checking out porn again? He could at least have waited until she was off the phone.

Her thumb quickly disconnected the call and Verity reacted with concern.

'What's wrong, darling?'

'It's my dad. He's acting weird. I think he's addicted to porn.'

'Oh no,' Verity replied with a resounding sigh. 'I hope

it doesn't give him any ideas. I don't think your mother's new face could stand anything strenuous or kinky.'

Talli pushed her plate away. For some reason that she couldn't quite put her finger on, her conversations over the last hour had resulted in a sudden loss of appetite.

Chapter Twelve

@minxandlenasauntiedot This is my 1st tweet. One important thing to know in life – where there's bingo, there's hope #jointhisDot

'What do I do now, love?' Auntie Dot handed the iPad back to Lena, who giggled as she posted up the tweet, then retweeted it on her own account.

'Just wait, Auntie Dot – by this time tomorrow, you'll be the most popular pensioner in Essex. Well, except for that Alan Sugar bloke, but he's on the telly so that doesn't count.'

'Yeah, you'll wipe the floor with him, Auntie Dot,' Minx added. 'I'll retweet your link too. I'll post up that pic of you snowboarding with me and Dale last year. Bet that Sugar bloke ain't ever stopped halfway down a mountain for a fag and a swig from a hip flask.'

'I'm a pensioner, love – I've got to stay hydrated.'

Auntie Dot nodded solemnly, then erupted into a raucous cackle.

Over in the corner of Spa Shiraz, Zac laughed as he swung around on a white leather swivel chair, detached from the conversation. He didn't have a Twitter account. He did have a Facebook page, but that was just for his training work and nothing personal was ever posted on there. He didn't get the need to tell everyone what he was doing. The other night he'd caught Kiki tweeting a picture of her dinner. Why, exactly, did the world need to know that she was having salmon and scrambled eggs?

But hey, if it kept his Auntie Dot amused, then it wasn't all bad. He was proud of the way his aunt refused to conform to the stereotype of an older woman. Unless a sixty-four-year-old woman normally had her white hair piled high on her head, a deep tan, and her finger- and toenails shaded in perfect coats of bright pink shimmer.

'All right there, Mrs Parker? Another five minutes and you'll be fine to put your shoes back on,' Fran told her, just as Porsche burst through the double glass doors, tears flooding down her face.

Zac automatically looked to see if a camera crew was following her. Nope, no one there. Whatever was causing the upset, it wasn't being done for show.

Auntie Dot jumped up on to her newly pedicured toes. 'What's wrong, darlin'? Deep breaths, sweetheart. That's it. Deep breaths.'

Her arm was around Porsche now, guiding her to the chair she'd just vacated. This was definitely where Lena got her caring side from. Lena was kneeling down next to Porsche, and over at the nail bar, even Shiraz had stopped applying Moonlight Black to Minx's fingernails and was leaning over, waiting to hear the problem.

Zac tuned in, doubtful that he could help, hoping that whatever was making Porsche cry was nothing to do with Kiki.

'It's that bitch Kiki,' Porsche wailed.

Zac's heart sank. Kiki had been ruffling feathers all over the place lately. A lot of it was just jealousy, but he couldn't deny that she was definitely getting used to the star treatment and had started to buy into the hype. The other day he'd caught her on the phone to a London photo agency passing on details of where she'd be for the next few days. When he'd chinned her about it she'd claimed she'd only done it because she liked the security of knowing there were always paps about to keep an eye on her. Zac wasn't so sure that was the whole truth.

Lena glanced over at Zac, raised her eyebrows apologetically and turned back to a wailing Porsche.

'Porsche, you have to calm down, babes. If you carry on like this you'll wreck those eyelash extensions, and you've only had them on for three days.'

That snapped Porsche right out of her hysterics and she immediately calmed down to just regular sniffs.

'I'm, like, proper raging. That devious cow has gone in and stolen my knicker line. Stole it! Gussets approached me months ago about endorsing their thong range and then I goes and tells Kiki a couple of weeks ago and today my agent gets a call to say they're going with her instead of me. It's so unfair. Ramone does those boxer shorts ads and I could just imagine the two of us next to each other on the billboards up the High Street. We'd have been, like, proper Posh and Becks.' Her shoulders were slumped now, misery engulfing her. 'I could have been fucking huge in knickers.'

The sniffs increased in volume to a minor wail, but without the tears that could threaten the glue on her lashes.

'Porsche, sweetheart, I'm sure there's an innocent explanation for all this,' Dot assured her, then gave Zac a pursed-lip look of total cynicism that suggested she didn't believe that for a minute. He had no idea why his aunt wasn't enamoured with his girlfriend. He had a hunch that it was because Kiki's ways got right on Lena and Minx's nerves and Auntie Dot was staying true to the trade union movement from her cleaning days and coming out in sympathy with her comrades.

He decided to make himself scarce. This was between the girls and he knew better than to get in the middle of their bust-ups. That could never end well. Besides, he was training Edwina upstairs in half an hour and they had serious work to do. He'd started adding super-sets into their workouts, high-intensity exercises that utilised more than one major muscle group at a time. There was just over a month to go now and he didn't feel they were making quite enough progress. That four-grand carrot was at the end of the stick and there was no way he wasn't reeling it in. Too much depended on it.

'Stay right there, Zac Parker.' Auntie Dot's words. Delivered in the tone of an assassin right before he put the barrel of a gun to his target's temple. 'Did you know about this?'

His hands went up into a surrender position. 'I swear I didn't. Kiki hasn't mentioned it. Look, let me ask her.' He pulled his phone out of his pocket and was about to press the speed-dial key when Kiki herself breezed in and stopped.

'What?' she asked, instantly aware that every pair of eyes was on her, and not in a good way.

Porsche attempted to jump up from the chair but Dot pulled her back down. 'That's not the way, love,' she warned her. 'No matter how bloody tempting.'

Dot pulled herself up to her full five-foot-two-inch height. 'Kiki, Porsche here is a bit upset because she's under the – surely mistaken – impression that you've swiped one of those endearment deals . . .'

'Endorsement deals,' Lena corrected her.

Dot carried on regardless. '. . . from under her nose.'

Zac watched as Kiki flushed a pale shade of Auntie Dot's toenails. Shit, she'd done it, right enough. This was going to cause frigging carnage. Out of the corner of his eye, he saw Shiraz picking up her phone to video the conversation. He wasn't thrilled with Kiki, but there was no way this was going on YouTube. 'Shiraz,' he said quietly, the reproach in his tone unmistakable. She replied with a 'can't blame me for trying' shrug, then settled for typing something instead. No doubt keeping her Twitter fans abreast of the situation.

'You are, like, proper evil,' Porsche spat.

Kiki accelerated from defensive to combative in 2.4 seconds.

'Look, it's not my problem if they wanted me to do it instead. They felt I was just a better fit for their brand values. Don't be so touchy, Porsche. It's business.'

Zac felt the pulse on the side of his neck beat just a little bit faster with irritation. Business? When did she get to be so cold? When all this started, the girls were friends, and now they were stealing each other's knicker lines. Not a sentence he'd ever anticipated thinking.

'Business?' Porsche screeched, echoing his thoughts and sharing them in a voice that could be heard by astronauts in orbiting space stations.

'Holy fuck,' Shiraz whistled. 'Like proper holy fuck.'

Kiki's attention never wavered from Porsche.

'Yeah, and what of it?' she fought back. 'I get more shoots than any of you lot so it's only natural that they want to use me. It's all about the brand.'

'Brand? You're Kiki fucking Spooner from Billericay, not Kate bloody Moss,' Porsche snapped back.

'Have any of you lot checked Twitter?' Shiraz interrupted again. Staring transfixed at her phone screen, something in her voice was serious enough to grab their attention.

Like a synchronised swimming team, everyone except

Zac performed exactly the same motion at the same time. Even Dot peered over to Lena's iPad screen.

The same message had appeared on all of their feeds.

@minxandlenasauntiedot @lenaparker @minxparker @shirazmoore @ramonesPorsche Kiki Spooner needs stopped. Bitch. Will end soon.

A whimper escaped Kiki's lips, but Porsche was a tad more definitive.

'Stole another knicker line from someone else lately?'

Chapter Thirteen

34 November 3013

Talli stretched and yawned at the same time, before flopping her arms down with a contented sigh. Pressing the button on the headboard behind her resulted in a low humming noise as the blinds on the floor-to-ceiling windows to her left swept back, revealing a stunning view of the Thames and Tower Bridge in the distance. Beside her, Domenic murmured, stirred, then lifted his eye mask, squinting into the light.

'Morning, darling,' she chirped as she leant over to kiss him, ridiculously happy to be lazing in bed on a Saturday morning, with no plans to see Edwina, contact suppliers or do anything even remotely connected to weddings all weekend.

She didn't even mind that he quickly turned his head, resulting in her kiss landing on his cheek. Domenic didn't do morning breath. He claimed that that was when mouth bacteria was at its highest.

If ever an apartment was reflective of the owner it was this one. A large penthouse loft, ten storeys up on the bank of the river, it was a real mix of styles and influences. The rich American walnut floor and Conran furniture demonstrated wealth, the subtle eggshell-white paint on the walls and sparkling white gloss kitchen indicated clean surfaces and lack of germs or clutter. The huge promotional prints displayed in black metal frames that punctuated the wall facing the window advertised the tours of Big Up D and a handful of other artists handled by Domenic's label.

The stone fireplace in the middle of the room was testimony to . . . what? Dom's warm and romantic side? OK, so that had been a little lacking lately, but it was completely Talli's own fault. If she hadn't gone tearing off to Essex and immersed herself in the world of weddings, they'd have been as close and happy as always. And anyway, after five years together they were past all the gushing, soppy stuff. Dom had been that guy once. He'd whisked her off to Paris to see the Killers for her eighteenth birthday. They'd made love in the moonlight after skinny-dipping in Antigua. It didn't matter that they'd cut the swim short because he was worried about the potential for a deadly stingray bite in the water.

Slipping out of bed, she padded across the walnut floor to the bathroom, her outsize T-shirt skimming the top of her toned legs. Working out at Density had kept her in great shape, and years of undressing in communal changing rooms at sports events had left her with no shyness about her body at all. She'd decided it wasn't nearly as sexy as the curves and boobs on the girls in *Lovin' Essex*, but everything was more or less where it should be and small breasts were bound to come back into fashion one day.

After a quick pee and brush of the teeth, she climbed back into bed, her honey hair wild and unruly. Pushing the covers to one side, she took the remote control out of Domenic's hand, switched off MTV, and straddled him, bending over to nuzzle at the corner of his Madness T-shirt. Underneath her, she felt the stirrings of an erection in his striped boxer shorts.

'Hang on, darling, be right back.'

'But I don't care about the teeth thing,' she replied, as he shimmied her across the bed and slipped out from underneath her. He looked at her like she'd just admitted to murdering a litter of puppies.

'Er, right. Back in a tick.' He completely ignored her objections as he disappeared into the bathroom, leaving Talli quite literally twiddling her thumbs.

She heard the shower go, then his electric toothbrush, a silent interval while he flossed, followed by the skoosh of deodorant spray, before the door opened again and he walked towards her, fully naked except for a condom on his semi-erect penis. Not the most erotic sight in the world, but Talli was suddenly very aware that it had been weeks since they'd had sex. She blamed her new-found addiction to *Lovin' Essex* for this realisation. She'd watched both series and was up to date with the episodes now, and it seemed like the characters in the show were always either planning to have sex, having sex or discussing the sex they'd already had. And the kind of sex they were having . . . Domenic was strictly a missionary position guy, but maybe a bit of variation would do them good. The show definitely made her feel like life was passing her by in a wave of floral arrangements, crystal glassware and conservative sex.

As he climbed on to the bed, a completely unfair comparison to his physique suddenly hit her. Yesterday she'd watched Zac training with Edwina, his top off, wearing just a tiny pair of black Nike shorts. They'd been alternating sets on the military press, pushing a bar from behind their necks until their arms were fully extended above their heads. With every slow, controlled movement, his delts and obliques at the side of his torso rippled, flexing and contracting with almost hypnotic rhythm, tiny beads of sweat running down the centre of his tanned back.

'OK, darling, let's go,' Domenic murmured, as he moved on top of her, the sun bouncing off his slender pale frame. From the neck up he was entirely cute in a floppy-haired, young Hugh Grant kind of way, but maybe it was time to suggest that they start working out together. Not to get as big as that muscled oaf Zac. That was excessive. Took far more dedication than any normal person would have time to give. Those arms didn't come from doing a few bicep raises once a week. And that chest wasn't the result of twenty minutes with a pec deck. And . . .

'Munchkin, you're damp down there,' Dom said with a sexy grin. His announcement took her by surprise, as did the fact that he was between her legs now, his cock probing at her vagina, his fingers guiding it in.

She gasped with pleasure as he entered her fully. Now that he was fully erect, she felt the whole of him push into her. The thought of Zac's shoulders wouldn't leave her. Reaching down, she cupped Dom's balls and he murmured his approval, groaning louder, louder. *Zac's thighs, huge, strong.* Pushing his body up on straight arms, Dom thrust his pelvis against hers. As the pace increased, his mouth came down and he kissed her, their tongues intertwining, both panting. *Those abs. Zac's abs.* Talli felt the tingle of an orgasm start at the small of her back, then spread across her stomach and pelvis, pulling him in hard to her. Domenic was pounding now, his tongue demanding, persistent, their sweat seeping together. *Zac's hips. Narrow, ripped, strong.* Talli brought her legs up and twisted them together across his back, the position letting him even deeper inside her. It was all they both needed. When it took control, her orgasm was strong and glorious, making her legs spasm and grip him even tighter. Domenic reacted to the entrapment with a loud 'Yes! Oh fuck yes!' pummelling against her as he came only seconds after her.

Sliding off her, he pulled her in tight to him and kissed her. 'That was amazing. Christ, I've missed you,' he announced. 'We really need to do this more often.'

Shame prickled her conscience as she dismissed all illicit images from her mind. He was right. They just had to do it more often, maybe even be a bit more adventurous, starting today. All she wanted to do was lie here cuddled up with Dom, watch TV, make love again, read a book and generally have a lazy day that didn't involve moving more than five feet from this bed.

A whole day in bed. A long, luxurious, sexy . . .

'Where are you going?' she asked, realising he was halfway across the room.

'Shower, munchkin.'

OK, so that wasn't out of the ordinary. He always showered straight after sex.

'But are you coming back to bed? I thought we could have a lazy day.'

His expression told her he had a different plan.

The front-door buzzer gave him the opportunity to escape. Talli flicked the TV on to the security camera channel, to see Verity, India, Dessi and Dom's brother Jake waving at the screen.

Bugger.

She buzzed them in, then jumped out of bed and grabbed the T-shirt she'd discarded on the floor. She pulled it on, covered it with Dom's black terry towelling robe, then headed for the door and opened it just as they alighted from the lift and swept past her in an orderly line, each one kissing her on the cheek as they passed.

'Oooh, you look like you've just been ravished,' Dessi announced. 'You have! Wow, your shagged hair actually looks better than your not-been-shagged-in-weeks hair.'

Talli leaned over and flicked the back of Dessi's head, eliciting a dramatic 'Ouch. Sibling battery!'

All three girls were in their standard weekend casual outfits. Skinny jeans in varying shades (black for Dessi, indigo for Verity, white for India), knee-high boots, jackets and scarves. Jake looked dark and mysterious in his black roll-neck jumper, cords and leather Crombie coat.

At twenty-eight, Jake was the complete opposite of Dom. He was a . . . Talli struggled to define it. A grown-up, from the top of his swept-back, immaculately styled black hair down to his Italian leather shoes. He was in the family business, a fine wine export company, and spent most of the year travelling, sampling new produce and checking on their offices throughout the world. He and Dessi occasionally hooked up when he was in town, but they both treated it as purely recreational, no strings attached.

Dom emerged from the bathroom, fully dressed, shaved and scrunching his hair into something resembling a style with his fingers. 'We thought we'd catch a movie this afternoon, then go out for a few drinks and dinner. I have to head over to Camden for a gig later – there's a singer called Luna Ma Dame who they're calling the next Amy Winehouse and I want to get in there and check her out.'

'Look, Dom, I don't want to do any of that. It's the first day we've spent together in weeks. I want to stay in bed all day and perhaps have a long bath together, then head out for a nice dinner somewhere quiet and romantic. Maybe Italian.'

At least that was what Talli thought. What she actually said was, 'Erm, OK then, I'll just go grab a quick shower.'

'I'll come with you,' Dessi offered. Or rather, she stated, given that she was already on her feet and following Talli across the loft. In the bathroom, she parked herself on the loo – thankfully the seat was down, due to the fact that Dom had once read that keeping the lid up while flushing spread germs all over the room. He now put the seat down and stepped back a few feet before pressing the flush button. With his big toe.

Talli pulled off her robe and T-shirt and stepped into the smoked glass cubicle. 'God, I wish I had your bum,' Dessi told her as she slid the door closed.

'I'll swap you for your confidence and hair,' Talli offered, laughing, determined to keep the subject on neutral territory. This was the first time she and Dessi had been alone together since the night at Delaney, and Dessi had a no boundaries when it came to recounting the details of her sexual exploits. The last thing Talli wanted to hear was anything even remotely connected with Edwina, Essex or Zac bloody Parker.

'So how's Muscles doing?' Dessi asked.

Talli opened the screen and popped her head out. It was a bit of an effort, but she kept her voice light and breezy. 'Seriously? You want to discuss him? I'd have thought you'd have known better than me how he was. Didn't you keep in touch?'

'I don't have his number. Besides, the guy is, like, a total party pooper. He missed the night of his life and it didn't even seem to bother him.'

The hands that were soaping Talli's hair stopped and slid the door open again, and this time a head wearing four inches of shampoo suds appeared through the gap.

Dessi giggled. 'Great look. It was on all the catwalks this season.'

'Rewind a minute,' Talli replied. 'What do you mean, he missed the night of his life? Didn't you sleep with him?'

Dessi was looking in the mirror now, reapplying lipstick from her tiny Chanel cross-body messenger. She paused mid pout. 'Nope. I might have suggested it, but he was out of there with sparks coming off his heels. I had to explain to Theresa the next morning why one of her kitchen chairs had a chip out of it. I had a choice between admitting that he knocked it over in his hurry to leave, and saying you did it. I blamed you.'

Talli wasn't listening. Back in the shower, she let the water pound her head, washing away the soap and her weird feeling of discontent with it. There was definitely a slice of self-reproach in there too. She owed him an apology. All this time she'd been giving him the cold shoulder because . . . actually, she wasn't really sure why. It was absolutely none of her business what he did with anyone. She'd just felt really uncomfortable about the whole situation. But now . . .

'Talli, darling, I love you madly,' Dessi chirped. 'But honestly, singing just isn't your strong point. What is that anyway?'

Talli clamped her jaw shut, mortified that she hadn't even been aware that she was humming a tune.

'Oh, nothing. Just an old song from a movie.'

'That's it! That film you always used to watch when we were younger. *Dirty Dancing*!'

Embarrassment be damned. Just because she bloody well felt like it, Talli broke into a loud, slightly out-of-tune chorus of 'I've Had the Time of My Life'.

Chapter Fourteen

'Happy birthday, dear Dottie, happy birthday to you!'

Zac, Minx, Lena, the whole cast of *Lovin' Essex* and three of Dot's closest chums were singing, glasses of champagne swaying above their heads. They were in Dot's favourite restaurant, a buffet-style place – £9.99, all you can eat – with a swirly carpet and fake beams on the ceiling. All the staff knew her by name and were joining in with the song as they passed, carrying three-foot-diameter trays above their heads. The manager had even splashed out on free Asti Spumante for the whole party in the hope that one of the *Lovin' Essex* cast would tweet their location. None of them did.

Dot blew out the candles on the cake to a thundering ovation.

'Speech! Speech!' shouted Den, with a couple of the others joining in.

Auntie Dot came over all bashful before finally

nodding her head. 'All right, all right. Stop heckling a woman of my age or I'll be giving your names and addresses to the authorities at Age UK.

'First I want to thank all of you for coming. It's not often a women turns forty-five.'

There was a wave of laughter and drum rolls on the table.

'No sarcasm, please,' Dot ordered. 'Any cheek will also have repercussions. Now that I've got my bus pass, I can hunt you down for free.'

More laughter.

'And I want to thank Jessie, Minnie and Ena, my bingo buddies, who live their lives by the same motto as me.'

Every single person in the room shouted, 'Where there's bingo, there's hope!' Since Dot had posted her mantra on Twitter, with the cast of the show retweeting it, it had gone viral. The company that made the show's merchandise had even made an approach about releasing a T-shirt range sporting the slogan, and Edwina had asked Dot if she'd consider appearing in a couple of episodes. Dot declined. Last thing she wanted was to be famous, she said. Attracted all sorts of unsavoury types. And the drug dealer up the road would only target her for cash.

'Lastly, I want to thank my Zac, Minx and Lena.'

Zac sat on one side of her, Minx and Lena on the other, all of them with beaming smiles. 'You know, when these three came to live with me, a few of my so-called pals didn't approve. But we proved them all wrong. I was told that taking on three kids would be an inconvenience. Too much. But they've been a joy since the moment they came to me. I might not have been lucky enough to have my own babies, but my God, I'm the luckiest aunt in the world. I love the bones of all of you.'

Dot raised her glass, and everyone else followed, cheering as they did. Zac tried and failed to swallow the lump that appeared to be wedged in his throat, Minx welled up, while the tears slid down Lena's face.

It was Zac's turn to speak. Standing up, he smoothed down the creases on his black trousers. He'd teamed them with a formal charcoal shirt, left open at the neck. Auntie Dot had a thing about dressing smart on special occasions. Normally he hated speaking in public with a passion, but tonight was no hardship.

'Ladies and gentlemen . . .' he started, triggering a chorus of whoops and hollers. 'And Auntie Dot. On behalf of me, Lena and Minx, I just want you to know that it wasn't you who got lucky, it was us. We couldn't thank you enough or love you more. Happy birthday.'

He sat down to another wave of drum rolls on the tables and took a couple of deep breaths. If he teared up in front of this lot, he'd never hear the end of it. A hand squeezed his knee and he turned to Kiki, sitting on the other side of him, looking killer in a white crêpe mini-dress with chiffon floaty sleeves. The front view was all virginal purity, but at the back was a V that plunged so low you could just see the very top of her butt cleavage.

She'd squealed when Auntie Dot had tried to persuade her to let her sew it up an inch.

'Aw, that was so cute, babes,' she told him as he pulled his chair back in, glancing over to Auntie Dot and Lena, who were hugging on his right. Belatedly, he realised that Kiki was still talking.

'Sorry, babe, didn't catch you there,' he said, leaning in closer to her.

'I said can we go now?' she repeated, pulling a pink lip gloss out of her diamante-studded bag and applying the 453rd coat of the night.

'Go where?' he asked, confused. He was positive they didn't have any other plans. It was Dot's sixty-fifth birthday; there was no way he was leaving.

'The Beach Box, babe,' Kiki said, like it was obvious. 'Tobes is heading over there too and it's Saturday night so the paps will be out in force. I've already missed the Sundays, but if I don't go, there will be no chance of making next week's *Heat*.'

The Sundays. Most real celebrities lived in fear of being spotlighted in the Sunday papers because it usually meant some sort of scandal had been uncovered. Kiki looked on it as a personal failing if she didn't feature in the first five pages. However, non-inclusion in *Heat* could have her sulking for days.

'What does it matter if you don't?' he asked tersely, trying not to show that he was annoyed. He got that this was her career and it mattered to her, but lately he had to admit she'd been taking it way too far. The need for publicity had almost turned into a battle between her and Porsche, both of them determined to outdo each other. It was out of control – especially with that weirdo stalker out there. He'd have been much happier if Kiki had agreed to keep a low profile until they'd tracked down the source of the letters.

They'd reported that tweet threat to the police and her management company's security team, but it had been made on a brand-new account, using fake details, on a pay-as-you-go mobile and they'd been told it was pretty much untraceable. Everyone kept telling them it was just some weirdo who would never actually do anything. Apparently loads of the reality TV stars had stalkers. That and getting papped with no knickers on were occupational hazards.

'Babes! Of course I have to go. It's my job.'

'And this is my family,' he told her calmly. He'd never lost his temper with Kiki. Wasn't his way. But he was no pushover either. He'd let her go so far, but there were some things that just didn't wash. Cue exhibit number one for the defence – her expression of pure outrage.

'Look, babes, I'm not being, like, a proper bitch or anything, but I want to go.'

'I'm staying here.' Calm again. Almost matter-of-fact. That seemed to annoy her even more.

'So you'd let me go out there when that crazy person could attack me or anything and you wouldn't be able to do anything about it.'

Bloody hell, was she really using the stalker as emotional blackmail to get her own way?

'Then stay here. I'll look after you. You really don't need to go there tonight, babe.'

Her face clouded over. 'I didn't spend all day getting ready and a fortune on this dress to sit in some dive restaurant all night.'

Her words stung.

'You know what, Kiki – if you want to go, then go. I'll call your management and get them to send someone over to meet you there, and I'll call a few of the boys on the door and have them look out for you too. But I'm staying here. It's a special birthday for Auntie Dot and I'm not ditching her.'

Her face was thunderous now. 'So you're choosing your Auntie Dot over me.'

'It's not my choice. You're the one that's leaving.'

'I don't know what's happened to you, Zac Parker, but you've, like, totally changed. Or maybe we've just outgrown each other.'

In a moment of sudden clarity, he realised that she was absolutely right. He was knackered. Physically he was shattered with training Edwina and his other clients, sometimes up to eighteen hours a day. Mentally he was burnt out with trying to look after Kiki and get this fucking money together. She was right. Maybe he'd changed. Maybe he'd changed too much for them to work now.

This wasn't even worth discussing any more.

He got up from the table and headed a few feet to his left, to where Den, Max, Ramone, Dale and Toby were sitting. The five main guys in the cast had been offered free veneers by a national chain of cosmetic dentists, so watching them all break into a grin at his approach was like being flashed by a strobe light.

'All right, guys?' he greeted them, putting an arm around Den's shoulders as he crouched down so that he was on the same level as them. 'Listen, are you lot going over to the Beach Box?'

'Yeah, like, later. You know, when Dot calls it a night,' Dale answered. Unlike the others, in their sharp suits and expensive watches, Minx's boyfriend stayed true to his extreme-sports spirit. His long, tousled brown hair was just right with his Bogner T-shirt and Zegna jeans. Zac was glad Minx had found herself a decent bloke. He just hoped that Max turned out to be good for Lena too. The fact that he was thirty, a few years older than her, definitely helped. Lena might only be twenty-two, but she'd always had her head screwed on.

Zac looked over his shoulder. Dot was now wearing a flower in each ear and throwing back a peach schnapps shot.

'Yeah, I think that might be a while. Look, Den, I'm going to hang around here tonight, but would you mind taking Kiki over to the Beach Box now?'

Den smiled at him knowingly. 'Getting the DTs from the flash bulbs?' he asked.

'Something like that,' Zac answered, not wanting to

bad-mouth his girlf . . . actually, as of a couple of minutes ago, he wasn't sure what she was. This was an almost surreal situation, but she'd forced his hand and he was just too annoyed to go along with her, yet too tired to fight. Easier just to let her go and work it out later.

'Man, she's getting out of control,' Toby threw in. With his fifties-leading-man black hair and cheekbones that looked like they'd been chiselled from shiny stone, he was the most handsome of them all. He had a huge fan club, and had already been offered his own spin-off show. Female hearts would break all across the nation when he came out in the series finale. 'I'm almost looking forward to blowing her off for the male model they've lined up for the big showdown. Sure you don't want to volunteer, Zac?'

'Nah, mate, you're fine. I make it a policy not to go out with anyone who wears more aftershave than me.'

The blokes all laughed, Toby the loudest.

'Tell you what,' Den said. 'These three are waiting for the girls,' he gestured to Dale, Max and Ramone, 'but me and Tobes will head off now and get Kiki out of your hair.'

'You're a pal,' Zac told him, then led the way back to the top table. Den stepped in to smooth the situation over. 'Dot, you know you can have my body any night of the week,' he teased her.

'Yeah, love, but I'd only want it to make me a cuppa and turn the telly over so I can watch those nice young men on *Grey's Anatomy*.'

Den leaned in, gave her a huge bear hug and then turned to a pouting Kiki. 'Come on then, Kiki – we're going over to the club. Coming with us?'

Kiki glowered at Zac, then stood up, flicked her hair back. 'Bye, Dot, bye, Lena, Minx.' Not a word to the supposed love of her life as she strutted off towards the door. The guys finished their goodbyes, both of them hugging Dot and wishing her well, before following in Kiki's wake. As soon as they were gone, Zac sat back down and immediately felt Dot take his hand.

'You know, son, it's been a long, long time since I gave you any advice or interfered in your life . . .'

Zac chose not to point out that she gave him advice and interfered in his life on a regular basis. It was just one of the reasons that he loved her.

'But mark my words, my darlin', that one is not for you.'

Taking a long, slow sip of his Jack Daniel's and Coke, Zac finally admitted to himself that perhaps he knew that already.

Chapter Fifteen

Talli was totally wiped out. After waking at six a.m., she'd run through her to-do list, checked on the progress of all the outstanding items, hopped in a cab, then a train, then another cab, arriving at Highdrow Castle for a nine a.m. meeting with Edwina and the castle's event manager, Trevor Highdrow. Over the last few weeks, Talli had discovered that he was the black-sheep nephew of Lord Highdrow, and had only been given the job to keep him out of trouble following a long stint in an Arizona rehab centre.

It was the perfect November morning. The air was cold and crisp and there was a layer of twinkling frost covering the gardens and grounds, making even the maze in the centre of the landscaped terraces look like it had been formed from ice crystals.

They ran through the schedule of events.

1 p.m. Sound check ends.

3 p.m. Guests begin to arrive. String quartet provides the music, mulled wine to be served.

4 p.m. Wedding ceremony followed by photographs.

6 p.m. Guests seated for dinner. Edwina and Simmy enter to the sound of the theme tune for *Lovin' Essex*. Edwina thought it was 'hilariously ironic'.

7.30 p.m. Speeches and further toasts.

8 p.m. Billy and the Brass take the stage. Party starts.

8.05 p.m. Talli leaves. Finds a bed. Crashes out. Then phones therapist to discuss treatment for post-traumatic stress disorder. OK, she might have been making that last bit up.

The replies to the invitations had been flooding in and they were now up to 350 guests, with many more yet to answer. With every passing week she had to up the numbers for the chair covers, the catering, the bar, the gifts . . . almost every single aspect of the day.

The only consolation was that all the main items were sourced and booked. The bride, groom and immediate family were being chauffeured to the castle the morning before the wedding, having a rehearsal dinner that night, then staying in the ten castle bedrooms. On the morning of the wedding there would be a lavish breakfast, before the family retired with a hair and make-up team to get ready for the big occasion.

The happily married couple would be the first to leave. Edwina and Persimmon were heading off to the Maldives on Christmas Day, so a Rolls-Royce was booked to take them to the airport after breakfast in the castle dining room. A fleet of cars would then take the families back to London, depositing them early afternoon to enjoy Christmas in their own homes.

The table settings had been finalised, although the linens and crockery wouldn't arrive from Italy until the week before the ceremony. Yes, the theme had changed again for what Talli desperately hoped was the final time.

Monochrome out. Traditional Venetian in.

Simmy had whisked Edwina off for a weekend in Venice when they got engaged and Edwina now wanted to replicate the table settings, flowers and ambience at the hotel they stayed in.

Talli was wondering how she was going to find a way to slip the florist some Prozac before she broke the news. They had exactly one month to go. Technically there was still time to get everything done, but it was getting so close, she'd taken to carrying around a brown paper bag in case she felt the need to hyperventilate.

Even Trevor, the wonderfully camp Highdrow liaison, was beginning to look nervous, and all he had to do was make sure that everything in the castle was in full working order and that the staff were on hand to put everything where it was supposed to be.

'Right, darlings, that's fucking fabulous,' Edwina declared as they wound up the meeting, all three of them confident that they were on the same, if ever-changing, page.

Talli needed more than that. 'Edwina, promise me on this bible . . .'

'That's not a bible. It's a copy of *House Beautiful* magazine.'

'It's all I've got,' Talli told her firmly, 'so it'll have to do.' She held out the magazine again. 'Swear on this Christmas 2012 edition of *House Beautiful* that you will not change your mind, alter plans, revisualise the scene or generally push me a single step closer to the edge than you already have done.'

'Count me in on that too,' added Trevor. 'My counsellor says I'm always just one high-pressure situation away from going back on the coke.'

'Or upset Trevor in any way,' Talli added.

Edwina screeched with laughter, agreed, then marched Talli to her car. 'Need to get to the gym pronto,' she informed her. 'I'm training at two, and if I'm not there, Zac will be even more grumpy than usual. I don't know what's got into him these days. I always had him down as happy-go-lucky.'

Talli's interest pricked at the mention of Zac's name. She owed him an apology and it was only right that she deliver it. The thought didn't fill her with pleasure. He might not have had sex with Dessi, but he was still rude, arrogant and obnoxious. She made the conscious decision not to add gorgeous to that list. The guilt of thinking about him while having sex with Domenic was still sitting heavily on her shoulders.

'And he's going to be even worse today if he caught the papers this morning. Honestly, Kiki's fan-fucking-tastic for our show, but the girl's middle names are Drama and Queen.'

'After my own heart,' Trevor added as he kissed them goodbye.

They were speeding down the driveway before Talli had a chance to delve deeper. 'So what has Kiki done that could have upset Zac?'

'Talli, do you not use Twitter?'

Talli shook her head.

'Facebook?'

'Yes. But I only check it every few weeks and even then it's just to send pics or messages to Fliss.'

'And the newspapers?'

Talli shrugged, shamefaced. At home she'd always read the *Guardian* and the *Telegraph* because they were both delivered, but she'd just been so busy lately.

'Kiki got caught with her tongue down Dean Braden's throat coming out of the Beach Box in the early hours of Sunday morning. He's that DJ who does all the celebrity gigs here and in Ibiza. Shame it missed the Sunday editions. That would have been fucking fabulous publicity. Having said that, the video went viral, so I reckon even your friend in the wilds of Ethiopia . . .'

'Malawi,' Talli corrected her. Edwina didn't stop for breath.

'. . . has probably seen it by now. Fucks things up a bit for us because she was supposed to be seeing Toby until the final episode of the series. I hope he can play heartbroken until we work up the "Kiki's Betrayal Forced Me to Seek Solace in the Arms of the Bloke Who Models for Armani" angle.'

Talli marvelled at her future sister-in-law's highly pragmatic take on it all. It was hard to believe these were people's actual lives they were dealing with.

Edwina spent the whole journey back barking orders to a series of colleagues, agents, managers and cast members.

By the time Talli reached Density Fitness, there were parts of her brain that were trying to tunnel through her skull to escape. She jumped straight in a cab and headed back to the hotel, spending the rest of the day contacting every single supplier and updating the details and numbers, then searching catalogues and online websites for the few smaller items she'd still to source. Where exactly did one find miniature gondolas that could be filled with sprays of flowers and line the entrance to the ballroom? It was almost nine p.m. by the time she'd finished, and every muscle ached from sitting hunched over and cross-legged on the bed. The choice was twofold – a double bill of *CSI: New York* on TV, or nip back to Density for a workout.

Den was the first person she saw when she arrived.

''Ello, duchess, how's tricks?' he greeted her with an exaggerated double air kiss.

'Don't think I don't know you're taking the piss out of me with all that air-kissing stuff, Den,' she bantered.

'I'm not! That's the way we all greet each other down my street,' he retorted indignantly. Talli giggled as they headed over to the circuits section. She'd been alternating her workouts between cardiovascular and weight training. Tonight was definitely one for the weights. She needed to stretch the muscles that had been inactive all day.

Den was counting her reps on the incline fly, an angled bench on which she sat holding a dumbbell stretched out at each side of her, just below shoulder height, then brought her arms up in a slow, controlled movement until her two weights touched in front of her chest. It would never give her boobs like the Essex girls, but it should give the ones she did have a fighting chance against gravity. She was doing three sets, reducing the reps from fifteen, to ten, to eight, while increasing the weight from five kilos, to eight, to ten. Den was alternating with her, doing his sets in her rest periods, using much heavier weights. Working out like this was the one thing she'd miss about this whole experience.

'All right, mate.' She didn't think anything of Den's words, given that he greeted everyone like that. It was only when a large shadow crossed her, then the body of Zac Parker came into her eyeline, that she paid attention.

He was in front of her now, and she realised that Den had disappeared from behind her, off to answer a plea from a woman on the treadmill for help in setting a program.

'Lift your arms a little when they're fully extended

and don't let them fall back just as far. You'll maintain the tension better if you don't let the muscle relax.'

Talli knew that. She did. She just wasn't paying attention enough to execute the movement properly. Instead, she got flustered, dropped a ten-kilo weight, and watched as he jumped out of the way, escaping injury by the approximate width of one little toe.

'Oh shit, I'm so sorry. SO sorry,' she stammered, delivering an apology but not the one she intended.

'It's OK, no harm done,' he told her, the closest they'd come to a conversation since that night in the restaurant. On the surface, he looked as great as always, but when she paid a little more attention, she could see that he looked tired. He had shadows under his eyes and he hadn't shaved today. The result was a rugged, handsome look, but somehow she didn't think the new image was intentional.

OK, apologise. Raise the issue. Get it over with.

'Listen, I just wanted to say sorry—'

'Shit, not you too,' he blurted, taking her by surprise. He might not have come close to dropping a ten-kilogram weight on her foot, but the shock was enough to stun her into silence.

'You're about the hundredth person that's doled out the sympathy today. Look, I can handle it, OK? I don't need the sympathy vote.'

It was either the adrenalin caused by the weights or some kind of out-of-body experience, but the apology Talli had been working up to came out as, 'Do you know what? You're a totally obnoxious twat. You really are. And did I mention arrogant? Oh yes, throw in arrogant as well, and perhaps a side order of oh-so-fucking-vain.

'I was about to apologise to you for the way I've treated you the last couple of weeks. I've been unspeakably rude. I didn't even thank you for helping with my dad that night, and that was unfair.' Her voice was raised now, courtesy of the emotions 'furious' and 'uncharacteristically explosive'. And even though a rational part of her brain was telling her to stop speaking, the other synapses were on a roll and refusing to take direction.

She'd had enough.

Enough!

Enough of every bloody person walking over her and living in their own precious world, not giving any thought to the people around them.

Apparently Zac was feeling just as frustrated, because he wasn't handling this with his customary coolness either.

'Look, it's fine. So you're "unspeakably rude". I don't expect anything else from you. Since the moment you came here, you've acted like you were too good for us all, so let's just say you being a moody cow for the last fortnight isn't exactly a newsflash.'

She reeled back like she'd been slapped.

'I'm not rude. I'm not. I've just been . . . under pressure and a bit overwhelmed.'

'Why? Did your servants not leave out the right knickers in the mornings?'

'Oh. My. God. You really are unforgivably obnoxious. And judgemental. You know nothing about me or my life.'

'Likewise. Although I do know that I helped you that night and you've treated me like a leper ever since. Never heard of manners?'

Talli snapped.

'I thought you'd slept with my sister!' she bellowed, so loudly that everyone around them stopped what they were doing to stare, until embarrassment caught up with them and they went about their business again, while trying really hard to listen to what came next.

There was a bit of a wait.

Zac stared at her for what seemed like an eternity, his blazing eyes locked with hers. Finally, he spoke.

'I didn't sleep with your sister,' he told her, his voice low and surprisingly calm. 'But why would you care if I did?'

Chapter Sixteen

'I . . . I don't care,' Talli stammered.

'Good. Then I guess we're back to where we started.'

Zac picked his towel up from where it had fallen when he'd jumped out of the way of her attempt to mangle his toes with a ten-kilo dumbbell, and headed off to the locker room, furious with himself for getting involved. Shit, she was some piece of work. Slept with her sister? He'd practically had to call in a SWAT team to fight her sister off.

Why were women such fucking hard work?

This one barely even knew him and she was giving him grief. He'd only gone over because Den was there. And, yeah, so what if maybe he'd felt like saying hello to her too? There was something about her that intrigued him a bit, and not just the fact that she had been looking amazing in a pair of bloke's running shorts and a white vest. It was just something about the way she didn't go for the dramatics, never tried to be the centre of attention.

Well, she'd blown that bloody theory tonight, hadn't she? It was the last thing he needed. Wasn't there enough shit going on?

After two hours of boxing training with some of the blokes that worked the door at the Beach Box, his workout gear was soaked with sweat and resisted as he tried to pull it off, before stepping into the shower.

The blokes had been sound, even when he'd asked them what actually happened on Saturday night. Seemed the reports hadn't been far off the mark. Kiki had basically snogged that DJ guy inside, fallen out of the club with him, then enjoyed a blaze of flash bulbs before getting into his Ferrari and heading off around three a.m. Zac had been in bed when she arrived home so he had no idea what time it was when she slipped in beside him.

She was already up and away when he woke up yesterday, then texted him to say she was staying at her parents' house last night. Now he wondered if she already knew what was hitting the papers this morning. Good of her to give him a heads-up.

There was a definite knot in his stomach as he towelled off. This was all such bullshit. If he was entirely honest with himself, he really didn't think Kiki had slept with the DJ bloke. It was far more likely that she was motivated by the desire for publicity than the need to be unfaithful. That was the persona she'd developed for the show – the wild child, crazy girl – and he'd gone along with it. Big mistake, he realised now. It was one thing flirting with Toby, or spreading rumours of flings with other celebs (which were, of course, never confirmed or denied), but snogging someone else went too far. And that was before he even started to pile on his annoyance about how she'd acted at Auntie Dot's party.

He threw on a clean T-shirt and a pair of grey jersey shorts, and headed out to the car, not even looking to see if Posh Bird was still hanging around. Definite exclusion zone required there, he decided.

As the car pulled out of the car park, he went on to automatic, his mind back on the Kiki situation. It wasn't working. The stuff she'd said to him at the party was true. He'd been telling himself it was just one of those phases couples went through and that it was all caused by the weird, fucked-up set of circumstances they were in. The TV show had changed all their lives and there were bound to be mistakes as they tried to deal with it all.

But this was more than that.

He loved Kiki. He just didn't like her much any more.

The muscles across his torso tightened with that thought.

Was this it? Over? Done? Sure, she'd blurted out some pretty harsh stuff the other night, but had she already made the decision? Or was it going to be down to him? The one thing he was sure of was that if he wasn't going to be around her any more, he had to know for sure that someone else was looking out for her. He wasn't a violent bloke, but the thought of anyone scaring her or hurting her made him want to kill them.

He exhaled wearily as he pulled into the parking space outside his block of flats, grabbed his kit bag and headed upstairs. They needed to sit down and talk about this. They were both adults. It didn't matter which one of them actually made the decision – the important thing was that they both walked away from the last two years regretting nothing.

As he opened the door of his flat, two things struck him. The first was the sound of the Wanted coming from the docking station in the open-plan lounge. Auntie Dot hadn't let herself in to check on his cleaning standards, then. Dot preferred a bit of Bon Jovi or Oasis.

The second was the smell of food. Chinese. Or maybe Thai.

Dropping his bag as he closed the door behind him, he turned to the right. As soon as the kitchen came into view, all else was forgotten except the view in front of him. It was safe to say Kiki hadn't decided to call it a day, given that she was sitting on the black granite worktop of the island that separated the kitchen and lounge area wearing nothing but a pair of eight-inch Louboutin mules.

'Hey,' she purred, opening her legs just a little and leaning forward so that her incredible tits were squeezed between her forearms, making them look even more amazing.

It was the oldest trick in the book, he realised. Using sex as a tool to manipulate him. Unfortunately, no one had informed his cock of the intricacies of psychological warfare, because he was crossing the room and it was leading the way.

'Kiki, we have to talk.'

Her only response was to open her legs wider, then bring both hands up to massage her breasts, her eyes never leaving his. She leant down, took one of her nipples in her mouth and started to suck.

Game over.

He was principled, but he was also human.

In less than ten seconds he was naked, between her legs, his hands underneath her gorgeous arse, pulling himself even further in. Moaning, she lay back on the counter, her arms now stretched out, holding on to the edges. He moved his hands round to each side of her hips, holding her tightly as he fucked her, every thrust emitting a low moan of 'Yes. Oh fuck yes, that's it, babes. Oh yes.'

When he could sense that she was feeling the first stirrings of an orgasm, he pulled out, making her yelp with surprise. She raised her body, but he gently pushed her back down, grabbed an open bottle of champagne from the nearby counter and slowly poured it over her torso, letting it flow between her legs and into her pussy.

Down he went, licking every drop of moisture off her with long, languorous strokes of his tongue, paying extra attention to the droplets that flavoured her clitoris with the sweet taste of Cristal. Only when it was all gone and she was crying for him to enter her again did he hook his arms under her legs, raising them so that her ankles were over his shoulders, giving him even more depth as his pelvis pounded against her, his cock going deeper with every thrust. Her body still flat against the worktop, he watched as her tits bounced up and down. Her smile widened, her eyes on his. He pulled out again, unwilling to come yet, not ready for this to be over. 'Stand up,' he whispered, holding her hand as she climbed on to her heels, standing, hands on hips, on the worktop now, the top of her head only inches from the chrome light fitting. He climbed on and twisted around, letting her place one foot either side of his torso, then she lowered herself down on to his throbbing, engorged dick and began to ride him, his hands on her hips now, supporting her every move.

Throwing her head back so that her hair trailed down to her butt cheeks, she grabbed her tits again and squeezed as she rose and fell, sweat glistening through the glitter gel that covered her body.

Zac always held off until she came first, but he suddenly realised that tonight it wasn't happening. He could feel his dick swelling with the need to explode and he let it go, making her cry out with the force of his climax. As soon as he was done, she lifted herself off him, rose on to her knees and began to rub her pussy, lasting only moments before her back arched and her whole body shuddered as an orgasm ripped through it.

Done, spent, she lowered her face and kissed him on the lips, making speech impossible. There was so much he wanted to say, things that were going to have to be discussed.

But right now, as he felt his muscles sag with weariness, and his eyelids sting with fatigue, he decided that all he wanted to do was sleep.

Chapter Seventeen

3 December 2012

'So how . . . wedding . . . going?'

The image on the screen kept flickering and the sound was intermittent but Talli didn't care – she couldn't be happier to see Fliss, even if it was over Skype and the signal would have been better if they were using tin cans and string.

'Don't ask. Edwina is the bridal equivalent of Ebola – rapidly changing and potentially deadly.'

Fliss laughed. Then didn't. Then laughed. Then gone again. After a few seconds she was back.

'Tell me about the school. I want to hear everything you're doing there.'

Fliss launched into a ten-minute description of the village she was living in and the conditions there, deprivation set against an incredible spirit of community. She was one of two volunteers, the other one a Dutch medic who was establishing childcare and immunisation programmes.

'I'm so proud of you, Fliss, I really am,' Talli told her, thinking not for the first time how brilliant her best friend was for doing this.

Her world shared, Fliss demanded news about the rest of their friends, laughing until she cried when Talli told her the story about Cosima Carlton and the birthday party from hell.

'And what about Dom? How's he doing?'

'Great, yeah. He's just signed a new singer called Luna Ma Dame. Says she's going to be huge, so he's really tied up with that.'

Fliss rolled her eyes. She'd never really bought into Dom's job, calling it an excuse to hang out in bars, get pissed and claim it all on expenses.

'I hear they're all going to Courchevel. Dom going too?'

'Yeah, but it's fine. Really, I told him to go. It's not fair that he doesn't get a break just because I'm working. I honestly don't mind.' Talli realised she was trying to convince herself as much as Fliss. Truth was, she did mind a little. It would have been great if he could have held off and they could have grabbed even a week in the sun after the wedding was over. No, that was just being selfish. Why shouldn't he go and have a great time?

'And what about the crowd you're with now? I can't believe you know the girls from *Lovin' Essex* – I used to love that show.'

'They're all really nice,' Talli told her. 'Or at least, the twins are lovely. Porsche is a total publicity junkie.'

'I knew it!' Fliss blurted.

'And Kiki is a bit . . . well . . . fake.'

'No way! She comes across as so sweet.'

Talli decided not to linger there.

'And Shiraz is fairly terrifying. I wouldn't like to fight her over the last pair of shoes in the sale. Not that she'd shop in the sales. Den says you can't throw a stone around here and not hit something her father owns.'

'Ooh, get you with the "Den says". Do I detect that mingling with the stars has left you with a crush?'

'Nooooo. Den is lovely, but he's in his forties. A sweetheart, though – I think he's my favourite of them all.'

'What about the rest of the guys? That Toby is . . .'

'Gay.'

Talli watched as Fliss bumped her screen. 'Bloody thing. For a minute there I thought you said he was gay.'

'He is.'

'Noooooo.'

Talli giggled at the absurdity of it all. 'Darling, do you realise you are thousands of miles away, living in a desperately poor country, risking your life amongst disease and famine, and you're wailing because a reality TV star is off the market?'

Fliss's head became just a mass of hair as she flopped it down, 'You're right. I'm a disgrace.'

Her beaming smile filled the screen again.

'No other talent? Nothing catch your eye?'

'No, of course not!' Talli retorted, feigning outrage.

The screen froze. Then Talli noticed that Fliss's left eyebrow had risen to a quizzical position.

'Talli?'

'OK, OK. So there's one guy . . .'

'God, you'd be rubbish under interrogation. Rule out a career as a spy, darling.'

Talli ignored her. '. . . called Zac. Looks great but he's so not my type. Overconfident, rough . . .'

'You like him.'

'I don't.'

'Yeah, right, darling. Talli, you never dislike anyone, so either this guy is some kind of evil serial killer or you have a thing for him. I'll bet my watercan you'll have hooked up with him by Christmas. In fact, I insist on it. Unless he's a serial killer, obviously.'

'Fliss, I love you. But your water can is safe. I promise you,' Talli replied, incredulous at Fliss's suggestion. There was no chance. Even putting to one side the fact that she loved Dom, she'd never been unfaithful in her life. On top of that, both she and Zac had made their feelings about each other perfectly clear.

Fliss looked off to the side and then said something to someone off camera in a language Talli didn't understand. 'I have to go, darling. That's our guide to say the Jeep is ready to head back to the village. I'll try to Skype again next month. Love you.'

'Love you too!' Talli blew kisses into the screen, then sat back, feeling a strange combination of happiness and sadness. She missed Fliss so much. If her friend was here now, she'd have thrown herself into helping with the wedding plans and she'd be loving all the intrigue surrounding the cast. Talli checked her watch. Five p.m. She could head over to the gym for a training session, but it was the busiest time, with all the after-work office staff arriving for a workout. After another day at Highdrow today going over arrangements with Trevor, she didn't have any more meetings until Wednesday, so she toyed with the idea of heading home and spending tomorrow chilling out at Chelsea Square. Again, though, the trains and cabs would be mobbed with commuters.

She paused, realising that she was chewing one of her nails. That, combined with thoughts of Fliss's enthusiasm for the whole *Lovin' Essex* world, gave her an idea. She'd been so wrapped up in organising this wedding that, other than her workouts with Den, she hadn't really spent any time getting to know anyone.

Over the last few weeks she'd occasionally chatted to the girls in the cast, and they'd invited her down to the salon, but she'd never had the opportunity or, if she was honest, the inclination to go. High maintenance wasn't her thing. She didn't even wear nail polish unless it was a special occasion, her tan came from running outside in the summer, and she was strictly a razor girl – waxing was entirely too much fuss. Now she had a night to spare and getting maybe a manicure and some chat seemed like a great way to spend it.

She grabbed her short leather jacket, Gucci, a hand-me-down from Dessi, threw it on over her long-sleeved boat-neck white top, and tucked her phone into the back pocket of her skinny jeans. After pulling on her trusty black leather biker boots and grabbing her Mulberry, she was on her way. The fact that it wasn't raining made her decide to walk, so twenty minutes later, when she pushed open the door of Spa Shiraz, her face was flushed from exertion and cold, and her hair looked like an explosion in a streamer factory.

'Hey! Come on in, babes.' Lena jumped up from the white leather pedicure bench, foam pads keeping her deep navy toenails apart, and greeted Talli with a hug. It was hard to believe that this warm, friendly girl was the sister of that oaf.

'Hi! I'm just . . . just . . . well, I thought I'd maybe get something done.'

Over in the corner, Shiraz stopped mid pluck on Minx's left eyebrow, stood up and applauded. Lena laughed. 'I knew we'd get you over to the glam side sooner or later. What do you think, Fran?' she asked the girl sitting on a stool who had, until a few minutes before, been applying coats of paint to Lena's toes.

Fran looked Talli up and down and whistled. 'It might take a bit of work, but we can do miracles here,' she joked, immediately dissipating Talli's apprehension with a chorus of laughter.

'I'm always up for a miracle,' Talli agreed, plumping herself down on the second pedicure bench next to

Lena. 'But let's start with a small wonder and work up to it. How about nails today?'

'That we can do,' Fran assured her, tucking Lena's foot into a white plastic contraption and pressing a button that switched on a purple light.

An hour later, Talli had ten deep red nails, each one with a tiny diamanté in the right corner of the tip, and had been assaulted with a full run-down on all the latest news and gossip.

Shiraz had received confirmation that the police weren't going to press charges regarding the whole naked-bike-ride-through-Lakeside fiasco, so Porsche was now considering naked trapeze at the Beach Box. Naturally.

Oh, and Porsche and Ramone had had a blowout, and she was responding by designing a new trademark vajazzle to replace his initials, dotted across her privates in a mix of emeralds and rubies.

Den had a new girlfriend, a retired stripper/body-builder called Bonny, whom the other girls – except Shiraz – seemed to like.

Lena and Max were still an item, and it had finally been revealed on the show that he'd split from his wife a month ago. Edwina had made it the big storyline for this month because Lena had been getting a backlash in the press and was desperate to let the nation know that Max and Coco, his glamour model wife, had split before they started seeing each other. Coco dealt with it by selling a story to the *Mirror* – 'My Marriage

Breakdown Hell' – and was soothing her heartbreak by shacking up with an Arsenal player in his Southwark penthouse. *Playboy* had offered her a hundred grand for a full-frontal photo shoot.

'I'd have done it for fifty,' Porsche announced curtly.

'Babe, you'd have done it for a front page and a vodka Red Bull,' Shiraz replied.

Fran applied a tiny dot of oil to the skin surrounding each of Talli's nails, then massaged her fingers one by one, while Shiraz sharpened her claws.

'Yeah, but at least you're upfront, Porsche. More than I can say for a certain lying tart who is, like, proper devious, yeah.'

'Oh here we go,' Lena warned, the corners of her mouth edging up. Talli couldn't help thinking that although all the girls were stunning, there was something about Minx and Lena that set them apart, other than the pink tutu Lena wore with endless bare brown legs. In December.

There was definitely a resemblance between the twins and Zac. The same green eyes, the same cheekbones, the same straight, perfect nose.

Over in the corner, Shiraz was working up a head of designer steam. 'Well, I'm just saying what we all think. Can't believe your Zac puts up with it.'

'Shiraz . . .' Lena said, the warning in her voice utterly explicit.

'Just sayin' . . .' Shiraz started.

'Well don't.' Lena cut her off.

Talli was so engrossed in the exchange that she didn't notice that her buttock was vibrating until the third or fourth ring. Snapping back to the present, she fished her phone out of her pocket.

'Hello? Oh hello, darling. No, I'm not there. I'm over at the salon having my nails done. I'm . . . oh.'

She stopped speaking, clearly cut off by the voice on the other end.

'No, of course I don't mind. Absolutely. Of course. I'll be so tied up anyway. Darling, I understand, I promise. You go. Don't work too hard. Bye, sweetie. Love you.'

She snapped the phone closed, then noticed that the salon was in complete silence and all eyes were on her.

'My . . . erm, boyfriend,' she said. More silence. Apparently short explanations were not sufficient within these walls

'Erm, Domenic.'

Still silence. Clearly not enough yet. She decided to go for full disclosure.

'He works for a record company and he's just signed a new act, and now he's decided to take the singer to Norway for two weeks to work with some producers over there, so he was just letting me know.'

'Female?' Shiraz demanded.

'Who?'

'The singer!' Lena clarified. 'Is it a female?'

Talli nodded. 'Yes, a girl called Luna Ma Dame. Apparently she's the next Amy Winehouse.'

'I know her,' Porsche added. 'She's from around here.

Went out with one of my brother's mates when he was a promoter for a few clubs in the city. She looks like Kim Kardashian but without the arse.'

There was a collective intake of breaths, all eyes still on Talli.

'What? What's the problem?'

Lena again. 'Look, I don't want to be, like, a downer or anything, but you're going to let your boyfriend go away with a gorgeous, fit young sort who knows that he can make her career and turn her into a star, and that doesn't worry you?'

'No, of course not. Domenic would never do anything for me to worry about. I trust him.'

At that very moment, Edwina marched in. 'Great timing,' Talli told her. Edwina had known Domenic for five years; she'd back her up on the matter of his character. 'I'm just assuring the girls that even though Domenic is going away for a fortnight with a female singer, he's not going to turn into some mad shagger. Is he, Ed?'

Edwina looked at her like she was deranged. 'You keep telling yourself that, darling. He's male. No telling what they'll do unless you have a camera implanted on their cock.'

Talli's face burned when she noticed that Kiki and Zac had followed Edwina in the door and heard every word. She suddenly found herself unable to tear her eyes away from her newly painted toes.

'Right, my little fucking darlings, here's a newsflash,'

Edwina announced. 'I know we weren't supposed to be shooting tonight, but there's been a change of plan. Lena, Coco has been dumped by that football guy and she's about to make a play to get Max back.'

Everyone saw the panic on Lena's face.

'Don't worry, he won't go for it. But Coco has agreed to take part in two episodes for a ridiculously cheap fucking fee so that she can milk the weeklies for a dozen exclusives. At the same time, that plank of a DJ that Kiki hooked up with has agreed to let Toby punch him in the face on condition that we arrange for him to get a set of veneers and some Botox and he gets to air his latest dance track on the show. It sounds like a car crash between a bin lorry and a klaxon, so we'll have to edit the fucking thing out later. So there it is, folks. We're shooting it over tonight and tomorrow, so there will be long hours but extra cash because we'll need all of you in the group scenes. That OK with everyone?'

Edwina didn't stop to check, given that she'd used the dual incentives of airtime and cash.

'Great. And Talli, what are you up to tonight?'

Her inability to come up with a quick lie had always been one of Talli's most disturbing failings.

'I'm . . . I'm . . . I'm . . .'

'Listen, darling, huge favour. I've been thinking. For the wedding, I want the rock that Simmy and I sat on when we had our first kiss.'

'A rock,' Talli repeated for clarification.

'Yah, you know the one – it's in your garden at Beeches.

173

I thought I could sit on it when Simmy takes my garter off. Amazing symbolism, no?'

Talli fought for the right words and could only come up with an echo of 'no', so instead she went for further clarification.

'You want me to go to Brighton and bring back the rock from our garden?'

'If I send anyone else, they're bound to get it bloody wrong. Do you mind, sweetie? I promise I'll make it up to you. In fact, look – go tonight, you can take the Merc. I'll be working anyway so I won't need it.'

'Edwina, number one, I'm not driving that Merc. It's huge. I'll cause a ten-car pile-up on the M25. And number two – how am I supposed to lift a ruddy great rock? The gardener won't be there, and even if he was, he's eighty-six – it could kill him.'

There was no denying the validity of her points. There was no escaping the pause that followed. And there was no stopping the feeling of dread that seeped through every iota of Talli's being when Edwina's head swivelled towards Zac.

'Right, Muscles, five hundred quid for your time, and you drive the car,' she bribed him.

Everyone had a price, but as Talli watched the horrified expression that crossed his face, she realised that wasn't his.

'No.'

'And I'll knock two pounds off your bonus target.'

Talli had no idea what that meant, but given the serious

thought he was apparently giving her offer, it might be enough to swing the deal.

'Done,' he eventually replied.

Chapter Eighteen

The five hundred quid had been sorely tempting, but it was the two pounds off the target that had sealed the deal. There was no bonus he wouldn't take if it got him closer to guaranteeing that the outstanding four grand would reach his bank account. Not that it would stay there for long.

How hard could this be? All he had to do was drive less than two hours to Brighton, collect a rock, drive back and not give in to homicidal thoughts regarding Posh Bird.

Talli's face had been a picture when Edwina had asked him to go. It would almost have been worth doing it for free just to wind her up.

Checking that he was still sitting at just under seventy, he chided himself for his childishness. What was it about that girl that made him act like this? It was like she walked into the room and a chip the size of a large baked potato instantly sprang up on his shoulder. Pathetic. Especially since he was pretty sure it was driven by his ego. Since he'd met her she'd ignored him, insulted him, misjudged him and accused him of things he hadn't done.

He found her confusing and deeply irritating.

Even Kiki didn't set off those kinds of feelings.

Kiki. They'd barely seen each other since the night in the kitchen, and when they did, it was like they were skirting round the issues, acting as though nothing was wrong, although they both knew that was not the case. She'd assured him that the whole thing with the DJ was just a snog for the cameras, a bit of provocative publicity, and he'd taken it at face value while coming to a decision. He was going to get Christmas out of the way, get the money problem sorted out, make sure she was OK and then call it a day. They were done, and he was pretty sure that she knew it too.

Beside him, Talli stretched as she woke up. She'd been sleeping since shortly after they left London. For the first half-hour or so he figured she was probably faking it, but that suited him fine so he didn't question it.

'Hey,' she said. 'Where are we?'

He'd programmed in the destination in the sat nav and it told him now that they had just under thirty minutes to go.

'Shouldn't be much longer. Maybe half an hour at the most.'

The pause that followed was long and uncomfortable,

but he didn't feel the need to break it. 'Thanks for doing this,' she said quietly. She had the poshest voice, like all those birds from that *Made in Chelsea* show. He'd watched it once at Kiki's insistence, to check out the chick who had beaten her in the *Heat* poll. He could see the appeal, but he'd been honest when he'd assured Kiki that she should have come first.

'It's OK. Wasn't doing anything tonight anyway. May as well earn a bit of cash.'

'What was that whole two-pound thing about?'

'Got a weight-loss target with Ed. It's now two pounds less.'

Another pause. Zac didn't bother filling the silence. What was the point?

'I saw you've introduced supersets into her workout. She's looking great. Her glutes are amazing. Is it weird that I noticed?'

He almost crashed the car.

'How come you know that? About supersets?'

'Sports degree. I'm obsessed with all that stuff. Always have been.'

Suddenly, other little things he'd noticed started to make sense. The rocking body. The workouts with Den. The fact that he'd passed her running to the gym some days.

Despite his vow not to engage her in conversation, he couldn't resist asking the obvious question. 'So why are you a wedding planner, then?'

'I'm not. I'm just doing this as a favour to help out my family. My mother is the event manager, but she's dealing with complications after surgery and can't do the wedding. I was at a loose end, so they asked me to help, even though I'm the worst organiser in the free world. To be honest, I'm freaking out in case I mess it up.'

It was the longest speech he'd ever heard her make, and it suddenly explained so much. 'Is that why you've always got a face like a wet weekend?' he asked, causing her to collapse with laughter.

'Have I?'

'Yep. I thought you were going to top yourself in Vera Wang.'

'Oh my God, that was a nightmare. I was so terrified she wouldn't find a dress she liked and I was just praying for some kind of divine intervention the whole time we were there. I'm not being dramatic and I know it's not really important in the whole life-and-death big scheme of things, but you've no idea how much pressure I feel to pull this off.'

He chose not to point out that actually he knew exactly how much pressure she was feeling.

In one swift, graceful movement she dived over the back of her seat, and returned clutching a Yorkie and a bottle of full-fat Coke.

'You're health-obsessed yet that's your idea of sustenance?' he asked, incredulous.

'I know. It's a flaw in my genetic make-up. Drives my boyfriend nuts.'

'Ah, the skinny guy,' Zac said with amusement.

'He's not skinny. OK, I suppose he is,' she contradicted herself immediately.

More silence. Shit, he shouldn't have said that. That tentative truce had been coming along nicely and then he had to go and slag off her boyfriend.

'Look, I'm sorry. That was rude.'

'You're always rude,' she said, quite matter-of-fact.

He was about to bite back when he suddenly realised that she probably had a point. He'd just twigged that there was an obvious cycle here. She was stressed out about this job so she was withdrawn. He thought she was being a bitch so he got defensive and treated her with disdain. She then thought he was rude and became even more withdrawn. And so it went on.

'Hang on, I know exactly where we are now,' she yelped. 'Turn right here.' He followed the instruction, turning into a long lane. Although it was pitch black outside, the smell of the sea air told him they were at the coast. They bumped along the road, trying as much as possible to avoid the potholes and banking at the sides.

'Sorry, we should have fixed this road years ago, but Daddy swears it's a deterrent for boy racers in speeding Corsas using it as a short cut to the beach.'

'He's probably got a point.' On his right-hand side the beech hedge suddenly stopped, replaced by huge iron gates, with a long red ash driveway leading to a picture-perfect white cottage.

'That's Slates,' Talli said. 'Edwina's family's beach house.'

He had to bite his lip to stop the 'You have to be fucking joking!' that the occasion deserved. He'd been expecting a beach hut. Maybe even a cabin. He hadn't for a single moment been anticipating a house that looked like it was straight out of a fairy tale, complete with thatched roof and shutters on the dozen or so windows.

'And this is Beeches,' Talli added, as they pulled up outside the house next door to Hansel and Gretel's.

This one was gorgeous too, Zac decided, even more so because it wasn't so perfect, so had more character than its neighbour. There were no huge gates here, just a waist-height wooden fence, with a winding flagstone path behind it. The front door was painted red, and the gardens were more unruly than the manicured grounds next door.

'This is the summer house? One that just lies empty all year round unless you're on holiday here?'

'I know, it's a complete waste,' Talli agreed. 'But it belonged to my grandparents, so I don't think Mummy and Daddy will ever sell it. It's like part of the family.'

If ever there was a reminder as to how different their worlds were, this was it. Who had a house like this that just lay uninhabited for fifty weeks of the year?

If he owned it, he'd want to come home here every single night.

He pulled the car over so that it was snug against the fence, leaving just enough room for Talli to climb out.

'Edwina's rock is round at the back,' Talli told him, stepping out into the dim sheen of the moon and leading the way. When they got to within about twenty feet of the front of the house, the security light came on, guiding them to a path that took them along the side wall. The white pebble-dash render came to an end, and another light, this time at the back corner of the house, flashed on, illuminating a large square of lawn with a huge tree in the middle and, in the distance, a small fence separating the grass from the beach on the other side. There, in a gap in the middle of the wooden slats, was a long rock, about three feet wide by one foot deep and the same tall, perfect for sitting on and watching the waves roll back and forward. He'd never thought of himself as particularly romantic, but this was something special.

'OK, so I suppose we should roll it back around to the front.'

Talli's words barely registered. Zac was too busy watching the waves crash up on to the sands. 'Is it wrong that I just want to go dive in there?' he said, more thinking out loud than anything else.

'Yes, it's bloody freezing. The shock will probably kill you and I'm rubbish at CPR.'

That was the sensible answer. It was December, the

temperature was nudging the bottom of the thermometer and – as if God had decided to back up her opinion – he felt tiny droplets of rain on his face.

'Bugger, it's going to pour down,' Talli said urgently, pushing up the sleeves on her leather jacket. 'Let's get this done and get back on the road. If we shift, we should still make it back before the Beach Box closes. Are you impressed that I know that?' she joked.

He couldn't help smiling. She wasn't that bad now that she'd chilled out a bit. He positioned himself next to her at the other side of the rock. 'Right then, let's go. I think rolling it is probably the best bet.'

The two of them hunched down, pressed their palms against the damp stone and started to heave. It moved slowly, but their hands were slipping with the moisture. With his white Nike trainers sliding as they pushed against the wet grass, Zac could see they needed a change of plan.

'You know, I think we'd be better lifting it. One at each end. What do you reckon?'

Talli eyed the grey mass, her expression saying that she wasn't convinced.

'Look, it can't weigh any more than eighty pounds. You can dead-lift that without breaking sweat.'

The rain was getting heavier now, starting to soak through his T-shirt. A jacket might have been one of his better ideas.

'I don't know. I think we should stick to rolling it. You've no idea how clumsy I—'

'We'll be here all night,' he argued. 'Let's give it a try. You grab that end.'

After a moment's hesitation, Talli mimicked his actions by squatting down and slipping her hands underneath the jagged edge of the stone.

'OK, on three,' he told her. 'One. Two. Three.'

With simultaneous grunts, they both straightened at the knees, lifting the rock a clear three feet from the ground. The weight was bearable as they turned, and Zac could already see that if they manoeuvred it well, his plan would work. 'OK, sideways is probably best; that way neither of us is walking blind.'

Like a pincer crab homing in on its prey, they crossed the wet ground, both of them concentrating on gripping the surface while the rain, heavy now, battered against them.

'Zac, I think I'm going to drop . . .' There was a sudden jolt as the rock slipped a couple of inches at Talli's side.

'You're fine!' he told her. 'Let's just get to the front of the house and then we can—'

'It's too heavy.'

'We're doing great.'

'But I think . . .'

'You're OK. Just a few feet further and . . .'

She wasn't OK. The rock slipped clean between her hands, plummeting to the ground, forcing Zac to drop his side too.

It would have been one of those silly things they

might even laugh about later, if it wasn't for the fact that the rock's landing was broken by an unexpected obstacle.

'Fuck!' yelped Zac, his voice strangled with pain. 'I think I've broken my toe.'

Chapter Nineteen

For the second time in a month, Talli wanted to cry. However, in this situation, she didn't want to be accused of stealing Zac's thunder. Because also for the second time in a month, she'd dropped something in close proximity to his limbs, and this time she'd hit the bulls-eye.

They'd managed to push the rock off his foot – not such a windswept symbol of romance now – and he was leaning against the side wall, one knee bent, unable to put any weight on the damaged limb. If this was a cartoon, she was pretty sure the offending toe would be bright red and visibly throbbing.

To make matters worse, the rain had now become a proper storm and was absolutely drenching them. For someone who didn't react well to stressful situations, Talli nonetheless realised it was time for a new strategy.

'Come here, put your weight on me,' she ordered,

taking charge and pulling Zac's arm around her shoulder. The support allowed him to hop, wincing all the way, around to the front door. There, she stretched up and felt along the door lintel, eventually producing a small silver Yale key.

'You've got to be kidding. You leave the key above the door?'

'Getting in is only half the battle,' she told him. 'The alarm is connected to the local police station, so even if someone gets in, they have to know the code. Having said that, my dad sets it off at least once a year because he can never remember it.'

With a twist of the key, the door flew open, and Talli immediately punched some numbers into a beeping keypad to the left, then flicked on a light switch.

Everything was exactly how it was left last time she was here, which was exactly how it had been on every visit she could ever remember. The huge, slouchy brown leather sofas faced each other on either side of the stone fireplace, a low, dark oak coffee table between them. The flagstone floor was randomly covered with rugs in shades of deep coffee. Lamps were dotted around the room, on the oak side tables at both ends of the sofas and beside the two huge armchairs that sat in the corners to her left and right.

It was picture perfect, she'd always thought.

However, in no perfect picture was there a bedraggled woman standing in the doorway with a bloke holding his throbbing toe.

Shit. Bugger. Shit. How bad did she feel about this? She'd tried to warn him, but as usual he was too bloody stubborn to listen and . . .

''Scuse me, but any chance we can actually make our way over to that couch there?'

Shit. Bugger. Shit. She'd dropped the rock and now they were stuck in a scene from a bad movie that definitely didn't star Patrick Swayze.

They hobbled over to the sofa and Zac sank down with a murmur of pain. She supposed he was being pretty brave really – that must hurt like hell.

'I think I should drive you to the hospital. It's only about twenty minutes away and they'll be able to X-ray that,' she said, pointing to the toe that had just been liberated from a Nike trainer and sock.

'Yeah, that will work,' he answered. 'After you cripple me, I'm supposed to let you drive me in a vehicle weighing several tons, in the rain, so you can stand an excellent chance of actually finishing me off.'

Talli tried to clench her teeth. She really tried. It shouldn't be too hard. Her twenty-three years had been a whole lifetime of letting people offload on her and staying silent while taking flack, yet . . .

'There you go again with the bloody rudeness! What is it with you? I didn't mean to drop the bloody thing, I warned you it was a possibility, and yet when the bloody inevitable happens you act like it was a huge bloody surprise. Sometimes you're not the sharpest tool in the bloody box, are you? Now there are two choices,

Einstein – you either let me drive you to the hospital or we stay here tonight, see how your foot is in the morning and then take it from there. Your choice. I'm not making the decision in case it leads to further injury or death.'

Or more furious repetitions of the word 'bloody'. Her charity swear box would be overflowing this month.

His head went down and she immediately felt awful. What the hell came over her when she was around him? She'd launched into a tirade exactly twice in her life and both times he had been the target. And he was injured. Oh shit, she was abusing a man in pain – this was what she'd come to.

It was only when his shoulders started rocking that she realised he was actually laughing. Laughing! At her. Or this situation. It was hard to say and she didn't trust herself to ask in case she started hurling abuse at him again, so she just stood there, hands on hips, waiting for a response.

It seemed like a lifetime before the hilarity had stopped long enough for him to resume speech.

'We should probably stay here,' he said. 'As long as you promise not to stab me in my sleep.'

'I don't make promises I can't keep,' Talli muttered, hiding the fact that she was starting to see the funny side of this too.

Deciding that the only way to deal with this was to be practical, she went around the room turning on the lamps, then knelt in front of the fire, flipped a concealed lever and pressed a tiny button in the hearth. With one click the flames roared to life, looking for all intents and purposes like a real wood-burning fire. It had been her mother's one insistence. Apparently beach chic didn't extend to chopping logs and using kindling to get a real fire going.

She disappeared into the kitchen, coming back with two boxes of chocolates, a packet of frozen roast potatoes and a family pack of prawn cocktail crisps. 'This is all that's in the cupboards,' she told him, plonking the crisps and chocolates down on the coffee table, then throwing the potatoes in his direction. 'And there's no milk, so it's either black tea or coffee or . . .' Over at a huge sideboard on the far wall, Talli opened a door and checked the contents. 'Wine or Scotch. That's it.'

Back on the couch, Zac had lifted his leg and put some pillows underneath it to elevate it, then placed the packet of frozen roast potatoes on top to halt the swelling. It was exactly what she'd have told him to do. The thought unnerved her.

'Wine,' he replied. 'Any kind. Doesn't matter.'

'Great. We finally agree on something.' Marching back into the kitchen, she returned with two glasses and a corkscrew, then set them down on the table, uncorked the bottle and poured the deep red liquid into the glasses.

Some of it splashed as she pushed it towards him. The urge to cry had now been replaced by an urge to scream. Aside from the fact that they enjoyed the companionship of, say, North and South Korea, they were marooned in soaking wet clothes miles from bloody anywhere.

Wasn't this normally the time in a movie when the brooding hero noticed that the leading lady's wet clothing gave her fabulous tits and swept her off her feet for a frantic night of passion?

Not that she thought for a minute he found her attractive – not when his girlfriend was officially the second most beautiful reality star on TV – but she just wanted to make it clear that even if he had a glimmer of interest, this wasn't one of those 'any port in a storm' situations. She was not that kind of port.

'Be back in a minute,' she murmured, and disappeared up the wooden staircase to her right. She returned wearing an ancient tatty jumper that her father refused to part with even though threads dangled from the bottom and it smelled of fish. She tossed a pair of jogging trousers and a sweatshirt in Zac's direction. They belonged to Simmy, so they had the added bonus of being purchased in the last five years. And not smelling of fish.

'Nice jumper,' he said, gesturing with his already half-empty glass of wine.

'I'll be in the kitchen for the next five minutes if you want to get changed out of those clothes.'

In the cosy rustic kitchen, Talli searched the rest of the cupboards and the pantry, increasingly ravenous and aware that other than a Yorkie, she hadn't eaten since lunchtime. In the freezer she found a loaf of bread, which she popped into the microwave to defrost. In the back pantry there was a large jar of strawberry jam, next to an unopened jar of peanut butter. It was her idea of the perfect three-course meal. When the microwave pinged, she loaded up the breadboard and headed back into enemy territory, pausing as she glimpsed familiar markings on the door frame, inch-long scores with a running narrative next to each one. Simmy, aged ten. A little higher, Desdemona, aged thirteen. Further down, Tallulah, aged eight. A wave of nostalgia washed over her. She loved this place. More than the townhouse in Chelsea Square, more than their farmhouse in Provence, this was the place that felt most like home.

'Don't say a word,' warned Zac as she approached him from behind. Only when she was facing him did she understand. Despite the fact that he was semi lying down, the tracksuit bottoms were a good six inches too short and the T-shirt was hugely baggy and bore the slogan 'This isn't a fat gut, it's a storage centre for a beach ball'.

'I swear if you drop that board on my other foot I'm going to sue you.'

God, this was priceless. 'I'm not saying anything,' she promised. 'But you'd better sleep with one eye open, because I'm dying to take a picture and send it to Lena, with the request that she tweet it to the world. I reckon even your parents would disown you,' she giggled.

'Too late for that,' he quipped, then fell silent as he reached for a piece of jammy bread.

'Oh God. What have I said now?' Talli groaned.

'Nothing, it's fine,' he replied. 'It's not a big deal . . . the whole "no parents" thing.'

'Oh for the love of God,' Talli said wearily. 'Why, Zac? Why can't we ever have a normal conversation, without insults, misunderstandings or injury? I'm sorry. I didn't know.'

'Honestly, don't worry. Lena and Minx deliberately keep it out of the papers so no one really knows about our family situation. But it's fine,' he assured her between bites. 'And you'd know that if you'd ever met Dot.'

The thick layer of peanut butter on top of the dollop of jam already on her bread threatened to slide off as his words distracted her. 'Who's Dot?'

Two hours and a bottle of red later, she knew it all.

'Your Auntie Dot is going to want a serious word with me for damaging your toe.' Was it her imagination, or were her words slurring slightly? Reaching behind her, she plumped up the cushion under her head, careful to keep it out of reach of the fire.

'Nah,' he assured her. 'But buying a bulletproof vest on eBay might be a sound investment. So what about your lot then? Your dad's a pretty good guy. When he's not unconscious.'

Her glare might have been slightly lopsided, but it made the point.

'Bollocks, sorry. I meant that as a joke. Is this a good time to remind you that you broke my toe?'

'God, you're sinking pretty low,' she murmured, although the last part of the sentence was swallowed up as she pulled the jumper over her head. 'Sorry, but I can't stand the smell any more. The fire is making me reek like grilled haddock.' Thankfully the white vest underneath was now completely dry. And only a little fishy.

After uncorking another bottle, Talli gave him a run-down of her family and the whole debacle behind the wedding. It was surprisingly non-embarrassing considering it involved a mother with a Kate Middleton fixation.

When she'd finished, she realised that a momentous occasion had just taken place.

'Wow,' she said, holding out her glass in a toasting motion. 'We've just managed to have a whole conversation without offending each other. Maybe there's hope for world peace next.'

Chapter Twenty

Of all the ways he could possibly have anticipated this day ending, this wasn't one of them. Miles from home, suffering from a mobility-thwarting injury, wearing a slogan T-shirt, lying on a sofa in a beach house with Posh Bird.

Not that she was on the couch. She was definitely on the floor, sprawled out in front of the fire. It suddenly struck him that if there was a competition between Talli and that girl from *Made in Chelsea*, Posh Bird would be lying there with a tiara on her head.

And that was without make-up or any other help. Although those bright red nails were definitely sexy.

He'd never have believed they'd actually have anything to talk about, but he'd spent the last half-hour telling her about the gym he hoped to open and she totally got it, understood exactly where he was coming from. Why had he never realised before how much she knew about this stuff? Tonight just got more bizarre by the minute.

On the table, his phone beeped and he reached over for it, mentally preparing himself for the onslaught. He'd texted Kiki an hour ago to tell her he'd be away overnight, explain he had broken his toe and assure her that he'd be back in the morning. Her reply was straight to the point.

'Fucker.'

Sighing, he slumped back against the arm of the couch.

'I take it that didn't go down well then?' Talli asked.

He turned the screen and she stretched over to read it. 'Oops. I think flowers and chocolates might be required to fix this.'

'Only if they come from Versace,' Zac replied. 'Kiki has expensive tastes.'

'She'd love Dessi, then. We should introduce them. I'm sure Dessi won't feel the need to share the fact that she tried to have her wicked way with you in our kitchen.'

Zac choked on his wine as he laughed. 'That was well scary,' he confessed. 'I mean, she's gorgeous, your sister, but she's not backwards at coming forwards.'

'What does that mean?'

Zac noticed that when Talli frowned, she got little lines between her eyebrows. It was beyond cute.

'It means she's not afraid to go after what she wants. Shit, if she was here now, I'd be doomed,' he added, gesturing to his elevated foot.

'So why weren't you interested?'

He shrugged. 'She's gorgeous, but you know . . . Kiki.'

'The one who just called you a fucker?' Talli teased.

'Yeah. It's her way of showing her love.'

There was a comfortable silence as he pondered Kiki's text, thinking he should feel more – panic, dread, sympathy – than he actually did.

'Sorry?' He'd completely missed what Talli had said.

'I asked you if you've ever been unfaithful,' she said. 'Or is that too personal? Sorry, I think it's the wine.'

'No, it's not too personal, and no, I haven't. Don't see the point. If it's done, then it's better to move on, not mess around.'

'Me neither. God, we're boring. Dessi swears it's a flaw in my personality. But I've been with Dom so long, and it's always been great . . .'

'And now?'

'It's still . . . great. Although obviously we're five years down the line and it's not all champagne and roses – actually, there never were roses, they affect his sinuses – but we're still going. Although your sister and the rest of the girls are horrified that he's gone off to Norway for two weeks with a new singer. Apparently she's the next Amy Winehouse. Or so he tells me in every conversation.'

Another sip of wine slipped down Zac's throat, the anaesthetic effects of the alcohol and the ibuprofen Talli had found in the bathroom having long kicked in on his foot.

'Do you ever think you're too young to be settled already? Not worry that you're missing out on anything?'

She shrugged. 'Never really thought about it. I guess I've just been getting on with things. You know, like wrecking parties and insulting men I barely know. I find that keeps me fairly occupied these days.'

He watched as she stretched up on to her knees and reached over for one of the boxes of chocolates. Unwrapping the cellophane, she peered at the box.

'They're a month past their sell-by date, but I'll take my chances if you will.'

'So this is, like, some kind of chocolate suicide pact?'

'Absolutely. We could be struck down by a Turkish delight at any moment.'

The wine caught in his throat, making him instinctively buckle over as he began to choke. 'Oh fuck, I've done it again,' she wailed, jumping a little unsteadily to her feet and reaching over to repeatedly thump him on the back.

'Stop! Stop!' he begged after the tenth thump. 'My ribs can't take it. Shit, you're strong!'

Swatting her away, he inadvertently flicked her hand. 'Aaaaw,' she wailed.

'Sorry!' he blurted, then paused as he realised she was giggling, her injury a pretence.

'Hey!' This time he reached for her playfully and she leaned back, misjudged the distance from the table and landed with a loud thud in the middle of a box of out-of-date Milk Tray, a fact that sent both of them straight to Hilarity Central. His jaw ached as he laughed like he hadn't laughed for a long, long time. Kiki, the money, the pressure . . . all of it gone. Right now his life came down to the scene in front of him – Posh Bird sitting three feet away from him in the middle of a box of chocolates, tears of laughter streaming down her face.

Until she wasn't any more.

Until she was just staring at him and he was staring back and they were having a whole conversation while saying absolutely nothing at all. Soon the silence was too long to take any of it back.

'Please take them off,' he said, his voice husky after all the laughter.

'What?' she replied slowly, her gaze not leaving his.

'Your jeans. They're covered in chocolate.'

'Oh.' She snapped out of the trance she'd slid into. 'Right. I thought you meant . . .'

'I did.'

'Oh.'

This was a mistake. It really was. She'd probably whack him with a family packet of prawn cocktail crisps. Or smash her wine glass and then he'd stand on it. She'd leave. She'd definitely leave and he didn't blame her.

Only she wasn't leaving.

She stood up, the fire behind her giving the illusion of a beautiful silhouette. Then slowly, but with no hesitation, she flipped open the button on her jeans and gradually, very gradually, slid the zip down. She slipped her fingers into the waistband and pushed, bending as the denim fabric eased down her thighs. This time her balance was perfect as she slid out one foot, then the other, and tossed the jeans to one side.

'The fire!'

'Oh shit!' she squealed, grabbing them back and patting down a couple of burning embers on the hem of the left leg.

Then she was back, standing in front of him again, wearing a white vest and white cotton hipster boy shorts. Her hair fell in loose waves over her shoulders and her lips glistened with wine.

He'd never wanted to kiss anyone more.

'This is a mistake,' he murmured.

'I know,' she agreed, as she slid down to her knees, so that her face was only inches from his.

Chapter Twenty~one

It was a mistake. She knew that. And if she'd really thought about it, she could have come up with a dozen reasons to back up that theory, but right now she was choosing not to because right here, right now she wanted to kiss him more than she'd ever wanted to kiss anyone in her life.

'Talli, are you sure?'

'No,' she whispered as she lowered her mouth to his and tasted him, softly licking his lips before kissing him, her deep breaths coming out as low murmurs as his mouth opened and his hand reached up to touch the side of her face.

Neither of them spoke as she pulled back, stared at him, looking at his beautiful face, spellbound for a long, long time, then leant down to kiss him again.

He didn't need an excuse to pull off that T-shirt and toss it over the back of the couch.

This had to stop. It had to. Nothing too terrible had happened yet. They could just forget about it and no one ever needed to know. They could go back to ignoring each other tomorrow, no damage done.

They could do all that.

Yet instead she was tingling with anticipation as he traced a finger down one side of her face, then the other, before pushing her hair back and leaning over to kiss her forehead, her eyelids, her cheeks. His hands cupping her neck now, he kissed her chin, her nose then her mouth again, deeper and more urgently this time, yet still their bodies hadn't touched.

With only a small wince of pain, he swung his legs around into a sitting position and she knelt in front of him.

'I'm scared to touch you,' he whispered, every trace of that overconfident, arrogant twat long gone.

'It's OK,' she told him quietly, realising that she truly meant it. She took his hand from her face, her boldness surprising her, and slid it down to her breast. He left it there, just holding her, his other hand on her face, their eye contact still not broken.

'Take everything else off. I want to watch you.'

Talli bit her bottom lip as her natural shyness made her recoil just a little, before something else kicked in. Perhaps it was the wine, or perhaps it was just the look in his eyes, but she felt . . . safe.

Standing up again, she took a step backwards, still watching him. Slowly she crossed her arms over her body and pulled her vest over her head, rewarded with Zac's audible intake of breath. Just as slowly, relaxing now, she pulled down her knickers and stepped out of them.

'Hang on,' she told him, then flew into the bathroom and returned clutching a condom. 'I know where Dessi keeps her stash,' she told him, face flushed with embarrassment.

He watched as she took a deep breath. 'OK, now you,' she said, staring as he lifted his butt from the sofa and slid the trackies down, carefully lifting them over his swollen foot.

He reached for her and she stepped forward, then gasped as he kissed her thin strip of pubic hair. Oh. My. God.

'Lie down.' His voice was little more than a croak now. 'I need to touch you.'

She should be panicking now, seriously freaking out, and yet it felt so, so good.

Sliding down on to the thick rug, she watched as he pushed himself off the sofa and knelt by her side. For the first time she noticed his dick, huge and only a foot or two away from her face. She quickly closed her eyes, then fought the single twinge of embarrassment and opened them again, to see him smiling at her.

As she lay there with him kneeling at her side, only their breathing interrupting the silence, she felt the touch of his fingers on the hollow in the middle of her neck, slowly moving down across her chest and abdomen. Then they moved back up again, stroking each breast, running down the contour from her arm to her hip. For long, ecstatic minutes, he touched, stroked, massaged every part of her. Then his lips repeated the trail his fingers had already taken, stopping when he reached the top of her thighs.

Slowly, gently, he eased her legs apart to allow his tongue to slip inside her, a sensation she had never experienced. Dom didn't go down on her because he swore it set off his hay fever.

Yet now she was allowing this guy she barely knew to nudge her legs a little further apart and run his tongue along the inside of her thighs, then enter her, again and again.

Only when her breath started to come in short, sharp rasps did he stop, before slowly rolling her on to her front and doing the same thing all over again, to her back, her legs, her shoulder blades. Then his tongue was running across her buttocks and her legs were wide again, allowing his tongue back inside her, the long, slow strokes the most indulgent sense of pleasure she'd ever known.

Talli turned her face to one side, watching the dancing flames of the fire as he licked every nerve ending. This wasn't how she'd thought it would be. She'd always thought of illicit sex as being frantic and fast and sordid, and yet this was . . . hypnotic.

His mouth was at her ear now, his breath heavy on her cheek. 'Are you OK?' he asked, raising up to allow her to roll on to her back, then lowering himself back down so that every bit of their bodies touched, his cock hard against her stomach.

'I know we shouldn't be doing this, but . . .' She shrugged, not needing to finish the sentence. Zac did it for her.

'I need you,' he said softly.

And then it happened. The frantic bit, the biting, the grappling, the insistent press of their mouths against each other, the heat as their sweat merged and the flexibility of two athletes with the kind of stamina that takes serious training. She dug her nails into his shoulders, buried her fingers in his dark blond hair, pressed the palm of her hand against his perfect chin. She couldn't think or plan or stop – every position she'd ever wondered about, every sensation she'd ever read about, now she was indulging in it all. He bent her forwards over the sofa and took her from behind, his chest against her back, his hands around her, holding on to her breasts. A few moments later, she was in charge, sitting on top of him, her hands behind her, clutching on to his knees as she slowly, tantalisingly raised and lowered herself on to him. They made love on the sofa, on the coffee table, against the door, on the sideboard and finally, back on the floor, in front of the fire where, exhausted, they came together and then lay side by side, silent again, Zac turned towards her, stroking her even then.

'You're crying,' he said, his alarm written all over his face. 'Are you sorry?'

Talli realised that now all the incredible physical feelings were gone, she wasn't sure what to call the emotions that were replacing them. Two tears slid slowly down her face.

'It was a mistake,' she answered honestly. 'But I'm not sorry. That was amazing.'

His eyes glistened and crinkled as he smiled. 'It was.'

Her attention was taken by the sight of something white on the edges of the fire, almost entirely consumed by the flames.

'Oh bugger, that's my knickers,' she blurted, her laughter pushing away the tears.

The irony didn't escape her. Talli Caston-Jones had the feeling that she'd just burnt her knickers in more ways than one.

Chapter Twenty~two

Fucker.

Kiki's text came back to him as he opened his eyes, and he knew he didn't have many grounds for argument.

How the hell had that happened? How? How?

The word kept swirling in his head as he pushed his eyes open properly and realised that Talli wasn't in the room.

They had slept in her bedroom, a cream-walled room with a picture of the athlete Michael Johnson on the wall above her bed.

Again, how?

And Jesus, how sore was his foot? He stuck it out from under the pale blue duvet cover and saw that the navy hue of his foot coordinated with the bedding. It wasn't broken, he decided, as he had full movement, even if the pain was excruciating.

However, it wasn't his toe that was concerning him now.

Last night. And again, how?

They'd lain downstairs for another hour or so, drunk another couple of glasses of wine, then he'd carried her upstairs – hobbling – her arms wrapped around his neck and her legs crossed around his waist. They'd made love again in the bath, and again in her bed, before falling asleep what was probably only a few hours ago.

He rolled on to his side and took in the most incredible view. The branches on the tree at the bottom of the garden swayed in the wind, under a sky that was light grey and peppered with clouds. The tide was out, but still he could see the waves rushing to the shore. This was about as far away from Chelmsford as it was possible to get.

Chelmsford. Kiki. Fucker.

Talli.

How?

In the distance, a shape came into the far right of his peripheral vision, a black shadow moving across the sands. Talli. Jogging in black Lycra running pants and a grey sweatshirt, her hair partially covered by a beanie hat pulled down close to her eyes.

He was as fit as it probably got, but he doubted he could catch her even without a mangled toe.

As he pushed up from the pillow he spotted his clothes, folded over the arm of a cream cord winged chair by the door. They'd been dried and perhaps even ironed.

The irony wasn't lost on him. Kiki wouldn't iron his clothes unless it was going to get her a double-page feature in *OK!* magazine.

Flashbacks kept ambushing his thoughts. Talli in front of the fire. Talli on the stairs. In the bath. His morning erection was alive and well as he stood up and stretched, watching her again as she switched direction and turned towards the house. After limping to the bathroom, he'd just made it back to the bedroom when she came in behind him. He turned to face her and watched her flinch as she got a full-frontal flash.

He grabbed his jeans and quickly pulled them on with a hasty 'Sorry.'

'Don't worry. I think it might be a little late for modesty. How's your foot?'

'Sore. I don't think it's broken, though. I took another couple of painkillers, so they should kick in soon and we can take off. I'm just glad Edwina's car is an automatic.'

The relief on her face was palpable. It was no big surprise that she was hating herself this morning. From what she'd said last night, this was way outside her normal behaviour. And his.

'Do you want to . . .'

'No,' she blurted. 'I don't want to talk about it. But I suppose we should. It was a mistake.' Her eyes were bloodshot – he wasn't sure if it was from running or from tears that were waiting to spill again.

'I think you already told me that. Look, Talli, I'm not

that guy. I'm really not. I don't shag around, I don't do one-night stands and I don't screw people over. It's not me. I can't explain last night.'

Plumping down on the bed, she pulled up her bare feet so she was sitting cross-legged.

'And I'm not the girl who does the secret affairs and the sneaking around. I'm happy with Domenic, Zac. You're with Kiki. Last night is all it's ever going to be.'

There was no doubt she was absolutely right. What was it he always told himself about staying away from distractions? Even before last night he'd had way too much going on to deal with anything else, let alone this.

Lowering himself on to the bed next to her, he gave in to an irresistible urge to touch her, to run his thumb across her cheek, before a sudden urge to laugh took control. 'This is crazy, Posh Bird.'

'What did you call me?'

'Posh Bird. That's what I always call you. Just not to your face.'

'Bugger, I wish I'd known. I'd have dropped something on your other foot. I'm not really posh.'

'You weren't last night.'

'Don't! Oh lord, I'm mortified. I know this will totally play to your overblown ego, but last night was pretty good.'

'You mean in-fucking-credible?'

'I do.' The tension was now well and truly gone.

'So what happens now? Think we can go back to the way we were before?'

Talli shook her head. 'I hope so. I enjoyed passing the time thinking up ways to hire a hitman.'

Her grin kicked off an instinctive need to touch her again.

'Regret it?'

'No. But it won't happen again. I don't know how I'm going to face Domenic. I'm just glad he's away for most of this month. After Norway, he's heading to Courchevel to meet up with the rest of our . . . friends.'

'I'm sorry you feel bad.'

'Do you?' she asked him, her blue eyes wide and clear now.

'Yep. To be honest, I don't think me and Kiki will be together much longer. It's not been right for a while, but she didn't deserve this.'

There was a prolonged silence, both of them absorbing the enormity of their actions and realising there was nothing left to be said.

Looking at her watch, Talli smiled sadly. 'We'd better go.'

'We should.'

'How long did you say it would take before the pain-killers kick in?' she asked shyly.

He reached over, cupped his hand around her neck and pulled her towards him. 'Long enough for this . . .'

Chapter Twenty-three

Things that were wrong with this situation, number 1: everything. She'd become an unfaithful, hedonistic tart who cared only about living in the moment and exploiting a situation for her own physical pleasure with absolutely no regard for the consequences. In other words, she'd turned into her sister. Woe.

After pushing the lever of the shower to the off position, she waited while another stream of water dribbled from the chrome head. The shower had been installed some time in the seventies and only worked when it felt like it, so things could take a while. However, this time her reluctance to leave had nothing to do with the plumbing.

She'd give anything to be able to phone Fliss right now and tell her what had happened. She would admit she'd messed up, tell her how bad she felt and then let her in on the secret that she'd just had the most mind-blowing sex of her life.

Mind-blowing.

It was a total cliché, but she'd had no idea it could be like that. He didn't even stop to check his pulse halfway through or shower within a two-minute window of orgasm like . . .

Domenic.

The noise of the shower was replaced by her groan. What was she going to do about Domenic? Yesterday she had been in love with him – what was she saying? She was *still* in love with him. But how could she look at him again knowing the things she'd done with Zac? The guilt was pressing down on her chest, squeezing the air from her lungs, but at the same time her stomach was spinning and she was fairly positive it was her ovaries doing the samba at the thought of him.

Enough. Enough of this bloody craziness. In a few hours they'd be back in Essex and he could go back to being arrogant and rude and she could go back to being a stressed-out wedding planner with a boyfriend who was currently in Norway with the next Amy Winehouse and no one would ever talk about this again.

As she came down the stairs, he was standing looking out of the window in the living room. He'd already put the furniture back to roughly where it was before their exertions. She appreciated the effort – it must have hurt like hell shifting heavy furniture with a foot in that state. Picking up her jacket and bag, she cleared her throat.

'So. Ready to go back to the real world?'

When he turned around and nodded, she realised he was looking at her differently from yesterday. Softer. More open. Not surprising, she supposed, given the whole naked intimacy thing.

'Guess so. Remember to put the key above the lintel. Can't have the criminals of this area having to actually devise a cunning plan to gain entry.'

Rolling her eyes, she headed for the door. 'My best friend Fliss would adore you.'

'What, in the way that your sister and your other friend wanted to adore me?'

'No! She would just think you were a pretty cool guy, Zac Parker.'

'And you?'

She grinned. 'I think you're a pretty cool guy too. There. Your ego happy now?'

'Very.' Grabbing the lapel of her jacket, he pulled her close and kissed her gently, before letting her go and opening the door to let her past. Outside, he opened the double gate, reversed the Merc up to the rock and pinged open the boot – a plan that Talli realised might have come in handy the night before. She was glad they hadn't thought of it.

Between the two of them, in the daylight and without negotiating wind and rain, it only took one large heave to get it into the car. Zac pressed the red button on the door of the boot, and they both watched as it closed and locked.

'Let's go,' he said, all businesslike and efficient now,

apart from the very definite limp. He was embarrassed, Talli could tell. He probably regretted it all already and was just dying to get home, have a shower and go back to his big-boobed girlfriend. Sure, he'd said they were on shaky ground, but that was probably a line. Not that it mattered.

They'd both been equally wrong to do what they'd done last night and she didn't blame him for handling it in whatever way he chose.

She jumped in the passenger seat of the car and waited as he set the sat nav and pulled away. The crunch of the red gravel was deafening as they headed to the road, stopping at the gate to check nothing was coming.

'It's OK, nothing ever . . .' She'd been about to tell him that nothing ever came down this way except the postman, when a flash of yellow appeared on the left, grinding to a halt only inches from the wing of the Merc.

A woman in her mid forties, wearing a bright blue skirt and matching jacket, waved as she jumped out of what Talli could see now was a small mini van, then went to the back door of the vehicle and pulled out a long wooden post with a sign on the top.

'What the . . .?' Talli muttered, climbing out.

'Morning, lovey,' the woman chirped. 'Sorry, I didn't expect anyone to be here today. We'd been told the house was only used in the summer.'

'It is, it's just that . . . Sorry to be rude, but who are you?'

'Oh for goodness' sake, excuse my manners,' the

stranger told her with a friendly giggle. 'Mandy Cockburn. Of Chandler Estates. I've got a card here somewhere . . .'

'No, that's OK. But, again, sorry to be rude, but why are you here?'

'Just putting the sign up, lovey.' As if supplying mitigating evidence, she gestured to the large sign in one hand and the mallet in the other.

Talli shook her head. 'I'm sorry, there must be some mistake. This house isn't for sale. It belongs to my family. Have you perhaps got the wrong street? It's an easy mistake to make. This is Holly Lane, and there's a Holly Crescent further up the road.'

Ms Cockburn was clearly hit by an uncomfortable realisation, as she paled slightly, while still standing there brandishing post and mallet like an estate agent warrior.

'I'm afraid not, m'dear. I actually met Mr Caston-Jones here myself. I advised him that we were better to wait until after Easter – it's dead around here until March – but he gave me strict instructions to get it on the market immediately. Perhaps now that we've met, you can reassure him that I'm carrying out his instructions. Lovely place. I imagine you'll all be quite sorry to see it go.'

'Yes, we . . . erm. Thank you. Right then. I'll be off,' Talli finished weakly and clambered back into the car.

'Everything OK?'

Talli pulled her mobile out of her handbag and

pressed a button. 'No. I don't know what's going . . .
Daddy? Daddy, it's me,' she said into the phone. 'Yes,
I'm fine. I'm . . . Daddy, what's that shouting? Are you
watching *Jeremy Kyle*? You're what?'

She put her hand over the speaker. 'My father is
watching last night's episode of *Lovin' Essex*. He says he's
taking an interest in Edwina's career. I swear the world's
going mad.'

Hand off the mouthpiece now. 'Daddy, I'm down at
Beeches and the strangest thing just happened. A
woman appeared and put a For Sale sign up. Daddy?
Daddy?'

A sickening feeling engulfed her. Shit, where had
he gone? Had he keeled over again? Of course, it
would be a shock to him. Beeches had been in his
family for generations, so the thought of someone
accidentally listing it for sale – and she was still sure
this was some kind of mistake – would shake him to
the core.

'Oh, thank God. I thought you'd fainted there. Daddy,
shall I go back and expl . . . What? I'm heading back to
Essex. I've got a rock to . . . It doesn't matter. Yes, of
course. I can do that. No, it's no trouble, I'll come right
now. I'll see you soon.'

She pressed the off button on the phone and slumped
back in the seat.

'Talli, what's up?'

Turning to face Zac, her expression was somewhere
between worry and confusion. 'I really don't know. But

could you drop me at a station with a direct line to the city. I need to go and see my father straight away.'

Chapter Twenty-four

First stop, the gym. He was five minutes away when he called the direct line to the office. Den answered on the second ring.

'All right, mate?' said Zac. 'Listen, can you nip downstairs to the car park sharpish? I need a hand to lift a bit of a weight.'

As he drew into the car park, Den was just coming out of the door. Two minutes later, it was difficult to distinguish what Den found the most amusing – the fact that Zac was hobbling while wearing only one shoe, or the fact that he was hobbling wearing one shoe while trying to lift a rock.

'We'll stick it in reception,' Den decided, as he manoeuvred his end without any strenuous effort whatsoever. 'Health and Safety will have a field day, but at least no bugger will steal the ruddy thing.'

'How was the shoot last night?' Zac asked, a twinge of something slightly flushing his face.

'Carnage, mate,' the older man replied. 'Toby smacked that DJ bloke in the face. It was supposed to be more of a show punch than anything else, but he misjudged it, caught him a cracker and broke his nose. Edwina was going fucking ballistic, especially when Toby fainted and cracked his head on a lamp post. The two of them ended up in casualty and the rest of filming got suspended until tonight. We wound up at midnight – haven't shot any of Lena's scenes with Max and Coco yet. I'm sticking around for that one, just in case Coco needs a shoulder to cry on. I'm known for my advanced sympathy skills,' he joked.

On the outside Zac was laughing, but on the inside he was curling up with dread. If they'd finished at midnight, chances were Kiki would have gone home to get a good night's sleep before today's shoot. His only hope was that she was already at the salon for an early call.

'What time is kick-off today?'

Den looked at his watch. 'Everyone's due back here at two o'clock.' Couple of hours yet, thought Zac.

With involuntary grunts, they dumped the rock in the corner of reception and headed back outside.

There were two choices. Stay here until just before Kiki was due to arrive and then head home, avoiding passing her on the way. Or head home now and face the music. All he wanted to do was get back, have a bath, strap his foot up and take another couple of painkillers because the ones from earlier were wearing off. A few hours' sleep wouldn't go amiss either. Every muscle in his body ached with fatigue.

Too late, he realised that Den was still talking to him. 'Sorry, mate?'

Den reached up and pinched his cheek. 'Man, you're wasted today – what's up with you? Are you gonna tell me what happened last night or what?'

'Nothing. Nothing happened. Listen, could you give Edwina these keys? I'm just going to head off.'

Taking the Merc keys but refusing to be swayed from his investigation, Den eyed him suspiciously. 'So you went off with the duchess, didn't come back until morning, your foot is wasted and nothing happened? If it didn't, you're a fool, mate. She's something special.'

With another pat on the back, Den was off, leaving Zac to hobble to his car. Fifteen minutes later, he pulled up outside his door. Last time, when she'd messed up, Kiki was waiting for him, naked, on the breakfast bar. Somehow he didn't think he was going to get the same welcome party this morning.

When he opened the door, the open-plan kitchen/ lounge was empty and his mood soared with the hope that she'd already left. Almost instantly, the noise from the TV in the bedroom indicated otherwise. There was nothing else for it. Face the music, his Auntie Dot always said. Better to get things over and done with and sorted. The worry would kill you before the punishment. It was no wonder that her tweets under the #jointhisDot hashtag were going down a storm and getting massive attention. She already had 132,000 followers. Not bad for a woman who only actually socialised down the bingo with Jessie, Minnie and Ena.

He pushed the bedroom door open and Kiki's gaze flicked in his direction. On the dog-house scale, that was somewhere above 'I'm ignoring you because you've fucked up big-time' and 'Hi, babe', said in a non-enthusiastic tone that indicated a minor strop.

'Hey,' he said casually, dropping his kit bag and leaning against the door frame. There was definitely no naked titillation this time. Her hair was pulled into a purple turban, her face was the same mahogany shade as Dot's garden shed, and she wore a pink onesie, zipped up to the neck.

He waited for some kind of reaction, but there was nothing. Her eyes were once again fixed on the most recent episode of *Lovin' Essex*, playing on the plasma on the wall facing the bed.

OK, so the guilt should kick in big-time now. Seeing her face should cripple him with remorse about last night and maybe even prove to him that what they had was worth another shot. Still nothing.

'Look, Kiki, I'm knackered, so if you're pissed off with me, I understand. But last night was unavoidable and there was nothing I could do about it.' If there was a lie detector within earshot, it would be going off like the alarm in a shop being ransacked by looters.

Last night was absolutely avoidable. There was plenty he could have done to stop it. He'd just chosen not to.

Her face distorted, scrunching up with annoyance and anger, an expression her fans would never have recognised as belonging to their gorgeous, light-hearted, fun-loving, pouting star.

'I can't believe you would treat me like that. I just can't believe it. Who the hell do you think you are?' Every word was spat out with pure, unadulterated venom. Shit, she knew. She knew. But how had she possibly managed to find out when the only people there had been him and Talli? Even thinking her name made his nine good toes curl with . . . what? Surprise? Regret? Happiness?

'Like what?' It was the obvious next question and he braced himself for the full-on assault of abuse that he absolutely deserved.

After taking a deep breath, she enunciated each word. 'You. Didn't. Even. Phone. Me. To. Ask. How. The. Shoot. Went.'

It took him a moment to process her reply. So hang on – she didn't know that he'd just spent many hours, naked, doing flexible things with another woman? She didn't know that he'd kissed Talli's eyelids and sat with her swapping stories and laughing as the sun came up over the sea? And why did even remembering all that make him want to confess everything right now, not out of guilt but because he just wanted to tell the whole sodding world? Sleep deprivation and painkillers were definitely having a strange effect on him.

Right now, he just needed to get the immediate problem over with so he could climb into bed and get some shut-eye.

'Kiki, I'm sorry. It was a bit of a night last night, what with the injury and all. I was wiped out.'

Cue aforementioned pout. 'You could still have called me. I mean, it's like you're not even interested in my career any more.'

'I am interested.' He could only hope that the weariness in his voice wasn't too obvious. 'But like I said, I was wiped out.' It took him a few seconds to hobble over to the bed, then he bent down and kissed her quickly on the pout.

'OK, I suppose you're forgiven,' she said grudgingly. 'But I tell you something, Zac Parker, you're lucky it was that wedding girl you were with or you'd have been in major trouble. God, she does nothing with herself, does she? Not even a bit of lip gloss. And that accent goes right through you. And she's always so bloody sour-looking. What did you even find to talk about?'

'Erm, nothing. We didn't talk about anything much.'

'See what I mean? Really, like, proper stuck-up. Can't stand girls like that. They think the world owes them something. S'not how it works, though, is it? Probably never done a hard day's graft in her life. Just swans around spending Daddy's money. They're loaded, you know. That Edwina has millions, and they all stick together, don't they?'

The urge to argue in Talli's defence was only quelled by clamping his mouth shut really tightly.

224

Distraction was the only answer. As Kiki chattered away, he stripped down to his Armani boxers and tuned out her voice, choosing instead to rejoice over the fact that he'd dodged a bullet and acknowledge the snippets of flashbacks that were once again firing across his mind. He'd watched Talli for ages when she fell asleep. The weird thing was that she looked exactly the same asleep as awake. For a man who'd spent many years with a girl wearing full-face make-up during waking hours, only for her to strip it off and climb into bed a completely different person, it was a weird experience. As was waking up during the night and discovering her wrapped into him, her head in the crook of his arm. Kiki didn't ever sleep that close in case it matted her extensions.

But this wasn't about comparisons. It was about one night, not to be repeated, and the sooner he got over it the better. What was it she'd said – ready to go back to the real world? Well, this was reality and hers was some skinny bloke called Domenic, posh pals and a nymphomaniac sister.

Seeing her around over the next couple of weeks was going to be weird, but after Christmas Eve she'd be gone, and it was a pretty safe bet that their paths would never cross again.

Fine.

He could deal with it.

Kiki had got out of bed and stripped off the onesie, and was now completely naked except for a pair of fluffy pink mules that she wore as slippers, standing in front of her open wardrobe.

The sight of it made him itch. His side of the closet was ordered and tidy, all of his clothes pressed and hanging with plenty of space to breathe. Her side looked like a collection of designers had shot their clothes into it with a cannon. There was stuff on hangers, stuff on the floor, all of it a messy, non-coordinated shambles. And yet still she whinged about having nothing to wear.

His eyes were almost shut when something in her tone made him refocus his attention.

'What was that, babes?' he murmured.

'I can't believe you're not even listening to me, Zac Parker. I swear even Toby listens to me more than you do and he's not even my real boyfriend. God, did you hear he fainted? I had to act totally concerned, even though he bled all over my new Roberto Cavalli. I'm billing Edwina for the cleaning.'

'Babes!' His impatience grabbed her attention. 'What were you saying before that?'

'Oh. Some bloke phoned this morning. Said something about a debt but wouldn't tell me the details. What's all that about then?'

No amount of flashbacks could distract him from the chill that rose from his stomach to his throat.

'No idea, babes,' he told her. 'Must be a wrong number.'

Chapter Twenty-five

The house was eerily silent when Talli let herself in. Her first stop was her father's office, but his brown leather desk chair was empty. She resisted popping her head round to see if his computer was on, in case the image involved porn or Westlife – either would be yet more evidence of the change in his behaviour.

She checked the lounge, to no avail. The next choice was the kitchen, and there he was. Sitting at the twelve-seater light oak table in the middle of the room, indulging in yet another new vice. He at least had the grace to remove the spoon from the carton of Ben & Jerry's Caramel Chew Chew and smile as she entered.

His general demeanour proved that this called for serious action. After enveloping him in a hug, Talli pulled a spoon out of the cutlery drawer and joined him, deciding not to mention that he looked like he'd spent the last hour ploughing a field. His hair was dishevelled.

His maroon wool sweater was bobbled with wear and he was wearing his gardening cords that had soil patches on the knees.

'So. What's new?' she asked with a breezy smile, acutely aware that whatever was going on required a light touch. A bit of humour always worked well with her dad.

Not so much this time.

'Tallulah, darling, you know that I'd never do anything to hurt this family . . .'

'Of course you wouldn't!' she said, coughing as a piece of chocolate stuck in her constricted throat.

Another silence. Her stomach churned with real fear. Whatever was going on here wasn't some minor issue that could be easily rectified or her father wouldn't be seeking solace in the bottom of an ice cream tub – he'd been on a low-fat diet since his doctor warned him about his cholesterol in 1998.

'I don't know how to tell you this, darling . . .' He hesitated, clearly finding words a struggle.

'Daddy, are you or Mummy having an affair?' It was the question that had been foremost in her mind from the minute she'd met the woman with the signpost. One of her parents had been caught being unfaithful, they were separating, splitting the assets, so the summer house had to go. Yesterday, she'd have been outraged at the thought of either of them getting involved in an illicit relationship. Today, her more sympathetic view was cushioned by a thick layer of guilt.

This time it was Giles who almost choked on a

chocolate-covered nugget of caramel. 'No! Of course not! Your mother would bloody kill me!'

His newly pink face gave her cause for concern and she made a mental note to give their family doctor a call.

'OK! Daddy, anything else can be fixed. It can.'

He shook his head wearily. 'Ah, but that's where you're wrong, my darling. This can't be fixed. Everything is gone.'

Talli looked around her, expecting to spot exactly what was missing. Was he hallucinating? Was his mind wandering? That had happened to their grandfather, who'd died swearing he'd assassinated Napoleon.

'What's gone, Daddy?'

'Our wealth, darling. It's all gone. Everything.'

His whole body sagged, and Talli felt a piece of her heart break – not for the money, but for the man in front of her, the father who had never been anything but strong and positive, even when they'd gone through the normal family trials of difficult teenagers, the long hours he'd worked when she was growing up, and the deaths of her grandparents. Daddy was the constant. The backbone of the family. The one who kept everything solid while their mother pursued the jowls of a twenty-year-old.

'We moved everything into an investment fund years ago. There's been a steady return, above the base rate, our clients were happy, we were happy, all was good. Today there's nothing left. When the downturn began, it transpired that a substantial amount of the capital had been put into US stocks and property, and when it all went south across the Atlantic . . . well, it was only a matter of time. It's all gone. The FSA will investigate, but the stable door is shut.'

Now that he'd started telling her the story, it was as if he couldn't stop.

'I'm not letting our investors down, Talli. My father would turn in his grave. The houses have to go, as do the cars and everything else we own, but at least we'll walk away with our heads up. It'll be all we have left.'

Right. This wasn't a time to panic. Although she felt physically sick – not at the thought of losing their life-style, but at the likelihood of what this would do to her parents – she had to stay calm. Dear God, her mother would never cope with this. Never.

'Does Mummy know?' she asked weakly.

Giles shook his head. 'Only you, darling. I'm going to break it to her when the time is right.'

They sat in silence for a few moments, both of them picturing that scene. In Talli's mind, it resembled something out of a horror movie, in which a perfectly respectable middle-aged woman suddenly exploded, turning into a crazed, demonic monster spewing green vomit over her Louis XVI ottoman.

Choosing not to share that particular image, she reached over and took her father's hand, squeezing it tightly. 'What can I do to help you, Dad?'

His face brightened just a little as he lifted her hand

and kissed it. 'Nothing, darling. Although you might want to be here when I break the news to your mother.'

'So that I can disarm her if she gets violent? I'll buy one of those Taser things on eBay.' Talli tried desperately to bring a tiny ray of levity to the situation, even if she recognised that her words probably weren't a massive departure from the truth.

A memory niggled at her mind, then came into focus.

'The band! That's why you were so hesitant when I called about the fee for the band at the wedding. I'm so sorry, I didn't realise. I'll cancel them tomorrow.'

'No. That would definitely kill your mother. We'll find our share of the cost of the wedding somehow. I don't want to put you in an impossible position, darling, but I've decided I'm not going to tell Arabella any of this until after the whole wedding affair is over. Let her enjoy her day. She's looked forward to the weddings of her children for years. She deserves to have her moment.'

Wow, Talli thought, sitting back in her chair. His whole life had collapsed yet there was no self-pity or recriminations or rage – just the resolute need to let her mother have her swansong. Her parents' relationship had always been a mystery to her; now she saw that, on her dad's side at least, there was a ferocious strength to his love for his wife. She could only hope that her mother's feelings were just as solid.

'And Simmy and Dessi? Do you want them to know?'

Giles shook his head sadly. 'Can I ask you to tell no one? To keep this between us until the time is right?

This should be such an exciting time and I can't . . .'
His voice wobbled slightly and Talli felt the crack in her
heart open wider.

'. . . I can't take it away from any of them. Do you
understand?'

Talli was already nodding when she realised that tears
were streaming down her face.

'We'll work something out, Dad. We will. It's not the
end of the world.'

He tried to smile again, not quite succeeding. 'Let's
just hope your mother sees it the same way, eh?'
Talli reached over and kissed him on the cheek, then
got up and went into disaster-recovery mode. 'Cup of
tea, Dad?'

The De'Longhi kettle was flicked on, and the clanging
of mugs provided a distraction, but by the time the
steaming cup of tea was placed in front of him, Giles
was lost in thought, his expression solemn, staring into
space as he hummed the first few bars of 'You Raise Me
Up'.

Chapter Twenty-six

10 December 2013

> @minxandlenasauntiedot Keep your friends close but your enemies closer – preferably locked in the shed #jointhisDot

Zac tried to bite into the slice of carrot cake but immediately realised that Dot had managed to achieve something that would defy even the smartest scientists: she'd created a carrot cake that was harder than the actual carrots used to make it.

Beside him, Lena coughed and checked that Dot hadn't arrived with the tea yet. 'Zac, you have to get rid of this,' she said, shoving her plate into his lap. 'There's no way my veneers will cope with it.'

At that exact moment, Auntie Dot banged in the door, using the tea tray as a battering ram, yet not spilling a drop. It was a talent honed over decades of practice. Straight away she spotted the cake pile on Zac's lap.

'Two pieces, son? You always did love my cakes. I'm sure that's what's built that body of yours.'

Zac decided not to tell her that her cakes could also be used in the construction of walls. Or tunnels. Or anything requiring extra-solid foundations.

Lena nudged him and he struggled not to laugh. 'He was just saying how ace it was, Auntie Dot. I reckon he could manage a third bit.'

Dot beamed with pride as she unwrapped a Penguin, then took a bite and washed it down with a drink from her I Heart Magaluf mug. Jessie, Ena and Minnie had been her annual travel companions to the sunshine resort for the last decade, despite it being renamed Shagaluf by anyone under twenty-five.

'Where's our Minx today then?' Dot asked.

'Out looking at jet skis. Minx has decided she'd rather have one of those than an engagement ring. I don't know whether Dale's dead chuffed or a bit worried. Not as if she can flash her jet ski at another bloke to fend off an unwelcome advance, is it?'

'No other boy could keep up with that girl. She's like that actress . . . you know . . . the one that Brad Pitt went off with.'

Zac somehow managed to swallow a morsel of cake, thereby regaining partial movement in his jaw. 'Angelina Jolie.'

'That's the one. Did all those action movies. Past it

now, of course. They should have our Minx in the films. Wouldn't even need a stunt double.'

After brushing some crumbs off her pale pink skinny jeans, Lena stretched up on to her eight-inch nude stilettos. 'You're right, Auntie Dot. And we could get new frocks for the Oscars and everything.' She held back her hair so that she could lean down and kiss Dot without risking a wavy lock falling into the cup of Tetley.

'Right then, have to be off. Got to be on set in an hour, and I haven't even got my eyelashes on yet.'

Auntie Dot pursed her lips while eyeing Lena warily. 'Not saying I approve, Lena. I mean, a married man? Didn't do that in my day.' Obviously one of her buddies had filled her in on the story.

'Auntie Dot, I promise, he's proper separated. Coco is shacked up with some Chelsea player now. Apparently the Arsenal bloke launched her out 'cause she told his ex-wife to bugger off on Twitter. We've already filmed the scenes where she, like, begs him to come back and he's having none of it.'

Auntie Dot's expression was sceptical. The two-week delay between shooting and the episodes airing was a permanent situation of puzzlement to her.

'Well, I'm just saying. It's not right. Doesn't deserve you if he's not even divorced that other one yet and he's already playing around.'

Lena grabbed her cream Marc Jacobs Stam bag from the sideboard, before leaning in for another hug. 'Auntie

Dot, it'll be fine, I promise. It's just the way nowadays. He's a good bloke. Zac knows him, don't you, hon?'

Lena's expression pleaded for back-up. Zac didn't mind stepping in. 'He's OK, Nan. I've known him for years and I train down the gym with him sometimes. He's been separated from his missus for ages and he's not messing Lena about. You know I'd never let anyone do that to her.'

The irony was as hard to swallow as Dot's cake. His application to join the fidelity police had just suffered a major setback.

Lena smiled gratefully and gave her aunt another hug. 'I'll bring him round one day – let you meet him.'

'Good,' said Dot, her tone ominous. 'I'll make a special batch of my Christmas mini logs.'

Zac decided to make sure he was as far away as possible from that particular meeting. Lena blew him a kiss and then was out the door. He automatically leaned over and watched at the window as she went down the path, climbed into her white convertible Volkswagen Beetle and roared off, Jezzer taking pics the whole way and then jumping on to his motorbike to follow her. Just another normal day on Planet Reality TV. It was a strange scenario when the sight of a familiar paparazzo was actually a comfort, reassuring him that there was someone there to look out for his sister's safety. There were so many nutters out there, he couldn't help but worry about the fact that all the girls attracted attention. They were still no further forward in identifying the creep who was sending that bollocks to Kiki, and it made his jaw clench just thinking about it.

It was as if Auntie Dot read his mind.

'So what's going on with that streaker, then?'

'Stalker, Auntie Dot. It's a stalker. There was another letter a couple of days ago. The TV people have decided to use it in the show and see if it flushes out the person responsible. I dunno. I think maybe they're so twisted they'll enjoy the extra attention.'

'Well, put your foot down, son. Say it's not happening.'

Zac shook his head. 'Nothing to do with me, Auntie Dot. Kiki decides all that stuff with her management and the producers of the show. They call the shots.'

He checked his watch. He had a one-hour gap between clients over at the gym and would have to be heading back there soon.

Dot contemplated her Penguin for a moment, then took a deep breath, her mind made up.

'You know, love, there's no point staying with someone when you're not happy. I'm just saying. Not interfering, like. Just saying.'

The last bite of her biscuit disappeared.

'I know, Auntie Dot. And I could sit here and say it's all OK, but . . .'

'I'd know you were lying, love. Your left eye twitches. Same when you were eleven and got caught with that fiver. Found it, my arse.'

The memory made him laugh. He'd raised the cash by selling his England top to another kid in his class. Dot had marched him up to the boy's mother, thrust the fiver into her hand and demanded that the top be returned, washed and ironed, within twenty-four hours. It was.

'It's not working out,' he said simply, absent-mindedly pulling at the neck of his Nike T-shirt. It was all the confirmation Dot needed – he always fidgeted when he had something on his mind. 'But calling it a day ain't that easy. It's been a long time. She's got all this stalker stuff going on. I don't want to upset the girl or leave her when she's dealing with all this flak.'

Dot's snort of laughter took him by surprise. 'Don't you kid yourself, son. That girl could survive anything. What is it they say? When the world ends, there'll only be cockroaches left? Yeah, right. Cockroaches and Kiki – and she'll still be looking for someone to take her picture. Don't think I didn't see that stuff in the paper about her with that DJ bloke. Didn't look like that was staged for the cameras to me. Her tongue was so far down his throat she was licking his lungs.'

Time was ticking on and Zac knew he had to get moving, but somehow, sitting here was making him feel a whole lot better. Density Fitness was open nineteen hours a day, between five a.m. and midnight, and he was there with clients for almost every hour of that. At least it meant he didn't see much of Kiki, though. The last week had been hard – flitting between worry, guilt and pressure to rake in as much cash as possible. The thought twanged another wave of guilt, and he knew Talli was feeling the same.

They'd bumped into each other just twice since . . . well, since that night. Both times in the gym, both times surrounded by other people, and both times they'd just smiled awkwardly and then carried on with what they were doing. She was obviously totally regretting what had happened, because she'd flushed bright red as soon as she'd spotted him. He just wished he felt the same.

'Is that all that's on your mind, love?' Dot asked pointedly.

Man, she was like some kind of paranormal force, able to penetrate the brain and mind-warp her helpless victims. There was no way he was telling her about Talli. She'd be outraged. Disgusted. Kiki might not be top of her popularity poll, but she wouldn't put up with him messing around – not on her watch.

And his other worries? Dot was the last person on earth he could tell about the cash situation. The last person. That was definitely one he had to keep to himself.

'Yeah, Auntie Dot, just that and work stuff. Nothing I can't handle.'

'You work too hard, Zac. You and Lena – you both got my work ethic. Minx got the sense of adventure. Not that I could do much about that in my day. None of that abseiling or ski-diving stuff then. Too busy grafting.' Zac knew it was true. Dot had had at least two jobs when they were growing up so that she could provide for them. Where was the fairness in that? His mother fucks off and leaves them and Auntie Dot gets an extra twenty years' hard labour. Not that she ever complained – not once.

The ringing of his mobile phone interrupted his thoughts. Blocked number. 'Hi,' he answered warily, breathing a sigh of relief when he heard the voice of Karen Smith. Or rather DC Karen Smith, one of his clients. A thirty-year-old cop, she could bench-press her own body weight and had more stamina than half of his other clients put together.

'Sorry, Zac, but I'm tied up at the station today. Won't make our session this afternoon. My bad. See you tomorrow at the normal time?'

'No worries, Karen. See you then.' As he hung up, he realised he was exhaling with relief. Karen had been booked in for a two-hour session this afternoon, so now, for the first time in over a week, he had some spare time before he had to be back at the gym for a four-hour workout with Edwina.

'Everything all right there?'

'Yeah, Auntie Dot. Just got a couple of hours off that I didn't expect. Could do with it, to be honest.'

Was it wrong that his first thought was to wonder where Talli was? Frickin' crazy. One night. Over. Done. There was nothing, absolutely nothing between them other than a pissed few hours of sex. She had a boyfriend that she was loved up with. Her life was nothing to do with his. He'd lost the plot to even be thinking about her. Lost it.

'Mmm. And where's that Kiki one now?' Auntie Dot asked.

'Home,' Zac replied. 'They've got a night shoot at the Beach Box tonight.'

'Well you know, son, sometimes opportunities present themselves and you've just got to get things over with. Bite the bullet. Not that I'm interfering,' she repeated, clearly aware once again that that was exactly what she was doing.

He put his head back against the brown fabric of the sofa and took a deep breath. Dot was right. He'd been planning to wait until after Christmas to talk to Kiki, but what was the point? Why not just get it over with now, then it would be one complication he didn't have to worry about?

'You know what, Auntie Dot, you're right. Thanks. I'll get off and catch her at the flat. For an old bird, you're pretty good at this life stuff,' he joked with her, and earned a clip on the ear.

'Hang on a minute, Zac – I'll go put some of that carrot cake in a Tupperware for Kiki. Might soften the blow.'

Before he even got as far as the door, Zac decided he'd be leaving the cake in the car. No point arming his soon-to-be-ex-girlfriend with a lethal weapon.

Chapter Twenty~seven

Four hundred and twenty wedding guests. And Zac Parker naked.

Four hundred and twenty doves now required. And Zac Parker naked.

A week and a half of avoidance measures – to prevent her from bumping into Zac Parker, naked or not.

What an idiot she'd been. Talli still couldn't believe how she'd behaved. She'd always thought there was no price on loyalty and fidelity. Now it seemed that it could be bought for two bottles of red wine and a large bucket of lust.

Lust or not, Zac Parker was off her priority list at the moment, given that it was fully booked by the wedding and the fact that her family were headed for a life-altering shift that would devastate them.

On the days Talli had been in Chelsea, she'd done everything she could to cheer up her dad. They'd wrapped up in parkas and gone for walks in the park. She'd ordered his favourite movies on Netflix and bought his favourite foods to encourage him to eat. And on the days she'd had to travel to Essex, she'd made sure that Theresa was on hand to keep him from hanging out too much with Ben & Jerry.

Today was one of those days. The plan was to go to Essex later in the afternoon, so that she was there for an early meeting with Trevor at Highdrow Castle the next morning.

When India had called and suggested lunch before she left, she'd thought about resisting, but the girls were all off to Courchevel the next day for a week, and it would be good to see them before they left.

Besides, over the next couple of months they were going to need all the stability and friends they could find. Hell, they'd also need padded soundproofing and a therapist when they broke the news to Dessi that her Harvey Nicks charge card had been cancelled.

Talking of which . . . 'Darling!' Dessi strutted into Bon Auberge in black leather boots with fierce heels, black skinny trousers and a padded jacket belted at the waist with a huge gold buckle. Her caramel hair was pulled back in a low ponytail, with tendrils escaping at the temples. If there was a cross between a Bond girl and a kinky riding instructor, this was how it would look.

India and Verity were right behind her, both of them in dark jeans that looked like they'd been sprayed on, India in a white jacket and Verity in red, their designer bags colliding as they squeezed between the tables, ever aware that the eyes of every guy in the place were on them.

A flurry of air kisses later, they were all seated and the first bottle of Bollinger had been ordered. 'Sparkling water for me, please,' Talli requested from the smiley waiter. 'Any kind, you choose.' As always, he eyed her like it was a trick question. Years of serving Domenic every lunchtime had understandably given him the impression that his girlfriend should be as fussy as he was.

'It's been a fucking age!' India announced, leaning over for another hug. 'I thought we'd lost you. Nice nails, by the way. A little . . . bright?'

Talli couldn't help smiling as she looked at the red nails with the diamanté tips. They were still absolutely perfect – not so much as a chip. It was like a miracle.

Verity pondered the menu, an act that was superfluous to requirements because she, India and Dessi would all order the same. Grilled sea bass. Green salad. Dressing on the side. They'd pretend not to care when Talli's relish dripped out of her burger.

'How are things going with the wedding plans? All under control?' Verity asked, spearing an olive from the tiny tray of hors d'oeuvres in the centre of the table.

Talli felt a surge of anxiety. On the one hand, she so wanted the wedding to be over, her job done and the weight of expectation lifted from her shoulders. On the other, the stress for the other members of her family would be just beginning.

Nodding her head, she pulled a large chunk from the loaf that had appeared in front of her. 'Dessi, remember your dress fitting this afternoon at Vera Wang.'

If Dessi hadn't already followed her mother on the Botox path to a wrinkle-free face, she'd have been frowning with puzzlement. 'Are you not coming with me?'

Talli shook her head. 'No, I have to get back to Essex this afternoon. I popped in this morning and checked my dress was OK. It just needed to be taken in slightly at the bust and hips, but apart from that it's fine.'

'God, I'd kill for your figure,' Dessi moaned, despite the fact that she was a perfect size 8 thanks to surviving on fish, vegetables and a pack of Marlboro a day. 'So what's so important that you have to head back to Essex today?' she added.

India piped into the conversation. 'If all the guys there look like Zac Parker, I might just come with you. Not that he's relationship material, but I don't think I'd care much about conversation or compatibility for the first few months.'

Dessi took up the mantle, looking directly at Talli as she spoke. 'Yes, but there's definitely something odd about him. India felt him up that night we met . . .' In her peripheral vision, Talli could see India nodding while wearing a matter-of-fact expression. '. . . and I attempted to jump his bones, but he was having none of it.'

'I know, it's . . . weird.' Talli stammered, wondering

why it was suddenly hot as a Swedish sauna. Change the subject. In the name of God, change the subject.

'I'm heading back today because I've got a meeting with Trevor Highdrow first thing in the morning,' she answered honestly. It took her a few seconds later to realise that they were all staring at her. 'What? What have I done?'

Verity snorted. 'Gone bright red!'

'No I haven't!'

'You have, darling,' Verity confirmed.

'And your eyes have gone all shifty, like when you know you've fucked something up and can't bring yourself to tell Mummy.'

'They haven't!'

India's eyes narrowed, then she sighed wearily. 'Darling, I really hope you haven't developed a crush on Trevor Highdrow. He's a sweetheart but he's as gay as they come. Raging coke habit too, although that last stint in rehab seems to have done the trick.' It was a glimmer of an escape route, so Talli went for it.

'But he's . . . really nice.'

'I know, darling,' Dessi laughed, 'but if he had the choice of which bridesmaid to shag, I'm pretty sure he'd ask if he could do the best man instead. Not that you ever would, even if you got the offer.'

'Of course I wouldn't.' Talli's faced burned again. 'I'm missing Domenic terribly.' Change the subject. Change the subject. 'So are you all excited about Courchevel tomorrow?' she asked. 'Who's there already?'

Verity reeled off half a dozen names, most of them guys from their long-standing circle of friends.

Relieved at getting the conversation back on safer ground, Talli was determined to keep it there. 'And when is Domenic coming over to meet you all? He said he was leaving Norway as soon as he had a few tracks laid down, but I haven't managed to speak to him this week. You know how crazy the hours are when he's in the studio.'

If she hadn't been blustering her way through, trying to avoid suspicion, she might not have been scrutinising their reactions. She might not have noticed the slight jolt of tension in Verity's shoulders. And she might not have picked up on the look that passed between them all.

But she was, and she did.

'What am I missing now?' she asked, praying that whatever was changing the vibe in the room was a long way from Chelmsford and the finely toned body of Zac Parker.

'Oh fuck it, I'm telling her. India, get the laptop out,' Dessi blurted.

Talli attempted to batter back a feeling of dread with another bread roll bomb.

'Tell me what?'

India slipped her hand into her YSL shopper and pulled out a MacBook Pro. On the front was the advertisement banner for her blog, Rich Cows and Cartier, home of all gossip and speculation in the Chelsea and Knightsbridge set. She flipped open the top and waited as it booted up, filling the silence with some recently acquired gossip. 'Meant to say, my contact at the FSA tells me that another four investment houses are going to bite the dust over the next month. Some big names apparently. He wouldn't tell me any more than that, but I'm working on it. Cost me a bloody fortune in drinks at Soho House last night.'

A glass of water, Evian as it happened, went flying across the table, and only India's swift reactions saved her MacBook from a watery grave.

'Sorry! Oh shit, sorry.' Breathe, Talli told herself. Just breathe. Now she knew how people in a siege situation felt. Zac. Their impending bankruptcy. Too many secrets to keep. This wasn't her. She didn't do secrets. She did gold confetti and table centrepieces and she didn't even do those particularly well.

Breathe. Just breathe.

India's deep grey nails were now click-clicking away on the keyboard.

Talli met Verity's eyes and saw true concern there. 'Have you been looking at Facebook lately?' Verity asked her.

'No, I never do. Only if I'm posting things for Fliss.'

India swivelled the laptop around so that they could all see the Facebook page on the screen. It took Talli a few moments to realise what she was looking at. Luna Ma Dame's picture finally gave it away.

'Luna's page? What's that got to do with me?'

'Read the last few posts,' Dessi ordered, her annoyance coming across loud and clear.

Talli's eyes scanned the content, starting at the bottom of the page.

Having the most amazing week. Stoked to be working with amazing people.
Learning so much. Feel like this week will change my life.
DSL taking unbelievable care of me. Sometimes in life you meet the right people at the right time.
Didn't know this kind of feeling existed.
So overwhelmed to be experiencing this right now. Moving to another level in every way.

And then finally, in an update from earlier that day, a notification that no amount of bread could soothe.

Luna Ma Dame changed her relationship from 'single' to 'it's complicated'.

Chapter Twenty-eight

It was ridiculous, but as he pushed open the door, he almost hoped she wasn't there. What was that all about? He'd specifically come here to talk to her, to get things sorted, and now he was hoping she was up the shops or doing a magazine shoot or off dreaming up some new crazy publicity stunt with that DJ bloke or . . . just anywhere but here.

The music coming from the bathroom told him otherwise. Time to man up. God, had he really just told himself to man up? What the hell had happened to him? If this was a mid-life crisis, it had come too soon, yet he was definitely displaying all the symptoms. Irrational decisions? Check. Unusual behaviour? Check. Change in sexual activities? Check. And if any bloke in Britain could see what he was about to do right now, they'd confirm that he had, most definitely, lost the friggin' plot.

Katy Perry's voice was blaring out of the bathroom. It

was one of Kiki's favourites. Zac was more of a Rihanna kind of guy.

He pushed the door open to see Kiki lying in the bath, her hair wet and swept back from her face, not a scrap of make-up on. And by the looks of things, she'd been there a while, because only a few bubbles remained in the otherwise clear water – enough to conceal everything from the waist down, but leave her gorgeous, stunning tits floating above the water. Shit, she was beautiful. It would have been the easiest thing in the world to put off the conversation that had been turning in his mind for days, and just climb in there with her.

Yet strangely, he felt . . . nothing. He didn't have a twinge of a reaction, emotional or sexual.

'Babes!' Her face darkened. 'You scared the crap out of me there! My heart is totally beating now. Could have given me a heart attack.'

Not the best start, then.

'Why're you not at work?' she asked, then continued without giving him a space to answer. 'Actually it's good, 'cause you could give me a lift over to the salon later and save me taking my car. Gonna be a late night at the Beach Box tonight and I'm going to be, like, so knackered tomorrow. Don't know what I'm going to wear, though. Got that new dress from Gucci last week, but it makes my thighs look massive.'

It struck him that if he really put his mind to it, he could perhaps remember when they used to have conversations in which they both participated. In fact, many of them had taken place in that very bath, with him at one end and her at the other, talking about everything and anything, invariably ending with them making love and flooding the floor.

When had they let all that slip away?

'Kiki, I need to talk to you.' He closed the lid of the toilet and sat down.

Kiki immediately reacted. 'Oh. My. God. What have you done? You look so serious, babes. Has there been another one of those letters? There has, ain't there? What's it saying this time? I'm letting my agent know about this because it's time they sorted out twenty-four-hour protection, Zac. I mean you can't always be there to—'

'Kiki, I think it's time for a change . . .'

'Yeah, I mean totally. 'Specially if some psycho is out there, we should definitely have a change of scene. When I get out of here, I'll go online and book the hotel in Marbs. I could do with some sun. We could stay there for Christmas. They were going to do the Christmas shoot in Dubai, but since all that stuff with Toby and Dean, they've decided they want to really build that up before Toby comes out and it's best to do it—'

'Kiki, that's not what I meant.' He took a deep breath and braced himself. 'I'm so sorry. We've had a great time together but I think maybe this isn't working the way it used to. I think it's time we weren't together any more.'

'But . . . but I live here!'

Of all the things he'd expected her to say, that wasn't in the top ten.

'If you want to stay here for a while longer, that's fine. I'll move back into Auntie Dot's for a week or two.'

The beautiful face of the second hottest chick in reality TV suddenly twisted into pure fury.

'Don't you do me any favours, Zac Parker. So who is it? There's no way you'd be leaving me if you hadn't met someone else. Who is it?'

OK, so this was definitely in the top ten. In the spirit of many childhood afternoons watching *Blue Peter*, he had an answer he'd prepared earlier.

'Kiki, there's no one else. I just think that your career is really taking off and you should be with someone who can dedicate more time to you, make you their number one priority.'

'You can do that!' she told him.

'I can't, babe. I'm trying to build the business and that's going to require long days and total focus. I'd be short-changing you. Holding you back.'

Shit, he was starting to struggle now. He'd done everything but say 'It's not you, it's me.'

If she continued to object, that would be his next strategy. What else could he say?

Tell the truth? That she'd become a spoiled, self-centred prima donna and he was sick of the demands and the drama. That she'd lost all the softness and fun that he'd loved about her in the first place. That he'd changed too and wanted a different kind of life. That he wanted an existence that wasn't controlled by TV shoots and next week's celebrity mags. That he'd spent the night with . . . No, never that. She'd stab him next time his back was turned.

'You can't handle it, can you? You can't handle the fact that I'm getting somewhere now. Jealous, Zac. You're pure jealous!'

'Kiki, it's not that, really it's not. It's just . . . we want different things now.' Oh for fuck's sake, this was, like, where bad bloke clichés came to die.

She stood up in the bath now, giving him a full view of what he was saying goodbye to. Still no reaction, other than a real gut feeling of sadness.

Pulling a towel off the rail, she wrapped it round herself, and that was when she did the most unexpected thing of all – she burst into tears. Great big racking sobs, so loud that he jumped up to comfort her, letting his shoulder muffle her wails, not caring that he got soaked in the process.

The fury he could handle, but this was making him feel like the biggest shit that ever walked the face of the earth.

He put his hand under her legs and whipped her out of the bath, carrying her through to the kitchen. There, he gently put her down on the granite top of the island, sitting so that her legs dangled over the edge. Sticking a mug on to the chrome tray on his Breville One Cup, he shoved in a tea bag, pressed the button and then scooped in two sugars. Bloody hell, what was he doing? He was acting like he was tending to a shock victim, not breaking up with his girlfriend. During the minute it took for him to make a cup of hot, sweet tea and place it down next to her, she just sat there, crying.

'Drink some tea. And you know I'll take you over to the club later for the shoot.'

Don't say you'll still be friends. Do. Not. Say. You. Will. Still. Be. Friends. Or you will go to cliché hell.

'I mean, we'll still be mates and we'll still see each other.'

The tears got heavier at that point, falling down her gorgeous face and accompanied by big, loud, heart-breaking sniffs.

Say nothing else, he warned himself. Nothing. It seemed no one had notified his gob of that particular instruction.

'And you know, babe, I'll always love you.'

Stop speaking or kill me now, the logical, non-pathetic part of his mind pleaded.

'I know that,' she finally stuttered between sniffs, 'but that's not the point, is it?'

The point? Oh shit, of course it wasn't. The point was that they weren't going to be together any more. That all their dreams for the future had just been wiped out. That he'd pulled the love rug from under her feet and devastated her. The point was that he'd been a complete arse and he deserved everything that she threw at him. The point was that he'd changed too, and in doing so he was now prepared to take away years of promises and plans.

'Point is,' she sniffled, 'who's going to look after me now?'

Chapter Twenty-nine

'Push! Come on, you weakling, push!'

Talli lay on her back on the bench press, attempting to manoeuvre what felt like the weight of a small car from directly above her chest to the elbows-straight position. Only when she managed it did Den take the weight of the bar and pull it back to rest on the metal hooks above her.

Talli looked up at the smiling face of her favourite man in Essex. The other one didn't count on the grounds that he'd seen her naked and she was trying her damnedest not to think about him. Den stood right behind her, his upper thighs level with her head.

'Den, you do realise that from this position I can threaten your future fatherhood if you continue to abuse me.'

His roar of laughter made everyone in earshot turn. 'You're right, duchess, but that would suit me fine. Save a fortune on condoms.'

Grinning as she rose from the bench, he chucked her a towel so that she could wipe away the thick rivulets of sweat that were pouring down her face. Her biceps, delts and pecs ached after an upper-body session that felt like it had worked every single muscle to snapping point. She was glad she'd chosen to wear a black vest and stretchy shorts because as Dessi would probably say, visible sweat marks were so last year.

The gym had been stacked when she'd arrived at seven, but it was quieter now, just a few faces she recognised as stalwart bodybuilders and a couple of women who'd nipped out for quick workouts now the kids were in bed.

There had been much deliberation on whether or not to come. The last person on earth she wanted to see was Zac, so she'd decided to stay in her hotel. After an hour or so of trying and failing to concentrate on a book, then flicking through dozens of channels showing nothing she wanted to see, the restlessness got the better of her. It was either jog on the streets on a cold dark night or come here, see Den and hope that Zac was somewhere else – out on the town or home with Kiki. Ouch, that one came with a small sting.

In the end, her optimism had been rewarded as she hadn't seen him here all night. He obviously had better things to do, like socialising or having a life.

'What is gnawing your knickers today, duchess? Dunno where your mind is, but it ain't here.'

Den's voice penetrated her thoughts, and after a

delayed reaction she realised that he was holding out her plastic water bottle. 'Sorry, Den, got a lot on my mind. Stupid stuff.'

And Talli Caston-Jones wins Oscar for Best Understatement in a Drama.

All day she'd been mulling over the Facebook page the girls had shown her at lunchtime and she'd come to the conclusion that it proved absolutely nothing. It was just the witterings of an aspiring singer who was excited to be finally on the verge of a career break-through. There was absolutely nothing to say that Domenic had done anything wrong at all. Luna Ma Dame could have hit it off with one of her production team or another performer working in the same studio complex.

What if he had done something that he shouldn't have? What could Talli say? Last time she checked, she'd slid off the moral high ground on top of a six-foot-two personal trainer.

A couple of phone calls to Domenic's mobile had gone straight to answering machine, so she'd left a message asking him to call her back. Hearing his voice would make her feel better in one respect, but she had no doubt it would up the guilt factor. One question had been on her mind since that night at Beeches. Could she continue with their relationship without confessing what she'd done? Would it be better to keep him in the dark and carry on, spending the rest of her life making sure she made him happy, without ever telling him about the disloyalty? Or should she confess what she'd done, devastate him and hope he could find it in his heart to forgive her? One stupid, crazy night could have blown the whole life that was mapped out in front of her. If she chose to let it.

'Duchess! If this crashes down on me 'cause you're dreaming, I'm reporting you to Health and Safety.'

It was her turn to 'spot' Den, to stand by, lift the bar into the starting position, support him if he struggled, and then return the bar to the stand when his repetitions were done. He was lying on the bench now, arms up in front of him at chest level, ready to take the weight.

'Sorry, Den! I'm . . .'

'Hey.' The voice came from behind her, and Talli could only think that if she had heard it a few seconds later, after she'd heaved the bar from its starting position, there was every chance that Den would now be in possession of several broken ribs.

As it was, Den sat up on the bench and reached out to shake Zac's hand.

'All right, mate? Finished downstairs?' he asked.

Zac nodded. Talli was suddenly very aware that her stomach was flipping like an eel. Don't let it show. Do not let it show.

Over at the spin bikes, she could see one of the mums nudge the other and gesture in Zac's direction. Suddenly they were both grinning and sitting up straighter, bosoms out, teeth on show. He had that effect, even now, when he was glistening with sweat, his hair wet and slightly messy. None of that detracted from the angular jaw or the eyes that had watched her . . .

Thump. Her shins were suddenly damp as her water bottle fell and exploded at her feet, sending a gush of water over her socks and trainers. Great.

'Edwina will be up soon. She's really coming on in the ring. Could whip a few of those guys down there.' So that was where he'd been – downstairs in the boxing gym. She hadn't thought to check there on the way in.

'Mate, she could do that just by opening her gob,' Den joked. 'The weaker ones would drop like flies. Anyway, what's new? Anything happening?'

Zac shrugged. 'Not much.' Talli felt the Oscar for Best Understatement slipping from her grasp.

'I'm just heading for the showers. Catch you later,' he told Den, and only then did he look at her. 'See ya, Talli,' he said quietly.

'Yeah, erm, see you.' The last couple of words were muffled, as she'd already started preparing her grip on the bench press bar, apparently keen to get back to the training session. Den, who had still to return from the sitting position to flat out on his back on the bench, looked at her quizzically, then switched his gaze to Zac's retreating back, and back to her.

'Nooooo!' he cooed, his eyes wide with surprise.

'What?' Talli yelped with what she hoped was a healthy dose of incomprehension.

'You and Zac? Nooooo!' Den didn't even try to hide his amusement.

'No, of course not!' she said firmly. 'Why would you say that? Now lie down. Didn't you say I was talking too much? Let's take that on board and cut the chat.'

He was laughing hard now as he manoeuvred into position.

'Well I tell you something, duch. If you haven't already then you bloody should. You two would be freakin' amazing together.'

'What two?'

For the second time in ten minutes, Talli almost caused serious injury to her workout partner. What was it with people sneaking up on her tonight?

'Nothing,' she told the newly arrived Edwina, who was still in her workout clothes, towel around her neck. 'Wow, you look great,' Talli told her, absolutely meaning it. Zac had done a fantastic job. Edwina had lost stones and inches. Her stomach was now flat as a gym bench, her hips were narrower than they'd ever been and from Talli's side view she could see that her butt was looking incredible.

'Thanks. Another two weeks to go. Should be enough time for the last half a stone if Mr Masochist keeps up the punishment. I swear when this is over I'm going to kiss him then beat him until he bleeds after all he's put me through.'

Edwina perched on the edge of the next bench. 'Darling, we have to up the numbers again. Got a few more acceptances through.'

'Edwina! I thought we agreed that you wouldn't send out any more invitations!' This was a nightmare. Every time Talli checked the numbers, she discovered that another dozen people had been added to the list. The invitations were the only thing she'd left to Edwina and they'd spiralled out of control. They'd started at 200 and now were way over 400.

Edwina had the decency to look mildly apologetic. 'I know, darling, but I told my father he could invite whoever he wanted and, well, he did.' She used the yellow towel around her neck to rub the sweat from her forehead, then threw in a fact that was obviously meant to cheer Talli up. 'One of the acceptances from the Stritch-Leesons.' It didn't cheer her up at all.

Domenic's parents. They were in the same social circle as her parents and Edwina's father, so it was only to be expected that they would come. The thought made her stomach flip again. If she decided to confess all to Domenic – which she was sure she would have to do in order to move on with their lives together – then no doubt all the parents would get to hear and it would be the absolute scandal of their social circle. The only bonus about that was that it would take the heat off Dad's imminent bankruptcy and public humiliation. Actually, that wasn't how it would work. It would compound their misery – the Caston-Jones family, disgraced, destitute and their daughter a harlot.

'I'll speak to Trevor in the morning. I'm meeting him at ten. If it tips him over the edge, I'm taking no responsibility.' Talli went for light-hearted and Edwina smiled.

'He'll be fine. I'll buy him something fabulous to

thank him when this is over. And we'll hold the christen-
ings of every one of our children at Highdrow – the
repeat business will make them a fortune.'

'I'm not organising those,' Talli quipped, making
Edwina chuckle again. At least it was supposed to be a
chuckle. How did Den describe her laugh again? Like a
tank reversing over a set of bagpipes.

Edwina's eyes flicked to the huge black and white
station-style clock above the nearby door. 'Right, Den,
you make sure you leave enough time to beautify yourself. You're in the Beach Box scenes tonight. Bonny still
OK to make a guest appearance?'

Den nodded. 'Yeah, she's ready.'

'And she doesn't mind the costume?'

'Costume?' Den countered. 'You mean the two nipple
tassels and a G-string? Don't worry. Bonny views that as
being overdressed. She's in touch with her inner nudist.'
The grin on his face suggested he approved of Bonny's
inner nudist too.

Edwina headed off to the showers, taking the same
route Zac had taken a few minutes earlier, before staging
a last-minute detour into the door marked Female
Changing.

'Right, duchess, let's call it a night. And for what it's
worth, m'luv, you're in pretty good nick yourself these
days.'

Talli leaned over and ruffled his hair to a wail of
protest. Den's hair was so perfectly styled and such a
national obsession that it had its own Twitter page.

Deciding not to shower at the gym, she took the stairs two at a time and bleeped open the car as she crossed the car park towards it. Deciding to bring her mum's Audi this week had been a decision born of convenience and the need to transport wedding paraphernalia from various suppliers to the storage areas of Highdrow Castle.

The car was within touching distance when a shadow a few cars away made her jump. Zac? Was that Zac? No one appeared and she decided that the rustling sound she heard between two cars must have been a cat or dog searching for food. Or maybe a fox. Whatever it was, it definitely wasn't Zac bloody Parker. Furious with herself for thinking about him again, she wrenched open the door of the car, almost hitting the Saab parked next to it

That was when she saw another shadow coming towards her, this time from the direction of the gym. Tall, broad, with an athlete's swagger. Description fitted half of the guys that trained there. It wasn't Zac. Definitely wasn't.

'Hey. Again.'

It was.

Now they were standing three feet apart, with the door of an Audi A3 between them, yet the breach seemed so much wider.

'Are you OK?' he asked her, to his credit seeming genuinely concerned.

'Of course, yes!' Talli went for breezy, but was very aware she might have hit 'slightly deranged and borderline hysterical'. What was she supposed to say? She'd discovered her family was on the edge of destitution, she'd soon have no home, her boyfriend was currently missing in action with a twenty-year-old aspiring star and she was planning a wedding that was swelling to such biblical proportions that pretty soon feeding them all would require a backup plan involving loaves and fishes.

Oh, and incidentally, she was going insane with guilt over the fact that she'd cheated on her boyfriend with a currently present hulk of physical perfection.

So it made perfect sense that she followed up the claim of contentment with 'Absolutely fine. You?'

'Yeah, I'm good.'

There was a toe-curlingly long pause as neither of them could find the words to express their level of discomfort with this situation.

Eventually Talli broke it. 'Well, I'd better go. Early meeting in the morning.'

'Yeah, me too. See you around.'

'Yep, see you,' Talli agreed, then slipped into the car, accelerated out of the car park and slammed the wheel while repeating the words 'Shit. Bugger. Shit' all the way to the hotel. After opening the door to her room, she walked directly to the bed and flopped down on it, tempted to put her head under the pillow and refuse to emerge until life took a turn for the better.

After a few moments, she got bored of waiting and phoned room service to order a pepperoni pizza and a large slice of banoffee pie instead.

This was torture. She now had a new respect for Dessi, who had been dealing with – in fact *encouraging* – this level of drama her whole life.

Domenic. She had to do something about Domenic. Even just speaking to him would make her feel so much better.

Without getting up from the bed, she slipped her hand to the floor, felt around for her bag, and once she had it, groped inside for her mobile phone. Holding it out in front of her, she pressed the speaker button and then speed-dialled Dom's number.

Answer. Please answer. Please know that I need to speak to you, to hear your voice. Just answer the phone.

'Hi!' Her spirits soared, and she was just about to babble a greeting when the message continued. 'This is Domenic Stritch-Leeson. I'm afraid I'm rocking out somewhere and can't take your call. You know what to do.'

Yes. She did. Toss the phone back into her bag and return her head to the under-pillow position.

The plan was foiled by a knock at the door. Room service was on the ball tonight.

Lunging off the bed, she grabbed a couple of pound coins from the tip stash on the dresser, swung the door open and . . .

'Oh.'

'Hey.'

Zac. And no sign of either a pepperoni pizza or a banoffee pie.

Their eyes connected, this time the silence neither uncomfortable nor awkward.

'I've no idea what I'm doing here,' he said softly.

'Me neither,' Talli replied, the words catching in her throat.

Another pause.

Then Talli Caston-Jones stepped back and let Zac Parker trespass on her life for the second time.

Chapter Thirty

The door hadn't even swung shut when he reached for her, put his hand on the side of her neck, his thumb on her cheek and pressed his lips down on hers, his urgency reciprocated by the hands that found their way under the back of his T-shirt.

'I need you,' he said simply, holding her against the wall now, her hands above her head as he peeled up her gym vest and unzipped the front-fastening sports bra. When her breasts were unleashed, he leant down, taking them in his mouth, one, then the other, listening to her groan her approval. She kicked off her trainers; he did the same, then pulled his own T-shirt above his head, returning his lips to hers before the top even hit the floor.

He pushed her hands above her head again. 'Leave them there,' he whispered, before moving downwards, once again stopping to kiss her breasts and take her nipples in his mouth, circling with his tongue, nibbling with his teeth.

More groans, this time from them both.

Down further, he hooked a finger into the waistband of her gym shorts and pulled them off, revealing the simple strip of hair between her legs. Once again she gasped as his tongue went there for a few tantalising moments before he stretched back up to standing.

'I haven't showered since the gym,' Talli murmured.

'I don't care,' he told her honestly, loving the musky taste of sweat on her skin.

'I do,' she chided him, smiling.

'Demanding,' he observed.

'It's the new me,' she countered, biting his bottom lip. 'But it only seems to happen when you're around.'

Taking his hand, she led him to the bathroom, pulled open the glass and chrome pivot door of the shower and flipped the lever, releasing jets of water that gushed from the rain shower head.

Their lips pressed together again, he slid off his own shorts before following her inside, watching her throw back her head, eyes closed as the warm water soaked her face and hair. He was about to lift her on to his stiff, waiting cock when he realised he didn't have a condom. Damn. But then none of this had been planned, and until he'd actually knocked on the door he still hadn't been sure if he'd have the nerve to do it.

Turned out the condom issue didn't matter, because Talli had other plans.

She sank to her knees and took all of him in her mouth, sliding her lips back and forward across the shaft of his cock, sucking with every stroke. The sensation of her mouth and the water was incredible, and it was all he could do not to come right there and then.

But no, he wanted this to last so much longer.

Gently he pulled himself from her, and steadied her as she rose to her feet again. 'God, I want to be inside you, but I don't have a condom.'

Her face fell, then instantly the corners of her mouth headed upwards again. 'The bathroom cabinet! I saw a couple in there. The hotel provides them. Very conscientious of them.' She was playing with him now, her arms around his neck, kissing him between words.

He disentangled himself, put one foot outside the shower for balance, reached into the mirrored vanity unit and returned with a condom.

Talli swiftly snatched it from him and put it on the chrome shelf to her left, swapping it for a huge bar of soap. 'Don't move,' she whispered, as she took the bar and lathered him from his neck to his feet, then worked her way upwards again, rotating around his body easily despite the confined space of the shower. When she got to his cock, she slowly ran the bar along it, then again, this time circling it in a spiralling motion. Again. And again. Until the urge to come had returned and he had to fight it by clenching his teeth and stepping backwards out of her reach.

He reached for a bottle of shampoo and squeezed a

circle into his hand, then let it drip on to her hair, watching her smile with enjoyment as he massaged it into her scalp, before moving her head back into the stream of water and rinsing it away. Only then did he take the soap from her hand and repeat the cleansing ritual she had performed on him. Soaping her shoulders, her breasts, her stomach then down to her pussy, slipping his fingers inside her, making her bite his chest as she moaned.

When every bit of her was covered in soap, he turned her round and placed her hands against the shower wall, his own hands sliding over her skin as he stretched around to massage her soapy breasts.

'So good, Zac, so good,' she repeated countless times, her voice low with longing.

Only when he was sure he could enter her without coming immediately did he take the condom from the shelf, tear it open and slip it on. Then, pulling her hips back towards him, he entered her from behind, his mouth on her shoulder, sucking in time with his thrusts.

Every synapse in his brain raced pleasure signals around his body, making his nerve endings feel like they were on the outside of his skin.

The water soaked them, running over his head and down over his face, dripping from his nose and chin as he threw his head back. 'Talli. Oh fuck, Talli.'

'Now, Zac. Don't stop. Come now. Right now. I'm . . .'

He jerked her tighter to him, his pelvis hard against her ass, then roared as the ferocity of the spasms that ripped through her trapped his cock in a vice. It was all he needed. His hands quickly left her hips and enveloped her, holding her tightly, his mouth on the side of her neck as he came in long, glorious, leg-trembling waves.

As they both sank to the floor, their limbs entwined, he reached over and kissed her, holding his lips perfectly still against hers for a long, long time. It had never been like this. And he wasn't sure it would ever be again.

Eventually unlocking their mouths, Talli reached up and switched the water off, then brought her head down to rest on his shoulder, staying like that until their skin started to show goose bumps.

'You're cold,' he told her.

'But I don't want to move,' she said simply.

He pushed open the pivot door, grabbed a thick white towel from the back of the door and wrapped it around her, then for the second time that day carried a woman from a bathroom.

But this time was different.

This time he carried her to the bed, pulled back the duvet and gently placed her down, then climbed in beside her, their bodies automatically finding a way to merge. He kissed her, softly at first, then more urgently, rolling on top of her, supporting his weight on his elbows.

'Again?' she laughed.

'Again,' he told her, before pausing to listen to a muffled sound coming from somewhere in the corner.

'Is that your phone ringing?' he asked her.

'It's OK,' she told him. 'I'll get it later.'

Chapter Thirty~one

'Talli, I have to go,' he murmured.

After a half-hearted attempt to creak both eyes open, she settled on a one-eyed squint. He was standing at the side of the bed, dressed in the shorts and T-shirt he'd arrived in last night. The very thought of his face at the door sent a shiver of adrenalin coursing through her. It was enough to get the other eye open.

'What time is it?'

'Eight o'clock. I've got a client at half past.'

It was a struggle, but she managed to raise her shoulders from the mattress. 'Bugger, I have to get up too. I'm due at Highdrow at ten. And I'm guessing I don't look like Professional Wedding Planner of the Year,' she added, gesturing to her hair and face.

She loved it when he laughed. In fact, there were many things about the last ten hours that she'd loved. They'd shared the pizza and the banoffee pie while watching old

274

episodes of *Friends* on Comedy Central. They'd drunk a couple of beers from the minibar and then he'd used the last of his to . . . It was probably too early in the morning to revisit that thought, but she'd definitely loved it. Later, they'd fallen asleep, naked, and slept that way all night. It struck her that she was twenty-three years old and she'd never slept naked all night with a guy. Domenic said he was wary in case it gave him a chill.

Domenic. The phone. It had rung last night when they were . . . well, busy, and she hadn't even checked to see if it was him.

'I have to go.' Zac leaned over and kissed her yet again. 'I'm not sorry I came last night. I know it's complicated for you, but I hope you're OK with it too.'

'I'm OK.'

'Sure?' His voice was full of concern.

'I'm sure.'

Picking up his bag, he came back for one more kiss, then he was gone. The duvet was so tempting and she came close to just snuggling back down and nodding off to sleep again, but anxiety kicked in just as her eyes began to close. Missing the meeting with Trevor at Highdrow would be a huge mistake. Every detail of this wedding had to be checked, double-checked and then checked again. The pressure had been racked up yet another notch by the fact that this was going to be her family's last cause for celebration for a long, long time. If it was all going to go horrifically wrong for them, the least she could do was to make sure that they had the memory of an incredible wedding. It was down to her, and that thought made her tremble. For Edwina and Simmy's sake, for the sake of her dad and Dessi, for the sake of her mother's newly formed face, she couldn't let them down.

She pulled on the oversize Dallas Cowboys T-shirt she normally wore in bed and staggered to the bathroom, carefully avoiding looking at her reflection in the mirror. There was only so much stress she could take in the morning. As she poured a glass of water from the tap, she noticed that Zac had picked up all the towels they'd left scattered around, folded them and put them in a neat pile on the counter.

In her peripheral vision she noticed a discarded condom wrapper in the tiled corner and swiftly grabbed it and stuck it in the bin. The action spurred another thought. Going back into the bedroom, she searched the room and spotted what she was looking for. One, two condom wrappers, one of them sitting on top of the ice bucket. It was probably best that she had no idea how it had got there.

She mentally ran through events in her mind. Shower. Bed. Bed again. Bath. With a phone call to housekeeping to send reinforcements halfway through. Oh, the shame. The staff room would be abuzz with rumours about the raging nymphomaniac in room 61.

But there should definitely be four condoms.

A knock at the door interrupted her search. 'Room service!'

She was about to answer that she hadn't ordered any when she realised Zac must have done it before he left. Sweet. Thoughtful. Grabbing three pound coins from the tips pile on the dresser, she swung open the door. The first thing she saw was a brown McDonald's bag. The second was the smiling face of Domenic Stritch-Leeson.

'Surprise!' he said. And there, right at the last minute, came the third and final nomination for Biggest Understatement in a Drama.

'Dom! What are you doing here? I mean, hi!'

He stepped forward, picked her up and swung her around, stopping halfway with a loud 'Ouch!' Then, 'Bugger, think I pulled something there,' he winced, rubbing the small of his back.

'Come in. Come in!' Talli stuttered, standing back to let a bloke past her for the second time in twelve hours. A room service waiter heading down the corridor caught her eye and winked. There was another story for the staff room rumour mill.

Domenic had plumped himself down on the unmade bed – God, just the thought of him sitting where she'd been with Zac made her feel physically sick – and pulled off his denim jacket to reveal a retro Ramones T-shirt underneath. Talli had bought him it on his last birthday. Another wave of nausea hit. What the hell had she been doing?

'Are you feeling all right, darling? Look awfully pale.'

'Just a stomach bug, I think,' she replied, gesturing to the room service tray. 'Or maybe the pepperoni pizza.'

'You ate a whole pizza? You're unbelievable!'

Not strictly by myself, no. Actually, I only ate half. The rest was eaten by another man. After he shagged me until I couldn't feel several muscle groups.

Naturally, none of this was vocalised. Instead she said, 'I'll be right back,' and ran into the bathroom. She stood with her forehead against the cold tile until she was sure she wasn't actually going to vomit, then quickly jumped in the shower, brushed her teeth, pulled on a robe and was back out in the bedroom in five minutes.

Domenic was still on the bed, flicking through the channels on the TV. 'Six porn channels, darling,' he said with a suggestive grin. 'You could be having a wild old time here with this lot.'

Not trusting herself to come out with any form of intelligent reply, Talli offered the best smile she could muster and distracted herself with the business of pulling on her jeans, then searching in the wardrobe for a clean top. She settled for her favourite white shirt, adding a black leather belt, her trusty biker boots and a long silver necklace that jangled down almost to the bottom of her shirt. Den had jokingly told her that she was as far removed from an Essex girl as it was possible to get. She took that as a hint to smarten up and put a bit more effort into her clothes, but hadn't got around to actually doing anything about it yet.

'You still haven't told me why you're here,' she said casually. 'Not that it's not wonderful to see you, because it is. It really is.'

'Just a pit stop,' he told her, clicking off the TV and turning so that he was lying on one side in the tangle of sheets. Oh God, the tangle. If she didn't get him out of here soon, she was going to pass out.

'I finished up in Norway last night, flew into Gatwick this morning and my flight to Courchevel doesn't leave until tonight. What else could I do but come and see my girl?'

'Oh. Right. And, erm, how did the sessions in Norway go?'

'Great,' he enthused. 'Absolutely first class. That girl is the next—'

'Amy Winehouse. Yep, I heard.'

Talli grabbed her wedding folder, shoved it in her bag and cast her eyes around for the room key. 'Thing is, though, darling,' she said as she searched her pockets, 'I've got a meeting at Highdrow today that will take most of the day and I really can't change it.'

His expression turned almost mutinous. 'But I'm only in town for a few hours,' he objected. 'Surely you can reschedule?'

'I would love to. Absolutely. But we're on such a tight deadline and everyone involved is meeting me there in . . .' she checked her watch, 'less than an hour, so it's too late to cancel.'

Her subconscious added, and I have to get you out of here before the throbbing blood vessels in my head explode.

'Bugger,' he said, his irritation clear. Rising from the

bed – finally, thank God – he reached for his grey canvas Diesel man bag. 'Well, I suppose I'll tag along with you then.'

'Sure!' Anything to get him out of here. Anything.

He pulled open the buckle on his bag and opened it wide, searching for something inside.

'But before we go, darling . . . Well, this isn't exactly how I'd planned it. I was going to take you out to lunch and maybe for a walk in a park, or . . . do they have parks out here?'

'Erm, yes,' Talli replied, confused, yet feeling a tiny sliver of dread starting at her toes. Surely he wasn't . . . oh fuck.

A little red box. In his hand. Flipped open now. A huge ring inside. Details blurry as panic was making her vision fade in and out.

'Well, look, I'll make it more romantic another day, but Talli, darling, I've been thinking about you so much while I've been away. Really soul-searching. And I know now that I absolutely want to spend the rest of my life with you. Every minute of every day. Talli, my love, will you marry me?'

Chapter Thirty~two

Zac had hated lying to her, but telling Talli the truth hadn't been an option. There had been two more phone calls on the flat's answering machine yesterday and one on his mobile this morning. Thankfully Talli hadn't noticed because his phone had been switched to silent. That was when he realised that he had to deal with this today. Now.

His grip on the wheel of his car got tighter as he drove, his fury escalating with every mile.

Bastards.

Anger didn't come often to him. After his mum had left, Dot had been so worried that he'd lash out or develop rage issues that she'd enrolled him in a boxing club and a martial arts academy, forcing him to divert any negative emotions into sport. No amount of judo or tae kwon do could defuse the lump of fury that was stuck in his gut this morning.

The clock on the dashboard clicked to nine o'clock. Early, but there was no way he could go another day with the harassment and this hanging over him.

The rain lashed against the windscreen as he negotiated the last of the morning rush-hour traffic, finally reaching his destination on the outskirts of Chelmsford, a unit in an old industrial estate that was mostly populated with disused warehouses and crumbling offices, all of them with grilles on the windows and metal roller shutters on the doors. It was as bleak as it got.

Skidding to a stop, he pulled on the handbrake and sat back in the seat for a moment, forcing himself to calm down. Much as he wanted more than anything else in the world right now to go in there and kill the smug bastards, he wasn't stupid enough to do it. It would only make matters so much worse. How could he fix this if he was banged up? Not to mention that it would break Dot's heart and she'd no doubt follow up his incarceration with a swift slap across the back of the head.

When his heart rate had declined to something near normal, he took a deep breath and climbed out of the car, still fighting to control his temper as he pushed open the steel door.

Behind it was exactly the same scene as the one and only time he'd been here before.

The smoke-yellowed walls were filthy, the rank, patchy carpet reeked of years of use. On a threadbare couch to his left sat two men, both of them overdeveloped, with the pockmarked faces that told of years of steroid abuse. One of them gorged on a bacon roll, the other didn't even bother to look up from the porn mag on which he balanced a white polystyrene cup of tea.

In front of him, another man, behind an ancient desk, patches of its wood veneer missing, legs held on with gaffer tape. This one bore no physical resemblance to the other two. His greasy hair was swept back, failing to cover his bald patch and sticking out in random tufts over the neck of his shirt. His emaciated face was close in colour to the yellow of the walls and in his hand was a cigarette, almost burnt down to his brown-stained fingers.

Zac wanted, really, really wanted, to take it and stub it out in a way that would make him scream.

The man behind the desk smiled as Zac stepped into the room.

'Mr Parker, what a surprise. Always like it when we get visitors, don't we, chaps?' He spoke to the two hulks in a languorous East End drawl.

'We had an agreement,' Zac told him, his calculated speech masking his ever-growing urge to take the slimy bastard's head and force it, at speed, towards the desk. Repeatedly.

'And we still do,' he was told.

'So what's with the phone calls? Part of the agreement was no contact until the seventh of January. That was what we agreed.'

'We did. Let's just call the phone calls friendly reminders.'

'You are fucking scum,' Zac hissed, dangerously close to losing it.

The man behind the desk held his hands up, clearly amused by this little interruption at the start of his day. 'Look, Mr Parker, I think you're overlooking the facts here. We provide a service. That service was called upon for an agreed fee. That fee is now due to be paid. I think that's entirely reasonable, isn't it, lads?'

On cue, the other two nodded.

Zac took a few more steps towards the desk. One of the goons made to rise, but the boss held up a hand, gesturing him to leave it.

Zac leaned on the desk, his face only inches away from those repulsively stained teeth, the smell turning his stomach.

'You will get your money. You will get it when we agreed. And every penny will be there. But if I receive another phone call in the meantime, I will come back here and I'll take his porn mag and insert it where it will need surgery to be removed. Stay away from me. Stay away from my family. Do you understand?'

This was more than crossing a line, it was pole-vaulting so far over it he couldn't even see the line any more, but he didn't care. He'd had enough. And if he was going to suffer repercussions for it later, he'd deal with them then. Right now, he just wanted to make sure they both knew exactly where they stood.

'I understand, Mr Parker,' the other man replied, with a well-practised edge of menace. 'But I hope you do too.

The money, here, on the seventh of January, or the consequences are going to be the kind of hell that you couldn't even begin to imagine. And now that we've got that sorted out . . .' His new smile was even more chilling than his threats. '. . . get the fuck out of my office and don't come back until you're ready to pay.'

Chapter Thirty-three

Speechless.

Domenic sat there on the bed, looking at her expectantly.

Still speechless.

'Talli?' he said, more to jolt her out of her stupor than anything.

'Oh God, Domenic, I'm so sorry, you've just totally taken me by surprise and I'm still half asleep and . . . It feels like I'm dreaming this.'

And not in a good way, she realised.

She plumped down next to him and he instantly paled. 'Grapefruit,' he said. 'Did you just use shampoo with grapefruit? Eurgh, that sets off my sinuses.'

'Sorry. I . . . forgot.'

'Anyway, darling, I know it's a bit of a shock, but after five years we know what we want, don't we? We should probably have got round to doing this ages ago.'

'It's just such a . . . huge step.'

Talli's mind hurled from panic to despair. What to say? She had to tell him. She really did. But looking at his face now, she honestly didn't have the heart to do it. What a coward. Suddenly, the pressure of the last few weeks overwhelmed her and she felt the tears spring to her eyes, then rapidly coughed them away. She had no right to feel sorry for herself, not when she'd behaved so terribly. She'd absolutely betrayed him and there was nothing else to do but confess everything and hope that he could forgive her. But . . . oh God, she couldn't do this to her parents. Not now. Not two weeks before the wedding, when they were all coming up to one of the most special events in their lives. Not when it was all going to go so horribly wrong afterwards.

There was absolutely no doubt in her heart that she loved Dom. But then there was also absolutely no doubt that she hadn't loved him enough to close the door to Zac.

She'd messed up so completely and right now she felt like the lowest of the low.

'Dom, I have to get going to this meeting, so can we talk about this later? Properly? When I'm not rushing away. It's just that . . .' She scrabbled for words. 'I feel like I'm not giving you the romantic moment that this should be. Stuff has happened – with my family and this wedding and . . . well, just so much really. I want to tell you about it all and then perhaps we can start this conversation again.'

He looked momentarily surprised, then quickly recovered. 'Of course, darling,' he smiled. 'Let's go. Let's get all this stuff out of the way and then we can have dinner before I head back to the airport. Is there a good fish restaurant near here?'

'I'm sure there is. I'll ask around today. Are you sure you want to come with me?'

The thought of him being by her side all day made her nerves jangle, but the image of him lying in this room where only a few hours ago . . .

'Of course, darling.'

Thank God.

With her bag fully loaded on her shoulder, she pulled open the door and then waited until he was past. That was when she saw it. Sitting on top of one of the two reading lamps on either side of the headboard was one bright red foil condom wrapper.

'Let's go.'

If he noticed that her voice was a high trill, he didn't mention it.

An hour later, they pulled up outside Highdrow and ran inside, shielding themselves from the pouring rain with an umbrella they found in the back of the Audi.

'If I get a cold now, I'll be bloody furious,' Dom told her in the hall, as they shook off errant droplets of water.

'Domenic!' Trevor's greeting was warm and effusive.

'Bloody hell, Trev, it's been ages.'

'Oh. I didn't know you two knew each other.'

'Same hockey team. Years ago. Before I discovered

crack and the joys of hedonism,' Trevor told her, sighing wistfully. 'How I miss the gutter. Normal life is highly overrated.'

For the first time since Zac had walked out of her hotel room, she felt a little ray of levity. The thought resonated, and she realised that as long as she was in company, she wouldn't have to face the inevitable. It took a bit of manipulation, but she managed to drag a three-hour meeting out to five, then suggested Trevor join them for a late lunch at a local themed restaurant afterwards. The only fish they sold came in batter. Domenic ordered a Caesar salad, dressing on the side, and they sat for a couple of hours afterwards nursing coffee and swapping stories of mutual friends.

By the time they dropped Trevor off at Highdrow and headed back to Chelmsford, the late afternoon darkness was closing in and the temperature had dropped to close to freezing.

'We're going to pass the salon, so I'll just nip in and ask Edwina to recommend a restaurant for dinner.'

It was an attempt to delay the inevitable that came with little risk, she'd decided. The girls were shooting in Spa Shiraz, so even if Zac was in the gym, there would be a flight of stairs and several walls between them.

Domenic automatically assumed that he was invited and jumped out of the car. Talli didn't correct him, aware that it would delay even further the moment when they were alone together and back on the subject of that ring.

The door of the salon jangled as she pushed it open. She immediately spotted Edwina, locked in conversation over at the nail bar with Shiraz and, although she could only see the back view, she was guessing it was Kiki.

The camera crew were setting up the lighting and dotted around the room the other cast members studied sheets of paper in front of them. Lena was the first to notice Talli's arrival and stood up to give her a hug. 'All right, honey? Haven't seen you for days. Thought you'd had a better offer and deserted us.'

Talli fought to stop her laugh descending into ironic hysteria. 'No, just been busy. You know, with the wedding.'

'Why don't we have lunch this week? Get a proper catch-up. You up for that, Minx? Porsche?' she said to the two girls nearest to her.

'A hundred per cent,' said Minx, as Porsche nodded in agreement. Talli was going to miss them when she left, but she couldn't help thinking that they wouldn't be so friendly if they knew what she'd done. She had shagged the boyfriend of one of their group. They'd hate her. And Lena and Minx – Zac was their brother! They'd be absolutely mortified.

Belatedly, she noticed that the girls' gazes were flicking between her and Domenic, their perfectly formed eyebrows raised in anticipation. 'Sorry! This is my boyfriend, Domenic. Domenic, this is Lena, Minx and Porsche.'

Dom's eyes widened as the three girls, all stunning, all smiling and all showing cleavage that could be used to harness a flagpole, waved their hellos.

'So you're the one that buggered off with some singer and left this lady all alone,' Lena teased. 'You're lucky she's still here. They're queuing up in that gym to ogle those muscles.'

She gave Talli's biceps a squeeze as the three of them laughed. Dom joined in, a little hesitantly. Meanwhile, Talli wondered if there was anyone in the room who was medically qualified and could resuscitate her when she fainted.

'How was Luna?' Porsche asked, going on to explain the background to Dom. 'She went out with my brother's pal when he was a club promoter.'

Domenic nodded. 'Yah, she's . . . she's very talented. Definitely the next . . .'

'Amy Winehouse,' Porsche finished for him. 'Yeah, they've been saying that since she was doing talent shows when she was twelve. I heard she tried out for *X Factor*. Didn't get in. Must have been thirteen or fourteen. She's much better now, though. I bet it was Dannii Minogue that knocked her back.'

Despite herself, Talli was actually enjoying this little exchange. When it came to local gossip, Porsche had encyclopaedic knowledge. 'She was, like, so confident, though. Ruthless. Like Madonna, only she's not the same age as my nan.'

Dom's coughing fit lasted at least ten seconds, before he wafted away some invisible toxic cloud. 'Allergies,' he explained. 'Must be the hairspray.'

'Talli, darling! And Domenic – what the fuck are you doing here, my lovely?'

291

Edwina crossed the room like a six-foot missile, locked on Domenic, who was still trying to regain his composure.

'Just passing through on the way to dinner,' he stammered eventually. 'Thought we'd pop in and say hello.'

'Aren't you supposed to be up a bloody big mountain somewhere? Never saw the point of skiing. Up a hill, back down a hill. Really? Far more important things to be getting on with in life.'

'How's the drama queen doing?' Porsche asked, gesturing over at the nail bar, where Kiki and Shiraz were still sitting. 'Have the tears dried up yet or should we ask her agent to set up an endorsement deal with Kleenex?'

'Porsche . . .' Lena said softly. 'Give her a break.'

'What's happened?' Talli asked, clutching at the opportunity to keep the subject off the next Amy Winehouse, but unsure if they were referring to Kiki or Shiraz. Oh God. What if it was Kiki? What if Kiki had found out about . . . No. Zac would have warned her. Surely he would have let her know? Despite the heat of the lights, she was suddenly cold to the core.

'It's Kiki,' Porsche said, with a roll of the eyes. 'We think Zac has finally seen sense and made a bid for escape.'

'Porsche, come on. Don't—' Lena tried to stop her.

'Lena, it's true. Her ego gives the rest of us a bad name. She totally acts like a bitch and then everyone thinks we're all like that. And we're not. Well, except

292

Shiraz, but that's 'cause she likes being a bitch. Anyway, Kiki says it was her who ended it.'

'It was her – Zac told us that, didn't he, Minx?' Lena sought confirmation from her sister, who nodded. 'Yeah, he said they talked about it yesterday and she decided it wasn't working any more. Still hard for her, though – they've been together for ages.'

Talli tried desperately to process the information, but no matter which way she interpreted it, she reached the same conclusion. Zac Arrogant Prick Parker had got dumped by his girlfriend yesterday, then came to her for a cheer-up shag.

And she'd fallen for it.

What an idiot.

What a raging bloody fool she'd been.

To her right, Edwina and Domenic were deep in conversation. She caught his eye, sick with another wave of realisation as to what she'd done.

How could she?

'Darling, Edwina has given me directions to a restaurant not far from here.' He consulted the Rolex on his wrist, a twenty-first present from his parents. 'If we go now, we'll have time for dinner before I need to head off.'

Later, she'd be unable to recollect the car journey. She would struggle to remember the face of the person who seated them, or the decor on the walls. Domenic spending several minutes in negotiations while ordering his food would be a blur.

Her only vivid memory would be him pulling out the ring box once again, and her looking properly this time at the large square sapphire surrounded by diamonds. It was so far removed from the thin silver band she currently wore as her only piece of jewellery. But the ring didn't matter.

'Marry me,' he said.

For the rest of her life she'd remember the weight of pressure not to hurt or disappoint him, not to devastate their parents and add to the heartache her mum and dad were about to face.

It was the right thing to do, and all her life, other than two completely out-of-character incidents, Talli had always done the right thing.

'Yes,' she said.

Chapter Thirty-four

The first clue was the banging at the door at six o'clock on a Sunday morning. It was the only day he didn't start early, due to the fact that most other people had better things to do than sweat in the gym at that time of the weekend.

He grabbed his phone and headed for the door, ready to press 999 if it was his favourite goon friends doing a house call. After checking the spy hole, he immediately swung the door open.

'Lena! What's up? Is it Auntie Dot? What's happened? Why didn't you let yourself in?'

His sister covered her eyes with the stack of papers she was holding in her hand. 'Your keys were in the other side of the door, Auntie Dot's fine, but eeeew – eye burn! Weren't those made illegal sometime in the nineties?'

He looked down at the tiny briefs he was wearing and groaned with embarrassment. 'I'm working such long hours, I'm behind with the washing. They were all I had left.'

He reached for the towel on the kitchen island, attempted to wrap it around his waist and realised it was a tea towel.

'Hang on, I'll be back in a minute.'

He disappeared into the bedroom and returned moments later wearing a pair of jeans, running his fingers through his dark blond hair.

'A T-shirt was a step too far?' Lena asked drily.

'All in the wash as well. Honestly, I'm down to three jumpers and a parka. Anyway. Pot. Kettle. Have you seen your get-up?'

It would seem his sister viewed a bright orange Victoria Beckham dress with shoulder strapping as appropriate outwear for a Sunday morning visit.

'Shut up! I haven't been home yet. We didn't get out of the Beach Box until after three, then we went to an all-night café for coffee, then I went to Max's for an hour . . .'

'Too much information!' he told her.

'And then I picked up the early papers at the petrol station and . . . OK, don't freak. I mean, you are going to freak, but don't go completely off on one.'

In the time it had taken her to explain, he'd made two cappuccinos using his black and chrome Dolce Gusto coffee machine. He handed one over to her.

'Kiki?' he asked, knowing that the Sunday press was her biggest target of the week. 'Man, what's she done now?' he said wearily. Not that it affected him any more, but he still cared about her, still wanted her to be happy.

Lena put down a copy of the *Sunday News*, the biggest-selling tabloid in the country, the one that had chosen to bombard the British paper-buying public with the headline: MY PREGNANCY HELL – DUMPED BY LOVER by Kiki Spooner. Underneath was a picture of Kiki sitting on her bed in her mum's house, wearing a long white jumper and matching socks, her bare legs crossed, her sad face resting on her knees. Next to it was a smaller picture, a grainy one of Zac sitting on the guy who'd pulled out the scissors and tried to cut Kiki's hair that day when they were leaving Perfect boutique.

It was the sub-heading that delivered the killer blow: *Pregnant reality babe deserted by thug only days before Christmas!*

'Fuck,' was the only word he could manage for a good ten seconds or so. Then, 'But it must be a set-up – there's no way she would have done this. For a start, it's not fucking true.'

Lena took a sip of her coffee before speaking. 'That picture has been taken in the last few days. She bought that jumper last week when she was out with me and Minx.'

No. None of this made sense at all. It had to be a mistake. Why would Kiki be so crazy as to make this up? And if she hadn't made it up, why hadn't she told him, given him a chance to help her? It couldn't be true. This paper had to have set it up. Or made a mistake. Or . . . was he actually going to be a dad?

'Is she . . . is she pregnant? Is that bit true?'

Lena shrugged her shoulders. 'I dunno, Zac. I phoned Shiraz on the way here 'cause her and Kiki always come on at the same time, but we couldn't work out if she mentioned it last month. Shouldn't you know?'

Both hands were in his hair now, running back and forward, trying to help his brain make some kind of sense of this.

'Yeah, I should, but . . . things have been really crap in that area for the last couple of months. To tell you the truth, it's all been crap for a while. That's why I asked her to go. Did you do what I said? Tell everyone else it was her who ended it?'

Lena nodded. 'Yep, me and Minx told everyone that story. She was saying that anyway so it wasn't such a stretch. Look, Zac, I didn't want to say anything before 'cause she was your girlfriend, but she's, like, a real devious cow. She lies constantly about everything. Nothing that comes out her mouth is true.'

'But why this? Why?'

Lena put her mug down, reached over and gave him a spontaneous hug, before carrying on, her voice thick with concern. 'For what it's worth, the rest of us were expecting her to pull a major "victim" stunt. Too many rumours were going around about her being a total bitch and she needed to soften up public opinion again. Guess this was one way of doing it. Girl's got no shame, Zac. Wish you'd seen that before.'

He pulled out a bar stool from under the counter, sat down and turned to the next page for the full story. The details were incredible.

Kiki Spooner wept with joy when the blue line appeared on the pregnancy test. It was the baby she'd longed for and she thought long-term lover Zac Parker felt the same.

The actress and TV star (22) had been forced to conceal her relationship with Parker (25) for the sake of her role in hit show Lovin' Essex. *One of the original stars of the show, her on-air relationship with Toby Mallard was a ploy to cover up her off-screen long-term love, who refused to be associated with her career.*

'He never wanted me to be a star,' Kiki said last night. 'I honestly think he was jealous of all the attention I was getting. People would stop me in the streets and I've had approaches from many famous names, but I was never unfaithful to him. I loved him.'

Kiki sobs quietly, the pain of her trauma etched on the face of the woman voted the Hottest Chick on Reality TV.

The heartbreak becomes even more apparent when she tells of how her thug boyfriend reacted to the news that she was pregnant.

'I thought he'd be happy, I really did. We'd talked about it so many times – even had names picked out. But when I told him, he said he wasn't ready to have a family. I couldn't believe what I was hearing. I had to leave. I

couldn't bring a baby up knowing that he didn't want us there.

'I'm back with my mum and dad now and I know they'll take care of me. Me and my baby will be fine. I'll love it enough for the two of us.'

Little is known about Zac Parker. The brother of Kiki's Lovin' Essex *co-stars Minx and Lena Parker, he was brought up by his aunt after being abandoned by his mother as a child.*

Parker was questioned by police after he attacked student Jason Hinds, who had approached the star to ask for her autograph. Mr Hinds said last night, 'The way he went for me violated every right I have as a human. He was like an animal and I am consulting with legal advisers with a view to suing him. People like that need to be stopped.'

Kiki agrees. Devastated as she is over this traumatic time in her personal life, she seeks consolation in the fact that her career continues to go from strength to strength. Her Christmas calendar is currently outselling the other Lovin' Essex *stars by two to one, and her range of glitter gel bra inserts have taken the cleavages of the nation by storm.*

'I'm also launching a new thong line and a range of car accessories. I need to work harder than ever now because I'm determined to give my baby the best life possible.'

With that, Kiki wipes away the tears and wraps up the interview, ready to head off for another Lovin' Essex *shoot.*

Parker was unavailable for comment last night.

*Kiki's Elevation Cleavage Enhancers are on sale now
– for a list of stockists see www.kikispooner.com.*

'Christ, what has she done? Not one thing in this story
is true.' Zac's voice was barely audible, his throat strangled by the shock of what he'd read. 'Does Minx know
about this?'

'Yeah. She's up some bloody hill somewhere, but she'll
be back later today. I've warned Dale to keep her locked
in the house, because if she meets Kiki, it won't end
well.'

Even the fact that his sisters were so protective and
supportive didn't raise Zac's spirits. He prepared himself
to ask the hardest question of all.

'Does Auntie Dot know?'

Lena shook her head. 'Nope, she was up the bingo
last night with the rest of her crew. She'll still be in bed.'

'Thank God. Will you come with me? We'd better get
over and tell her about it before she hears from someone
else.'

'Only if you put a top on. And not the parka.' Lena
tried to lighten the mood, but it was hopeless. Zac felt
like his guts had been ripped out.

'Look, Zac, in the big scale of things, it doesn't really
matter, does it? Who cares what anyone else thinks?
Everyone you care about knows it's a pile of crap.'

Not everyone. Talli would read this and she'd think
every word of it was true, and he realised, without a
single doubt, that he cared what she thought.

'Anyway,' Lena continued, 'it'll all blow over in a few days.'

'Not if she's pregnant,' he answered. Pregnant. A dad. That was the thing about this story that hurt the most. He knew what it felt like to grow up with absent parents and he'd never, under any circumstances, desert his kid. 'Shit, how could she say that stuff?' he said again.

The buzzer for the security door downstairs rang and Lena turned to check the camera.

'Hate to tell you, bruv, but I think you're about to find out. Will I let her in?'

Chapter Thirty-five

The noise of the tray clinking at the other side of the door woke Talli up before the accompanying knock. Reaching over to her right, she switched on the overhead reading light. This hotel had been home for so long now, she was actually going to feel weird waking up anywhere else.

The early morning call had been booked because this was her last day here and she wanted to get everything packed up. Trevor had very kindly offered her a bedroom at Highdrow Castle for the rest of the week, and she was free to arrive any time after two, when the wedding guests from the night before would have vacated their rooms.

Taking her last few pound coins from the dresser, she opened the door to let Jack, the morning room service waiter, enter. She thought he was a lovely, hard-working boy who was a credit to his family. Thanks to staff room gossip, he thought she was a high-class hooker who used to date one of the minor royals and was now on the game to fund a coke habit.

'Morning,' he said with a wink, and Talli thought again how friendly he was and decided to leave a nice comment about him on the guest feedback card. She wrote it in her head while he was putting the tray down on the end of the bed: 'Very accommodating and always goes the extra mile to ensure guest satisfaction.'

Tip given, she waited until the door closed behind her before crawling back on to the bed and pouring a coffee from the large pot on the tray. A chunk was liberated from the bowl of fresh pineapple, and toast was next – two thick slices that she slathered with butter and jam. May as well enjoy her last couple of hours here and her last week or so of luxury, ever aware that the only pine-apple she'd be able to afford in a couple of weeks' time would come out of a tin. Worry about that particular subject had been deferred for now. She'd made the decision that if she was going to get through the next week without ending up rocking backwards and forward in the foetal position, she had to compartmentalise her prob-lems and deal with the issues on a priority basis. Right now, her number one priority was Edwina and Simmy's wedding. When that was taken care of, she'd open the vault containing the other trifling issues of her family's financial situation and the fact that she had somehow dealt with the guilt of being unfaithful by getting engaged.

That one threatened to escape the compartment into which it had been locked, so she quickly swallowed another chunk of pineapple and picked up the paper, looking for a distraction.

Her first reaction was that it must be some mistake – she'd definitely ordered the *Times*, but the *Sunday News* had been delivered.

Her second reaction was an involuntary gasp that came close to lodging a pineapple chunk in her trachea.

Kiki was pregnant. Zac was the father. He'd rejected the baby. She'd left him. And there, just to put the final cherry on top of the whole fuck-up of a cake, was that picture of him attacking the young man who had asked for Kiki's autograph.

Every word of the story burned into her brain, as she read about someone she didn't recognise in any way. His version of the incident with that young guy had been totally believable, but now, reading the other side of the story in black and white, she wasn't so sure.

Had she been a complete fool?

The guy she knew, however briefly, just wasn't capable of this stuff. He'd never attack anyone, never.

But then wasn't that what the families of serial killers always told the police?

Unable to eat any more, she pushed the tray away, sat back and closed her eyes. What a fool. Bad enough that she'd been unfaithful to Dom, even worse that she later found out that the second time was just a rebound shag for Zac, but now it seemed like she'd been with a guy who belonged on a Channel 4 documentary about the menaces on Britain's streets.

Her period of meditation didn't last long. Like a fixated spectator, she had to revisit the scene. It didn't sound any better the second time. Nor the third. By the fourth, she knew it almost verbatim, and still there wasn't a shred of evidence in his defence other than her gut instinct that this didn't describe the man she knew. Her mother's voice echoed in her head, giving her a dressing-down after Cosima Carlton's party and bemoaning her gullibility. Had she been ridiculously naive as well as rash and stupid? A new view of her future played out in her mind, in which she was destitute, Domenic dumped her, and she ended up an old lady who hit the headlines after marrying a lifer called Axeman Archie, whom she swore was innocent despite there being CCTV evidence to the contrary.

The insistent buzz of her mobile phone forced her to tear her eyes away and divert her frazzled brain to wondering who it could be at this time on a Sunday morning. Dessi, Dom and all the gang were still in Courchevel and not due home until the twenty-third. Her mother would be back on the same day. Her dad would be sleeping off his indulgences of the night before and she'd told Den she wouldn't be back in for a workout this week.

So that left . . .

'Hey, I'm on Skype. You around? Fxx'

Like an angel shipped in for the occasion by the powers of the internet, Fliss had charged in as the Malawian cavalry.

Talli quickly fired up her iPad and connected, just seconds later seeing her best friend's face on screen.

'Hello, my darling,' Fliss grinned, performing a cheery wave.

'Good morning!' Talli chirped back, attempting to infuse her words with enthusiasm and *joie de vivre*. 'How are you, Fliss? You look amazing!'

It wasn't a false platitude. Fliss's eyes were shining and her skin was tanned, her deep chestnut hair in two plaits, one falling over each shoulder.

'You'd better be careful. If my mother sees you looking so young and shiny, she'll be over there demanding a five-day spa break.'

Fliss roared with laughter. 'I'm loving it, Talls, I really am. Apart from a week ago last Wednesday when a random gang invaded the village, but the men pushed them back and they're gone now.'

'Oh, that's fine then. As long as the threat that you could be murdered in your sleep has passed for now,' Talli said, only half joking. The truth was she was terrified that something might happen to her friend, but if Fliss was determined to take the risk, Talli felt she had no right to introduce worry and fear into the equation.

'So tell me everything else,' Talli prompted, and then listened for ten minutes as Fliss updated her on every facet of her life there. It was only when she'd moved on to an explanation of their new irrigation system that she suddenly stopped.

'Hang on, you're doing that thing again, Talli,' she said suspiciously.

'What thing?'

'The thing where you keep someone talking, asking loads of questions, so that you won't have to get around to talking about yourself.'

'I'm not! So anyway, the water supply . . .'

'Talli! OK, what's going on?'

'Nothing. I'm just really happy to see your face and hear your voice. So tell me about the sustainable wells . . .'

'Talli, stop. What's happened? Tell me.'

Talli cracked, compelling her own personal irrigation system to send tears shooting to her eyes. 'Dom went away to Norway and I've met a guy here and I don't know how it happened but I slept with him. Twice. The first time it was because of a rock – it's a long story – but the second time I had no excuse and it was the best sex of my life, Fliss. He's so incredible and not just in bed but the way he touches me and holds me and the things he says and I can't stop thinking about him and then I found out that the second time we slept together his girlfriend had just dumped him so I was clearly a rebound shag and now he's all over the Sunday papers today because he's left his pregnant ex-girlfriend in the lurch and they're calling him an irresponsible thug and I can't stop thinking about it because I want to believe he's not, Fliss, I really do. I'm such a tit. Stupid, unfaithful tit.'

She finally stopped to draw breath. 'And in the middle of all that, my family has lost every penny they have and I somehow got engaged to Dom.'

Fliss sat open-mouthed, staring, for so long that Talli thought the screen had frozen again.

Eventually she recovered the power of speech.

'Talli, are you making any of that up as some kind of prank?'

Talli shook her head. 'You've no idea how much I wish it was a bad joke.'

'Bugger, I thought it was me who was living on the wild side. So hang on,' said Fliss, clearly trying to form this news into some kind of cohesive story. 'You slept with a rock star?'

'No! I slept with him because of a rock. Honestly, you don't want to know.'

'So who is the guy?'

'Zac.'

'OMG – the one from Essex that the girls pounced on a few weeks ago?'

Talli nodded. 'I know. How predictable am I?'

'Completely un-bloody-predictable by the sound of things.'

'I know, Fliss – I'm sorry. I really am.' She'd disappointed her best friend and she now officially wanted to crawl back under the duvet and stay there. She was a disgrace. And this was only a tiny taste of what would happen if her family and other friends found out.

'Don't you dare apologise!'

Talli lifted her head to see Fliss's face, pinched with annoyance.

'How great was the sex?'

'I don't have the words,' Talli said.

'Oh well, bugger it. Look, darling, if you ask me, it's

about bloody time. Your whole life you've done everything to please everyone else or look after people and they all take dreadful advantage of that. You're allowed to do as you bloody well please, Talli, you're twenty-three, not bloody sixty-three. This is when you *should* damn well be having riotous sex.'

'God, Fliss, I love you. Even if you're making no sense whatsoever.' Talli laughed through the tears.

'I am making sense. Great sex should be compulsory in life, so banish the guilt. Although dealing with it by getting engaged is a bit radical. Talk me through that one.'

'Are you sure you don't want to go back to discussing irrigation?'

'Talli!'

'OK, OK! Dom came here to surprise me and produced a ring and all I could think about was not hurting him . . .'

'There you go again.'

'. . . and about what my parents would say . . .'

'And again!'

'. . . and I felt so bad and stupid about what I'd done.'

'Talli, stop beating yourself up! You're human.'

'And as I said, I found out that his girlfriend had left him the day we'd had sex so I was obviously just a cheer-up shag.'

'Talli, you're nobody's cheer-up shag. For God's sake, he probably couldn't believe his luck.'

Talli shook her head, fully aware that this was situation

normal, classic Fliss. Their whole lives she and Fliss had defended each other, supplying support and confidence in equal measure.

'So I said yes to Dom. Although we've agreed not to announce it until after the wedding. I didn't want Simmy thinking we'd tried to steal his thunder.'

For a few seconds there was silence, making Talli check the signal indicator.

'Do you want to marry him, Talls?'

'Yes!' Then a pause. 'No. I don't know. I haven't got the foggiest idea what I'm doing here, Fliss.'

Fliss took a deep breath. 'You're helping your family out because that's what you do . . .'

There was the unmistakable sound of someone shouting her name in the background. Just like last time, her gaze went off to the side and she uttered a few words in another language before returning her attention to the screen.

'Darling, I have to go. You're totally free to ignore everything I'm about to say, but here's what I think. You're a good judge of character, so trust your instincts. Don't give a damn what anyone else thinks, because you've spent your whole life trying to please and look where it's got you. Rethink marrying Dom. I never liked to say it before, but he's a wet bloody blanket who doesn't deserve you. Forget the hot-sex guy if his situation is complicated, because you don't need that kind of stress. And oh, we didn't get on to what's happened with your family's finances.' She took a deep breath. 'Think about where I am, Talli. They've got nothing, yet life goes on. You're all healthy, smart and you'll find a way to adapt. And if all else fails, come here and be with me. We could do with someone as fit as you to climb up bloody great mountains for supplies!'

A man shouted her name again.

'Have to go. Love you!'

'Love you too, Fliss,' Talli told her urgently, then watched as the screen went dead and her friend was gone.

The guy on the reception desk had no idea why the high-class hooker had red-rimmed eyes when she checked out.

Chapter Thirty-six

'Want me to go and leave you two alone?' Lena asked.

'Are you kidding?' Zac blurted. 'She could say that anything happened. Stay here, sis – I know it'll be awkward, but I'd really appreciate it.'

'No worries. Just don't let me smack her on the mouth,' Lena drawled, unable to hide her disdain. 'It would just give her an excuse for a headline and a new set of teeth in bling-bling white.'

The knock at the door was muted, yet it felt like the loudest noise Zac had ever heard. Lena answered, rewarded by the shocked expression on Kiki's puffy face.

In spite of the spin cycle of emotions gripping him, Zac could see how hard it was for his sister to stand back and say nothing as Kiki walked in. They'd protected each other their whole lives – it was tough to stop now. Lena's restraint didn't apply to non-verbal communications, however, and she gave Kiki the filthiest look before turning around, crossing the room, plumping down on one of the grey leather sofas and picking up a copy of *Men's Health*, which she pretended to read.

Still sitting at the kitchen island, wearing just his jeans and a bad case of bed head, Zac struggled to find the words, finally settling on a quiet, devastated 'Why?'

Kiki just stood there, her hair scraped back into a ponytail, her face bare. She was dressed in jeans and Ugg boots and an old baggy sweatshirt he recognised as being one of the ones he wore to the gym. Her thousands of fans would struggle to recognise her, yet she looked exactly like the girl he had fallen in love with. Except this girl had started to cry, wail really. Zac didn't move, didn't comfort her, just waited – moment after long moment – until she'd stopped.

'I'm sorry, Zac, I didn't mean it.'

He ignored Lena's snort of disbelief from the couch. Anger welled inside of him, but he fought to stay calm. For all he knew, this was just another one of her games. She could be recording it or a bloody camera crew could burst in at any moment. Nothing would surprise him.

'How could you not mean it? For fuck's sake, Kiki, this is serious shit!' He braced himself for the most important question of his life. 'Are you pregnant?'

There was a terrifying pause before she shook her head. 'No,' and then a quick, desperate, 'but I thought I was, I really did.'

The relief was instant, and for a moment Zac struggled to swallow the lump that had formed in his throat.

After using the sleeves of his sweatshirt to wipe away the last tears from her face, Kiki approached him, pulled out another bar stool and sat down.

'I was in my manager's office on Friday and I fainted. Real proper fainted, not acting or anything. When I woke up, she said that I looked awful and the only time she'd fainted was when she was preggers. So I started thinking and realised I was late, and when I told her, she said we owed it to my fans to explain, and then the reporter was there and this whole story came out and . . . fuck, what have I done? I'm so sorry, Zac. It was all just like a bad dream and I was so upset and my manager was telling me how we had to handle it and . . .'

Excuses exhausted, she fell silent.

'But you're definitely not pregnant?'

'No. I came on right after the interview.'

'And you didn't think about retracting it?'

'It was too late,' she argued weakly, both of them aware that she was lying again.

'I can't believe you would do this. I would never have believed you could stoop this low,' Zac said, his voice calm, devoid of emotion. Once again, they both ignored a snort of derision from the sofa.

The beginnings of another wail were emitted. 'Stop,' he warned her. She did.

Silence again, this time caused by weariness on his part and fear on hers. She was the first one to give in to her emotions.

315

'What are you going to do, Zac? Are you going to tell the press I lied?'

'Yup,' said a voice from the couch.

'Lena, don't,' Zac said softly, despite the annoyance that was building again inside him. So that was what Kiki really cared about – whether or not she'd be made out to be a liar in the press.

'Because, you know, that could destroy everything for me.' Her words confirmed his thoughts, perversely dissipating his anger and replacing it with absolute pity. That was all she had, wasn't it? Her career. Her fans. She didn't have a friend or a lover – nothing but a great wardrobe, money in the bank and 250,000 followers on Twitter that she'd never met.

'Zac? What will you do?' she repeated, nervously pulling at the cuffs of the sweatshirt.

'You know what? I've no idea.'

'But Zac . . .'

'Don't say another word, Kiki, because I don't care. I honestly don't care. I don't give a flying fuck what you want or what's best for you because right now, you're the last person I'm thinking about. Right now I need to go see Dot and . . .' He caught himself, unwilling to give too much away. 'I just need to sort out the carnage you've caused by being a selfish bitch. Stay away from me, Kiki. I honestly never want to see your face again. Now get out.'

He pushed off the chair and headed for the bedroom, not even turning to see if she was doing as he asked.

Lena took it as her cue to jump from the couch, dive to the door and hold it open. 'I think he asked you to leave,' she said, her breezy tone displaying outstanding acting talent.

Reluctantly, Kiki walked towards her, head down. It was only when the two women were level that Lena gave her verdict on the matter. 'You're lucky my brother is such a nice guy,' she said quietly. 'I'd have knocked you out.'

The next sound was that of the door banging shut.

'I heard that,' Zac told her, grinning from the bedroom doorway. He had a top on now, a black jumper and a pair of black socks in his hand.

'She deserved it and more,' Lena replied. 'I'm not one for confrontation or bothering with silly cows like that, but she's crossed a line. In fact, she crossed it a long time ago. No one hurts our family, Zac.'

'I know, and I appreciate it, I really do. Listen, you've been brilliant this morning, but can I ask you for another favour?'

'Sure.'

'I don't reckon Dot will be up yet and there's someone else I've got to see. Could you head home and I'll catch up with you there? If Dot's up, explain to her what happened and tell her not to worry. Then lock all the doors so she can't get out, 'cause if she goes after Kiki, she'll bloody kill her.'

'Might just let her,' Lena said with a smile, before adding, 'Kidding!'

The buzzer rang again and she pressed a button on the security system. 'Oh shit,' she murmured. Three or four paps were visible, gathered at the front door.

'Wonder if they got Kiki leaving here?' Zac pondered aloud.

Lena scowled. 'She probably tipped them off that she was coming. Come on, let's get out of here – it's only going to get worse. I might go stay at Minx's and send Auntie Dot over to Ena's for a couple of days till it all dies down.'

The two of them left the apartment together, and were halfway down the stairs when Lena issued the orders. 'Give me your car keys. You can't go out like that – you look like a police mug shot.' Zac realised about ten minutes too late that he hadn't shaved or brushed his hair. Right at that moment, he didn't care. 'I'll go get your car and bring it round the back. You wait for me out by the bins.'

There was a flurry of activity when Lena strutted out the front door, head held high, questions firing at her from the group of press that had now increased to eight or nine.

'Lena, is Zac inside?'

'Is he coming out? Will he talk?'

'How could he leave his baby?'

That one stopped her in her tracks.

'My brother will speak to you when the time is right. But in the meantime, I'd suggest you speak to Kiki Spooner, that self-proclaimed actress, for the latest update. God knows, she's never knocked back a request for an interview yet.'

With that, and a beaming flash of her perfect pearlies, she jumped into Zac's car and roared around to the back of the building, re-emerging a few minutes later to climb into her own Beetle convertible and shoot off. The press realised too late that they'd been duped. Even Jezzer knew that by the time he jumped on his bike and gave chase, Zac would be miles away.

He was.

Thankfully the early Sunday morning streets were quiet as he raced through them, running over in his mind again and again what he needed to say, yet painfully aware that he couldn't expect her to believe a word of it.

He needed her.

In his whole life, he'd never said that to another soul, yet he'd said it to Talli twice and meant it.

He just needed her.

He pulled up at the hotel with a screech of brakes and jumped out, slamming the door behind him, startling the concierge who was leaning against the marble wall, half asleep. Dashing past him, he headed straight for the lift, pressed floor number 6 then drummed his foot impatiently as it took an excruciatingly long time for the doors to reopen at the right floor.

Seconds later, he was just a large wooden barrier away from seeing her face. He knocked. No answer. He knocked again. No answer. 'Talli? Talli, it's me. I need to talk to you.'

A room service waiter appeared from a room a couple of doors down.

'You looking for the . . . ahem . . . lady in that room?'

'Yeah, is she in?'

'Nope, checked out this morning.'

'Shit!' Zac spat, leaning against the wall, breathing deeply, trying to work out what to do, clearly distraught.

'Man, she must be good,' muttered the waiter as he wandered off down the corridor.

When the strength returned to his legs, Zac pushed off the wall and headed downstairs, bypassing the lift this time and taking the steps two at a time. Back in the car, he snatched his phone from the tray between the driver and passenger seats and dialled a number.

'Edwina, hi, it's Zac.' He held the phone away from his ear as she questioned at length and considerable volume the need for him to call her early on a Sunday morning when their training session wasn't booked until evening.

When it was safe, he returned the phone to the side of his face.

'Don't tell me you're calling about all that stuff in the papers this morning? Most transparent load of tripe I've ever read. Honestly, some of those bloody journalists should be shot. They know she'd sell her granny for a story, yet they still write that stuff.'

'I think she got carried away – got into a situation she couldn't get out of.'

'Oh, listen to it – Mr Bloody Gentleman, defending the cute girl despite the fact that she's fucking monstrous.'

'Edwina, look, I don't want this to . . . you know . . .' Man, he couldn't believe he was about to go into battle on behalf of someone who had just had a good go at wrecking his life. 'I don't want it to be a problem for her role on the show.'

On the other end of the phone Edwina cackled. 'Oh don't worry, darling – I'm as much a media whore as the rest of them. Viewing figures will rocket this week thanks to this little stunt, so trust me, Kiki will be on *Lovin' Essex* for the foreseeable future. Now was that why you were calling me? Can I hang up now and go do illicit things to my fiancé?'

'Erm, no. The thing is . . . do you have Talli's number? I need to get hold of her pretty urgently. It's about a training thing. You know, at the gym.'

'She's staying at the Essex Pulton hotel. Have you tried there?'

'Yes, but she's checked out.'

'Oh. Right. Look, I've no idea where she is, but I'll send you her mobile number. I'll text you Dessi's number too. She's abroad, but those two don't do much without letting the other one know.'

'Thanks, Edwina, appreciate it.'

His fingers tapped against the phone casing as he waited impatiently for the text to arrive. As soon as it pinged through, he pressed the highlighted number next to Talli's name.

'This is Tallulah Caston-Jones of Grand Affairs Event Management . . .'

Tallulah Caston-Jones? Holy crap, no wonder she'd shortened it. It was typical of Talli – she'd hate all the ceremony that came with a name like that. For a posh bird, she didn't seem to care much about posh stuff.

The conversation he needed to have wasn't one for an answering machine, so he hung up, then steeled himself before dialling the next option.

The ring tone was long and sounded different. Definitely abroad then.

'Hello?' The voice on the other end was unmistakably groggy and unmistakably Dessi.

'Dessi, this is Zac, Zac Parker. I don't know if you remember me, but . . .'

'Ooooh, I remember you,' she cooed, sounding much more awake now.

'Right. OK. Well, thing is, I'm looking for Talli and I just wondered if you happened to know where she was. Or maybe you've got a home number for her?' he added, clutching at straws.

'Oh, hang on, I need to light a Marlboro. Can't think without a cig.' There was the unmistakable sound of a lighter barrel, then a deep inhalation, before she was back.

'Brain fog lifted,' she announced. 'First, is anything wrong? Has she gone missing? Should I be worried?'

'No! God, no! I've just been . . .' he scrambled for an explanation, 'looking out for jobs for her. You know, something in sport. And a bloke I know wants to speak to her this morning about . . . about . . . helping out with a football team and her mobile is ringing out. Nothing to worry about at all. It's just that she's checked out of the hotel and I'm not sure how else to get in touch today.'

Sweat beads were actually popping out of his forehead now. He was rubbish at lying. Rubbish. It would be a bloody miracle if she believed any of this nonsense.

'Hang on, I'll call you right back. Your number is stored in my memory now.'

The line went dead. Zac realised she was probably on the blower to the coppers, alerting them about the strange bloke who was hunting down her sister.

His mobile rang and he snatched it up immediately. 'Hello?'

'Right, she's not at Chelsea Square and Theresa says they're not expecting her today or for the rest of this week. If she's checked out of the hotel, the only thing I can think of is that perhaps she's on her way here for a few days. Don't say anything, but Domenic got pissed last night and announced that he'd proposed and she'd accepted. That's probably it. Actually, I'd better go warn him . . . Last time I saw him, he was dancing on the bar in his Y-fronts. Overdosed on his anti-flu medication.'

Zac wasn't listening any more. In fact, he'd tuned out at the word 'accepted'.

Talli was getting married.

He was too late.

In more than one sense of the word, she was gone.

Chapter Thirty-seven

'Promise me one thing,' Trevor Highdrow begged Talli as they sipped their coffee from large mugs in the freezing cold doorway of the castle. 'When this is over, we'll go out and you'll take personal responsibility for getting me so wasted I'll be sucking my own toes.'

'Can't,' Talli replied, watching him stub out his cigarette, delighted that they could now head back inside. She was wearing three sets of long johns but still didn't stand a chance against the coldest snap Essex had experienced in fifty years. 'I'll be dead by then. Your cig habit will have given me hypothermia.'

Shaking off the cold, they headed back inside, slipping through the first door on the right in the huge imposing hallway to a small conference area used for discussing events with clients. Edwina was already sitting at the stunning rosewood table in the middle of the room, poring over a thick stack of papers, including an A3 sheet with a kaleidoscope of circles on it.

'OK, campers, I'm ready to go,' she barked. 'Incidentally, nice bedroom, Trevor. Simmy will be thrilled with that when he gets here.'

Talli winked at Trevor, who had been on tenterhooks until Edwina's arrival half an hour before as to whether or not her bridal nerves would have turned her into a raging bridezilla, roaming through the castle picking fault with every little thing. So far so good.

Edwina continued to examine the documents in front of her, eyes darting from circles to the lists placed by her side, back to the circles, to the lists. Talli bit her bottom lip with apprehension. The linens had arrived in the nick of time this morning. The gondolas were lined up and ready to go. The florist promised she was on schedule. As did the caterers, the castle staff, the car hire company and the musicians. All that was left to check was the table plan, which had taken weeks to do, and had required the brains of a mathematician and the diplomacy of the United Nations. Talli had almost fainted when she'd realised that the Carltons and the Deloites were on adjoining tables, with the Abercrombies within viewing distance of the inevitable carnage. They were now all at opposite corners of the ballroom.

'Darling, I hate to pick holes when you've obviously worked incredibly hard on this, but where are the *Lovin' Essex* cast and crew sitting?'

Talli paled. 'What?'

'I need another fag,' Trevor murmured.

'The cast and crew,' Edwina repeated.

'But . . . but . . . they weren't on the invitation list.'

'Of course they were! I just didn't bother actually sending them invites because I see the whole bloody lot of them every day. They're all coming, though. So that makes . . .' She counted the numbers in her head. '. . . another twenty.'

Talli did a calculation of her own. Five hundred. The wedding that had started at two hundred was now at five hundred guests.

'Can you accommodate that?' she asked Trevor nervously.

Clearly resigned to the fact that arguments would be futile, he nodded, then picked up his iPad and pretended to be busy on the grounds that hopefully it would stop Edwina changing anything else.

Talli thought it through in her head. There was space near the entrance for another two tables of . . . Shit, Kiki would be coming. The thought almost paralysed her vocal cords.

'Is it just cast and crew or partners as well?'

'Just cast and crew.'

Relief.

'No problem, I'll sit them here,' she pointed to a slight gap on the page, 'in two tables of ten.'

Rising from her chair, Edwina leaned over and hugged her. 'Thank you, darling. You've done such an outstanding job on this. Simmy and I can't tell you how much we appreciate it.'

'You're very welcome, but please tell me that again the day after the ceremony.'

'Stop fretting. You're such a worrier.' Her gaze switched to Trevor. 'I don't know where she gets it from – none of the rest of the family is like that.'

Back to Talli now. 'It will be wonderful and we'll all have a blissful time. You've been through every single detail so many times. There's nothing that could possibly go wrong.'

Trevor Highdrow cleared his throat. 'Ahem, ladies,' he interrupted.

Ed and Talli both turned to face him, as he flipped the iPad around so that they could see the screen.

'Have either of you thought to check the weather?'

Chapter Thirty-eight

'How much is that, mate?' Zac asked, fishing his wallet out of the pocket of his jeans.

'Eighteen quid.'

Zac handed over a twenty and told him to keep the change.

'Thanks, guv. Merry Christmas.'

As the cab drove off and left him standing in the middle of the car park, Zac reflected that it had never felt less like Christmas. Or less merry.

He was about to head inside when Den appeared from the revolving door.

'Did I just see you getting out of a taxi? Motor problems?'

Zac shook his head. 'Sold it. Had been hoping to hang on to it another week, but the bloke wanted to give it to his missus on Christmas morning.'

That much was true, as the five grand that was nestling

in his pocket would testify. The next line, however, was more on the side of fabrication. 'Got something lined up but I can't collect it till middle of January.'

The truth was, it would depend on whether he could find a deal offering zero deposit, or track down a bank manager willing to give him a loan for the lot. In the big scheme of things, it didn't matter, though. All he needed now was the cash from Edwina and he was sorted. Twenty grand.

Done.

He noticed Den scanning the car park. 'Everything OK?'

'Yeah, just . . . thought I saw someone over at the bottle bins there.' He shook his head. 'Imagining it. It's my age. They say it's all downhill after forty-five.'

'Yeah, right. Nothing about you is going downhill unless it's in a ski suit. Anyway, better get inside. Big weigh-in with Edwina today. If she hasn't hit the target, try to stop me from topping myself, will ya?'

'No need. She got called away. Had to go over to Highdrow to meet the duchess about the wedding plans or something.'

Zac's visceral reaction was on two counts: the mention of Talli and the realisation that Edwina's weigh-in wasn't going to happen. No! He needed that dosh. Everything depended on it, and if she was gone now, he wouldn't see her until she got back in January and it would be too late. He fought the urge to buckle over and vomit.

This couldn't be happening. It couldn't.

'You OK?' Den asked.

Zac nodded. No point in spilling his problems to Den. He was a good bloke but this wasn't his battle to fight. 'Fine, yeah. Just wanted to get the weigh-in done before she headed off.'

Den's grin stretched almost from ear to ear. 'Just as well your mate here did it for you then. Wasn't gonna let her fill up on wedding cake and cocktails and blow the result. She weighed herself in the gym this morning. Camera crew filmed it. One pound under target.'

Two grown men, in padded jackets the thickness of duvets, danced in the car park outside a gym in Chelmsford.

'Yes! Thank you, God.'

'And thank me too,' Den corrected him. 'In fact, just me.'

Two grown men danced some more.

'So what are you going to do with the cash?'

Zac shrugged. 'Probably use it for the new motor.' Another fabrication, but he knew Den would be horrified at the truth of it. 'Speaking of which, did she leave the payment with you?'

'Nah, didn't have her chequebook on her. Said she'd post it to you tomorrow. Might get held up what with Christmas and stuff, but you should still get it next week.'

The dancing stopped as Zac did some calculations. If he got it say the twenty-seventh or twenty-eighth, put it in the bank, three days to clear over the New Year holidays, it should be ready for the third. It was close, but it could work. It had to work. After nothing but disasters and crap, good things had to start happening here.

'And the whole car thing,' Den said, 'that will be a nightmare over Christmas. Tell you what, d'you want the Mitsubishi? It'll just lie there for the next fortnight anyway. I'll make the call, put you on the insurance.'

Zac spun his head round to the focus of Den's gaze. A black Mitsubishi Warrior, the 4x4 that they used to transport their kit to the park and corporate venues for boot camps and demo sessions. Two rows of seats in front of a covered storage space. It wouldn't win any medals for being sporty and sexy, but it would be the biggest blessing to him right now.

'Den, I don't know what to say. That would be different class, mate.'

Someone upstairs must have been listening, he decided, because finally something good was happening and he couldn't afford to slip back on to a losing streak.

There was way too much to lose.

Chapter Thirty-nine

23 December 3013
It was like being in a big, fluffy white cloud. Only that conjured up images of fun and wonder, as opposed to dodging death on a British motorway while thick snow fell all around. Not that Talli could see the snow. The dense fog was currently winning the battle for supremacy in the war of life-threatening weather.

Only minutes from Gatwick now, they were one of the few parties insane enough to be on the roads.

'I'm going to die,' announced Trevor, sitting beside her in the front seat of the Highdrow Castle minibus. 'I've taken drugs all over the world, fucked male hookers in Rio, experimented with S & M in a brothel in Venezuela, had heart surgery due to a lifetime of chemical abuse and I'm going to die on the outskirts of Gatwick airport in a minibus the castle staff call Vera.'

Despite the whole lavish amount of dread and fear, Talli creased with the giggles.

'Vera?'

'Vera the Volkswagen. Don't ask. I didn't make it up.'

When Talli finally stopped laughing, she nudged him. 'We're not going to die. Don't worry. We're almost there.'

A series of orange and red flashing lights guided them towards the terminal building and then into an underground car park. As they climbed into the lift and pressed the button for the arrivals hall, Talli crossed her fingers, clutched a lucky rabbit's foot and said repeated prayers for some kind of divine intervention.

What a nightmare.

The worst snowstorm in decades. On the eve of the wedding. Causing mayhem and chaos and forcing the British infrastructure to grind to a halt. She'd been calling Gatwick repeatedly all morning but the messages and website just continually advised them that the situation was changing on an hourly basis, and that flight disruption was inevitable. It was the final line of the warning that worried her most. At the moment the runways were open, but should the weather deteriorate further, closure was possible.

The majority of their friends had decided to stay on longer in Courchevel, but in a few minutes, Dessi, India, Verity and Domenic were due to land. Fortuitously, in a masterstroke of travel planning by Theresa, Arabella's flight was due to touch down ten minutes later.

Simmy, Giles, Theresa and Edwina's father, Charles

Gambond, had all arrived earlier that morning, deciding to err on the side of caution. Talli didn't even want to think about how the other guests were going to get to Essex for the wedding the following day. Right now, collecting the rest of her family and friends and getting them back to the castle safely was all that mattered.

In an eerily quiet terminal hall, they joined the small crowd in front of the arrivals board, watching with horror as, from the bottom of the screen upwards, the dreaded words started to appear.

15.05 Milan – cancelled

Next . . .

14.38 Vancouver – diverted to Manchester.

On they flicked . . .

14.10 Prague – cancelled

13.55 Rome – cancelled

13.22 New York – diverted to Manchester.

Raising her eyes north, Talli counted . . . seven flights between the last cancelled one and her mother's flight from Geneva.

Flick.

13.12 Amsterdam – cancelled

13.05 Paris – cancelled

12.52 Los Angeles – diverted to Manchester.

Stop. Please stop. She checked her watch. Still ten minutes until Dessi's flight.

Flick.

12.47 Bermuda – diverted to Manchester.

12.40 Barbados – cancelled

'I once swallowed a whole fish when I was off my tits in Barbados,' Trevor declared helpfully.

Oh lord, two to go until Geneva. Do not flick. Do not . . .

Flick.

12.32 Grand Cayman – diverted to Manchester.

'And in Grand Cayman I—'

'Trevor, don't make me kill you,' Talli warned.

Don't flick. Noooooo.

Flick.

But it wasn't Arabella's flight, it was the one above it, the one containing several people she loved.

12.15 Grenoble – landed.

'Yes!' She threw her arms around Trevor and covered his face in kisses, not caring who was watching the tall, skinny woman in the pink and blue striped woolly hat lavish affection on her companion.

The next ten minutes lasted a week. A couple of times the board seemed to flicker, to suggest that it was going to change, but it didn't move. Come on. Come on. Through the huge floor-to-ceiling windows Talli could see that visibility was zero. There was no way they'd land another plane in that. No way.

Flick.

12.05 Geneva – landed.

Rushing to the doors from the baggage reclaim, Talli nervously hopped from one foot to the other.

'Will you stop that? People are staring. They'll think you need to pee.'

Suddenly the doors swept open. First through was a trolley containing at least a dozen bags, a tower so tall there was no sign of the people propelling it forward. Talli shrieked with relief. It could only be . . .

'Darling!' Dessi ran towards her and swung her around, swiftly followed by Dom, his brother Jake, India and Verity.

'Dear God, we nearly fucking died on that landing,' Dessi wailed.

Talli grinned. 'Then meet Trevor. You two will get on just great. Ask him about Grand Cayman.'

'Munchkin!' Domenic's arms were around her, hugging her, and she flushed with embarrassment when she realised that her first thought was how different that felt from when Zac's strong arms wrapped . . .

'Munchkin, are you all right? You look so pale. It's OK, we're here now. Stop worrying. Shall we go?'

'No, my mum's flight has landed too. She should be here any minute.'

'Fabulous!' Dessi chirped, then paused, taking in the sight in front of her. 'What on earth are you two wearing? Talli, that's horrific. You look like a sleeping bag with limbs.'

Neither Talli nor Trevor argued, on account of the fact that it was true. They were both sporting ankle-length navy blue padded coats, borrowed for the occasion from the castle groundsman.

'Those are truly horrendous,' India teased, surveying Talli from head to well-upholstered toe.

Millie Conway

Trevor was having none of it. 'Just remember that when we have to pull in to the hard shoulder on the way home and sleep in a man-made hole for a week until the snowploughs dig us out.'

'Where's Mum? Where is she? She should be through by now.'

'Munchkin, do you need to pee?'

There! Oh. My. God.

Swanning towards them dressed in head-to-toe white ski wear, a huge fake-fur hat on her head, face provided for the occasion by a thirty-year-old Hollywood starlet, was their mother. She looked stunning. Beautiful. Like a woman born to jet-set around the world, spreading her wealth and indulging in the finest things in life.

The navy blue sleeping bag with limbs burst into tears.

Chapter Forty

@zacminxandlenasauntiedot There are two sides to every story in the animal kingdom and one should never believe the side of that common breed the attention-seeking cow. #jointhisDot

'Auntie Dot, look, I really appreciate the support, but you have to stop putting up those tweets. Especially now that you've changed your name to include me. Everyone knows why you're doing it.'

Dot Parker folded her arms and widened her eyes in a gesture of innocence.

'Don't be so sensitive, son. Just spreading my experience, that's all. Woman of my age has learned a lot over the years and I'm just passing it on.'

There was no point arguing. He didn't do the whole Twitter thing, but Lena had phoned him twice this week already to tell him about:

@zacminxandlenasauntiedot The truth will out – but not in a double-page spread in a Sunday paper while wearing glitter balls to prop up yer knockers #jointhisDot

And . . .

@zacminxandlenasauntiedot Dear Santa, where do I find the perfect gift for a former friend of the family? And how do I wrap one of those polygraph machines? #jointhisDot

The press were making subtle innuendo about the meanings behind them, Dot's Twitter following had almost doubled, and the *Lovin' Essex* website had completely sold out of #jointhisDot T-shirts.

Zac pulled the Warrior into the kerb and waited as Dot gave Ena three rings on the mobile phone to tell her that they were outside. 'She won't be a second, love,' she told him. 'There she is now.'

Zac jumped out and was at Ena's side in seconds, taking the huge suitcase she was attempting to drag down the path. 'Ena, what have you got in here? You're only coming for one night.'

'Look, son, I remember the war . . .'

'Ena, you weren't even born in the war.'

She raised one eyebrow in what Zac recognised as the standard over-sixty stare of death. Auntie Dot used it on stroppy sales people and the drug dealer up the road.

'I was about to say I remember the war *movies*. It was all about being prepared.'

Deciding it was safer for his health if he didn't argue, Zac pulled the suitcase down the path and put it in the back of the truck, then helped Ena into the back seat.

'Jesus, Ena love, are you coming for a fortnight?' Auntie Dot echoed Zac's thoughts.

'Apparently she was influenced by war movies,' Zac replied, absolutely deadpan.

'Yeah, well I watched that Andes film, but no matter how long we're snowed in, I'm not planning to snack on Ena's liver.'

It was so long since Zac had really laughed that it took him by surprise. This day was just becoming all kinds of bizarre. It had started in the morning with a call from Dot, announcing that she was rounding up Ena and Minnie – Jessie was in Pontefract visiting her son, even though she called her daughter-in-law a 'jumped-up tart' behind her back – and bringing them to her house so that if they got snowed in they'd at least spend Christmas together. Then she'd dispatched him to Tesco for enough food and drink to sustain a seven-night Mediterranean cruise, and now he was acting as her very willing personal chauffeur-cum-rescue-service.

Half an hour later, the same rigmarole had been repeated with Minnie (two holdalls, one shopping trolley and seven full plastic bags) and they were back at Dot's bunker, fully supplied and candles on standby in case of power cuts.

'Right, Auntie Dot, I'll be off, but I'll be over on Christmas Day for lunch. Or to dig you three out.'

With all the drama, the whole festivities thing had pretty much passed him by, but he'd never missed a Christmas Day with Dot and he wasn't going to start now. First, though, he was going to head home, grab a shower, and then – for the first time in months – lie in front of the telly. In fact, since tomorrow was Christmas Eve and he had a four-day break with no clients, he might just lie on the couch all day tomorrow too.

'Are you sure you won't stay, son? You know you're more than welcome, and there's plenty of food. They've just said on the news that all travel should be cancelled for at least the next twenty-four hours.'

He leaned down and kissed her on the top of her head. 'Thanks, Auntie Dot, but I've got stuff to do. Love ya.'

He gave her a hug and headed for the door, jumping when the phone on the hall table burst in to life as he passed it. It was the only phone in the house – one of the old corded ones – so he picked it up.

'Hello?'

'Well, well, didn't expect to hear your voice. Was looking for that lovely Auntie Dot of yours.'

Zac's blood ran cold as the familiar leering laugh came down the line.

'What the fuck are you doing phoning here? We had an agreement. Stay away from me. Stay away from my family.' He could barely speak through teeth that were clenched with fury.

'Now that's not very festive, is it, Mr Parker? This is

just a courtesy call. We like to wish all our clients a merry Christmas. It's good to keep in touch, isn't it?'

The line went dead.

'Zac, I thought you'd gone! Who was that on the phone? Did you answer it?' Dot asked as he returned to the front room.

'Wrong number. And I'm just thinking, Auntie Dot. I'm probably best staying here after all.'

'Brilliant,' Ena said from the dining table, where she was sitting dealing out playing cards. 'That makes an even number for the game. Hey, Minnie, since Zac's playing, will we make it strip poker?'

Chapter Forty~one

'Bloody, bloody bollocks,' Edwina said as she joined Talli and Trevor Highdrow at the door of the castle.

Something immediately distracted her from her woes. 'Why are you two wearing sleeping bags?'

'It's a long story,' Talli told her. 'I can't believe how well you're taking this, Edwina.'

This was what it had come down to. All those years of dreaming of their perfect wedding. All those months of planning. Gondolas. Venetian table settings. A florist with a new anxiety disorder. And now, barely an hour before the biggest event of her life was due to begin, they were approximately 491 wedding guests and a couple of hundred doves short.

Still, at least they had a rock to sit on at the door.

Edwina took the cigarette from Trevor's woolly-gloved fingers and inhaled deeply before returning it. 'There's no point in moaning,' she said pragmatically. 'Lord Highdrow is here to officiate, everyone we count as family is here, and at the end of the day, all that really matters is that I'm marrying Simmy.'

Talli wondered if it would be churlish to wish she'd been privy to that particular nugget of information before the stresses and events caused by planning this whole affair had come fairly close to ruining her life.

'I was looking forward to a huge party as well, but fuck it, we can do that later,' Edwina added.

Talli smiled, despite her chattering teeth. 'Mum's back in charge now – I'm sure she'll be delighted to organise that for you.'

The three of them sat in silence for a while, looking at the miles and miles of white in front of them. The snowploughs and the ground staff had given clearing the driveway a go, but they were fighting against blizzard conditions. And now that the snow had stopped, there was no point in trying again because the entire south-east had pretty much ground to a halt. They'd spent some of last night watching report after report of closed motorways, deserted airports and army deployments to rescue the elderly, but after a while they'd switched off and settled for stiff drinks and Dessi on the piano instead. Talli had no idea when she'd fallen asleep, but she'd woken up on the sofa covered with three blankets and her sleeping bag coat at eight o'clock this morning. Her stiff neck was a small price to pay for avoiding being alone with Domenic, she'd decided, then immediately hated herself for being so disloyal. Guilt was definitely warping her thoughts these days. She had to speak to him, and she would. Soon. They'd sort it out. After five years together, they'd find a way through this.

'Well, fuckety fuck fuck,' whistled Edwina beside her. Talli was so used to her almost-sister-in-law's vernacular that she didn't pay much attention.

'Is that a . . . It's a . . . No!' Now Edwina was laughing, huge, deafening chortles.

'She's going to set off an avalanche,' Trevor sighed, stepping back into the doorway.

Confused, Talli turned to see what Edwina was looking at. It took her a moment to spot it. A black dot on the horizon, getting bigger and bigger with every passing second. It was a blob now. A bigger blob. A shape. A square shape. Slowly, it approached, trundling towards them. A big square shape. A . . .

'Is that the crew's truck?' Talli asked, before squealing with delight. Looking upwards with real concern, Trevor took another step back inside the door as Talli yelled, 'It is! It's the crew. Fuckety fucking brilliant!'

She threw her arms around Edwina, delighted that she had at least some of the people that mattered to her here.

The massive truck trundled to a halt and the driver jumped out – a grinning, suited, booted and very dapper Den. 'All right, duchess? All right, boss?'

Talli reacted with her newly developed standard of calm and restraint by doing a snow dance.

She moved towards Den to hug him, but he was already backing away, still smiling, heading to the rear of the van. With a mighty wrench of the metal handle, the door swung open. He pulled down a set of steps from inside.

'Ta-da!' he said, like a ringmaster delighted to be entertaining the crowd.

Talli watched, entranced, as person after person trooped out. Lena and Max, Porsche and Ramone, Minx and Dale, Kiki and Dean the DJ, Shiraz, Toby, the guys in impeccable suits, the girls in full make-up and beautiful hair, wearing shoes so tall they almost carried their feet above the snow.

It was the most amazing, wonderful sight Talli had ever seen. With the possible exception of Zac Parker's arse. Aaargh! She immediately blocked the thought.

There were so many screams of happiness that Trevor disappeared back inside, convinced he'd be buried under ten feet of snow at any minute.

After hugging everyone – yes, to her shame, even Kiki – Talli herded them all inside, steering them round to the drawing room, where she'd left the others lounging on the huge overstuffed chesterfields in front of the fire.

Simmy was the first out of his chair to welcome them.

'Bloody marvellous!' he beamed. 'Delighted you're here! Delighted!'

Despite being imminently betrothed, he was undoubtedly even more delighted when the girls removed their coats to reveal the sparkliest, tightest selection of dresses outside the costume department of *Dreamgirls*. Every single one of them was breathtaking.

Her dad was next on his feet, shaking hands with all of the new arrivals. 'Jolly brave to come out. Well done!'

'Takes more than a bit of snow to keep us away from a party,' Lena said with a cheeky wink. Zac's wink. Talli wasn't sure if she was holding her breath or if her lungs had stopped working due to a week of passive smoking outside with Trevor.

After the rest of the introductions were made, India, Verity and Dessi budged up to let Shiraz, Lena and Minx sit with them and immediately launched into a conversation about Shiraz's Louboutins. Porsche and Kiki sat on the edge of the coffee table in front of them and joined in. The Essex guys headed to the bar in the corner where Domenic, Trevor and Jake were already popping the caps of beer bottles, and the older members of the group, Talli's parents, Lord Highdrow (call me Percy, he'd told her with a twinkle in his eye), Edwina's dad and Theresa, sat watching it all with delighted amusement.

'So what's the plan?' Den asked. 'What can we do to help?'

Edwina and Talli looked at each other and shrugged. 'Lord Highdrow – sorry, Percy,' Edwina said to a charming nod from the dapper gentleman on the couch, 'is here to conduct the ceremony, so that's fine. There's loads of food and drink in the kitchen so we can help ourselves later, and that's about it really. We've no music or anything . . .'

'Billy and the Brass live in the city so they couldn't make it,' Domenic interjected from the corner, before Edwina continued.

'. . . but Dessi can give us a few songs on the piano.'

'That was my whole repertoire last night. If you don't like the Beatles, you'd best wear headphones.' Dessi laughed.

'What about thingy?' Minx spoke up.

'Who?' Talli asked, puzzled.

'Luna. The next Amy Winehouse. She only lives the other side of Chelmsford.'

A resounding crash at the bar interrupted the conversation.

'Everything OK over there?' Minx asked the guys, who'd all, thankfully, reacted with the reflexes of cats by jumping out of the way when Domenic dropped a bottle of Bud.

'Surely you could give her a shout?' Minx was targeting the question at Dom now.

'No, I'm sure that—'

'Brill idea!' Porsche butted in. 'Or if you, you know, feel a bit awkward about it, I'll get my big bruv to do it. He knows her from the clubs.'

Everyone in the room was now looking at Dom expectantly, but Edwina was one step ahead. She snatched Dom's phone off the mantelpiece, crossed the room and thrust it towards him. 'Go on, call her now. Fuck, this day is getting better and better,' she trilled excitedly.

Talli's heart went out to Dom as he smiled nervously

under the weight of Edwina's insistence. She was a formidable force to be reckoned with, yet with Simmy she was like putty in his hands. That was love.

'Luna? Luna, hi, it's, erm, it's yah, it's me. Listen, we're in a bit of a fix and I know you're probably really busy with your family and with this deadly weather it won't be possible anyway but I don't suppose you could make it over to Highdrow Castle today to perform at a wedding for my . . . friends.' He listened for a moment before shaking his head and putting his hand over the speaker. 'No can do, I'm afraid. Doesn't have any transport.'

Lena didn't hesitate. 'Don't you worry about that! You just tell her and her pipes to be ready in half an hour and I'll get her here,' she said confidently as she pulled out her mobile, pressed a speed-dial key and then put it to her ear.

Chapter Forty~two

It took him a while to realise that his phone was ringing, due to the fact that living in a house with his Auntie Dot and her two pals for almost twenty-four hours had apparently given him the skills to put himself into a trance-like state.

'Zac! Zac, that's your phone ringing,' Dot shouted, before galloping into the kitchen holding it out in front of her like it was high-grade plutonium. Despite her new-found Twitter addiction, she held a deep-rooted suspicion of mobile phones, ever since one of those Channel 4 health programmes had said they could cause a whole range of problems, including erectile dysfunction.

He smiled at the sight, glad that he'd stayed. There hadn't been any more dodgy calls and he didn't reckon there would be now that it was almost noon on Christmas Eve. He was starting to relax a bit. Even malicious thugs took Christmas off.

Before answering, he checked the screen just in case, his mood lifting even more when he saw it was Lena.

'All right, sis?' he said.

'Smashing, lovely. Listen, I know this is a bit of a big ask, but me and Minx and the rest of the *Lovin' Essex* lot are at Edwina's wedding . . .'

'Bit of snow won't keep you from a party, eh?'

'That's exactly what I said,' she replied with a giggle. 'But the band didn't make it. Actually, pretty much everyone didn't make it.'

Talli? Did Talli make it? It was all he wanted to ask, yet he couldn't say it.

'Anyway. Luna Ma Dame has agreed to come over. You probably know her. Used to hang out with Porsche's brother.'

'The next Amy Winehouse?' he said, quoting something he must have read over the last while.

' Yeah, that's her. Anyway, she can come but she's got no transport. Any chance you can bring her over? Den said you've got the truck, so I was hoping you'd help.'

Zac thought it through, weighed up every eventuality, considered every circumstance and realised that what it came down to was a choice between the slim possibility of seeing Talli and another night being threatened with the prospect of strip poker.

'No worries, Lena. Text me her address. I'll be there as soon as I can.'

Chapter Forty~three

'I've got déjà vu,' Talli said as she stood on the steps of Highdrow with Trevor, this time wearing her sleeping bag coat over her bridesmaid's dress.

'Enough about you.' Trevor swatted an imaginary fly away. 'That chap Toby. I've seen him in the papers with whatsername . . .'

'Kiki.' Talli filled the blank.

'But I swear to God he's got my gaydar going like a strobe at a disco.'

In deference to his fear of an avalanche, Talli tried not to laugh, but failed. 'Yep, he's gay. And lovely. A really sweet guy.'

'That's it – this coat is getting torched,' Trevor said, unbuttoning the duvet.

The butterflies in Talli's stomach received signals from her brain and went into full flight. A dot. Coming through the gates at the bottom of the half-mile-long drive. Getting bigger. Closer. Her chest tightened. There was nothing she wanted less than to see Zac Parker walking towards her. She knew who he was now. The kind of guy who came to her for a rebound shag after his pregnant girlfriend had left him. Although given the way Kiki was knocking back the vodkas inside, she wasn't exactly embracing motherhood either. Talli had had a lucky escape. Dom would never do that, never treat her that way. She was so much better off with him – if he still wanted her after she told him what she'd done.

Now Zac was in the vehicle that was coming closer with every second, until . . . Nope. That wasn't him. It was someone smaller. And they were doing a three-point turn now, heading the other way, right back down the drive. Must have taken a wrong turn.

Crazy being out in this weather, though.

The car was only a small dot again, heading through the gate, when a bigger blob passed it, moving steadily up the drive, stopping with a swerve right in front of her.

Her legs turned to mush as Zac jumped out of the driver's side and went around to open the door for Luna Ma Dame, who was even more beautiful than her pictures suggested. Why had Talli ever even entertained the slightest worry about this girl and Domenic? Luna had the kind of face and body that you would more likely see on the arm of a rock star.

'Thank you so much for coming,' Talli told her, ignoring Zac.

'I'll take you through,' Trevor offered, sweeping Luna

inside, leaving Talli no choice but to wait for the other new arrival.

Actually, that was new arrivals. Plural. Because Zac had now opened the back door and three older women were climbing out one by one.

As they straightened their coats and conferred over the positions of their hats, he bounded up the steps. 'I'm so sorry,' he whispered. 'But they've always wanted to see this place, and when I told them what had happened, they insisted on coming to help.'

Talli now recognised one of the women as Lena and Minx's – and Zac's – wonderfully notorious Auntie Dot.

'Don't apologise, really, it's fine. We appreciate you bringing Luna. I feel that I should warn you, though – Kiki's in there.'

'That's OK,' he shrugged. 'Unless those three decide to back her into a corner, in which case we'd better hope a SWAT team can get through the snow.'

His reply took Talli completely off guard. What the hell was that about? Why was he making jokes about something so serious? Urgh, she'd been so wrong about him. Much as she appreciated the help with Luna, she just wanted him to stay as far away from her as possible.

'One thing, though,' he said, suddenly a tad anxious and running his fingers through his hair. 'Can you do me a favour?'

'What?'

'For God's sake don't let my Auntie Dot rustle up a wedding cake.'

Chapter Forty-four

What the hell had possessed him to come here? He should have dropped Luna and just headed back home, even if it meant Dot would never forgive him. Out of the corner of his eye he could see his aunt holding court with Edwina and Talli's family and they looked like they were having a right old laugh. That was the thing about Dot. She took everyone at face value.

As soon as they'd arrived and the introductions had been made, it had seemed like the natural thing to do to join the blokes at the bar. Mistake. Huge mistake. He'd somehow ended up in a conversation with Domenic and he wasn't sure how to get out of it. All he wanted to do was get Talli alone, talk to her, explain, wish her well . . . anything. He just wanted to be with her. Instead, he was locked into a conversation with a grown man who was wearing a baseball cap backwards.

'So, training Edwina . . . That would take a braver

man than me,' Domenic told him, passing over another bottle of beer. 'Talli said you've done an incredible job, so well done on that.'

Yep, this was all kinds of bizarre. He was in a castle, Kiki and Talli were only feet away, and just to put the tin lid on it, he was making small talk with Talli's fiancé.

Great.

Smashing.

Fantastic.

Compared to, say, having his thumbs broken in a vice.

'She was dedicated, so that's half the battle. Prepared to put the work in.'

'Yah,' Domenic agreed. 'Talli's just like that too. Have you seen her shoulders?'

Yes. Naked.

'Works like a demon in the gym,' Domenic carried on. 'In fact, she's always trying to get me to start training.'

'You should. Definitely. Makes a huge difference to how you feel.'

'You're right. In fact, why don't you . . .'

Zac suddenly realised what Dom was about to say and every bit of him shot out subliminal requests to block it. Don't do it. Don't say another word. Stop now.

'. . . give me a call and we'll set up some sessions?'

This couldn't get any worse.

'In fact, we could do double sessions! You could train Talli and me together!'

It just got worse.

356

'Nothing like working up a bit of a sweat together, is there?'

Nope, Zac thought as he knocked back his beer. There's absolutely nothing else like it at all.

Chapter Forty-five

'Right, darling, give me half an hour and then head upstairs to my room.' Edwina, a bottle of champagne in one hand and a full glass of fizz in the other, gave Talli her orders.

'Are you sure you don't want me to come with you now?' Talli asked, aware of her responsibilities as both bridesmaid and wedding planner.

'Darling, I'm thirty-two years of age. I'm more than capable of inserting myself into a frock. Besides, I'm taking Simmy and I can't rule out a pre-marital shag.'

With that she was gone, leaving behind her a gathering of suppressed astonishment.

Minx was the first to lose it, collapsing into a fit of giggles. 'I bloody love her. Don't get me wrong, I'd rather take on a black run without a set of ski poles than go up against her, but you can't deny she's proper class. Makes you look like a pussy cat, Shiraz.'

Shiraz responded with a deadly glare, making Minx giggle even louder.

It had been over an hour since the new arrivals had descended, and the copious amounts of welcoming drinks had definitely broken the ice. The room was still split into three groups. The older members of the bridal party had been joined by Dot, Ena and Minnie and were sitting on overstuffed chairs and sofas in a picture-perfect reading area by the huge window that overlooked the gardens.

Over in the corner, the guys were all being very blokey at the bar. Trevor, who had now divested himself of his duvet coat and replaced it with smart black trousers and an impeccably cut silver silk shirt, was clutching a bottle of non-alcoholic beer and working his way around the group in Toby's direction.

Den, Toby, Ramone and Dean the DJ were laughing at something Den had just said. So that left . . . bugger, she couldn't look. Dom and his brother Jake were deep in conversation with . . . oh dear God. Zac. This was like watching the bit in a soap when it's all fun and games, right before someone divulges a huge secret, cracks, and uses a concealed weapon to take out half the cast.

'Are you OK, Talli? Looking a bit flushed there,' Lena said.

'Fine! Absolutely fine! Is there any more champagne in that bottle?'

If there was ever a time to go over her usual one-glass indulgence, this was it – at a wedding, feet away from two men who'd seen her naked, while surrounded by a group of gorgeous women wearing more designer gear than Elle Macpherson's wardrobe.

'OMG, who is that woman? The one in the cream trouser suit? Isn't she, like, famous? Did she go out with Peter Andre? Or maybe it was the long-haired one from One Direction,' Porsche mused. 'No, that's it! She was in the papers last week, had it off with a Chelsea player.'

There was a slight feeling of dizziness as Talli spun her head in the direction of Porsche's query, before responding, 'Erm, no, I don't think so.'

'It is! I'm sure of it! Said he snorted coke off her arse.'

'No, I really don't think . . .'

Verity, India and Dessi had now clicked on to the discussion and were doubled up with laughter.

Porsche didn't register their amusement; too busy focusing on her target.

'It is!'

'Not!'

'Is!'

'Not!'

'What makes you so sure?' Porsche challenged.

'Because that's my mother!' Talli blurted.

It took Porsche a few seconds to regain her power of speech. 'Well, whatever she's using, I'll have some.'

Shiraz's interest was piqued elsewhere. 'What about the guy at the bar, then. Who's he?'

Four Chelsea and the other four Essex heads turned to check.

'That's Jake, Domenic's brother,' Talli answered, a twinge of dread in her words. Despite the heat of the fire, the temperature dropped a few degrees. Jake and her sister Dessi had an ongoing casual thing, and she wouldn't be surprised if they'd been hooking up in Courchevel.

'Oh, I would,' Shiraz whistled, to the amazement of the Essex girls.

'Well I do,' Dessi challenged.

Shiraz put her hands up. 'Fair 'nuff. Wouldn't ever go near another girl's bloke. Some of us have morals. Kiki, I'll explain what morals means to you later, love.'

'Piss off,' Kiki retorted, more weary than annoyed.

Talli felt her stomach twist. She actually felt a bit sorry for Kiki. The poor girl was pregnant. She had some crazy stalker. She'd just split from Zac. Lena and Minxy were pointedly ignoring her. All in all, she had enough to worry about without Shiraz having a go.

With the darts of tension shooting around, the room started to feel claustrophobic. What had seemed like a fantastic thing just a short while ago suddenly seemed to have disaster written all over it. Talli had seen the show. When the girls all got together, chaos inevitably ensued. And even minor spats were followed by fury, drama and tears. Throw her own friends' propensity for outrageousness into the mix and this could definitely be the most antagonistic event in the history of Highdrow Castle. And wars had been fought here.

There was an uncomfortable pause, before Dessi

addressed Shiraz again, her tone sitting somewhere between amusement and nonchalance.

'Oh, don't worry about it, it's nothing major. If you like him, go ahead.'

'Seriously?' Shiraz asked.

'Sure! He's my "any port in a storm" guy. Good-looking. Great in bed. But he's a bit too intense for me. Only came to Courchevel for three days because he was working. Priorities are all wrong.'

Shiraz shrugged. 'I kinda like that. Can't tell you how bored I am with guys who just want the fame thing.'

'Then knock yourself out,' Dessi told her.

Shiraz eyed Jake like a tiger would peruse Bambi. 'If you're sure . . .'

'Tell you what, I'll swap him.'

'For what?'

Dessi gestured to Shiraz's shoes.

'If you get the guy, I'll have the Louboutins.'

'Dessi!' Talli chided.

'What? They're limited edition. I've been on the bloody waiting list at Harvey Nicks for months.'

Shiraz slowly shook her head and Talli felt sick. This was going to go horribly wrong. Visions of Cosima Carlton lobbing a Jimmy Choo flashed into her mind.

'That is the most immoral thing I've ever heard,' Shiraz told Dessi. 'You're treating that guy like an object. It's beyond shallow. It's insulting. It's absolutely ridiculous.'

'I know,' Dessi agreed.

'And I like that.' Shiraz broke into a grin, immediately flipping the atmosphere from tense to light-hearted. 'Talli, are you sure this one's your sister? Because from here, it's like looking in a mirror.'

Talli couldn't take any more. 'She is,' she replied, reaching over to Shiraz's side of the coffee table, 'but if you give me that bottle of champagne, she's yours.'

Chapter Forty~six

Zac had never considered himself an emotional guy, but even he'd felt a bit choked when Edwina walked up the aisle to the background of Luna Ma Dame singing an old song he recognised as being a Barbra Streisand one that Dot used to play.

'Evergreen', that was it.

The words were beautiful, and even from his position at the back of the room, he could see that most of the girls were having a sniffle.

Except Kiki.

A few minutes into the ceremony, she'd turned and tried to catch his eye, but he'd just shaken his head and looked away. He had nothing to say to her. What was done was done, and there was no point dragging it all up again. He didn't even hate her. There was just nothing, no feeling left there at all.

Now, as Edwina and her bloke exchanged their vows,

all he could do was stare at Talli's back. Her silhouette in that navy dress was stunning, her hair pulled back from her face and falling in waves past her shoulder blades. And a tiny mark on the back of her shoulder, that everyone else would think was just a blemish or the remnants of a bruise, he knew was where he'd sucked on her skin when they'd made love in the shower.

He felt behind him for the door. He couldn't do this. He just couldn't. He'd thought he would just see her, maybe talk to her, wish her well on the engagement and at least say goodbye as friends, but this was killing him, especially as she acted like she couldn't stand the sight of him. Not once since he arrived had she glanced in his direction; instead she was all over that skinny twat she called a boyfriend. Or should that be fiancé.

'Zac Parker, stop your fidgeting or I'll take my hand to the back of your legs,' his Auntie Dot hissed furiously beside him.

'Auntie Dot, I'm twenty-five.'

'I don't give a bugger what age you are, love – you're not showing me up at a posh do like this. Now stand still and behave.'

Chapter Forty~seven

'I didn't know she could sing like that!' Talli said to no one in particular as Shiraz belted out 'Twist and Shout', accompanied by Dessi on the piano. Luna Ma Dame was taking a well-earned break after entertaining them for two hours with a request show that then degenerated into a general singalong.

Shiraz and Dessi had gone from potential love rivals to an entertainment duo. Jake was back over at the bar, and Talli had caught him twice staring at Shiraz. Dessi might have to clear a spot in her shoe wardrobe for those Louboutins.

For a wedding snatched from the jaws of disaster, it had turned out to be a pretty special day. After the ceremony, Auntie Dot, Theresa, Ena, Minnie and Talli had headed to the kitchen, where, after a bit of strategic planning and a couple of bottles of champagne, they'd emerged victorious with huge tureens of soup (Heinz vegetable, but the rest didn't need to know), countless trays of sandwiches, platters of ham, cheese and salads, and three huge chocolate fudge cakes balanced on top of each other as a makeshift wedding cake. When Auntie Dot carried that out, Talli couldn't help but meet Zac's gaze and return his smile. Edwina and Simmy had cut the cake, then Luna had sung 'These Arms of Mine' as they slow-danced in a space they'd cleared in the middle of the drawing room. The others had joined in, and since then the time had passed in a whirl of singing, eating, drinking and dancing.

Now it was almost ten o'clock and everyone was a little bit pissed and a big bit happy. Talli felt exhaustion in every bone in her body and longed to call it a night, but she wanted to hear Shiraz finish the song first. 'She could be a professional,' she continued, realising that no one was in earshot except Auntie Dot, who grabbed her arm and pulled her on to the dance area, demonstrating the twisting abilities of a highly flexible woman half her age.

They went up and down and round and round until they were breathless, and fell off the dance floor with relief when Shiraz and Dessi, in perfect synchronicity, switched to 'She Loves You' and the Essex girls formed themselves into a line of backing vocalists and serenaded Simmy – with actions. Even Kiki seemed to be having a great time, knocking back the champagne and dancing on eight-inch heels.

Zac was over at the bar with the guys, and Trevor was

so engrossed in conversation with Toby that he didn't notice Ena and Minnie dancing in their tights on a coffee table that had been in the family for generations.

Talli sighed with relief and happiness. It had been a near-perfect night. Potential drama averted. No problems. And as long as she didn't look at Zac or Domenic, no stress. Now she just wanted to go to bed and remember it for the wonderful day that it had been. She was about to sneak off when a glass of champagne appeared from her right, attached to the arm of a grinning Dot. 'Here you go, love.'

Talli smiled as she took the glass and decided another five minutes wouldn't do any harm. If love at first sight existed, she had found it when she'd met Dot. Her humour and cheek had had her in stitches all day.

'So,' Dot said, linking her free arm through Talli's, 'what's going on with you and my nephew then?'

Talli almost spat her bubbles right back out again. 'Nothing! What . . . what makes you say that?' she stammered. Perhaps sneaking off to bed ten minutes ago wouldn't have been such a bad idea.

'Because you can't look at him and he can't stop looking at you. And every time he sees you he fidgets. He's always done that when he's anxious.'

Dot was now staring at her with a terrifying expression that demanded an answer. She was like a CIA interrogator with a beehive, and Talli capitulated immediately.

'We kind of . . . went out with each other a few times. It was nothing, really.'

It was so much easier than saying it was everything. 'We shouldn't have. I was . . .' God, this was hard. This woman hadn't said a word in the last few minutes, yet she was somehow forcing Talli to blab like a Mafia grass. '. . . seeing someone. My boyfriend, Dom. We're engaged now. And Zac was still seeing Kiki. But it was before the baby!' she added, needing to somehow prove that she wasn't entirely without scruples.

Dot snorted. 'Huh! Baby! There is no baby. That tart made the whole thing up. Zac dumped her and it was her way of getting back at him. Only reason I've not chinned her is 'cause he made me promise not to. Another one of these . . .' she held up her glass, 'and I might just develop that temporary amnesia that us old people get,' she added, her tone making it absolutely clear that she had the memory of a large elephant.

'Are you OK, love?'

Talli couldn't speak. No baby. He'd dumped her. It hadn't been a rebound shag after all. Why did she always seem to get things wrong? Not that it changed anything really. Hearing the truth just made her feel a bit better. Telling the truth would help even more.

It absolutely would. Dom. She knew she had to tell him everything.

Maybe it was time she was honest with the people she cared about, because the whole secrets thing clearly wasn't working out.

She took another sip of her champagne. Bugger, if she didn't do it now, she never would. 'Mrs Parker . . .'

'Call me Dot.'

'Dot, would you excuse me? There's something I just need to do.'

Scanning the room, she saw that there was no sign of Domenic. Damn. She'd finally decided to do the right thing and he wasn't there. Kitchen! He must have gone for food. A quick peek revealed nothing. Maybe he'd nipped up to their room. In fact that would be perfect.

Heart racing, she'd only taken a few steps into the hall when she heard voices coming from the small conference room near the front door. Knowing with every fibre of her being that she should stop, turn around, that no good could come of this, she was unable to resist being drawn in like a moth to a devastating flame.

'When were you going to tell me?' The female voice.

Then the male voice, weary. 'When the time was right. I just wanted to wait . . .'

'Wait until when? Until the whole bloody world knew about it?'

'I don't suppose it matters but how did you find out?'

The female voice was low now, utterly seething with anger.

'When my credit card was refused at the clinic. Thank God I had another one. But it didn't stop me making some calls and finding out the truth. How bad is it?'

'As bad as it can be. Everything is gone.'

A long silence.

'Why, Giles? Why wouldn't you tell me?'

'Because I thought you'd leave if I did!' Talli jumped as she heard her father shout for the very first time in her whole life. Her mother, however, apparently had the opposite reaction, as her voice was low, barely above a whisper.

'If that's what you think of me after all these years,' she said slowly, with absolute conviction, 'then you don't deserve me.'

Talli flattened herself against the curtain as her mother strutted past, the half-light concealing her presence.

Nooooooo. What should she do? Go after her upset mother? Console her devastated dad? Oh bollocks, she'd do both . . . but having somehow mustered the courage to face Dom, she had to see that through first.

She took the stairs two at a time, used the banister as leverage to swing herself around at the top, got to the start of the corridor where the bedrooms were and stopped suddenly.

Because there, in front of her, was Domenic.

And he was currently in the process of checking Luna Ma Dame's vocal cords.

With his tongue.

Luna spotted her first and froze, giving Dom the hint that something might be amiss. When he turned and saw Talli, his whole body physically slumped.

'Talli, I . . .'

Oh bloody . . . oh bloody . . . oh bloody hell this was wonderful!

'No, it's OK. Really,' she assured them, being rewarded with expressions of total confusion. 'Just tell me – this . . .' She gestured to them. 'Did it start before you asked me to marry you?'

Dom closed his eyes, then blurted, 'Yes. I'm sorry. I think the engagement thing was some kind of guilt trip. I'm so sorry. I don't know how to explain it.'

Talli's roar of laughter made them both jump.

'Me neither! Oh, we are both total dicks! You two . . . you two . . . be happy!' she blurted, before turning and running downstairs, along the hall, back into the drawing room, racing through the crowd and skidding to a stop in front of Zac.

'Zac Parker, I . . .' She paused, heart thumping.

Shit, what should she say? She'd never done this before, and now that the moment was here, she realised that a moment or two of preparation would have come in handy. Her mouth froze as her brain panicked.

His shoulders sagged. 'I know, you're engaged.'

'You're engaged?' said her father, who she now noticed was standing next to Zac at the bar. Consoling him was definitely next. But first . . .

'No! I'm not engaged! I . . .' Aaaargh, how did this work? And it didn't help that the singing had stopped and everyone in the room was now staring at her.

'Look, I know!' Zac butted in tersely. 'You and Domenic are announcing it next week. I know, Talli.'

'Zac, will you shut up!' she snapped, and if anyone hadn't been paying attention, they definitely were now.

'I'm rubbish at this and you keep interrupting and . . . just don't say anything for a minute, OK?'

He opened his mouth as if to speak, and then stopped.

Talli took a deep breath and then exhaled. 'OK, I can do this,' she said, mostly to herself, then she raised her head, pulled her shoulders back and looked him straight in the eye.

'Zac Parker, I . . . need you.'

Chapter Forty-eight

Zac cried.

Actually, he swept her up, spun her around, kissed her and then he filled up. In what he could only hope was a relatively manly way.

'Really?'

Her eyes were glistening too. 'Really.'

'What about that skinny bloke?' he asked, grinning.

Talli broke off and turned to the room full of onlookers. 'Edwina, Simmy, I'm so sorry for interrupting your special night.'

'Are you fucking kidding,' Edwina replied, tears streaming. 'I love this. Why is there never a bloody camera running when you need it?'

Talli took that as permission to proceed. 'Domenic and Luna will be down soon. They're seeing each other. Sorry, it got a bit confusing there for a while, but we're both with the right people now.'

She leant back and whispered in Zac's ear. 'We are together now, aren't we?'

'Yes,' he laughed.

'Great,' she replied, then turned back to the crowd. 'Please, everyone, back to the party. Shiraz and Dessi, if you could manage something slow so I can snog this man's face, that would be great.'

The audience reacted with a rousing ovation, as Zac grabbed her, spun her around again and kissed her, properly this time, to an ecstatic shout of 'Go, duchess!' from Den.

His hands instinctively moved to her face, cupping her cheeks. 'I don't believe you did that. Are you sure?'

'Couldn't be more sure.'

Their bodies pressed together and they moved around the room as Shiraz sang 'Something', Dessi playing beautifully in the background. India and Verity sneaked up to give them a hug.

'I'm so happy for you both,' Verity exclaimed.

India rolled her eyes, then fixed them on Zac. 'I'm bloody devastated. I was planning on hitting on you again later.'

'India, my muscles could snap you,' Talli warned, the ominous tone blown when they all got the giggles.

Zac took the opportunity to escape and whisked her to the side, realising too late that he'd taken her right into his Auntie Dot's line of fire.

He quickly murmured a heads-up in Talli's ear. 'She

never likes my girlfriends, so don't take anything she says personally.'

'I knew I was right,' Dot bellowed. 'Didn't I say that, Ena? Minnie, didn't I tell you too?'

Both women nodded in agreement. 'You were right, Mrs Parker,' said Talli. 'I love him. Even if he fidgets.'

Dot leaned over and hugged them both. 'Call me Auntie Dot, love. And come round tomorrow so we can chat. I'll bake a cake.'

This was almost too much for Zac to take in. This morning he'd woken up, single and unhappy, in a house with three over-sixties, and now . . . hang on!

'You love me?' he checked.

'Yes. Bugger, is that OK? Too soon?'

'Not too soon. Outside. Now. I want to talk to you.'

He had to tell her right now how he felt. Not in a crowded room, but just the two of them, alone.

Pulling her by the hand, he slipped around the corner and out into the hallway. They didn't even get as far as the main door, instead ducking into the folds of the huge ceiling-high curtains, where he kissed her until . . .

The noise. It wasn't loud, yet it was enough to make them both stop and turn around, squinting to see the figure in the shadows. Only when it moved forward a few steps did Zac spot what it was holding.

A brown envelope.

His muscles tensed and he felt Talli move forward, ready to engage the other person. He pulled her back, throwing his hand over her mouth, his eyes imploring her not to speak.

The brown envelope. The same kind that had contained every one of those death threats to Kiki.

Moving out of the folds, he stepped forward at the same time as the other person. Their eyes connected and they both froze. Zac squinted to get a better look, and as his vision adjusted to the semi-darkness, he began to see features, his whole body jolting with recognition and then pain. Real pain. The shape of the face. The lips. Those eyes.

Lena's eyes.

Minx's eyes.

His own eyes.

'Mum?' he whispered.

Chapter Forty-nine

'Talli, go get Dot. Just Dot, no one else.'

Talli slipped out from behind him and ran back to the drawing room, terrified to leave him alone but realising that there was only one person who could help.

Back in the drawing room, she tried to act cool as she sidled over to Dot, who was deep in conversation with Den, Ena and Minnie.

'Dot . . .'

'Auntie Dot,' she corrected.

Talli hugged her, taking the opportunity to whisper in her ear. 'Zac needs to see you outside straight away. There's a problem.'

Then, leaning back and taking Dot's hand, she smiled as widely as possible. 'Can I just borrow Auntie Dot for a second? Got a bit of a cake situation we need her help with.'

'I knew it!' Auntie Dot told the others. 'Bet Zac wants me to make my Victoria sponge. It's his favourite.'

The end of the sentence was lost as Talli swiftly manoeuvred Dot away and out of the room, turning the corner into the corridor and then the main hallway. The scene was exactly as she'd left it. Zac and his mother standing twenty feet apart, staring at each other silently.

He heard them approaching and turned. 'I didn't trust myself to speak,' he told Talli, then to Dot, 'Auntie Dot, I'm sorry . . .'

'What's going on?' Her gaze swivelled from Zac to the other woman. 'Leonore,' was all she said.

'Look at the envelope, Auntie Dot. It was her. She sent those letters to Kiki.'

For the first time, the newcomer became animated. 'She didn't deserve you,' she spat. 'Throwing herself at all those other men on that television show. I was just trying to scare her a bit. Make her see sense. Slags like that need to be stopped.'

'Really, Leonore? Again?' Talli could see that Dot was angry now. Furious.

'What do you mean, again?'

'It's why she left, son. Got banged up for threatening the wife of some bloke she was seeing. High, she was. And it wasn't the first time. Malicious phone calls to an old boyfriend's new gal. Threats to the barmaid down the pub. It was the drugs, love. Always too fond of the drugs. Tried to get her off them when she got out, but she disappeared.'

'Spain. I went to Spain,' Leonore said. 'Anyway, that bitch deserved it. People shouldn't be allowed to get away with stuff.'

'And what about you?' Zac spoke. 'What do you think you got away with? From where I'm standing, it looks like twenty years of motherhood.'

The other woman came back challenging. 'I wasn't cut out for that and I knew she'd do a better job. But whenever I was back here I'd check on you. And Lena and Minx. Nearly died when I saw them on that show. Knew then it was time to come back and help my kids.'

'Come back to cash in on them, you mean!' Dot exploded.

'I'm their mother! I've got rights! But then I saw that Kiki one. With you. Behaving like that. Made my blood boil. Needed sorting. Especially now I'll be sticking around for a while, making up for lost time.'

Dot took a few steps forward so that she was level with Zac. 'No you won't.' Her voice was deadly.

'Don't you dare tell me what to do,' Leonore countered angrily.

Zac wasn't having it. 'Don't you dare speak to Dot like that. Not ever,' he warned her.

'Everything OK here?' It was a new voice to the party.

'It's OK, Den,' said Talli, a spectator in this until now.

The anguish was clear on Zac's face as he explained. 'It's my mum, Den. She's the one that's been sending those letters to Kiki.'

'Want me to get Lena and Minx?'

'No,' Dot said, making a decision. 'They don't need to hear all this tonight. Tomorrow will be soon enough. Den, love, I hate to ask this, but would you drive that truck thing and take me and Leonore back to my house?'

'Leonore?' Den said, coming closer. 'It can't be . . .'

'What the fuck are you looking at?' Leonore growled.

'Den, it's fine, I'll go. Auntie Dot, I'll take you,' Zac pleaded.

Dot was absolutely resolute. 'No you won't. This is a special night for you and I'm not having her ruin it. And anyway, you'll be over the limit. Den, you been drinking?'

'Course not.'

'Then it's settled.'

Leonore didn't agree. 'No it's not. I'm going nowhere with you. Got my car outside.'

Her words jolted Talli's memory. The car, earlier. The one that had turned around in the drive.

To her credit, Dot stayed absolutely calm. 'Leave the keys. Zac will bring it back tomorrow. Den, go. Get Ena and Minnie too, they'll come with us. Tell Kiki I want to see her as well.'

She focused on Leonore again. 'And let me tell you, Leonore, if you don't do exactly as I say, if you make one move to cause any of these kids a single ounce of pain, I'll turn you in myself. Don't push me. Don't even try.'

Den was back in no time, with Minnie and Ena, who immediately sussed out the situation.

'Well, well, bad penny back for Christmas,' Ena snorted.

'I'm taking her home,' Dot told her.

'Then we're coming too,' Minnie assured her without even being asked.

'Where's Kiki?'

'I'm here,' Kiki trilled, skipping forward. When Talli had seen her last, she was dirty dancing with Dean the DJ in the kitchen. Apparently she was now under the impression that the party had moved to the hall.

Only when the atmosphere finally made it through her giddy mood and raised blood-alcohol level did she pause, look around, and sober up immediately.

'What's going on?'

'Kiki,' Dot said, 'our family owes you an apology. This is my sister, Leonore – Zac's mum. It's her that's been sending you those letters. I'm sorry.'

Leonore went on the attack again. 'Don't you bloody apologise for me. I'm not sorry.'

'Mum, shut it!' Zac warned.

'You fucking bitch!' Kiki was more than capable of fighting her own battles. 'I'm, like, so going to have your face in every newspaper. The press will love this one – they'll crucify you.'

'Kiki, love, what does it say about you that getting in the papers is the first thing you think of?' Dot said, weary now. 'If you want to give her name to the police, that's fine with me. But you won't go to the papers. You won't hurt Zac and the twins like that.'

'Named and shamed! That's what should happen to her!' Kiki argued.

'If you name and shame her, then I'll go to the papers too – tell them how you faked the story about Zac. What is it you've told them about that pregnancy test? False positive? I'll tell them everything. The truth. All of it.'

Checkmate.

Den put his hand on Zac's shoulder. 'Keys for the Warrior?' Zac handed them over.

Until now Talli had been a bystander, an unwilling spectator in this whole affair, but now she spoke up. 'Ladies, I know where your bags are in the kitchen. I'll get them.'

She turned and ran, heart hammering. Poor Zac. She just wanted to hold him, talk to him, but right now the only thing that would help was getting rid of his m— that woman.

Thrusting open the kitchen door, she almost knocked over a couple, arms around each other, embracing. 'So sorry. Sorry! I'm . . . Mummy?' No! Her mother and Lord Highdrow, entwined. This wasn't happening. The only way to deal with it was denial. She grabbed what she'd come for and sped back to the hallway. Minnie, Ena and Dot took their bags and Talli's heart melted as Den put his hand on Zac's shoulder as he passed. 'I'll call you tomorrow, mate.'

Zac hugged him. 'Thanks.'

And then they were gone.

Zac stood in the middle of the hall, staring at the empty doorway. Talli moved behind him, wrapped her arms around his waist, put her head on the back of his shoulder.

'I'd understand if you didn't want any of this. I would, Talli. You can walk away.'

'I'm going nowhere,' she murmured.

'Talls, my mother is a deranged junkie.'

'And mine's in the kitchen being a slapper. Guess we've more in common than we thought.'

Chapter Fifty

The noise of the spoon clanging on the side of the glass made Zac wince. His head hurt. Really hurt. As did his neck. A night spent spooning his girlfriend – yes, *girlfriend* – on a chesterfield sofa would do that. It wasn't how he'd imagined their first proper night together. Domenic and Luna had stayed in Talli's room. Simmy and Edwina had retired to the honeymoon suite. All the parents had gone to their beds. But everyone else had stayed up, dancing, drinking, singing, until one by one they fell asleep where they sat or lay. He'd woken up to see an ocean of blankets and sleeping bags and to hear a mass call for medical intervention for chronic hangovers.

Unable to stomach breakfast, the Essex crew and cast had headed off with two extra guests – Trevor had apparently been kidnapped by Toby and Shiraz had left in the arms of Jake. She must have lost her shoes, though, because he'd had to carry her barefoot over the snow.

Before they all left, Zac had spoken to Lena and Minx, who were now heading straight to Dot's house, ready to deal with Leonore.

'I don't care about her, Zac, I really don't,' Lena had told him, Minx nodding in agreement beside her. 'She left when we were three – she's nothing to us.'

He knew they were right. So much made sense now. Those times when he'd come out of the gym and had the feeling someone was in the shadows were down to Leonore. Watching. Waiting.

He shuddered. As he waved his sisters off down the drive, glimpses of green and brown on the horizon now that the snow had begun to thaw, he thanked God for Dot. If they'd been left with Leonore he couldn't even contemplate how different their lives would have been.

When he'd called her to let her know the girls were on the way, she had answered the phone on the third ring and assured him that everything was fine. She'd slept with one eye open, she'd said, claiming it was a skill she'd learned in the war. Zac had laughed and promised he'd be over soon. But for now he was sitting at a long table with his girlfriend's – yes, *girlfriend's* – family and friends. And a singer who was the next Amy Winehouse.

'Ladies and gentlemen,' Simmy bellowed, invoking winces and head-clutches from everyone under fifty. 'My wife and I would like to thank you all for coming yesterday. It was a wonderful day that we'll always remember.' A pause, then he cleared his throat, obviously scrabbling for something else to say.

'Oh darling, you're rubbish at this!' Edwina cut him off. 'Let me do it.'

'Thank God,' Simmy said, relieved. 'I thought for the first time ever you weren't going to take over and sort it out. I almost panicked there.'

Raucous laughter, followed immediately by more collective winces and hands to heads.

'Darlings, thank you all. Daddy, thank you for giving me the biggest wedding ever that turned into the smallest but best wedding ever. Simmy, thank you for putting up with me. I love you. Giles and Arabella, thank you for treating me like a daughter since I was thirteen years old. Dessi, thanks for making the rest of us look industrious . . .'

More laughs.

'And especially to Talli. Darling Talli, who put up with all my crap. We never did get to see the fruits of your labour, but I'm sure you would have triumphed.'

Talli bowed to a round of applause and cheers.

Edwina began to sit down, then immediately jumped up again.

'Oh, and to Zac, who gave me – and Simmy – this fabulous arse.'

More applause.

Due to tender heads, it would have been perfectly understandable if the rest of the breakfast was subdued, but no, the coffee and laughter flowed.

After all the anecdotes from the night before were done, when all the stories had been told, Talli whispered in Zac's ear. 'Ready to go? We could sneak off now to see Dot.'

How incredible was his girlfriend? Despite everything that had happened lately, despite problems that were still to be sorted, despite his mother causing carnage, he'd never felt happier than he did right now.

'Talli, before you go, darling . . .' Talli's mum had obviously clocked that they were getting ready to head off. 'While we're all together and before everyone goes off in different directions, Giles and I need to tell you some news.'

The room hushed down immediately. 'Edwina, Simmy, sorry about this, darlings, but I don't want you reading about it on your honeymoon and worrying.'

'What's happened?' Simmy put down the coffee pot and waited for the reply, as Talli reached out and slipped her hand into Zac's.

Arabella took a deep breath, glanced at Giles and then spoke again. 'We all know how dire the financial situation has been over recent years, and it seems we're not immune to the tribulations. Our family firm has . . .' Her voice caught and she cleared her throat, then carried on as calmly as before. '. . . suffered, but our clients will not. Giles has made plans to return their funds in full. However, we will be left with nothing.' Shaking her head, she reworded her last statement. 'We will be left with no assets. But we will still, of course, have you all. And each

388

other.' Reaching out, she took her husband's hand. 'Talli, I know what you think you saw in the kitchen last night, but that was just me letting Percy down gently. He's always had a thing for me. Understandable, really.'

Giles's laugh was the loudest.

'Talli . . . well, money has never mattered much to you. Simmy, you're a success on your own terms. Dessi, I know this will hit you the hardest.'

'Mummy, it's fine. I'll marry rich,' Dessi countered flippantly, and Zac could see that she was trying her best to be supportive.

'I appreciate that, darling,' Giles told her softly.

Arabella took over again. 'The house will have to go, as will everything else. I don't know where we'll be, but you know, Giles and I have been together for over forty years and he has always accepted my . . . foibles. I'm sure we'll both find a way to accept this and rebuild our lives.'

Zac heard a quiet sniff and saw one tear slide down Talli's face. She quickly wiped it away.

'Actually . . .' Edwina was speaking now. 'I was going to wait until breakfast was over to give Simmy his wedding present, but I think now might be the perfect time.'

Getting up from the table, she retrieved a folder from the nearby French dresser.

'My gardener at the beach house called me a couple of weeks ago to say that the house next door had gone up for sale. Giles, I didn't want to intrude on your reasons for selling, but it was where Simmy and I first kissed, where we spent a million wonderful times, so . . . Simmy this is for you.' She held out the folder, with a picture of Beeches on the front, then immediately swivelled around to Giles and Arabella. 'But I think under the circumstances, we'd like you to have it back.'

'Edwina, no . . .' Giles started to reply, but Edwina's father, Charles, cut him off.

'Take it, Giles. You and Arabella have looked after that girl like she was your own since my wife died. Your son has doubled the profits in my company since he took over. It's due,' he told them firmly. 'But Persimmon, this wedding has cost me a fortune, so I'm cutting your honeymoon short,' he joked.

The tension was broken again and Zac couldn't help but be taken aback by a world in which people bought each other houses. It was about as far away from his own life as it was possible to be. If Talli expected . . . He stopped the feelings of anxiety that were creeping in. She was as skint as him now. It was a level playing field. They'd be fine.

'Actually, that's not strictly true.' Shit, had she somehow read his mind and was now arguing back?

Best to check. 'What's not true?'

'The wedding. It didn't cost a fortune. I, erm, took out insurance.' Even as Talli was saying it, he could see multiple frowns of confusion around the table.

'Insurance for what, darling?' Arabella asked her.

'Insurance against the wedding being cancelled or changed. Wasn't entirely confident that I wouldn't mess something up. I, erm, even paid the higher fee to cover acts of God. And terrorism. And invasions.'

'That covers my Auntie Dot, then,' Zac added.

'So how much will that pay out?' Edwina asked.

'About a hundred thousand pounds. Give or take the odd thousand.'

'Fuck, you're bloody marvellous!' Edwina exclaimed, before her father interjected again.

'Giles, that's yours. Call it a dowry, from my family to yours. And now that you officially own my daughter, see if you can do something about her language.'

Talli leaned over and hissed out of the side of her mouth, 'Thought you had the monopoly on family drama? You sure you want a part of this?'

'I'm sure.' The pulse on the side of Zac's temple throbbed with pressure. It was time. While everything was getting brought out into the open. While they had a chance of starting with a clean slate. He had to tell her.

'But Talli, there's something else you need to know.'

Chapter Fifty~one

5 January 2013

'What do you have to remember?' Zac asked her as he pulled the Warrior into the parking space between Lena's convertible and the drug dealer up the road's Porsche Cayenne.

'Eat nothing that's not in a wrapper.'

'You're learning fast.' Zac leaned over, touched her face and kissed her. 'I love you so much, Talls.' He had never been more sure about anything. The last ten days had been incredible, spent down at Beeches, just the two of them, with nothing to do all day but eat, talk and make love.

'I love you too, Zac Parker.' As she said that, the tingles started in her stomach and spread instantly to the rest of her body. And how she loved him, she thought. This had been the most amazing time of her life. At Beeches, they'd been together twenty-four hours a day and they were still reluctant to leave each other's side – something that would be made easier by Den's offer of a job for her in his gym.

Now they were living together, working in the same environment and spending every other moment exploring each other and planning the life they knew they were meant to have. Together.

They held hands as they went up the path, and Zac let himself in with his key. It was a spontaneous visit. Since Leonore had gone off back to Spain – or rather, been packed off back to Spain by three very determined women – they'd been popping in regularly to keep an eye on Dot, reassured that she seemed to be her normal chirpy self.

She'd been through much worse, she'd told them. In the lounge, Lena was sitting on the couch, glasses on, reading through a pile of papers in front of her. Contracts, Talli noticed with a tug of pride. While Minx was the show's action woman, Lena was the best businesswoman in the cast. She'd avoided all the cheap endorsement deals and as a result had been offered a new job hosting the ITV2 spin-off of a major Saturday night prime-time talent show. Her career was about to go truly stellar.

'Hey, sis.' Zac leant down and kissed the top of her head. 'Where's Auntie Dot?'

'D'you know, I've no idea. She got a phone call, said she had something to take care of, called a cab and then she was gone.'

It took just a few seconds for the fear to reach Zac's gut.

He dived out and pressed 1471. He recognised the number.

'We need to go,' he told Talli. 'Right now.'

Lena put the contracts to one side. 'Is everything OK, babes? You're, like, freaking me out.'

Zac kissed her again. 'Everything's fine. Least it will be.'

And then they were gone.

Chapter Fifty~two

5 January 3013

Contracts. She'd never been particularly good at dealing with them. Not that she'd had much experience in these things. The man in front of her cleared his throat, impatient about the delay. If it was meant to intimidate her, it was succeeding.

She should sign. Definitely. But . . .

Her eyes flicked to the large black clock on the yellow wall. Noon.

The pen was making a ridge on the inside of her index finger, yet she couldn't release the pressure. This would change so much. Everything. It was too soon. She needed more time, but the expectant faces around her made it clear this was a one-shot deal.

Little beads of sweat popped out on the palms of her hands, natty accessories to the flushed face and the heart that was hammering louder than that ticking clock.

That bloody clock.

12.01.

OK, so it had to be now. She had to sign it right now and consequences bedamned.

The pen touched the paper, then moved with a flourish to complete the first letter of her name.

Suddenly, she stopped. Looked up. The guy with the obnoxious cough stared at her with puzzlement.

'I'm sorry, but I don't think this pen is working.'

He looked at her, then down at the page, then met her eyes again before repeatedly patting down all his pockets.

Everyone in the room was now mimicking his movements, searching their pockets, their anxious faces giving them the appearance of a stressed-out formation dance team.

Perversely, the situation was having the opposite effect on her as, for the first time since she woke up this morning, a sense of calm started at her perfectly manicured toes and worked its way north.

The paper in front of her was still blank.

It had to be a sign.

Chapter Fifty~three

The slam of the metal door against the yellow wall made everyone in the room jump, but the goons were too slow to react as Zac flew across the room and grabbed the guy standing beside the desk. He flattened him against an old grey metal filing cabinet, then, hands around the guy's neck, he turned his head back.

'Have you signed that, Auntie Dot? Have you?' he demanded, eyes blazing.

Dot looked grey, shaken. Talli rushed towards her, throwing an arm around her shoulder and holding her tightly, meeting the gaze of the two huge blokes to one side of her. She held up her mobile phone. 'Nine nine nine on the screen. You move, I'm pressing dial,' she told them.

'N . . . no, love. But the man here was just explaining what would happen if I didn't.'

'You. Piece. Of. Shit.' Zac spat in his face. 'We had an agreement!'

The fucking agreement. Auntie Dot's loan, taken out years ago, to help Lena and Minx buy their first cars and help Zac put his deposit on his flat. She'd told them it was a big bingo win. It was only when he'd picked up the phone at Dot's one day that he'd learned the truth.

A loan shark. High compound interest. Her house as security. Now a five-grand loan had swelled to twenty and it was time to settle or hand over the house.

Zac thought he'd sorted it when he'd paid them a visit. Made the agreement.

Twenty grand. On the seventh of January. Don't tell Dot he was involved, but just tell her on the eighth that they'd waived the debt. Relief would be so great she'd accept it, no questions asked.

But the bastards had tried to take the house instead – told her to come in two days early, sign over a house that was worth far more than twenty grand.

Bastards.

Reluctantly, he let go of the sneering face in front of him.

'Can't blame a businessman for trying,' said the mouth full of rotten brown teeth.

'I can't tell you how much I want to kill you right now,' Zac threatened him. He took a step back and reached into his pocket

For the first time the other man looked scared. 'Stay!' Talli warned the two goons.

'But scum like you isn't worth doing time for.'

From his pocket Zac took out a wad of notes and threw them down on the desk. 'Twenty thousand pounds. It's all there. Don't ever come within fucking miles of me or my family again. Come on, Auntie Dot.' He took Dot's hand and they headed back towards the open door.

'Oh, and gentlemen,' Talli told the remaining participants, holding up her phone again. 'I've recorded the whole thing. If we hear from you again, it goes to the police.'

Her modulated tones made it clear there was no negotiation.

Back in the car, none of them spoke until they'd cleared the estate. Only then did Zac pull in beside a burger van. 'I'll get you some tea, Auntie Dot. You haven't spoken in minutes. Must be in shock.'

Dot Parker grinned, leaned over and hugged him, squeezing the air out of him. 'Less of your cheek, son,' she said, tears running down her face. 'You're not too big for me to take my hand to the back of your legs.

'And you,' she said, switching her embrace to Talli. 'You're some girl, you really are. Remind me of myself when I was younger,' she said with a wink, then seriously, 'Thank you. Thank you so much.'

Zac nipped out and came back with three teas.

'Just saying to your Auntie Dot, darling. Would be good to get back to normal life. No disasters, no worries, and definitely no more drama! Think we can manage that?'

'Course we . . . Hang on, that's Den,' he said, picking up his ringing phone. 'All right, mate?'

The two women only heard Zac's side of the conversation.

'What?'

'You're kidding me.'

'Oh fuck.'

'No way.'

'Yeah, I'll come now.'

Stunned, Zac turned back to the two expectant faces.

'Might have to cancel that promise about the drama. That was Den. Said he used to hook up with Leonore in his drug days. He wants us to go take a DNA test, 'cause he thinks he's our dad.'

Epilogue

The sun's rays beat down on Talli's stomach as she foraged her toes into the sand, looking for the damp, cooler layer underneath.

This was about as close to heaven as it got.

A soft tug warned her that Zac was toying with the string holding her bikini bottoms together at the side. She turned to face him, her smile automatic.

'Hey. I thought you were sleeping.'

'I was.'

His fingertips slipped under the string now, tracing across her hip bone.

Shyness made her quickly glance around to make sure no one could see them. Not that she was entirely sure it would have made a difference. If she'd learned anything in the last few months, it was that she was utterly incapable of resisting this man.

No doubt the fierce, irrepressible passion would wear off one day, but she was pretty sure it wouldn't be any time soon.

'Oh, look! They're filming the engagement scene!' Talli pointed to the sky. Minx and Dale were doing a tandem paraglide, a camera crew filming them, while the rest of the cast watched from the beach below.

Max stood behind Lena, his arm around her neck, both of them looking upwards. Porsche and Ramone were signing autographs and posing for photographs with fans. Toby and Trevor were playing volleyball with a crowd of guys they'd met at the beach bar. Kiki was giving an interview to a Spanish TV station, no doubt telling them that Spain couldn't progress as a country until the nation embraced glittery gel-filled bra inserts.

And lying under a white muslin canopy on a sunlounger for two, Shiraz and Jake were deep in conversation.

'Love that those two got together,' Talli said. 'Do you think it will last?'

Zac shrugged and flashed a cheeky grin. 'Dunno. One's from Chelsea, one's from Essex. Different worlds.'

She punched him playfully, then rolled on top of him so that she was planking his entire body.

A huge cheer went up as Dale and Minx kissed, a hundred feet above them.

Zac pushed Talli's hair back, his hands cupping her face as he pulled her lips towards his and kissed them, eyes open, their gaze never breaking.

'You know I'm going to marry you, Talls, don't you?'

She smiled and kissed him again. 'I know.'

There had never been any doubt. They didn't need rings or proposals or fanfare. They just needed each other.

They kissed again, slowly, their breathing coming quicker now. Time to get off the beach, to move somewhere private. In one fluid motion, Zac managed to get up and sweep her up with him. He carried her across the sands towards their hotel. Kissing her as they went.

'I love you,' he whispered.

'I love you too. But can I just ask one thing?'

'Anything.'

'When we get married . . .'

'Yes?'

'Promise you won't ask me to plan the wedding.'

Acknowledgements

Proper thanks to Sherise Hobbs, without whom this book wouldn't exist and I'd have missed spending a fantastic summer in Essex and Chelsea.

Thanks too, to Lucy Foley (for christening Zac) and the rest of the team at Headline for moving mountains.

Gratitude as always to Sheila Crowley, Rebecca Ritchie, Katie McGowan, Sophie Harris and all at Curtis Brown.

To Jan J, Frankie, Lyndsay, Linda, Jan McC, Wendy, Pam, Carmen, Gemma and Liz – for services to wine, gossip and texting.

To Sadie Hill, Rosina, Barry and Gillian, for their enthusiasm and encouragement – and because I promised I'd name a character Barry and he'll realise now that I didn't.

As always, thanks to J and our boys – and I'd like to propose that my sons be included in the *Guinness Book of Records* for making me 32,453 cups of tea while I wrote this book.

Huge love. Huge. xxxx

TASMINA PERRY

Private Lives

Rumours can be deadly . . .

A young associate with a glamorous media law firm,
Anna Kennedy is the lawyer to the stars, hiding their
sins from the hungry media. But when Anna fails to
prevent a damaging story being printed about heart-
throb movie actor Sam Charles she finds herself
fighting to save not only his reputation, but also her
own.

Soon Anna uncovers a scandal more explosive than
even Sam's infidelities. A party girl is already dead
and those responsible are prepared to silence *anyone*
who stands in their way. Not least a pretty young
lawyer who knows too much . . .

Step into a world where games are played to mask the
truth. Where there is no one you can trust. And where
being too good at your job could put your life in
danger.

'A thrilling, sun-drenched beach blockbuster' *Glamour*

'You won't want it to end! *****' Closer

978 0 7553 5846 5

headline
review

NICOLA DOHERTY

The Out of Office Girl

From London . . .

Alice Roberts is having a rubbish summer.

She's terrified of her boss, her career is stalling, and she's just been dumped – by text message. But things are about to change . . .

. . . to Italy

When her boss Olivia is taken ill, Alice is sent on the work trip of a lifetime: to a villa in Sicily, to edit the autobiography of Hollywood bad boy Luther Carson. But it's not all yachts, nightclubs and Camparis. Luther's arrogant agent Sam wants to ditch the book entirely. Luther himself is gorgeous and charming but impossible to read. There only seems to be one way to get his attention, and it definitely involves mixing business with pleasure. Alice is out of the office, and into a whole lot of trouble.

. . . with love

978 0 7553 8685 7

headline
review

Now you can buy any of these other bestselling
titles from your bookshop or
direct from the publisher.

FREE P&P AND UK DELIVERY
(Overseas and Ireland £3.50 per book)

A Walk in the Park	Jill Mansell	£7.99
The Out of Office Girl	Nicola Doherty	£6.99
Recipe for Love	Sasha Wagstaff	£6.99
The Summer of Living Dangerously	Julie Cohen	£7.99
Private Lives	Tasmina Perry	£6.99
The Statistical Probability of Love at First Sight	Jennifer E. Smith	£6.99
Destiny	Louise Bagshawe	£6.99

TO ORDER SIMPLY CALL THIS NUMBER

01235 400 414

or visit our website: www.headline.co.uk

Prices and availability subject to change without notice.